SHADOWS OF THE PAST

Secret of the Ankhs

ALSO BY NELLIE H. STEELE

SHADOWS OF THE PAST

A SHADOW SLAYERS STORY

NELLIE H. STEELE

A Novel Idea Publishing

For my parents, Paul and Stephanie

ACKNOWLEDGMENTS

A HUGE thank you to everyone who helped get this book published! Special shout outs to: Stephanie Sovak, Paul Sovak, Michelle Cheplic, Mark D'Angelo and Lori D'Angelo.

Thanks to Kaddour Boukaabar who graciously agreed to review my French phrases and provide feedback and corrections. Thank you for making sure my French was correct and sounds like a native speaker!

Finally, a HUGE thank you to you, the reader!

CHAPTER 1

*J*osie bolted upright from her sleep, drenched in sweat. She gasped for breath, her heart pounding. Glancing around, she recognized her surroundings. Her breath began to slow; she swallowed hard. She was at home. She had fallen asleep sitting on the couch next to her cousin, best friend and roommate. After hours of tossing and turning in her own bed, she snuck into Damien's room to see if he was awake. Dragging him from his slumber to the living room, they lounged on the couch, talking for a few hours about anything and everything on her mind before she dozed off somewhere between solving world hunger and expressing her craving for ice cream.

She glanced over her right shoulder. Damien was asleep on his side, facing her, left side leaning against the back of the couch, his head buried in his chest. He would likely have a stiff neck, Josie thought. He stirred a bit, groggily asking her if she was okay, still half asleep.

"Yes, I'm fine," she answered, standing.

He pushed himself up, becoming more awake. "Did you

have a bad dream?" He must have noticed the sweat on her brow and her elevated breathing earlier.

"Yeah, I'm fine though, go back to sleep. I'll tell you in the morning."

Damien took a deep breath, too tired to argue, and lay back on the couch. Apparently, he had no desire to go to his own room. He was asleep before she left the room. Josie returned to her own bed, feeling the cold sheets press against her as she lay down. It gave her a chill since she was still soaked with sweat.

She laid awake, still a little riled from the bad dream. It was a recurring dream that she had several times before. In the dream, she was running through a dark cave or cavern; the walls felt cool and damp to the touch; she was out of breath, terrified, being chased by something or someone. She clutched a book in her hands; she looked back over her shoulder, hearing something behind her then pushed her tired body to run forward away from the noise. She awoke before she ever reached the end of the cave. Each time it was the same, each time she woke up in a cold sweat, and each time she had trouble sleeping afterwards. She did not understand the meaning of the dream but it was so vivid that it felt as though she were living it.

Her friends, including her cousin, Damien, told her it must be a reaction to some stress in her life, perhaps with work or family and that she should try to relax, maybe get a massage or do some yoga. Nothing made it easier when the dream reoccurred; it was so intense that it would terrify her all over again. Even after waking up and realizing that she was in her own bed and her own home, the unsettled feeling that she had during the dream remained and she always had trouble going back to sleep afterwards.

As usual, Josie laid in bed pondering everything about the dream and learning nothing. The next thing she knew, her alarm was screaming at her. Groggily, she pushed herself up to sitting, looking at the clock. It was 4 a.m., her normal wake-up call. Most people wouldn't even consider getting up at this absurd hour but Josie did it daily. An avid jogger, Josie liked to pound the pavement before most other people started their day.

She considered hitting the snooze button but decided she'd feel worse if she didn't get up now. Sleepily, she made her way to the kitchen to make her normal breakfast of oatmeal. She put on a pot of coffee. Even though she didn't drink coffee, she prepared the pot for Damien whenever he crawled out of bed. She noted on her way to the kitchen that he must have dragged himself back to bed during the night since the couch had been empty this morning. She also set a bowl of oatmeal in the fridge for him to eat when he got up.

With her morning chores completed, she headed back to her bedroom and changed into her jogging clothes. She finger-combed her blonde hair back into a ponytail with the loose curls touching the nape of her neck after being pulled up. Grabbing her water bottle, she headed out the door for her run. Her head was still a mess after the sleepless night and the nightmare, she hoped the jog on the quiet road would help clear it.

Josie loved living on a country road. At most times of the day, the road was deserted, especially this early in the morning. They lived on the outskirts of a small town. The location offered them the privacy and rural feel they had grown up with coupled with a commute of less than an hour to the city. Josie owned her own cybersecurity business and often worked from home, but she made enough trips to the city to prefer a shorter commute. Damien's computer programming position offered flexibility to work from home also, but he often traveled to his office for coworker and client meetings.

Before Damien was even awake, she finished her run and

returned to the house. She was already changed and putting water on for a cup of tea when he staggered into the kitchen, rubbing his eyes and yawning. He headed straight for the coffee without a word.

"Good morning to you, too," she said jokingly.

He took a sip of coffee. "Ugh, I don't know how you do it. I'm exhausted."

"You should have come with me for a jog, it wakes you up," she answered.

"I'd rather shoot myself in the foot," he retorted. Damien did not care for anything athletic, choosing to get most of his physical activity from furious typing or video game playing. "I'm glad it's Sunday and I don't have to go to work."

"Me too!"

"Hey, you never have to 'go to work,'" he countered, "you work from home."

"I guess technically, I'm always at work then."

"Haha, hilarious, Josie."

"You have plans today?" Josie asked while pouring steaming water into her mug.

He glanced at her. "What do you think?"

Damien, ever the introvert, preferred his own company to most other people's, except for Josie. They grew up together, living next door to each other for the first five years of their lives. When Damien was five years old, his parents passed away in a car accident, and Josie's mother had insisted that she care for her sister's only child, taking Damien in as one of her own. Growing up together, they had been inseparable and were far more like siblings than cousins. While Josie's personality was like his in many ways, Josie was more self-assured, comfortable being alone or with others. She dragged Damien to countless social events throughout the years despite his constant protests. "It's good for you to get out, D," she always told him, and he always listened much to his chagrin on most occasions.

"I think we should go see that new comedy, we could both use a break."

"Or we could find something on Netflix?"

Josie rolled her blue eyes. "Come on, D, the popcorn is way better at the theater!"

"I don't know…"

"Come on, D!!! I need a break, you said it yourself, and no one wants to go to the movies themselves! Come on!"

"For you being the more independent one of us, Josephine Benson, you're co-dependent."

"Is that a yes?"

"Yes." He rolled his eyes. "It's a yes. Pick an early show so no one else is there," he called as she disappeared from the kitchen to look up movie times.

Returning with her laptop, she said, "I don't care how early we go. I'm still eating popcorn." Opening her laptop, she searched for show times at their closest theater. "Oh, here's a good time, starts at one fifteen, we'd be out around three. We could have an early dinner out, hole up for the night and play video games. I promise I'll let you pick the game this time."

Eating his oatmeal, he nodded in agreement. "That's good," he said, once his mouth was no longer full.

"Awesome, I'm getting tickets now. There's only like four other people in the theater, so this totally meets your 'no people' quota." He stuck his tongue out at her as a response. "Just sayin'!"

"And done! So, where do you want to eat?"

"Might as well go to the Mexican place next door. It's easy."

"Sounds good to me! Okay, I've got some work to do before we head out. Leave around twelve thirty?"

"Yeah, that's good."

Josie closed her laptop and, hugging it to her chest, disappeared from the room.

* * *

A dark-haired man studied the outside of the medium-sized Craftsman style home set in the middle of a wooded lot. It was off a country road; it took some work to find it. "Just like her to pick somewhere like this," he thought as he stared up at the light blue exterior trimmed with dark wood. He shrugged his trench coat around him tighter though he didn't really need it; it was warmer here than where he was from. He looked at the box in his hands. It was the first step. He waited until she left the house with a man who also lived there. She looked the same as he remembered: flowing golden blonde curls, bright, sparkling blue eyes, delicate facial features with high cheekbones, and a smile that could light up a room even on the darkest of days. She had been smiling a lot, so very unlike the last time he had seen her. She seemed happy, but he could not avoid this moment. He approached the porch and set down the box outside of the door. She would find it there when she got home, and she would remember, she had to remember. They were doomed if she did not remember.

CHAPTER 2

"*I* thought the movie was good, what about you?" Josie asked after they were settled in a booth at the neighboring Mexican restaurant.

"Yeah, it was okay, it was funny, I guess." Damien answered, shrugging his shoulders in his usual manner.

"I thought it was funny, too. It was one of the better comedies I've seen in a while."

Damien yawned widely. "Am I boring you?" Josie said, grinning teasingly.

"No, you're keeping me up all hours of the night is what you're doing."

Josie made a face. "Sorry, I just can't sleep, you know how I am."

"Yes, I do, but unlike you, I never get used to the lack of sleep. Did you say you had another one of those nightmares last night when you finally fell asleep?"

"Ugh, yes. Same nightmare, which meant that I couldn't sleep again after that. I'm annoyed with this dream to be honest."

"How many times is that this month?"

"That I've had that dream? Probably six, seven times?"

"It's only mid-month, so that's like every other night. What's got you so stressed out, Jos?"

"No idea! I can't come up with anything. Work's fine, I'm fine, there's no major project deadlines looming, nothing stressful in my personal life, no major decisions hanging over my head."

"Possibly the break-up with Michael?"

"Please." Josie rolled her eyes. "That was months ago, and I was having the dream before we broke up."

"But not as much. Plus, it was only like two months ago."

"I don't think that's it, D, the nightmare would have started after we broke up."

"You didn't seem to have a good reason. 'Not feeling it' doesn't seem like a good reason, anyway. Maybe it started before because you were planning on breaking up with him?" He phrased his suspicion like a question.

Josie rolled her eyes. "Will you let that go? First, that's a perfectly good reason. Something was just... off. Besides, that's not the problem. How is a dream about running through a cave holding a book related to breaking up with someone?"

"I have no idea? Trapped feelings? A chapter in your life? How would I know? I'm just saying."

"Is that your professional opinion, doctor? Okay, so then answer this: why is the nightmare worse now that we broke up?"

"Because you didn't have a reason? And he wants to get back together with you, that could be stressing you out? Perhaps you want to get back together with him? You may have some unresolved feelings?"

Rolling her eyes again she asked, "Can we drop this? As much as I'd like to figure out why I'm waking up in a cold sweat from the same recurring dream, I don't want to dwell on breaking up with Michael again and to be honest, I'm tired of talking about this dream, too. Let's just talk about something else." She waved her hands as though to dismiss the topic by shooing it away.

Damien shrugged his shoulders again. "Yeah, ok, fine, so what do you want to talk about?" he said, giving in to her like he usually did. They spent the rest of their meal talking about movies, work, friends, family, and whatever else that allowed them to avoid the subject.

When they arrived home, Josie found a small box on the porch. "Were you expecting a delivery?" she asked, retrieving the box.

"Nope, I'm not the Internet shopping queen, so my best guess is that's yours. Look, that's your name on the box!"

"I didn't order anything."

He raised an eyebrow at her. "I didn't ever expect to hear those words come out of your mouth."

"Very funny, D, very funny."

"Well, let's go inside, open it and find out what it is."

"I'm not sure I want to find out."

"Oh, come on." He pushed the door open and motioned for her to enter before him. "You probably ordered a dress, or a scarf, or a shirt or some article of clothing that you forgot about."

"I remember that stuff."

"You don't! You have so many clothes you don't even realize what you've got or what you've bought. Here give the box to me. I'll open it."

Josie handed him the package, and he sliced open the tape across the top of the box. Josie peered in as though she expected a rodent to come leaping out. "What's inside, can you see?"

"Some packing paper, so far," he said, carefully pulling the wrapping apart. "I see a shiny, metal-looking thing." He kept moving the paper around until the object revealed itself.

Josie peered in at the object. "What in the heck is that? I didn't order that."

Damien reached into the box and pulled the item out. "Looks like some kind of box? Jewelry box?" They both looked at the small gold box he held in his hands. Red, green and blue jewels embellished the top. "Man, this is heavy. This must have cost a fortune, Jos."

"I didn't buy it!" she insisted.

"Yeah right. You probably bought this thing on the home shopping network during one of your sleepless nights."

"I did not buy it, not then, not ever! Besides, it looks way too old to be something that they sell on HSN."

"Yeah, this looks kind of old, definitely looks used."

"Is there a note or packing slip in the box?" Josie peered in but found nothing. She searched around, pulling all the paper out, but finding nothing else in the box.

"Maybe the note's inside," Damien said, opening the box. As he opened the lid, a music mechanism was triggered and a tinkling little tune began to play. Neither of them recognized the song although something seemed familiar about the music to Josie.

"Wow!" Josie said as he opened the top, her eyes wide. Inside the box appeared to be a large ruby necklace. "Surely that's a fake."

Damien lifted the necklace out of the box. "Whoa, it's heavy, so it's a good fake, if it is a fake."

"Oh, there's a note underneath. Hopefully this will explain something. It's probably not even for me, there's probably a mistake or something." Josie lifted out the note and stared at it.

"What does the note say?" Damien said, still studying the necklace and the box.

Josie didn't answer.

"Jos? What does it say?" he persisted.

"Ah…" She paused, trying to make sense of what she read. "It says 'My dearest Celine, or as you are now known, Josephine, A piece of your past to help bring you back to us in your future.'"

Damien furrowed his brow in confusion. "Huh? What does that even mean?"

"No idea. Who is Celine? Is that me? And why are they calling me Celine like my name changed?"

"Let me see the note?" he said peering over her shoulder.

She repositioned the note so he had a better view. "As you are now known? Yeah, looks like Celine is you, at least that's what they think. Piece of your past…" He continued to read bits and pieces out loud. "Was this yours as a kid?"

"Not that I remember. I'd remember something like this, right? I mean you'd think I'd remember something like this, but I don't remember this at all."

He looked at the necklace and jewelry box. "Yeah, I think you would. I don't remember it either. Nothing about this is familiar?"

"No. Well…" She paused.

"What?"

"The music seemed familiar. But I bet I just heard that song somewhere along the line."

"I don't recognize this song? I'm surprised you do; it's not any well-known song that I can remember. Anything else about it?"

"Nope. Nothing." Josie was puzzled, not understanding the note or the object it accompanied.

"Try asking your mom."

"Yeah, good idea. She may know something. Here I'll take a picture, hold the box up," she said, opening her camera app on her phone. "I'll text her."

Josie attached the picture and typed: *Hey Mom–Found this on my front porch with a weird note that called me Celine and said it was a piece of my past? No signature on note, don't remember this at all. Any idea???*

"Okay, sent!"

Damien had moved on to studying the necklace. "I don't know much about jewelry, but if this is a fake, it's an awesome looking fake."

Josie took the necklace from him. "Wow, this thing is heavy. It's beautiful! Here, put it on me!" She handed the necklace back to him and swept her hair up, turning her back to him. After he clasped it, she spun around. "How does it look?" Without waiting for an answer, she headed toward the entryway mirror to admire the jewelry.

"Looks… big and fancy," Damien said as she made her way over.

"Yeah, wow, it's really something. It'd be crazy if this thing was real. No one wears anything this extravagant, right?"

"Yeah, it's really something. If that thing was real, it would cost a fortune!"

Josie's phone chirped to life, informing her of a new text message. "Oh, I bet that's your mom answering you, Jos," Damien said, carrying her phone to her.

Josie was still admiring the necklace in the mirror. She rubbed her hand across each jewel as she eyed it on her neck, her other hand still holding her hair up. Damien held the phone out for her. "Josie, I bet this is your mom, wonder if she knows anything." His efforts garnered no response. "Josie? JOSIE?" he almost yelled, poking at her arm.

"Huh? What?"

"Geez, obsessed much? Stop admiring yourself and check if this message is from your mom?"

"Oh, I didn't even hear that come in, thanks!"

Josie unlocked her phone and checked her messages, finding one from her mother: *Never saw that before. You sure it's for you? Wrong address? Sounds like it was for someone named Celine.*

Josie answered her: *The note has my name too. And box is addressed to me.* She sent a picture of the note and the address on the box.

Her mother answered almost immediately: *No return address?? Some kind of joke?*

Josie answered: *Nope, no return address... no postage either so someone hand-delivered... Yeah, could be a joke.* Then she let the subject drop. Her mother knew nothing about either item.

"So, she doesn't have any ideas either, said she didn't recognize the jewelry box and was wondering if it was a prank or a joke, but I noticed that there's no postage on this, so someone hand-delivered this to the house, D," Josie said.

"Oh, well, that doesn't help us. The hand-delivery might narrow it down. Who would do this as a prank? And why?"

"No idea. It says something about bringing me back to someone? Might be an ex? Michael?"

"What ex of yours would do something so weird, do you really think Michael would write a weird note calling you Celine? I mean unless you guys had some weird role-playing nicknames or something like that."

Josie laughed. "No, he never called me Celine for any reason at all, ever, so no. And none of my exes ever called me Celine. I've never heard that name mentioned before today."

"Okay, so your mom doesn't recognize it, you don't think an ex would do it. Anyone else with a weird sense of humor?"

"You?"

"Me?!?" he cried, his face incredulous. "I didn't do it, why would I do this?"

"No idea, why would anyone do it? This is just bizarre."

The pair of them studied the box and necklace, which Josie had now removed and replaced in the box but they weren't able to come up with any answers. After about a half hour of further discussion, they packed the jewelry box carefully back into the package and set the package aside, giving up on solving anything for the moment, turning their attention to unwinding before the start of the week with some T.V.

Before they headed to bed for the night, Josie was sure to check all the locks twice. "Paranoid?" Damien asked her, watching her jimmy the door to be sure it was locked tight.

"I'm just getting an uneasy feeling. Someone brought that box with the weird note right to our door. I mean, who does that? Some crazy person who thinks I was named Celine or am Celine or whatever was literally standing three feet from where I am right now. It just gives me the creeps a little."

"Why not text some other people? Someone may have a clue? Might settle your nerves?"

"And what if they all answer no? Then I might feel worse. The only one I could imagine might do this and it's really a stretch is Michael. You said he wanted to get back together, and the note says something about bringing us back together."

"So, text him now, maybe you'll sleep better."

"Okay," Josie said, grabbing her phone. She sent a text to her ex, Michael, saying: *Hey, super weird question for you but did you leave anything on the porch for me today?*

Michael responded within a few minutes: *No????*

Josie took a moment to consider her response. She didn't want to have a conversation with anyone now, especially not Michael. "He said no," she reported to Damien as she typed back: *Ok, thanks!*

Unfortunately for Josie, that was not enough to end the

conversation outright. Michael responded quickly: *Every-thing ok? What was dropped off?*

"Now look what you've done," she said to Damien, showing him the message, then typing back her own: *Every-thing's okay... some music box with a necklace inside.*

"Hey," he said holding up his arms in protest, "not my fault! Tell him you're going to bed. Speaking of, I can sleep in your room tonight if it makes you feel better? We still have that inflatable mattress in the closet, I can set that up."

"Uh, as much as I want to say no and I'm fine, I'm just going to lay awake thinking about who sent that and how creepy it is they were on our porch, so, yeah, I'll save you the midnight wake-up call and take you up on your offer."

"All right, I'll set up the mattress, you can finish texting with Michael." He winked as he darted up the steps in front of her.

Josie turned off the lights, made her way up the steps and into her bedroom. Damien was already dragging the inflat-able mattress out onto the floor as Josie climbed into bed. She checked her phone to find another message from Michael: *Wrong address? I assume you didn't order it?*

Josie sighed, it looked like she was in it for the long haul. Besides, it would help pass the time while the mattress inflated. She texted back: *No... I didn't order it. Wasn't sent through a carrier, someone put it on the porch, no postage on box, just my name and address.*

"What's he want now?" Damien asked, tossing himself across her bed as the mattress inflated.

"He's asking about whether it could have been a wrong address. I told him it wasn't even delivered; someone hand-carried that box to our house. It doesn't make sense." Her phone chimed: *That's weird, are you sure you're okay? I can come over.*

Josie rolled her eyes, sighing with annoyance. "Now

what?" Damien asked, noticing her expression. She held the phone out for him to read the message.

"I'm wondering if he didn't do this just so he could offer to come over," she said only half-joking.

"What if you never texted him though? No, nope, that one doesn't add up, next theory."

Josie was already answering: *I'm fine... D is here, all good... just about to go to sleep, good night!* She barely clicked her phone off when the response came back: *Ok, text if you need anything, good night!*

"No more theories, I am going to sleep!" Josie said after finishing texting with Michael.

"Sleep? You promise?"

"Well, I will try," she said, pushing her feet under the covers and playfully kicking at Damien to get off the bed.

"Okay, okay!" he said, leaping off the bed and testing the mattress for firmness. He turned off the inflator pump, tossed his pillows and blanket on top and settled into the mattress. "Good night, Josie."

Josie turned off the light. "Good night!"

The man watched the lights go out, plunging the house and its surroundings into darkness. She had gotten the package; he had seen her carry the box into the house earlier. He assumed she had opened it. He couldn't know for sure. Did it have the intended effect? Did she remember? Only time would tell. For now, he could rest, having carried out the first piece of his plan. He turned the key in his car's ignition and, without headlights, eased the car back onto the road from the service road he had hidden his car on earlier. Only after he was on the road did he turn his headlights on, heading to his motel. He'd work on the next step of his plan in the morning. For now, having finally accomplished something, he hoped for a good night's sleep. The first in a long time.

CHAPTER 3

"Good morning," Damien said, yawning as he walked into the kitchen and straight to the coffee pot.

"Good morning," Josie said, sipping her just-made hot tea. "Did you sleep okay on the air mattress?"

"Yeah, how about you? Any bad dreams?"

"Nope! Slept through the night, even with the creepy visitor thing looming. Thank you, by the way," she said, putting her hand on his arm, "for sleeping in my room last night. It really helped."

"No problem," he said, pulling her in for a hug. "I'm glad you slept."

"Me too," she answered as the doorbell rang.

They exchanged a puzzled glance. "Who would that be at this time of the morning? It's not even six thirty," Josie said.

"No idea," Damien answered.

They stood in silence until they heard a knock at the door.

"Whoever it is isn't going away," Josie said, her heart beginning to beat faster as adrenaline coursed through her body. She crept through the doorway toward the living room and the front door with Damien following her. They saw a figure looming at the front door.

"Here, let me go first," Damien said, pushing her behind him.

"Get the bat from the closet," Josie whispered. Damien grabbed the bat from the closet, holding it ready as he crept toward the door. "Who is it?" he called.

"Michael," a voice answered.

They both breathed a sigh of relief as Damien dropped the bat and began unlocking the door. Josie rolled her eyes at him and made a face that Damien recognized as her "are you kidding me?" face.

Damien pulled the door open. "Hey, man, how's it going?"

"Good, how are you? Hey, Josie," he said, stepping into the house, "I wanted to check on you. How are you doing with all the excitement over that strange package?"

"You could have texted, Michael," Josie said crossing her arms. "You scared us half to death after all that excitement."

"Yeah, well, I knew you'd tell me not to come, Josie, but I wanted to make sure you were okay, like for real okay."

"I'm fine, slept okay, no nightmares, no more weird packages."

"You're still having the nightmares?" Michael asked, smoothing his tie against his dress shirt. He used that matter-of-fact tone that irritated Josie to no end. The tone she had nicknamed his "Dad" tone.

"Shouldn't you be getting to work?" Josie asked, trying to avoid the question.

"I've got time," Michael answered. "Can I see the package?"

"Yes, it's right here," Josie answered, irritation dissipating a bit since she did not mind if he looked. She showed him the box on the table.

Michael picked it up, looking at the address and lack of

postage on the top of the box. He opened it and pushed the packaging aside to pull out the music box.

"Whoa, this is heavy, nice, it's beautiful." He opened it, looking at the necklace first, then the note. "So, are you Celine? Why would you think I sent this?"

"I don't know, I didn't think it came from you. It was more of a hope because it's disturbing to realize that some random person dropped it off."

"It was definitely not me. But it concerns me that some strange person who thinks you're someone else dropped stuff off on your doorstep. You should contact the police. And it may be a good idea if I stayed here, just in case."

Typical Michael, Josie thought, using the situation to his advantage to try to push back in. Growing up in a prominent family, Michael Carlyle had never wanted for anything. He was a savvy businessman, learning from his father and grandfather who had taken a small family business to a multi-billion-dollar international industry. Michael's split-second decisions and overconfident behavior sometimes drove Josie to the point of madness. "Neither is necessary. I mean it's creepy but I don't think it's dangerous."

"How do you know? This person sounds like a whack-job. Calling you Celine? Talking about this being a piece of your past and hoping it leads you back to …whoever this is? It's crazy."

"We'll be fine," Josie said, crossing her arms, trying to dismiss the conversation.

"I'd like to be sure. I can sleep in the guest room, you won't even realize I'm here."

"Won't I? Really?" She raised her eyebrows in disbelief.

"I'm not going to argue about this, Josie, I'm not taking any chances. Sorry, I realize it bothers you I still care, but I do. I can stop by my place after work, grab my gear and be over."

"You want to help out here?" Josie said turning to Damien.

He shrugged his shoulders and shook his head, unwilling to get into the argument. Josie threw her arms in the air, sighing. "Fine, whatever, the more the merrier, I guess."

"Great! I'll see you later then," Michael said, squeezing Josie's arm before turning to head out the door. "Damien, nice seeing you again." He nodded to him as he left.

"Thanks so much for the assist, D," Josie said, after Michael left.

"I'm not getting in the middle of that and besides, I wouldn't mind having someone else here, between your nightmares and the creepy stalker. Sometimes you listen to him more than me."

"He's not a stalker. We have no idea what's going on. Oh, never mind, never mind, let's just forget about this stupid thing," she said, stuffing the music box back in the box and shoving it into the nearby coat closet along with the discarded bat. "I've got some errands I need to run. I'm going to head out. I'll be back later."

"Okay," Damien answered, knowing when she needed to cool off. "I'm heading into the office for a few hours. See you when I get home?"

"Yep, have a good day, D."

Josie stormed up the steps, trying to push the morning's events from her mind. It was barely 7 a.m. and she'd already had enough of this day. Stepping in to her room, she closed the door behind her, shutting her eyes and taking a deep breath. She opened them and scanned the room, seeing the air mattress lying on the floor. She gave it a half-smile. She was glad Damien had stayed with her last night. Thinking about it, perhaps it wouldn't be half bad having Michael in the house, too. She hated to admit it but she had some unresolved feelings about him. Perhaps this would help resolve them.

She would not dwell on it now; she'd concentrate on getting dressed and out of the house to run her errands. One perk of self-employment was running errands when most other people were at work. She hopped into the shower, dried her hair, put on some makeup and was out of the house within the hour.

She made a few quick stops, picking up some various household items that she needed and a few food items from the store now that they would be entertaining and eating for three. She dropped everything off at home. Checking the time, she saw that it was only 10 a.m. She didn't have much on her work schedule for the day, but she figured she would get a start on them and clear them off her plate.

Upon sitting down at her desk, she found herself distracted. She pushed through a few items but found it difficult to focus. She checked her window often, which overlooked the front of the house, making sure no strangers were lurking around. After about thirty more minutes of work she found herself too distracted to continue. Despite her words this morning, she really was unnerved being in the house alone. Her mind lingered on the strange package that was delivered and on the person who had delivered it.

Not being able to focus, she gave up on work. She settled on getting out of the house and doing some shopping. Whenever she was stressed, she found that shopping was a great way to relieve her mind. With her mind made up, she grabbed her keys and headed out the door.

Josie eased her car into a parking space at the mall, parking outside one of her favorite department stores. She hoped the distraction would help ease her mind. She made her way through the store, stopping every so often to browse at a few clothing items or accessories. Finally, her mind began to relax at the expense of a new dress and a pair of shoes. Considering this a success, Josie decided to eat before continuing her retail therapy. She dropped her purchases off at her car and headed to the food court.

When entering the food court, she felt off. She chalked it up to waiting too long before eating lunch. As she considered what food appealed to her most, she began to feel worse. A stabbing pain above her right eye made concentrating difficult. She rubbed her head in the hopes this would relieve it until she sat down to eat.

She settled on pizza and made her way to the counter to order, practically running into a man along the way. She apologized to him, unable to take her eyes off him even after he began to walk away. He turned back, staring at her. Something about him seemed familiar to her, but she couldn't place it. Suddenly, the pain in her head became ten times worse, nearly blinding her with its stabbing sensation. Instinctively, she put her hand to her head; her mind was a jumble of thoughts. Her nightmare was pushed to the front of her mind, she remembered her hands on a cold wet stone, her labored breathing. She closed her eyes, trying to shut it all out. When she opened them she noticed the man she had almost run into still staring at her. She stared back for a moment before her vision narrowed to a pinpoint, blood rushed into her ears. Her limbs became heavy, and she sensed herself slipping away. Her eyes rolled back, and she slumped to the floor.

CHAPTER 4

The dark-haired man saw her go limp. Josie, as she now called herself, had almost run into him moments before. Had she recognized him? There was an instant where it appeared as though she remembered then a confused look prior to her grabbing her head, as though in pain. She had shut her eyes and when she opened them she had focused on him before fainting. He ran to her, catching her just before her head hit the hard floor. He eased her onto the floor. "Celine," he said, trying to call her back to consciousness. "Celine!" He remembered she no longer used this name. "Josie... Josie, wake up, Josie." The woman moved, a moan escaping her lips. She was coming to, would she remember now?

* * *

Josie's eyes fluttered open. Her brain felt scrambled. She gazed at the man hovering over her. He was asking her something but she couldn't respond. She realized she was lying on the floor. A small group of bystanders had gathered around her. She recognized the man as the one she had almost run into moments ago. He asked her if she was okay. She tried to sit up, but he stopped her. "Yes," she said, confused. "I think so."

"Don't get up, we've got paramedics on the way, ma'am," a uniformed woman told her.

"Paramedics?" Josie said, starting to return to normal. "No, no, I'm fine. I think I waited a bit too long to eat. I'm fine." She again tried to push herself up to sitting, feeling ridiculous lying on the floor.

"Ma'am, please, stay where you are. The paramedics are on their way; we need to check that you are okay."

It dawned on Josie that the security officer viewed her like a lawsuit waiting to happen. She stayed put, realizing that they were only following their protocol. The paramedics arrived within minutes, pushing aside both the security officer and the concerned man who still hovered over her. They descended on her with all manner of medical devices, measuring her oxygen intake, blood pressure, heart rate and more. "Ma'am, can you tell us your name?"

"Josie, Josephine, Josephine Benson." Josie stammered, feeling ridiculous. They probably thought she didn't remember her own name given her response.

"Do you know where you are?"

"The food court at the mall."

"Can you tell us what happened, ma'am?" one paramedic asked her.

"I had a pain in my head, a stabbing pain and then I fainted. I think I waited too long to eat," she responded sheepishly.

"Did you hit your head?"

"Uh, I don't know…" Josie began to answer when the man who was hovering chimed in.

"No, she didn't. I spotted her falling and caught her before she did."

"Thank you, sir." The paramedics proceeded to fire the standard barrage of questions at her. Josie refrained from rolling her eyes as she answered them all.

"Vitals look good," one paramedic said to his partner. He turned to Josie. "Okay, we're going to move you onto the stretcher here. We're going to have you sit up slowly and shimmy onto it."

"Stretcher? No, I'm fine. I just need some food and some rest," Josie said, sitting up and waving her hand at them.

"Ma'am, Josie, we need to take you to the hospital to run a few standard tests."

"Tests? I don't need any tests. I'm fine! I just…"

"Ma'am, I'm sorry, but we have a protocol, we need to take you."

Josie sighed. Of course they needed to take her; they had to follow the procedure to clear her of any medical problems or identify them right away in the event of a lawsuit. "Okay, okay," she answered, beginning to shimmy herself onto the stretcher with their help.

"Besides, you get to ride in the ambulance! We'll even use the siren for you," one paramedic said, winking at her.

"What fun," Josie said, her words thick with sarcasm.

Within minutes Josie was strapped down onto the stretcher and they were wheeling her to the ambulance that sat waiting outside. She felt ridiculous but at least she'd soon be out of sight from most of the people gawking at her. Once she was in the ambulance and they were on the way to the hospital, sirens blaring as promised, Josie asked for her phone. Her purse was out of her reach and she wanted to text Damien.

"Here you go, hun," the paramedic said, handing her the purse.

"Thanks." Josie dug for her phone, retrieved it and unlocked it, navigating to her text messaging app. She sent Damien a text: *I'm fine, but headed to the hospital. Fainted at the mall... they're making me go to be sure I'm ok.*

Within moments, Damien, always connected, texted back: *WHAT??? ARE YOU OKAY? On way to hospital, meet you there.*

Josie texted back: *I'm okay. See you at the hospital.* She sent a second text: *Be careful... don't speed. I'm fine*

Damien text her back: *K, will be safe :)*

Josie put her phone back in her purse and waited to arrive at the hospital. Once they arrived, another massive amount of medical professionals descended on her, rechecking vitals, asking questions about what happened, drawing blood samples, and ordering tests. It wasn't long before she was sitting on her own, the masses who had greeted her upon her arrival disappearing to deal with their respective details. A knock interrupted the momentary lull. "Hey, Jos, how you doing?"

"D!" Josie reached out to draw him in for a hug. "Thank you for coming. I'm fine though. I'm fine. I think I just didn't eat soon enough."

"So, what happened?" Damien asked her, pulling up a chair, still holding her hand.

"I don't know. I was in the food court, felt strange and then I fainted."

"Did you hit your head?"

"No, thankfully, some nice bystander caught me before I hit the floor."

"Good thing." He rubbed her head.

Another knock announced the arrival of a woman in scrubs. "Ms. Benson? I'm here to take you for your CT scan."

"Okay, thanks."

"We'll have her back as soon as we can," she said to Damien as she wheeled Josie from the room.

The CT scan did not take long and Josie was returned to her ER cube to wait for results within forty-five minutes. As she was being wheeled back into the room, Josie smiled as soon as she caught sight of Damien. He gave her an awkward smile back, the reason for which she discovered as soon as the whole room was in her view. Standing opposite Damien was Michael. No one spoke until the attendant repositioned her bed and left the room.

"What are you doing here, Michael?" Josie blurted out as soon as the opportunity presented itself. "How did you even find out?"

"What happened?" was his response.

"I just fainted, that's all. I'm fine."

"We'll see," he said curtly. "But I'm not leaving until they tell me you are okay."

Not wanting to argue while in her hospital bed, they all sat in awkward silence for a few minutes. Damien broke the silence, trying to make some light conversation as they waited. After what seemed like an eternity, the doctor entered the room.

"Good afternoon, Ms. Benson. How are you doing, feeling okay?" He paused, waiting for her response.

"Yes, I'm okay. I feel fine."

"Great. I have your results here. Blood work all came back normal, CT scan looked great. Nothing's showing up that suggests anything is wrong. Anything causing stress at home or work?"

"No, nothing. I think I waited too long to eat. So can I go?" Josie asked him.

"Well, the nightmares," Michael said, before the doctor could respond. Josie seethed internally, reminded in an instant of why they had broken up. Michael had a bad habit of playing parent rather than a partner.

"Nightmares?" the doctor asked, pausing.

"It's nothing. I've had an occasional nightmare here and there, it's nothing outside of what all normal people have."

Sighing, Michael again chimed in, "She wakes up heart pounding, in a cold sweat, labored breathing from the same dream over and over and over." Josie was ready to spring from the bed and punch him.

"A recurring dream? That's usually a sign of stress, which could cause this type of reaction, particularly if you're having trouble sleeping. I'm going to recommend that you follow up with a therapist. We'll include a few names and phone numbers. I'll have the nurse get you some lunch. Other than that, physically, you are fine, so we're going to send you home. Take it easy, not too much on your feet for the rest of the day, we don't want any repeat performances where you may get physically hurt."

"Okay, thanks, yep, sure thing, I will rest, no problem!" Josie promised.

"Okay, we'll get you processed with discharge instructions, someone will be in to go over those with you shortly. Take care."

"Thank you." When the doctor left, Josie turned to Damien and said, "I told you I was fine."

"Yeah, I'm glad you're okay. I was kind of worried."

"Ah, I am so glad to go home, not what I expected when I started the day. I only wanted to shop and relax."

"Awww, so didn't you get any retail therapy?" Damien asked.

"Well, I bought a dress and one pair of shoes but nowhere near the amount of retail therapy I was longing for." Josie grinned at him.

"I think you should consider seeing the therapist about those dreams even if you are physically fine," Michael said.

"Well, thanks so much, buzzkill," Josie said, rolling her eyes.

"Josie, I'm just concerned, that's all. You told me you were having those dreams months ago before we broke up and you're still having that same dream? Something is going on."

"I just want to get home. I'll see how I feel in a few days. This experience exhausted me more than the dreams."

"Well, yeah, let's get you home and relaxed," Michael said, rubbing her shoulder.

As annoyed as Josie was with Michael, she agreed, she couldn't wait until she got home. She didn't even care if he was with her at this point; she wanted to decompress. She felt like she had run two marathons and was spent.

Thankfully, within a few minutes, a nurse joined them with a small lunch, went over several items of paperwork and told Josie she was free to dress and leave. Within about an hour, they retrieved Josie's car from the mall and had Josie home on the couch, feet up, relaxing as promised. She watched the boys buzzing around her like busy bees trying to be as attentive as possible after her "emergency" earlier. Once they got her as settled as they could, they joined her to watch movies, allowing her to have her choice. While she wasn't physically sick, she didn't complain about having free rein on viewing choices and took full advantage. They ordered in for dinner and kept their movie marathon going until Josie yawned and stretched, telling them she was ready to go to bed.

"Want me to bunk with you again?" Damien asked as she prepared to head upstairs.

"Yeah, if you don't mind the air mattress again." Josie winced.

"Nope, don't mind at all."

Michael listened to the exchange, seeming to want to join in but deciding it might be best not to. "I'll be in the guest room if you need anything. I hope you sleep, Josie."

"Thanks," Josie said.

They all headed up the stairs, parting ways outside of the guest room door with Josie and Damien continuing to her room. Within a few minutes they were both settled and Josie turned out the lights after exchanging good nights with Damien.

* * *

The man watched the lights go out at the house one by one, plunging the surrounding area into darkness. She seemed so close to remembering earlier today; before she fainted, he thought there had been a glimmer of recognition in her eyes. He did not know what her medical condition was after they wheeled her away on the stretcher, but he couldn't imagine anything being gravely wrong with her. Not Celine. Instead, he had come back here and waited, spying two men returning with her earlier this afternoon. Since then the house had been quiet. Another day was coming to a close. It might be time to enact phase two of his plan. Tomorrow was a new day. He'd hold on to the hope that the faintest glimmer of recognition had crossed her face and that she'd soon be the Celine that he knew. Hope, it was all he had.

CHAPTER 5

*J*osie sat on the edge of the bed, still shaking. She sniffled, wiping tears from her face. The latest version of the nightmare seemed more real, bringing her to tears. The commotion had awoken Damien; he sat next to her, rubbing her back. "I'm okay," she said, still sniffling. "But it was way more intense this time."

Damien remained quiet, offering silent support while she continued to recover. After a few moments, Josie grabbed his hand. "Thanks," she whispered. "Guess we better try to go back to sleep."

"Do you think you can sleep?" Damien asked her.

"Probably not. I don't sleep well even when I'm not having nightmares. But, at least I'll try."

"Want me to stay here 'til you fall asleep?"

She nodded, still ill at ease. She laid back on the pillow; he held her hand, remaining on the edge of the bed. After a few moments, she said, "Okay, I'm okay now, you can go back to sleep. Thanks, D."

"You sure? I can stay here 'til you're out."

She smiled and squeezed his hand. "I'm sure, yep." She was much calmer, although no closer to sleep. Damien squeezed her hand back and headed back to the air mattress. Josie lay awake for another hour before dozing off. Within the first hour of sleep, though, she was startled awake again, the nightmare making its second appearance that night. Although not as rattled as the first time she experienced it, she still startled awake, bolting upright in bed. This time she was quiet enough not to wake Damien, who was snoring quietly at the foot of the bed.

She checked her clock; it was 3:28 a.m. With a 4 a.m. alarm looming she would never sleep now. She got up and tiptoed around, grabbing her jogging clothes and sneaking out of the room so as not to disturb Damien's sleep. A few minutes after four, she hit the road. Feeling a little sleepy, she was hoping the jog would clear her mind. Josie was too stubborn to miss it.

She returned home to find two concerned faces sipping coffee in the kitchen. "Do you think that was wise? Jogging alone in the middle of the night?" Michael chided.

"I wanted to clear my mind, I couldn't sleep anymore."

"Why didn't you wake me? You said you were okay to go back to sleep," Damien said.

"I was, I did, but I had the dream a second time. It takes me a while to go back to sleep after it and it was already three thirty, so I got up. It wasn't that early."

"You could have woken me up. I would have gone jogging with you at least," Michael chimed in.

"I'm fine, guys, honest."

"You had the dream a second time you said?" Damien asked.

Josie started a kettle of water heating on the stove to make some tea. "Yeah, twice last night, lucky me." Michael and Damien shared a glance, one that didn't escape Josie. "What?" Neither answered. "Oh, come on, what was that look?"

Damien shrugged. "Nothing, just... well..." He stammered.

Josie crossed her arms. "Yeah?"

"Well, perhaps you should try a therapist. I mean, this nightmare is starting to affect more than your sleep. Perhaps it's smart to see someone and try to get a handle on this," Damien answered.

"I don't understand how a therapist can help, but..." Josie paused. "It is getting really aggravating. This limited sleep is going to lead to more problems."

"So, you'll make an appointment?" Michael asked.

"Yeah, I will make an appointment with someone from the list. I'll try it, can't hurt, right?"

"Good, I'm glad you're doing that," Michael said. "I'm going to work here today, that way I'll be here if you need me."

"I'm glad you're going to see someone, Jos," Damien chimed in. "Unfortunately, I can't work from home today so I'm going to head into the office but call if you need me, okay?"

"I will," Josie said, squeezing his shoulder. Damien was always protective of Josie and often considered himself responsible for her. She hoped the simple gesture reassured him she would be fine.

"Text me when you get an appointment made with the therapist, okay?" he said, patting her hand before standing and heading to his room to get ready for work.

"Okay!" Josie called after him.

"Just us," Michael said. "You should continue to rest today, too. Want your laptop on the couch?"

"Okay, will you stop with 'Dad mode,' I can work in my office, I am fine."

Michael held his hands up to demonstrate defeat and said nothing further. Josie left the kitchen, intent on getting some work done after dressing for the day.

When 9 a.m. rolled around, Josie decided she wouldn't put off calling for an appointment with one of the recommended therapists from her ER visit. Grabbing her phone she forced herself to dial the first number on the list and waited while the phone rang on the other end. After a few rings, the receptionist answered, dashing Josie's hopes that no one would pick up. She recounted a succinct version of her story of ending up in the emergency room after fainting and that Dr. Reed was one of the recommended therapists for a follow-up. Within short order, the receptionist was offering dates and times for the next available appointment. The doctor had an appointment open at 6 p.m. the following evening. Hoping Damien would go with her, she booked that appointment since it was well after he was home from the office.

The rest of the day dragged. Josie struggled to stay awake. She considered napping, but worried it would cause her to be unable to sleep that night so she opted to fight to stay awake.

When evening came, she elected to turn in early, hoping it didn't take long to fall asleep and that she would stay asleep. She told Damien he didn't have to sleep in her room tonight, hoping that her weariness would be enough to keep her sleeping through the night. A small part of her was almost afraid to close her eyes for fear of having the dream again, but within minutes of her head hitting the pillow she drifted off to sleep.

Regrettably, she did not remain asleep for the duration of

the night, as she hoped. Around midnight, she awoke out of breath, drenched in sweat, having dreamt again of running through the cave, frightened and panicked. As she took several deep breaths attempting to lower her heart rate, the dream raced across her mind. She hated to continue to think about it, but she couldn't help herself. Something was bothering her about it; something seemed different. She replayed it in her head over and over. As she lay back down, a new thought struck her. She bolted upright again. The difference in her latest dream was subtle. As she ran through the cave carrying the book, terrified and panicked, she turned to look behind her. That was usually when she awoke from the dream. In this dream, she did not have the book and continued running after her glance backward. As she began to run again in her dream, someone called her. Except they weren't calling to her, they were calling to someone named Celine.

Celine. There was that name again. She recalled that was the name used in the note with the music box. She wondered if her mind had added that detail; had that incident crept into her nightmare or did she wake up and add that detail? Either way, she had a strong urge to go look at the music box. She threw off her covers and crept downstairs, trying not to wake the others in the house. Where had she put that box, she wondered? She remembered she had shoved it into the closet after Michael had invited himself to stay. She made her way to the closet and retrieved the box. Sitting on the floor, she pulled it open and took out the music box, opening it. The tinkling music filled the air; it calmed her frayed nerves. A peaceful mood settled on her. Her hand rubbed the necklace inside. As if on autopilot, she took it out and put it on, sensing its weight around her neck. She pressed a hand against it as she listened to the music.

* * *

"Josie, Josie! Josie, hey, Josie!"

Was someone calling to Josie in the distance? She felt her body shake. As if being pulled out of a dream, she slowly came to her senses, blinking her eyes and glancing around. Damien and Michael were both standing above her. "Josie," Michael said again, "hey, are you okay?"

"I'm fine, yes, why, what's wrong?"

Damien and Michael exchanged a glance. "What's wrong," Michael began, "is that we found you here at two in the morning dazed sitting on the living room floor listening to this music box. We've been trying to talk to you for the last five minutes."

"What?" Josie remembered that she had come down after her nightmare looking for the object. "2 a.m.?" Josie was perplexed, had she been down here for almost two hours?

"Yes, it's two in the morning, what are you doing up and listening to this?" Michael asked.

"I…" She stammered. "I had the nightmare again, and I got up and I don't know, I was thinking of this music box."

"So you weren't sleepwalking?" Damien chimed in.

"No. I was awake. I remember coming down here, but it seems like I just did. But you're telling me that was hours ago."

"You were unresponsive, Jos, we were talking to you and you were just staring into space like you were sleeping with your eyes open," Damien said.

"I'm more fatigued than I realized, I must have been lost in thought," Josie answered. "I should go back to bed and try to sleep. The upset the nightmare caused has passed now."

Josie stood up to head back upstairs. "You going to sleep in your jewels, princess?" Michael asked her.

"Huh?" Josie grabbed her neck. "Oh, right. I don't know

why I'm wearing this. I must have been in a daze, I don't remember putting this on," she said, removing it and placing it back in the music box.

"You said you wanted to see the music box? Is there a reason?" Damien asked.

"No. Wait, yes. When I had the dream again, before I woke up, I could hear someone calling the name Celine. I was thinking of the music box since it came with that note addressed to Celine."

"Probably been on your mind since it was kind of disturbing," Damien said.

"Here give me that thing, I'll put it away," Michael said, reaching out to take the music box from Josie.

"No!" Josie snapped, snatching it back from him.

"Whoa, okay, sorry," he said, holding his hands up.

"Sorry, I don't know why I did that, sorry, I think I'm just drained. I wanted to take this with me. The music relaxes me, maybe it'll help me sleep."

"Okay, yeah, whatever helps you relax," Michael answered. "Hope you sleep."

"Thanks," Josie said, calming down and heading up the stairs.

Damien began to follow her when Michael grabbed his elbow and motioned for him to stay behind, holding a finger up.

"Have you ever seen her like that before?" he said, when Josie disappeared down the upstairs hallway to her room.

"No, and I've never seen her sleepwalk either."

"Why was she so worked up about the music box? The music calms her?"

"No idea. Like I said, I've never seen her like that before, never saw this music box when we were growing up, never heard that music 'til the day it showed up on our doorstep. I

don't know why she'd find it calming. I just know this therapist appointment can't come soon enough."

"Agreed. Not much longer now. All right, I'm heading
back to bed, see you in the morning."

"Yeah." Damien yawned. "See you in a few."

CHAPTER 6

*W*hen Josie awoke the next morning, she was amazed at how well rested she felt despite experiencing the nightmare again and being up for hours in the middle of the night. The little music box was still tinkling away on her nightstand. She shut the lid as the memory of how it got there flooded back to her. Sitting on the edge of her bed, she prepared for the day. Her therapist appointment was this evening. She dreaded going but if it managed to help her, she would do it.

Her run didn't help to clear her head, and she found herself distracted for most of the day. As much as she dreaded the appointment, she was relieved when they were finally on their way to the doctor's office. Damien agreed to go with her and Michael insisted on tagging along. Josie was rather nervous so she didn't argue, but was glad to have the support of both men.

The wait for her appointment seemed like an eternity for an apprehensive Josie. As her impatience reached its peak, Josie was called back. Both she and Damien stood to enter the doctor's office since Josie had asked him earlier to go in with her.

"Usually only the patient goes back," the receptionist said.

"I'd be much more comfortable if he came with me."

"Okay, right this way, Ms. Benson."

They entered the doctor's office. It was nicely appointed with dark, muted colors and comfortable looking chairs, probably designed to make a patient relaxed. The doctor sat at his desk. Upon their entering, he stood and motioned for them to take the two leather armchairs to the right of the desk. He took a seat across from them in another armchair. "Ms. Benson, nice to meet you, I'm Dr. Reed. Can I call you Josie?"

"Sure," Josie answered. The doctor's tactful manner was irritating her already. She wanted to cut to the chase.

"May I ask who your friend is?"

"This is my cousin, Damien. We've lived together since we were five years old. It makes me more comfortable to have him with me."

"Of course," the doctor said gently. "So, tell me, Josie, what brings you here?"

Josie recounted the story of how she had received the doctor's name after fainting in the food court of the mall. She also described the nightmares she had been having, telling him that they had been increasing in frequency. The doctor listened without interrupting. When she was finished he said, "Okay, let's start by talking about what's going on in your life, specifically, stressors. How is work?"

"Work is good. I'm self-employed, I run a cybersecurity business. I don't really have any issues, I have a steady stream of work but I'm not drowning in work, I've got a nice balance going on right now."

"Any issues with a boyfriend or husband?"

"No. No husband or boyfriend, no issues there."

"How is your relationship with your parents?"

"Fine. I've always had a good relationship with them, no issues lurking on that front. I know you probably are wondering if there is an issue between D and I, but there isn't, we get along great, we always have, no stress there. He's more like my brother than my cousin. We've always been close. I've dealt with far more stress before and never experienced anything like this. I wouldn't even consider myself to be stressed right now. There's nothing on my mind or worrying me."

"Stress can manifest itself in several ways. It may be something that you don't even realize is bothering you."

"I can't figure out what it would be."

"I'd like to try to get to the root of that through your subconscious with your permission. There are a number of methods we can use. I'd like to start with hypnosis. It's a noninvasive procedure. I'd like to determine tonight if you're susceptible to being hypnotized and if we can get any information that way about the dream or its source."

"Oh, um, I guess that's ok. I mean, I've never been hypnotized before but I'm willing to try."

"Great. Damien, I'm going to ask you to step out for this," he said, turning to Damien.

Josie was quick to answer, "Oh, no, he stays, even during this."

"Okay, if that's what makes you comfortable, Josie. I'm going to dim the lights a bit."

"Okay. Do I lay down or what?" Josie said, a bit nervous.

"No, that's not how we'll approach this. I will start this pendulum here. I want you to follow that, just focus on that, try to shut everything else out and listen only to my voice, okay?"

"Simple enough," Josie said.

"Okay, let's begin, Josie," the doctor said, starting the pendulum moving. "Now just try to relax, let your body sink into the chair, relax. Your limbs are beginning to become tired and heavy and your eyes are starting to close. You're starting to feel completely relaxed, and when I count backwards from ten, you will become even more relaxed. When I finish counting, you will be completely relaxed and asleep." The doctor counted backward from ten, pausing after each number. When he finished, Josie was under.

She sat motionless in the chair, eyes closed, limbs slack. "Josie," the doctor began, "I want you to find a safe place, a place where you are happy. Tell me when you've found one."

"I have one," Josie murmured after a moment.

"Good. I want you to remember this safe place. If you become afraid while we're talking, I want you to go to that place, okay?"

"Okay."

"Josie, I want you now to recall the dream you described to me earlier. Can you remember that?"

"No."

"Why not?"

"I don't want to remember that. I want to stay here."

"Josie, you can go back to your safe place anytime you want, but right now I want you to recall the nightmare you've been having. Tell me when you remember it."

"Okay," she said, after a momentary pause, "I'm thinking of it."

"Can you tell me what you see? Tell me what's going on."

"It's dark. I'm running; the walls are cold and wet, like a cave. I'm scared. I have to get out of here. He's coming. I can hear him. He's coming behind me. I have to run." Josie began to breathe harder. She pinched her eyes shut and wrinkled her forehead before speaking again. "Aidez moi, aidez moi. Il arrive. Aidez moi. Mon Dieu, aidez moi." Josie panted, gripping the chair, her voice rising to a fever pitch.

"Josie, Josie, you're okay, it's just a dream."

"Non, non, il vient. Je dois partir."

"Josie, please speak English."

"HE'S COMING, I MUST GO!" she shouted, tears rolling down her face.

"Josie, you're safe. It's just a dream. Can you tell me more?"

"NO! NO!" she shouted, wincing in pain as the tears continued to stream down her face.

"Josie, go to your happy place. Tell me when you are there."

In an instant, Josie's demeanor changed. While tears still streaked her face, her breathing slowed and the pained look left her face. "Are you in your happy place, Josie?" the doctor prompted.

"Yes, I'm there."

"How do you feel now, Josie?"

A smile crossed her face. "Happy, at peace."

"Good. Now, Josie, I'm going to wake you up. I want you to forget about the dream and I want you to remember how you are feeling at this moment, okay?"

Another smile. "Okay," she said, content.

"Okay, Josie. I'm going to count backwards from ten and when I am finished, you'll wake up as content as you are right now." The doctor began his slow count backwards.

When he said the word "one," Josie's eyes opened. She blinked a few times, glancing around the room. "What happened?" Josie asked. Realizing she had tears on her cheeks, she wiped her face with her hand.

The doctor answered, "Well, I was able to hypnotize you, and we did induce the dream."

"Did you find anything about what's causing my nightmare or what it means?" Josie asked.

"No. We witnessed firsthand how upsetting it is to you." Josie frowned, let down. "It takes time, Josie. This is a process. We're not going to solve this in one session."

"I was hoping to get SOME information," Josie said.

"We got some. But like I said, this takes time. It was upsetting to you, so we want to keep trying until we can get to a point where you can discuss the dream without becoming frightened. We'll get there. I'd like to see you back in a week; you can make an appointment with my receptionist. Until then I want you to relax, don't push yourself to overthink the dream. Would you like me to prescribe a sleep aid for you?"

"No, thanks, I'd rather not get into medication. I'll do my best, and if it's still an issue, we can address it next week."

"That sounds like a good plan, Josie. Do you have any questions for me this evening?"

"No, thank you, Dr. Reed." Josie stood to exit the office, along with Damien. After making an appointment for the following week, she left the office with Damien and Michael.

"Okay, so what happened in there, D?" she asked as soon as they were in the car.

"I'd like to know the answer to that myself," Michael chimed in from the driver's seat.

"Um, well," Damien started out, unsure, "you were having that dream or whatever. I mean first he asked you to find like a happy place where you felt safe and remember it so you could go back there if you needed to."

"Happy place? You had the dream? Did you go to sleep?" Michael said, rapid firing questions at them.

"No, he hypnotized me. And then I had the dream. I don't remember anything. Although, I woke up serene, nothing like when I wake up from the dream at night."

"Yeah," Damien said, "yeah, he hypnotized her, and like I

said, he had her find this happy place and then he asked her to remember her dream and then when she got super upset he asked her to go back to the happy place and forget the dream when she woke up."

"What did I say about the dream?"

"Should we be talking about this, Jos? He said not to push yourself," Damien said.

"D, I'll go nuts if I don't know what happened in there, so it'll be worse if we don't. Now come on, what happened?"

"Well, you started out saying the same stuff you've been saying, describing the dream. You're running in some kind of cave and you're scared and someone is coming after you. And then..." Damien paused.

"Yeah? And then?" Josie prompted.

"Umm, this will sound bizarre but..."

"Bizarre? More bizarre than the situation already is?" Josie asked, half joking and half serious.

"Yeah. More bizarre. You were talking as though you were in the dream. Like not telling us about the dream, just talking out loud. But... you were speaking French. At least, I assume it was French."

"What?" Josie asked, shocked. "I don't speak French."

"Yeah, I know, but I'm not kidding, you were speaking French. Fluently. Dr. Reed had to tell you to speak English again."

"I... I'm speechless. I don't even understand how that could happen. I don't speak French, I never have. What did I say?"

"I didn't understand you, I don't speak French either. We both took Latin together in high school, remember?"

"Great, so I'm rambling in French and we have no idea what I said," Josie said, throwing her hands up in frustration.

"Actually, though, I recorded it while you were under, just

in case, so we can try to find someone who speaks French to translate it?"

"I speak French. Well, not fluently, but I might be able to translate it," Michael suggested.

"I hope you can, I don't relish playing this for some random person," Josie said.

Damien unlocked his phone and navigated to his video files. "Ugh, you took a video? That's kind of creepy, D," Josie complained. "How did the doctor not notice?"

"I was discreet! And I thought it might be useful because now you can see it's really you speaking perfect French." He played the video. Michael listened while Josie and Damien watched as the doctor put Josie under hypnosis and asked her to recall her dream. As Josie began discussing the dream, becoming more and more upset, Damien said, "Here, it's right after this."

As if on cue, Josie began to speak in French. "Okay, that's just weird," Josie said after seeing the video. "Did you understand any of that?" she said, turning to Michael.

"Uh, maybe, play it again?" Damien replayed the part of her speaking French. "Okay, something like 'help me help me my God help me' I think. There's something else, too, play it again." Damien replayed this part. "Okay, it's 'help me help me, he's coming, my God, help me.' Go to the next part." Damien let the video play to the next lines in French. "No, no, he's coming... play that again? Okay, yeah, 'no no, he's coming, I have to go' is what you're saying."

"Okay, so that at least seems consistent with what I have described before but how the heck am I saying it in French? I doubt I could repeat that as fluently as I did while under hypnosis even after hearing it a few times!"

"Yeah, I'm not sure, I mean, if I didn't see it myself, I wouldn't have believed it but I was right there and saw it happen."

"Did you hear it on a movie somewhere?" Michael asked, turning onto their road.

"I don't know, I mean, not that I recall. I don't watch a lot of stuff with people speaking another language and if there was a small foreign language part, I don't remember it."

Within a few minutes, they were pulling down their driveway. "Maybe it's best we drop this, like Dr. Reed suggested. You're not supposed to be thinking about it, remember?" Damien suggested.

"Right, yeah, we can. I can't explain it, that's for sure. I'm not sure I can forget about it especially since it took a turn for the weirder, but I'll try. Perhaps some pizza will help?" Josie joked, hoping they'd like her plan for dinner.

"Pizza always helps!" Damien grinned.

"While I'm not sure that statement is valid, I'm on board with pizza," Michael agreed. They unbuckled their seat belts and gathered their things, heading into the house for the night.

The man observed them entering the house from his usual hiding spot. Where had they been, he wondered? He had not followed them, unsure of their destination. He preferred to follow Celine when she was alone. She was far less likely to notice him and, if she did, far less likely to cause a scene. There had been no miraculous moments that he could tell so far, no sudden flashes of clarity on her end. At least none that he was aware of. Impatience was growing in him, as it was in everyone else. He had received a text from his cousin this morning asking for a status and to learn if he had made any progress. While he couldn't offer much hope, he brought him up to date on the progress with Celine. The final text from his cousin rung in his head: *We're running out of time.* Running out of time, he thought. It was time to enact the next phase of his plan. The next opportunity that he got he had to take things one step further. He only needed a moment alone with her. His cousin was right; they were running out of time.

CHAPTER 7

*J*osie sat on the edge of her bed. Despite being relaxed, sleep would not come to her. She could not prevent her mind from darting from concern to concern. She tried to push away the thoughts of the video that Damien had captured of her hypnotherapy session but found herself unable to do so. It wasn't what she had said that bothered her, but how she had said it. She had spoken fluent French. How? She had never taken a course in French, never traveled to France; she had no knowledge of the language. Yet she had undeniable proof that she had, in fact, spoken it and in a way that made sense. Josie glanced around the room as if searching for answers. Her gaze fell onto the gold music box. She stared at it. Another mystery. Why give this to her? Whose was it? She picked it up, sensing its weight in her hands. She was sure she had never seen it before yet somehow it seemed so familiar to her. She opened it and the gentle tinkling music started to play. Yes, it seemed so familiar and comforting. She held it for a while longer, lost in thought. It brought her a sense of security, but her mind remained troubled. It seemed like it was reaching for something but couldn't quite fill in the gap. It was as though she was teetering on the verge of remembering some detail but she wasn't able to make the final connections.

She settled back in her bed, still holding the music box. She was suddenly sleepy. She closed her eyes, shutting out the world. Except for the music. The music kept playing as she drifted off to sleep.

* * *

When Josie awoke the next morning, the music box sat on her night table, closed and quiet. She hadn't remembered putting it back there; she must have been half asleep when she did. The silence in the room was deafening. She missed hearing the music. She opened the box and let the music play. What a lovely tune it played, she noted, as she changed into her jogging gear. She almost hated to leave it, but she wanted to get her jog finished. She closed the music box and headed out.

When she returned, Michael and Damien were both awake and preparing for the day. "How did you sleep?" Michael asked.

"Good, actually," Josie said, "I had trouble falling asleep but once I did I was out like a light."

"Did the music box help?" Michael questioned further.

"It did. How did you know?"

"I checked on you in the middle of the night. You were holding it. I closed it and put it next to you."

"Why did you do that?" Josie said, accusatory.

"I didn't want it to wake you or for you to drop it."

"You shouldn't have done that. Don't touch that, just leave it next time."

"Okay, sorry," he said, confused at her sudden outburst.

"Sorry, I realize you were trying to help," she said, softening a bit. "Are you both heading in to the office today?"

"I am, full day today, half-day tomorrow," Damien answered.

"Me too, unless you want me to stay home with you?" Michael said, directing the last statement as more of a question posed to Josie.

"No, no, I'm fine. I feel good. Perhaps the therapist was a good idea."

"Okay, great. See you when I get home then," Michael said, leaving the kitchen.

"You sure you're okay?" Damien asked once Michael left.

"Yeah, like I said, I feel good. About the best I've felt in weeks. It's amazing what a good night's sleep will do, huh?"

"Okay, if you need anything, call me."

"Okay, have a good day!" Josie said as she set the teakettle on the stove.

Josie had her morning cup of tea on the porch, enjoying the beginnings of what promised to be a lovely summer day. She swung gently on the porch swing as the warm breeze caressed her skin. She overlooked the front lawn edged with the forest that enveloped the house on all sides. The smell of summer hung in the air; closing her eyes, she enjoyed the scent and sounds of the season. She felt refreshed today, more like herself. As she sipped her tea, she hummed with happiness to herself. She recognized the tune; it was the one from the music box. The music box was beautiful. If she had received it by mistake, it was a happy accident because she was growing to love it.

She retrieved it from her bedroom, carrying it to the porch. As she drank the rest of her tea, she listened to the music, becoming relaxed. She almost hated to finish her tea and close the little music box to head in for work. Checking the time, she dragged herself off the swing and headed in to her office. She spent the rest of the morning processing jobs, checking logs, fixing issues and more of the typical cybersecurity work.

By lunchtime, she had made great progress. She headed out for lunch and a few work-related errands. She stopped by a local café for a salad and iced tea before making a few stops to pick up and drop off various things for work.

Her last stop was at the local office supply store, she had a list a mile long of supplies she needed. She took a cart and began to navigate the aisles, looking for everything she needed. As she rounded the aisle, she almost ran into someone on the corner. "Oh, I'm sorry, excuse me," she apologized, smiling at the person. Her smile faded as the man turned to faced her. He seemed familiar, but she couldn't place him. Then she realized. "Oh, oh my goodness, you're the man from the mall, you caught me when I fainted. Wow, this is the second time I've almost run into you, you should really stay away from me," she joked.

"Yes, how are you?" the man asked.

"Much better, thank you. I never got a chance to say thank you for the save. There was so much confusion."

The man smiled. "Anyway, thank you again." She gave an awkward laugh and started to push her cart away.

"I can help you more, if you'd let me."

"I'm sorry?" she asked, turning back to him, unsure of what he meant.

"I said I can help you more. I can help you remember who you really are."

"I'm sorry, I don't understand what you mean," Josie said, growing uncomfortable with the conversation.

"You've been struggling, haven't you? With the dreams? The nightmares?"

Josie eyed him with disbelief. How could he know about her nightmares? The man continued, speaking quickly, sounding almost desperate. "The music box, it's helping you isn't it?"

Josie's mind clouded, her brow creased as she tried to process the information but failed to do so.

The man continued, "You need to remember, remember who you are." He grabbed her around the shoulders. "You've got to remember, Celine. You've got to remember." He shook her a bit as though trying to jar loose something in her brain to help her remember.

Josie struggled against him. "Let go of me, let go." She wriggled out of his grasp. "You're crazy," she said, backing away. "Stay away from me." She turned and hurried toward the exit of the store, leaving behind her cart and intended purchases.

"Celine!" he called after her, "Celine, wait! You've got to remember!"

Josie hurried from the store, rushing out into the bright sun. She fumbled with her sunglasses, resisting the urge to break into a full run to her car. She was unnerved and her hands were shaking as she got into the car, locking her doors behind her. He was crazy; he had to be. But yet he knew personal details about her. Why did he insist on calling her Celine? Was it him who sent her the music box?

She took a deep breath and swallowed hard. She looked at the store's entrance; the man had followed her out and was staring across the parking lot at her. She pulled on her seat belt and fired the engine, putting the car into gear and driving away.

By the time she pulled into the driveway at home, she was no less unnerved. She entered the house, pushing the door shut behind her and locking it, she leaned against it, eyes closed, taking deep breaths.

"You okay?" a voice said.

She jumped, startled. She opened her eyes to find Michael

making his way across the room. "Sorry, I didn't mean to startle you, is everything okay? You seem upset."

She considered lying to him but she was so disconcerted by what happened she couldn't pull it off. She shook her head 'no,' unable to speak for the moment.

"What happened? Come sit down, are you sick, do you feel faint again?" Michael helped her to the couch. "I'll get you some water," he said.

"Water, yes, some water please," she managed, trying to compose herself.

Michael returned with a glass of water, handing it to her and sitting down next to her. He rubbed her back as she took a few sips. "Can you tell me what happened now?" he asked after she set the glass down.

"This man, at the office store, he just, he was crazy, he had to have been," Josie stammered, almost as though speaking to herself.

"Man at the office store? What? Josie, start at the beginning."

"I went to the office supply store. Oh my gosh, I never finished shopping, I just left," she said, placing her hand on her forehead as she remembered her folly.

"What about the man, Josie?" Michael persisted.

"I was shopping. I turned the corner and almost ran into him. The man that caught me when I fainted at the mall. I recognized him and I thanked him for helping me. He asked how I was feeling and I said I was better. Then he just started rambling about how he could help me and that I needed to remember who I was. He grabbed me and kept saying I needed to remember who I was."

"He grabbed you? Are you okay?"

"Yeah, yeah, I'm fine. I mean, he didn't hurt me, but he grabbed hold of me, but I'm okay."

"Probably some nut case. But I don't like the fact that he's showing up so often, that can't be by chance. Nor that he's putting his hands on you. We should call the police."

"Michael, he knew," Josie said, looking right into his eyes and ignoring his previous statement. "He knew about my nightmares and the music box. How would he know that?" she asked, turning pensive again. "It was so strange. I thought he was crazy too, but he knew things about me. How did he know those things?"

"Probably has been following you and overheard it. I don't like this, Josie. We should call the police and I don't think you should go anywhere alone or even stay here alone. Who knows how crazy this guy is. Did he follow you to your car?"

"He came out of the store. I was already in the car, I left. What are you doing?" Josie asked, seeing Michael with his phone in his hand.

He put the phone to his ear. "I'm calling the police."

"No, don't," she said, grabbing the phone.

"Why? Josie, this guy might be dangerous."

"I just, I feel stupid. He is just some weirdo, probably harmless. I mean, what am I going to tell the police? A strange guy caught me when I fainted and I ran into him later and he told me I needed to remember who I really am. I'm the one who will sound crazy at this point."

"Yeah, that's exactly what you're going to tell them. Okay, if you don't want the police involved yet, fine, but as much as possible, you shouldn't be going out anywhere alone or staying here, will you at least agree to that?"

"Yes. I didn't say I wasn't uneasy. I just don't think it's police report worthy at this point."

"Good."

"Shoot!" Josie exclaimed.

"What?"

"I told you, I never finished my shopping. I needed supplies for work."

"Order it, Josie. Don't go back to the store."

"I don't want to go back but I should order it now before I forget. I'm going to change and grab my laptop."

"Okay."

Josie headed up the steps and to her room. She was a little calmer, no longer shaking. She was home and safe and she focused on that. She started changing into more comfortable clothes. As she put away the clothes she was wearing, she spotted the music box. A wave of emotion swept over her. She remembered the man in the store mentioning it. He must have been the one who delivered it to her doorstep. That was before he had "rescued" her at the mall. Who was he and why was he doing this, she wondered? No matter what the reason, it now made her apprehensive. It reminded her too much of the scary experience she had at the store. She pulled on a change of clothes, grabbed her laptop and the music box and headed out of the room and downstairs.

"Feel any better?" Michael asked when she reached the landing.

"Yes."

"Why do you have that?" he asked, motioning to the music box.

"I'm getting rid of it. I don't want it. The crazy guy mentioned this, too. I think he was the one who left it here."

"Are you going to throw it away?"

Josie considered the question for a moment. "No, not yet. I'll put it back in the box in this closet. It seems really old, it's beautiful, perhaps it's a keepsake. He might be crazy, but I'd feel bad tossing it in case it belongs to someone."

"Here," Michael said, approaching her, "Let's put it up on the shelf. It will be out of the way." They packed it in the box and Josie watched Michael push it back on the shelf in the closet.

As he shoved it as far back as he was able, Damien came in through the front door. "Hey guys," he said. "What's up?"

"Just putting that stupid music box away," Josie said, arms crossed.

"I thought you liked it?" he asked, shedding his messenger bag and shoes.

"She did until she found out it came from a crazy stalker who attacked her today," Michael chimed in, closing the closet door.

"What?" Damien stopped dead from removing his second shoe in shock.

"I wasn't attacked. Some crazy guy was just talking nonsense at the office supply store. He was the same guy who caught me when I fainted at the mall. He was at the office store and was just saying crazy stuff to me."

"Like what?" Damien asked.

"Like I need to remember who I am and he can help me and on and on, weird stuff."

"And he grabbed hold of her and mentioned her nightmares and the music box," Michael added, "so we know who brought this to the door and we know he's not only been here at the house but in two other places she's been. So, he's stalking her and he could be violent."

"Really, Michael? Violent? That's quite a leap," Josie said.

"Josie, you were shaking when you got home, don't write this off."

"I'm not writing it off. I'm just saying he might be unbalanced but not unhinged."

"Did you call the police?" Damien asked.

Michael crossed his arms in frustration. "Nope, tried to, she didn't want to," Michael said. "But I'm insisting that she not be anywhere alone, including here as much as possible, until we know more or this guy crawls back under whatever rock he came from."

"I agreed to that, yes," Josie said.

"Yeah, sounds like a plan. I agree we should not leave you alone. But, are you sure we shouldn't call the police, Jos?" Damien prodded.

"If he shows up again, we will. For now, I'd rather not," Josie explained.

"Reason?" Damien asked, now removing his second shoe.

"I don't know. I just, I don't think he's dangerous. He seemed kind of..." Josie paused. "Sad, I guess."

Michael rolled his eyes. "He's crazy," he mouthed to Damien.

"I saw that. Let's drop it. I'm going to order my supplies that I didn't get when I ran out of the store."

Josie made her way to the couch and set up shop, retrieving her list and creating her order. She did everything possible to keep the incident off her mind for the remainder of the day and evening. As bedtime approached, she was reluctant to go to bed. An uneasy pall hung over her and she was sure as soon as she laid down her mind would dwell on the incident.

Damien knew her well enough to sense her hesitance and asked if she'd prefer him to camp out with his favorite air mattress in her room. Josie loved how he could sense her moods and told him that she would appreciate that gesture very much.

Even with Damien so close, sleep escaped Josie. Every time she closed her eyes, she saw the man, remembered the wild look in his eyes as he begged her to remember, felt his hands grasping her shoulders, heard his voice, feverish by the end. Each time she would snap her eyes open to make sure she was still safely tucked in her bedroom. Sometimes she peered over the edge of the bed to check that Damien was still there.

After hours of fretting, she dozed off, sleeping restlessly, dreaming of the incident with the man, the music box, and a woman named Celine. She walked through the office store, but the aisles became winding tunnels and she became lost. The man appeared begging her to remember her true self. Somewhere the music box played, and she followed its sound. She wound through passage after passage, finding it playing on top of a shelf. She approached it and found a mirror behind it. She looked at the mirror and saw her reflection. But yet, it wasn't her reflection. "No," the reflection said, "I am your true self. I am Celine."

Josie jolted awake, disturbed by the dream. She concluded that trying to sleep was useless. She rose from the bed and donned her robe. Tiptoeing out of the room, she made her way downstairs. She hoped some television would help distract her mind enough to fall asleep.

She flipped through the choices on her streaming network and settled for re-watching a comedy series. The show did little to distract her, only providing background noise for the questions churning in her mind. How did the man even find her? Why did he think she was Celine? Who was he? How did he know about her nightmares? Why did he give her the music box and what did it mean? Was it Celine's music box? Who was Celine? The questions would not cease racing across her mind.

Her thoughts converged on the music box. She had packed it away earlier, not wanting to see it. Perhaps that was a mistake. A sudden urge pushed her to want to see it again, to hold it in her hands and to hear the little tinkling song that it played. She went to the closet and struggled to pull the box down from the shelf. It was no use; she couldn't reach it. She sighed, frustrated. Heading to the laundry room, she grabbed a step stool and dragged it to the living room. She set it up outside of the closet, climbed up and grabbed the box. As she was climbing down, she heard a noise behind her.

"What the hell are you doing?" Michael asked, still squinting in the light.

Damien was behind him, rubbing his eyes. He yawned. "Yeah, what are you doing?"

Josie narrowed her eyes. "What are you doing up?" Josie asked.

"Ah, you woke everyone up with all your banging around," Michael responded. "Is that the music box?"

"Yes," Josie answered curtly.

"Why are you getting that?" Damien asked. "It's the middle of the night."

"I wanted to see it," Josie said, climbing down off the step stool and dragging it away enough to close the door.

"I thought you said you didn't want to see it anymore?" Michael questioned her.

"Well, now I do. I'm allowed to change my mind," she said, sitting on the couch with the box and beginning to open it.

"Josie, put that away. Go to bed. Try to get some sleep. You can see it in the morning," Michael prompted her.

"I couldn't sleep. I had a disturbing dream, not the same one, but a different one and I couldn't sleep anymore. After everything that happened yesterday, I think that's understandable."

"Well, okay, sure, let's put that down and we'll hang out and watch some T.V. with you or we could play a video game or something, get your mind off of everything." Michael sat down next to her and tried gently to remove the box from her.

"No, leave me alone!" she shouted, pulling the box back to her and away from Michael.

Michael shot a glance to Damien. This was not the Josie

he knew; he was growing concerned. The lack of sleep seemed to be taking its toll. Damien's concern equaled Michael's. He approached Josie, sitting on the coffee table in front of her. "Jos?" Damien said, putting his hand on hers. "You should try to get some rest, let's go to bed," he said gently.

"Stop treating me like a child. I'm not a child. I'm not going to bed. I prefer to be left alone," she said, pulling the music box from its package.

Michael and Damien shared another glance. Josie stared at the music box, running her hand over the top of it. She opened it and the bright music began to play. "Hey, didn't you say that helped you sleep? Maybe you should take it upstairs with you and lay down and see if you can sleep now," Damien suggested.

"Yes," Josie said, sounding almost dazed, "yes, I will." She stood and made her way to the stairs.

"Okay, that's weird," Michael said when she was out of earshot. "Her behavior around that music box is odd. One minute she wants nothing to do with it and the next she's rummaging around in the closet on a ladder to get it back in the middle of the night. And then she's so touchy about it."

"Maybe it's the lack of sleep?" Damien offered. "I don't know. I mean I've seen her at her best and her worst and I agree, this is odd behavior for her."

"We need to convince her to get rid of that box in the morning. Or at least after she's had a little sleep."

"Yeah, that might be a good idea." He yawned. "Speaking of, I'm going to try to get some sleep, too. I hope I can sleep with the mini concert playing in Josie's room."

"Yeah, I hope you don't start acting weird after a night of listening to that thing."

"Me too." He yawned again. "See you in the morning."

They both headed up for the night. Damien found Josie in

her room, already asleep. The music box played on the night table. He considered closing it but decided not to. The last time Michael did that, Josie had become annoyed with him the next morning. Perhaps it was better for him to wait until she had more sleep to approach the subject. He laid down, trying to tune out the music and fell asleep despite its constant droning.

* * *

The man nursed a drink at the local bar. His first attempt at getting through to Celine had failed, miserably. He must have sounded like a raving lunatic. He had to find a way to reach her, sooner than later. He had to keep at it; had to keep pushing until she remembered. So many lives depended on it.

CHAPTER 8

*J*osie groaned as her alarm chirped, tired from another restless night. The little music box tinkled away on her night table. Funny that she almost threw it away when it had such a mellowing effect on her. She decided she would take it with her to have her morning cup of tea on the porch again after her jog. Closing it for the time being, she got ready for her jog in the en-suite bathroom before tiptoeing out of the room and down the stairs.

She had returned, changed clothes, and made her cup of tea before anyone else was up. They must be sleeping in since neither planned to go to the office today. Retrieving the music box, she set it up on the porch along with her tea. It was another pleasant summer morning. With her shoes kicked off, she swung gently on the porch swing, the cool morning breeze caressing her skin. The music box tinkled away as she sipped her tea. She let the gentle movement lull her into a relaxed, dreamlike state.

She held her legs out in front of her as she swung, letting her gaze fall to her feet. She smiled, thinking how much she loved being barefoot in the summer. Without warning, another image dashed across her brain. It was fleeting but vivid. It seemed like a memory, yet she couldn't place it. She was swinging, watching her bare feet in front of her. The scent of flowers hung heavy in the warm air. She leapt from the swing and splayed herself onto the lawn below, the grass cool beneath her. Her curls fell around her, her hair much longer than she ever remembered wearing it. She stared into the crisp blue sky, with white clouds dotting it here and there. The bright sun shone down upon her. She closed her eyes as it warmed her face. "C'est un jour parfait pour être heureux," she murmured aloud.

Josie stopped the swing, snapping back to reality. Where did that come from? It seemed like a memory. But she did not recognize the place. And it was impossible for her to remember speaking in a language she didn't know. The so-called memory confused her; her head began to ache. The pain drove the memory from her mind. The music still playing from the music box began to irritate her. She slammed it shut, rubbing her temples.

"Ready to pitch that thing yet?" Michael asked, leaning against the front door jamb, coffee in hand.

Josie sighed. "Please stop startling me like that."

"Sorry," he said, making his way over to join her on the swing. "Did you end up getting any sleep?"

"Yes," she said, still irritated from the pain throbbing in her head.

"Doesn't sound like enough."

"I just have a headache. I need some aspirin and another cup of tea."

"Okay. Hey, I was thinking, we should get out of the house today, take your mind off of things, you know? We could see a movie. Or take a trip to the park. Whatever you want."

"Yeah, I'll consider it," Josie said, hovering in the door. "Let's see if my headache goes away," she said, disappearing to retrieve her aspirin and more tea.

She returned about fifteen minutes later, Damien in tow. "Look who I found," she said, sitting on the swing.

"Did your headache pass?" Michael asked.

"Yes, the aspirin seems to be working already. I think we should go out today. What about a movie? It'll be too hot for a hike today."

"Right, yeah, what's it going to hit over ninety today or something?" Damien asked, always willing to forego physical activity.

"Okay, I'll even let you guys pick the movie, as long as you promise not to pick something boring," she teased.

After having a lazy morning, the three selected a matinee showing of an action movie and planned to grab an early dinner after the movie before heading home. The darkened theater erased any traces of the headache Josie experienced earlier in the morning, leaving her relaxed. They left the theater, joking about a few scenes in the movie. Pushing through the exit doors, the heat and bright sun greeted them.

As Josie stepped out, the sunshine blinded her after being in the darkened theater. As soon as she pushed through the door, she felt like a brick struck her. She doubled over, clutching her head. Thoughts raced through her brain, but they made little sense to her. She heard her friends calling her but they sounded like they were miles away. The sensation, while intense, passed within seconds. She recovered, righting herself and taking a deep breath.

"Josie, are you okay? Get the car and bring it," Damien said to Michael. Michael disappeared, keys in hand to bring the car around.

"I think so," Josie said. "I got this intense pain in my head and my mind was so blurry. I guess from the sudden heat and sun," she surmised.

"Yeah, I'd believe that if you didn't just pass out and end up in the ER. I think you should revisit the hospital.

"No, no way, absolutely not. I'm fine!" Josie insisted.

"Okay, well, maybe we should head straight home, at least."

"No, no, I'm fine, let's go eat. I just need some food, my popcorn lunch may not have been a good idea."

"Are you sure?" Damien asked as the car pulled around toward them.

"Yeah, I'm sure, I'm fine." She smiled, trying to portray an air of confidence.

Damien opened the door for her and got her into the car, then hopped into the backseat. "Home?" Michael asked, pulling away from the curb.

"No way, I'm hungry, let's go eat!"

"Really?" he questioned.

"Yes, really. I'm fine, the sun just blinded me, that's all. I'm fine. I'm fine."

Michael shot Damien a glance. He shrugged his shoulders. Josie rolled her eyes. "Oh stop it, you two, I'm fine. I won't be fine if someone doesn't take me to get something to eat soon though."

"Okay, okay, we'll go get something to eat," Michael said, easing the car onto the road and heading for the restaurant they selected.

The three were seated quickly after arriving and ordered shortly after. Josie excused herself to use the ladies' room after ordering. She looked at herself in the mirror as she washed her hands. What had happened to her when she stepped out of the theater? Despite all her protestations, she wasn't sure she was okay. The thoughts that spilled through her mind during her attack made no sense to her. They were akin to the image she experienced this morning while sitting on the porch. It seemed as though she was remembering someone else's life. What was wrong with her? Perhaps she was overtired and her mind was playing tricks on her, she contemplated, as she dried her hands with a paper towel before exiting the bathroom.

No matter what it was, she decided, as she pushed through the door into the hallway, she would not let it ruin her dinner. She would do her best to push it from her mind.

"You're remembering aren't you?" a voice said from behind her as she entered the hall.

"What?" she said turning to face the person speaking.

"I said you're remembering, aren't you?" the man said again, smiling at her. Josie recognized him, it was the man from the mall and the office supply store. It was obvious now that he was following her.

"I don't know what you're talking about," Josie lied, "I told you to leave me alone." She turned to leave; he wouldn't dare follow her to the table with her friends unless he planned on getting into a world of trouble.

"I can help you when you're ready, Celine!" he called after her.

Josie returned to the table. "Everything okay?" Michael asked, as she sat down.

"Yep," she lied. "Even better now that the appetizer is here," she said, helping herself. Neither Michael nor Damien were convinced, but neither wanted to push it.

"Excuse me, miss? I believe you dropped this." Josie looked up as someone placed something on the table near her. It was the man who had been following her. He left as quickly as he came, turning slightly, giving her a half-smile as he walked away.

Although astounded, Josie said nothing to either of her companions. Instead, she called a 'thank you' after him and reached to put what he left into her purse. She glanced at it as she shoved the card in. It was the manager's card for the restaurant. On the back was scrawled 'Call me when you're ready' along with a phone number. Josie didn't understand why she didn't tell anyone else who the man was nor that he had left his phone number with her, but for reasons unknown, she decided it was the best course of action. Instead, she acted nonchalant and returned to eating and conversing as if nothing happened.

The man walked from the restaurant. For the first time he sensed progress. She was beginning to remember; he could see it in her eyes. She knew there was something more and she would soon be ready to accept that along with his help. She now possessed the means to contact him. He hoped she would do so soon. If not, he'd have to push her a little further. Time was of the essence. But even if time wasn't on their side, he couldn't help but leave the restaurant with a smile. She would soon be his Celine again.

CHAPTER 9

*J*osie sat on the edge of her bed, turning the card over and over in her hands. Questions raced through her mind once again. Why had the man given the card to her? Why did he insist she was someone else? Why had she not said anything to her companions? She let the man who had been following her, who had grabbed her while raving like a madman, walk out of the restaurant without mentioning even a word to them. Josie's own behavior was scaring her as much as the dreams and the recent visions she had been experiencing.

She heard a noise at the door and shoved the card under her leg. Damien knocked on the door. "Ready for bed?" he asked.

"Yep, I was just about to turn in."

"You sure you're okay sleeping alone tonight?"

"Yeah, I'm sure, thanks for checking though. I'm exhausted and I think getting out for that movie did me some good. I'm sure I'll sleep fine."

"Are you going to play the music box to put you to sleep?"

"No, don't even think I need it," she said, climbing under the covers, keeping the business card hidden.

Damien smiled. "Okay, good night, Jos, sleep tight."

"Good night." She smiled back. She closed her eyes, relaxing into her pillow. As soon as she heard the door click closed, she snapped her eyes open. She pulled the card from under the covers where she had hidden it. The same questions poured back into her mind. She was becoming concerned about her judgement yet she couldn't bring herself to tell anyone about it. She hoped her therapy appointment next week would help. Five days until her next appointment seemed like an eternity. She considered calling the doctor, but even if she did, she would have to wait until Monday. This didn't qualify as an emergency in her opinion; she would not disturb him over the weekend. She would have to do her best to remain calm before that appointment, as he had suggested.

She cracked the music box open enough to slide the card into it. Closing her eyes, she tried to push everything from her mind and drift to sleep. She willed herself to be strong. She had never been a quitter; she came from stronger stock than that. She would be fine. She kept repeating that to herself until she dozed off.

Despite her best efforts, Josie had a restless night, full of concern about the man following her and her lack of alarm over the situation and her refusal to tell anyone that he had approached her again. It seemed as though she was drawn to him. She had also found herself drawn to the music box again in the middle of the night. She opened it and left it play, finding it the only thing that helped her to get any sleep.

She dragged herself out of bed for her morning jog, afterwards slogging into the kitchen on autopilot to make a cup of tea.

"Bad night?" Michael asked, already up and heading to the gym.

"Not terrible but yeah, the lack of sleep is starting to be an issue."

"Why don't you try to go back to sleep now?" he suggested.

"I'm afraid that'll ruin any chance of sleeping tonight. I'll be okay," she said, yawning, "I just need some tea."

"Okay, if you say so. I'll be back later." Josie heard him leaving through the front door. She made it all the way to the porch with her tea before hearing Damien stirring in the house. He soon appeared with a cup of coffee in hand.

"Did you sleep?" he asked.

Josie knew everyone was concerned about her, but the constant conversation about her sleeping habits played on her last tired nerve. "Not really, no nightmares, but still couldn't relax, I guess."

He approached the porch swing where Josie sat and joined her without saying a word. They swung together in silence for a while, each lost in their own thoughts. Josie appreciated having family like Damien, his presence alone comforted her, there was no need for words.

She stared out at the brightly lit lawn. The sun was already heating the day; it was going to be another scorcher. Within an instant, Josie's view changed. She no longer looked at her front lawn and driveway with her and Damien's cars parked near the house. Instead, she saw a large home rising in front of her, white and stately looking with a long curving drive leading to it. Bright blue skies framed it across the top and a landscape of beautiful flowers on the bottom. The air smelled of the sea. The image lasted for a few seconds before it disappeared.

Josie's overtired mind tried to make sense of it. What were these things she was seeing? Her stomach became queasy and her head ached. Not wanting to panic Damien, she tried her best to recover in silence. A few minutes passed, and she hadn't recovered. "Hey, I'm going to lay down for a little while, I don't feel so good."

"You're sick? Do you need anything?"

"No, just my touchy stomach, probably my poor diet yesterday," she gave a weak smile, heading inside and up to her room. She laid down on the bed, closing her eyes, hoping it would help dull the pain in her head. It did nothing to stop the pain. Her stomach still rolled as though she were on a roller coaster. She considered retrieving some medication from the bathroom but she was too sick to move. She laid still on her back, hoping the sensation would soon pass.

Opening her eyes and turning her head she spotted the music box. Her hand reached over to caress the top of it. After a moment, she opened it. The small box's music filled the air. She lay on her side, staring at it. Reaching over after a few moments, she removed the necklace from the box, clutching it to her chest. After about ten minutes, she began to recover. Her head still had a dull ache but the queasiness in her stomach had started to pass. Thank goodness, she thought.

She closed her eyes again, her stomach and head beginning to ease. She began to relax, particularly now that the sensation that she may vomit at any moment had passed. She took a few deep breaths, relaxing as the cool air from the air conditioning unit blew on her as the unit kicked on. The tinkling music continued to fill her mind and lulled her off to sleep.

Josie bolted upright; she'd had the dream again, and it had produced its usual side effects: labored breathing, soaking sweat, quickened pulse and a racing heart. She clenched her fists as she took long, deep breaths to calm her nerves. She looked at her palms, they were damp and sweaty. The dream had been different this time, she recalled, prompted by the clamminess on her palms. She remembered the usual: running through the cave, walls damp, being chased, but this time there was more. After hearing Celine's name being called she had run toward a small ray of light. As she neared, she looked down at her hands. Blood covered them. She had awoken before she determined the source of the blood. She concluded that was a good thing.

She wasn't sure how much more she could take. The almost constant sleepless nights coupled with the terrible dreams and now the strange visions. She considered calling the therapist despite it being the weekend to request those sleeping pills. She was loath to do it; she solved nothing if she medicated her problems away. How long would she need to use pills before she was "cured?"

She glanced over at the little music box, still playing cheerfully away. She remembered having removed the necklace from it before falling asleep. She found it lying under the covers, discarded during her sleep. She placed it back in the music box. She caught sight of the business card she had placed inside. Picking it up, she turned it over, reading the note again. Her eyes clouded with tears. She needed help, but she didn't know where to get it. She didn't want to tell her therapist she was having visions, fearing she'd end up in a straitjacket locked away in a psychiatric ward somewhere. The man who gave her this note seemed to understand. Or was he just as crazy as she was? Why did the prospect of confiding in him appeal to her so much more than getting professional help?

She sniffled, letting a few tears fall to her cheeks. She heard a knock on the door. She wiped her face, sniffled again, and called out, "Yeah?"

Damien poked his head in. "Didn't wake you, did I?"

"No," she said, "I was getting up." She discreetly put the

business card back into the music box and closed it, standing up from her bed.

"Did you get any sleep?" he asked, entering the room.

"Yes, I did."

"That's good! How about a quiet movie day on the couch? It's going to be a real scorcher out there today and there's some severe weather blowing in this afternoon. Sounds like a great day for watching a scary movie to me!"

"Scary movie? I see enough of those when I sleep!"

"Rom-com? Action? Anything, Jos, you can pick," he said, trying to be supportive.

"I'm kidding. Maybe if I'm scared out of my wits, my mind will snap back into place."

"Nothing is wrong with your mind, Josie, you're just stressed out or whatever. I'm sure Dr. Reed can help you. In the meantime, maybe call him for a prescription or try an over-the-counter sleep aid."

"I'm fine, D. I'll just wait for the appointment. What movie do you want to watch? And is it too early for popcorn?"

"You can have whatever you want, Josie, no matter what time it is." Damien grinned.

Josie spent the rest of the day feigning relaxation on the couch when she was anything but relaxed. She felt guilty, both Damien and Michael were falling over themselves to make sure she was comfortable and stress-free, but she couldn't shake the residual emotions from the latest version of the dream. The dreams seemed to be intensifying and coming more frequently. They were lasting longer and including more disturbing information.

By the end of the afternoon, she found it difficult to keep her cool and jovial attitude. The movie marathon provided little distraction no matter what genre they tried.

"What movie next, Jos?" Damien asked. "We have time for two more. It's your pick."

"Ah, pass, someone else can pick."

"Come on, it's your turn."

"Actually, I think I'll get some fresh air."

"Fresh air?"

"Yeah, I'd like to take a walk, clear my head."

"Yeah, stretch the legs, that sounds good, then we'll do one last movie," Michael said.

"I didn't mean all of us," Josie retorted.

"Well, too bad," Michael responded, "You're not supposed to be going out alone, remember?"

"Oh, whatever, I'm too tired to argue, let's just go. First, I have to change my shoes."

"Okay, we'll meet down here in a few minutes," Michael said.

Annoyed, Josie trudged up the stairs. She just wanted five minutes alone. She knew everyone was concerned for her and doing their best to protect her from whatever was happening and she hated herself for reacting this way. But she was becoming overwhelmed with the entire situation and growing anxious about trying to sleep that night.

As she retrieved her shoes, sitting on the edge of the bed to put them on, she opened the music box. Its sweet music filled the room. She took a few deep breaths, closing her eyes, letting the music soothe her frayed nerves. She put her shoes on, tying the laces slowly and methodically as she let the music wash over her. She spent another moment listening to the music before heading down to meet the guys for a walk. As she closed the music box, she saw the business card again. Her hand reached for it before she stopped herself. She would not dwell on it, instead, she forced herself to go for her walk.

The walk did not clear her mind. She spent most of the

time trying to keep up with the pleasantries designed to keep her mind off of her troubles. She forced herself to sit through one more movie before feigning tiredness and excusing herself to go to bed.

Josie was not tired, but she needed to be alone. She opened the music box and curled up on her bed with a book. She wasn't able to concentrate on it and after a few pages she gave up on it, tossing it aside and grabbing her laptop. She browsed social media sites, news articles, and email before playing a few games of solitaire. She tried anything and everything to distract herself but none of it worked.

After running out of distractions, she tried to sleep. She was exhausted, but almost too terrified to close her eyes. She laid down and fought to stay awake but after a while her eyelids became heavy and she closed her eyes, drifting off to sleep. The dream came to her not long after, ruining her sleep early on. She awoke in tears, not only from the terror of the dream but in frustration.

The little music box continued playing its tune on and on, doing its best to soothe her tattered nerves. She reached for it, hugging it to her, wiping tears away. Her fingers ran over the necklace then the business card. She grasped it for the umpteenth time and studied it in the moonlight that streamed in through the window. How could he help her, she wondered? Then again, how could he hurt? She was a mess. Something seemed strangely familiar about the man, she thought, something that calmed her or drew her to him. In a moment of impulsivity, she grabbed her cell phone from the night table and texted the number: *How do you think you can help me?*

She regretted it as soon as the message was sent. Josie threw her phone down among the covers. Why was she texting a stranger in the middle of the night? What did she expect him to answer? The man was unbalanced at best, yet

Josie had texted him and asked for his help. What did that say about her?

She tried to push everything from her mind and concentrate on the music. She closed her eyes, focusing on it until another sound intruded into the night. Opening her eyes, she picked up her cell phone. She had a text message waiting: *Hello, Josie, or can I now call you Celine again?*

The prompt response surprised Josie. She waited a moment before responding, considering if she should answer and what she should say. Before she responded, a second message came through: *I can help you, you're not crazy.*

Uncontrollable tears streamed down her face. She didn't know why, perhaps from relief that someone didn't think she was crazy or perhaps she was just overtired. She let herself sob for a moment before grabbing her phone with a shaky hand to reply: *I don't see how you can help me.*

Within moments, the reply came: *You must have thought I could, you texted me.*

Josie answered: *Why are you following me?*

I need your help, but only after you remember who you are. I can help you remember.

Josie was lost: *I'm Josie Benson. I don't know what you're talking about.*

You're having dreams, nightmares... about that night, the night you changed... the night that changed your life.

The conversation unnerved Josie. She texted back: *I made a mistake contacting you, please leave me alone.*

A response came almost immediately: *Celine, please...*

Josie ignored it but within minutes another text came through: *I can help you... stop the nightmares and help you remember*

Tears rolled from Josie's eyes again as another message came through: *Celine... just meet with me once... please*

Then another: *I can help*

Josie was overwhelmed. She concluded that she had made a grave mistake in sending the initial message. What had she been thinking? As the messages continued to come through despite her lack of response, she became frustrated. She considered throwing her phone against the wall but she knew she would regret it and also wake up the entire household. She considered blocking the number, but she hesitated to do so. Besides, he had her number now, it would be as simple as getting a burner phone to contact her again so what was the use in blocking this number. Instead, she powered it down, preventing any further messages from reaching her tonight. She tossed it back onto her night table and curled in a ball under the covers. Tears continued to roll down her cheeks despite any attempt to stop them. After a while, sheer exhaustion overcame her, and she fell asleep, getting a few hours of sleep before the morning broke.

He set down his phone. The last several messages had gone unanswered; she was ignoring him. It frustrated him, every step he took forward seemed to be followed by three steps back. He checked his phone again, no answer. He doubted he would get a response tonight. The last thing she had sent asked him to leave her alone. But he couldn't do that. He would have to wait for her to respond or continue to send her messages until she did. He tried to focus on the good. She had texted him, she had reached out, she had opened the lines of communication. Not only did it mean that she was coming around but also that he could now get in touch with her without having to follow her every move and calculate when he could approach her. Things were moving in the positive direction, he had to believe that. Otherwise, he faced certain doom, they all did.

CHAPTER 10

*J*osie slept in the next morning, exhausted after another restless night. Before even considering breakfast, she lay with a cool, damp towel over her eyes, swollen from the crying overnight. She felt awful, exhausted both emotionally and physically, with a headache and a touchy stomach.

After about an hour, she dragged herself from her bed and down for breakfast. She was the last one awake, which was unusual. "No jog today?" Michael asked as she plodded into the kitchen.

Josie stifled a yawn. "No, took the morning off," she said, making herself some oatmeal.

"No jog? That's not like you! You must be sick!" Damien joined the conversation.

"I feel awful. I'm going to spend the day in bed."

Michael and Damien shared a glance, the news not sitting well with them. "Do you think you should call the therapist and see him earlier?" Michael asked.

"Yeah, or maybe get a sedative?" Damien added.

Josie realized they meant well but her sheer exhaustion

made the conversation tedious. "I'll see how things go after today," she said, hoping to end any further conversation.

She wasn't that lucky. Michael continued. "I wouldn't put it off, Josie. It seems like you're getting worse."

"Getting worse? What's that even mean?"

"You're getting less sleep, having the nightmares more often, you're having some physical symptoms now like headaches, fainting, I just…" he began to respond.

Josie cut him off. "I fainted once. It's Sunday. If I need him, I'll call tomorrow."

"He has an emergency line," Damien offered.

"And that line is for emergencies. This is not an emergency. Asking for a sleep aid is not an emergency." Josie sighed.

"How about an over-the-counter?" Michael asked.

"Those do the exact opposite of what they're supposed to do for me," Josie said, knowing that over-the-counter sleep aids made her jittery. "I'm just going to hang out in bed today, try to rest and relax and if I am this bad tomorrow, I'll call, okay?"

The men shared a glance. They weren't getting any further with this advice at the moment. "Okay," they both said in unison.

As Josie left the room with her bowl of oatmeal, Damien called after her, "Text us if you need anything, we can bring it up to you."

"Thanks, D," she shouted back.

Josie forced her oatmeal down before lying back in bed. She grabbed her remote and turned on the small T.V. she had in her room. She didn't care what she watched she just wanted some background noise. She started to perk up a little, but she didn't want to push herself. Maybe that was the problem, she was pushing herself too hard and needed a day of rest. She settled back into her pillows, determined that this would make a world of difference for her psyche.

Perhaps she would take Damien up on his offer to bring her something and trouble him for a cup of tea, she thought, grabbing her phone. As she picked it up, she recalled turning it off last night, having received several unwanted texts from the strange man who had been following her. She supposed it was stupid to have texted a stranger, but she had been so desperate last night.

She turned the phone back on, waiting for it to power up. As she waited, she hoped that she would find no messages waiting for her. She planned to delete the conversation from her phone and throw the business card away so she wouldn't be tempted to repeat something so foolish again.

As her phone came to life and connected to the network, she heard several chimes. So much for her wish being granted. Several text messages waited for her, all of them from the same person. She frowned; she had made a huge error in texting him. Unlocking her phone, she began by texting Damien, requesting a cup of tea. He answered her within seconds that he would have a hot cup up to her in a jiffy with a smiley face and a hug emoticon.

Josie smiled at the message before setting her phone down. She did not intend on reading the stranger's other messages but her curiosity got the better of her. She picked up her phone, opened the message app and selected the unread messages.

I'm sorry about the other day, I realize you are overwhelmed
The nightmares will stop or at least slow once you remember
I realize you don't believe me but I can prove that I know you

Josie stared at the messages. The first two sounded like typical messages in a disagreement where one person was attempting to draw the other to their side. The last one struck her though. Prove it, she thought. How could he prove to her that they were acquainted?

As she studied the phone, another message popped onto her screen: *Good morning, Josie... I hope you didn't answer because you fell asleep :)*

Josie clicked her display off, as though having it on allowed the man to see her and see that she was there. Josie pondered for a moment. Should she respond and if so, what should she answer? Was she crazy to respond to him? Perhaps it was best to let things drop, but she was intrigued to find out how he could "prove it" to her. Perhaps she could be finished with him once and for all if he didn't provide evidence.

As she pondered her options, Damien knocked and came through the door without waiting for a response. "Special delivery!" he said cheerily as he came through the door carrying a tray. "Tea, two sugars, just like you like it, nice and hot! And some cookies!" he said, setting the tray on her nightstand. She moved the music box out of his way, setting it on her lap. "Here, I'll take that," he said, reaching for it.

"No, leave it."

"You sure? I was just going to move it to the dresser."

"I'm sure, it's fine. Thanks."

"Oh, this episode is great," Damien said, noticing the T.V. show on her screen. "Want some company?"

Guilt consumed Josie about her borderline rude behavior earlier so she motioned that he was welcome to stay. "Awesome," he said, throwing himself onto the opposite side of the bed and grabbing a cookie.

"So, did you want to stay for my sake or for cookies?" Josie teased.

"Cookies, definitely the cookies," he joked back.

Josie took a sip of her tea and nibbled a cookie. "Hey, sorry about before, I was just super tired."

"Yeah, I understand, Jos. It's okay. We both realize that you're having a rough time, we just want to make things easier."

"I know, sometimes, though, I just, I don't want to deal with it or have anyone treat me like there's something wrong with me. Anyway, sorry."

Damien put his arm around her in a half hug and she let her head rest on his shoulder for a moment. After a short while, he reached around her as though he would give her a full hug. Instead, he snagged a cookie from the plate. She picked her head up, giving him a face. "What?" he said, stuffing the cookie in his mouth.

Despite her lack of rest, it was the most normal moment the two had shared since Josie had been struggling with her nightmares and visions in the last week. She tried to enjoy the moment as much as possible, seeming almost normal again. Perhaps this was just what she needed. "Hey, who is this guy? The actor, what's his name? What else was he in?" Damien asked.

"Um, I'm not sure, wait I look him up."

"Okay, you do that, I'll get more cookies," Damien said, grabbing the plate he had emptied and hopping off the bed. Josie swiped her phone open as he darted out of the room. The message from her strange stalker appeared on the screen. While alone, she responded: *How can you prove it?*

She closed the app and went back to searching the actor Damien asked about. He returned within a few minutes with a replenished plate of cookies. "Did you find it?"

"Yeah, I got it," Josie answered, telling him the actor's name and what else he had starred in as he settled back on the bed to finish the show.

Josie's cell phone soon chirped. She grabbed it to check the message. It was from her mysterious stalker. She did not want Damien to see the response, but she also didn't want to create suspicion, so she nonchalantly checked the message and responded. His message read: *I can tell you details about your nightmares*

Okay, so go on she responded to him.

Damien gave her the side eye. "It's my mom," she lied. "Just checking up on me."

"Did you tell her things are getting worse?"

"No, I didn't, and I'm not planning to," Josie continued to fib.

"Okay, sure. So, she thinks everything is okay?"

"Pretty much," Josie said, telling a small bit of truth. She hadn't told her mother anything in detail, only that she had been experiencing some sleepless nights. Her mother was not aware of the pervasiveness of the nightmares or the stalker.

Josie's phone chirped again. Satisfied with her explanation, Damien paid no attention, returning his full attention to the T.V. Josie opened the message: *You're being chased through a cave with blood all over your hands*

The details were close to her latest iteration of the dream, leaving her more than a little disconcerted. How would this stranger know this? Perhaps he had broken into the therapist's office and listened to the recording. He couldn't have gotten the detail about the blood from that recording. That piece of the dream hadn't developed until after the therapist's visit. Besides, that seemed a little farfetched. Although perhaps less farfetched than having a stalker following you around gifting you music boxes and telling you to remember your true identity. Josie didn't answer for a moment, setting the phone down to consider her response.

Another message came through: *I'm right, aren't I and now you're wondering how I know*

Josie found herself annoyed, not only was it disturbing that this stranger was correct about her dream but now he presumed to tell her what she was thinking. There had to be some reasonable explanation. Had he been spying on her and overheard her talking about the nightmare? Did he break into the therapist's office and listen to the tape Dr. Reed made? Josie wasn't sure, but she had an idea that she presumed might end the situation. She texted back: *No, you're wrong... that's not what my nightmare is about*

Josie waited for the response. After a moment, the phone chirped and Josie read the latest in the saga of text messages: *I'm not wrong... also here is more evidence...*

She waited for the supposed proof. Within seconds, the phone sounded again and Josie opened the message. She took an extra moment to stare at the latest message, her mind unable to wrap around what she was seeing. The message contained a picture of a photograph. The man, her stalker, stood in the photo. He was smiling, his arm wrapped around the woman next to him. Much to Josie's shock, she recognized the woman. It was Josie herself. Josie did not recall taking this picture, but the woman in the photo was identical to her, down to the mole on her cheek that she hated. She had her arm wrapped around the man's waist and her other arm rested on his stomach. Her smile beamed through the picture.

She turned off her phone display, disturbed by what she had just witnessed on it. She wasn't sure what to do. She didn't want to dwell on the photo at the moment, afraid that Damien might wonder what she found so interesting. It must be a fake. It couldn't be real; Josie had never met the man before. She needed to study it more, but she didn't want messages to continue to pour in while she waited for an opportune moment. She texted back: *I need time to think*

She received an immediate response: *I'll be here when you're ready, Celine*

Ignoring it, she set her phone down, pretending to watch

the show with Damien. Her mind buzzed from what she had just seen. She found it hard to focus. "Can I trouble you for a second cup of tea?" she asked.

"Sure, I'll be back in a jiff!" he said, hopping off the bed and grabbing her mug. He headed out of the room. Once alone, Josie grabbed her phone. She opened the messaging app and the picture. She zoomed in on the woman's face. If this wasn't her, it was a twin or a near-identical look alike. The hairstyle she had was slightly different from what she normally wore, but it looked like her hair color and texture. She didn't remember having a dress like the one the person in the picture wore; it was bright pool blue with six gold buttons on it from the neckline to the waist. The pair stood in front of what appeared to be a house, but Josie couldn't be sure since only a portion of it could be seen. She didn't recognize it as any place she had been, although there seemed to be something familiar about it. Josie zoomed in and out on various parts of the picture, trying to determine where it was taken or if it could have been doctored to make her appear to be somewhere she had never been. If someone had tampered with the photo, it must have been done by a professional. In addition to that, it was printed to appear aged. The picture was of an actual photograph that looked like it was printed decades ago based on the style of printing method used.

The plot thickened for Josie and she wasn't enjoying the new twist. She texted back: *I don't know you or how you created that picture but that can't be me*

He responded in less than a minute: *You don't remember but I can help you... This is the cause of your nightmares... well one cause*

Josie texted back: *There is nothing to remember*

She felt like she was going crazy. She had no memory of this man but it appeared to be her standing in the photograph with him. She considered for a moment asking her mother or Damien, but she didn't want to tip her hand. Why was she afraid though? What was forcing her to keep this a secret from her cousin and her mother? As she pondered this, Damien appeared, her mug in hand, carefully carrying it with steaming hot tea.

"A second cup, as requested," he said, setting it down on the saucer he left on her night table from the first cup.

"Thanks." She smiled appreciatively.

"Sure," he said, rearranging the pillows to get comfortable again.

Josie checked her phone, she had a message waiting: *I know you don't believe me... I've given you some proof... please give me the chance to convince you*

The image burned in Josie's mind. He had correctly identified her dream, and he had a picture of them together. She teetered on the edge of losing her grip on reality from sheer lack of sleep and from the strange visions plaguing her, particularly those that involved her speaking a foreign language that she didn't speak. Impetuously she answered: *It has to be in a public place... I'm not meeting with you alone*

Within seconds the man responded: *Just tell me where and when*

Josie pondered for a few moments before responding. She did not know how she could meet him given the close eye that Damien and Michael were keeping on her. She wanted to meet in a crowded spot. She had an idea and texted back: *The Roasted Bean Coffee House on West St... 10am tomorrow*

He responded: *I'll be there*

Within a few minutes, Josie received another text: *If you need anything before then, call or text... I promise this is a positive step for you... for us*

Josie tossed the phone down onto the covers, contemplating what she had just done. She tried not to dwell on it, it was over for the moment and she had almost twenty-four hours to deliberate about it before she had to show up at the café. Twenty-four hours to hope and pray that what she was doing was a positive step forward for her. She sunk back in her pillows and attempted to enjoy the show and the company.

* * *

He set his phone down. There would likely be no more messages from her until they met, if she came. He hoped she did, but he realized she might try to back out. He stopped himself from dwelling on that; she would come, and he would convince her. He had no other choice, he was out of options. It was not only a positive step for her but also for him. He checked his watch. Less than twenty-four hours to go. He'd use the time to plan what he would say to her, what the best way was to convince her of the truth. It wouldn't be easy but at least he had the opportunity. He would take full advantage; he could not fail. Too many people's lives depended on him succeeding.

CHAPTER 11

*J*osie poured her tea before anyone else appeared for the day. As she took the first sip she contemplated her plan, hoping it would work. She spent most of her sleepless night wondering if she was doing the right thing, vacillating between backing out and going through with meeting the stranger. At least her troubled mind and wavering decisions prevented her from having the nightmare again, most likely because she slept so little. What little sleep she got was tainted by nonsensical dreams splicing together any and every recent event in her life.

She was running on adrenaline, so fatigue hadn't set in yet. She turned to leave the kitchen, planning to take her tea onto the porch and watch the rain fall before checking the status of a few accounts prior to her meeting with the strange man who claimed to know her. She realized at that moment that she didn't even know his name. Shaking the nagging reluctance to go through with the plan from her mind, she headed out of the kitchen.

Michael was on his way down the stairs along with Damien. "Good morning," she said.

"Hey, good morning," Damien answered. "Did you get any sleep?"

"Good morning, yeah, same question here," Michael echoed.

"No, not really. I did contact Dr. Reed's office. He said to come by today around ten to discuss options. Maybe he can give me a script."

"Ten? Can you change it? I've got an in-office meeting," Michael said.

"I've got to be in the office today, too," Damien admitted.

"No, nope, can't change it. That's all he had. It's not an appointment per se, so it's fine if I go alone. He's probably just going to ask if I have any allergies or have used any sleep medications before and prescribe something."

"Well, treatment or not, the point was you're not supposed to be going anywhere alone since there is a madman on the loose stalking you," Michael said.

"First, I don't think he's a madman and second, I doubt I will get accosted at the therapist's office. Even if I do, there's plenty of people there to handle him or call the police."

"Yeah, but not at the pharmacy," Damien pointed out.

"I won't go to the pharmacy, I'll come straight home right after and send one of you if he prescribes something."

Michael grabbed his phone. "I'll see if I can change my meeting."

"No, no, it's fine. I will be fine. I'm not a child, you can't be with me twenty-four seven."

"Well, I don't like it but okay, deal, straight there and back," Michael said.

"Okay, dad." Josie teased. Michael sighed but chose not to pursue it further. Josie's plan worked, for better or worse. She was free to meet with the stranger or whoever else she chose.

Josie was a bundle of nerves as she went about her

morning routine. Her ruse had worked, making it all too possible that this meeting would occur. Although she wondered what she had been thinking when she agreed to the meeting, she was determined to go through with it. She needed to learn if he could help her like he promised. The therapist hadn't been able to, although she only met with him once. Following that session, though, the visions, as she referred to them, had developed, so she was worse not better.

After checking her job logs, noting anything that might need followed up on later and verifying everything else, she found herself distracted by anticipation. She paced the floor for an hour before deciding it was time to leave.

She arrived at the coffee shop early, parking outside and watching the entrance for about ten minutes before she found the nerve to enter. She forced herself to open her car door and walk toward the entrance. Her stomach was jittery, her palms were sweaty and her pulse was racing. Her heart was beating hard in her chest as she walked through the door. She scanned the room, not expecting to find the man there since she was early. However, he was there, sitting in a back corner with two mugs in front of him. He waved to her. She took a deep breath, swallowing hard. A last minute impulse screamed at her to turn and run but she squashed it, favoring the strange sense of acquaintance, and pushed herself to walk to his table.

He stood as she approached and pushed the chair in as she sat. "I bought you a tea, two sugars, just the way you like it."

Already unsettled, Josie became more so. He knew about her dreams, he had a picture supposedly of the two of them and he knew how she liked her tea. "You said you can help me. Tell me how."

"Celine…" he began gently.

"Josie," she snapped back. "My name is Josie."

"Okay, all right, Josie." He held up his hands.

"How can you help me? Why do you think you know me?"

"I realize you want me to tell you everything, but we have to start slow. I don't want you to think I'm crazy."

"And knowing everything will make me think you're crazy?"

"I'm concerned that knowing everything too fast might, yes."

"Okay, I'm leaving," she said, beginning to stand.

"Josie, please wait," he said, grabbing her wrist.

"Wait for what? For you to feed me another line about how you can help me and not follow through?"

"I CAN help you. Please wait. I'm not lying to you."

"So help me!" she exclaimed, sitting back down.

"Okay, all right. Now, you've been having the dreams? Being chased through the cave, hands covered in blood? Carrying a book, right?"

"Yes, I've been having dreams like that, sometimes in the dreams my hands are covered in blood, sometimes I have a book. And now I've been having, I'm not sure how to describe them, visions, perhaps? In an instant, it will be like I'm remembering something, I can see, smell, hear things but they are nothing familiar to me, but they seem like memories."

"Visions? Can you describe these visions?" the man spoke quickly, leaning forward toward her.

Josie was anxious because of his behavior but she pressed on. "Um, one was, uh, I was swinging, it smelled like flowers, it was a beautiful sunny day and…" She paused, trying to remember. "I was speaking French. I never learned French, but I was speaking French. That's the same thing I did when the doctor hypnotized me."

"You were hypnotized? When? By whom?" He appeared to become agitated.

"Yes, after I fainted the doctor in the ER recommended a therapist. He hypnotized me and apparently I spoke French while I was recounting my dream to him. Well, not apparently, I did speak French. My cousin has a video of me doing it."

"And you've experienced the visions ever since? Any other ones?"

"Yes, ever since that. There's one more that I remember. It was of a big white house, I remember smelling the sea. It only lasted a few seconds, so I don't have very many details."

The man sat back, lips pressed together, mulling over the information. "Well?" Josie said, impatient. He remained quiet. "Look, that's it, this is ridiculous, you have no way of helping me."

"They're memories," he blurted out.

"What?"

"Memories, the visions you describe, they are memories."

"Memories? Memories of what? Places I've never been? A language I've never learned?"

"Yes, memories. The hypnosis unlocked them. Although only one session probably wasn't enough," he mused as if to himself, then turned to her, "I have a family friend, a doctor. She can hypnotize you, she's familiar with your background, she can continue the treatment so you can remember everything."

"Remember what? There's nothing to remember. These aren't my memories. I've never been to a white house by the sea or swung in a garden while speaking French. I told you I don't even speak the language."

"They're not your memories, no," he admitted. "They're Celine's memories."

"Who is Celine? Why would I have her memories?"

"This will be difficult to understand, Josie. But…" He paused, reaching out to take her hand. "You are Celine. I realize you don't think you are, but you are. You are Celine, they are Celine's memories, but they are also yours."

"Okay, no, it's not difficult to understand. It's crazy." Josie pulled her hand away. "How am I this other person? You're crazy."

"I know what you're thinking, but I showed you the picture of us, I am familiar with your dreams, because I knew you when you were Celine. I knew you."

"I have never been Celine! I have always been Josie, from my birth until now. I have been Josephine Elena Benson for almost twenty-five years now. Never once have I ever called myself Celine, ever, not even as a joke or a screen name or anything. You have me confused with someone else."

"You were Celine long before you were Josie."

Josie sighed, exasperated, flinging her hands in front of her as she spoke, palms up. "How can I have been someone before I was me? I have no clue what you're talking about. Is this some kind of past life you're referring to?"

"In a way, yes."

"In a way? You're talking in circles and I'm guessing it's because you're crazy. I don't know why I came here," she said, shaking her head.

"Because you know," he said, grabbing her hand, "that I'm right, you can sense it, I'm sure of it. Deep down you realize this is true but until you remember everything you will continue to suffer from the visions and the dreams."

Josie sat for a moment, too confused to move. She let him take her hand and continue to hold it. Tears formed in her eyes, threatening to roll down her cheeks at any moment. It was too much to take in. He was right, there was something that kept drawing her to him and to presume that he could help, but she didn't understand what and she couldn't accept anything he was saying. "I can't do this, I need to think," Josie said, abruptly standing and bolting from the table and out the door to her car.

The man followed her. "Josie," he called after her when they were both outside. "Josie, please," he said when he caught up to her just before she climbed into her car. She wiped a few tears away that had fallen as she had made the mad dash from the café. "I'm not trying to hurt you, I'm trying to help you, please. You've got to trust me." He gently cupped her face in his hands, forcing her to look at him. She looked into his sea-blue eyes. He was so sincere and so tender with her. Still, she couldn't process what he was telling her.

She sniffled. "I can't believe I'm about to say this but I feel I do trust you. You're the only one giving me a specific explanation, however bizarre it might sound. I just... I need some time. Right now, this is too much for me. I need to process this."

"I understand," he said, dropping his hands to her arms, giving them a squeeze. "You go, get some rest, text me when you're ready to talk again."

She nodded, "Okay." Turning, she opened her car door.

"Josie," he said, as she climbed into the car, "it'll be okay. You'll be okay."

She nodded in place of a response, closing her door and starting the car. He watched as she pulled away. Josie took a deep breath as she watched him disappear in the rear-view mirror as she drove away. Focusing on the road, she concentrated on getting home; trying not to dwell on the strange conversation that had just occurred.

When Josie got home, she decided a soak in the tub might relieve some tension that had built up from the meeting earlier. Slipping out of her clothes and into her bathrobe, she started the water running into the tub. After she got the temperature right, she let the tub fill while she put her hair up and checked her email. Finding nothing urgent, she headed back to the bathroom, stopping along her way to grab the music box. She placed it on the vanity and opened it. The music filled the air as she disrobed and stepped in the tub, shutting off the water as she settled in.

She laid her head back on the rim of the bathtub, closing her eyes, trying to relax as she listened to the tinkling sound. The warm water surrounded her, wrapping her up like a warm blanket. Her thoughts drifted first to the man she had met then to their conversation. She realized she still had not learned his name; she never asked for it and he had never given it to her. Perhaps it would be helpful to establish that fact; maybe she could find some information on him and this Celine person he was referring to. She considered what they had discussed. It was surreal, the conversation made no sense to her even after trying to analyze each detail after getting distance from the event.

She took a deep breath and tried to push the thoughts from her mind. Opening her eyes, she stared at the music box playing on the sink. She reached over, her fingers just able to catch the necklace inside. Holding it up to the light she admired it, it really was beautiful. The red rubies sparkled in the light. She put it around her neck, careful that the water wasn't high enough to touch it when she settled back into the tub.

She closed her eyes again, letting her hand run over the necklace. This time she let her mind wander over more pleasant thoughts. The warm summer sun heating her face as it rose over the ridge while she sipped her morning tea on the porch. The quietness of the area during her morning jog. Another memory entered her mind and she let herself dwell on every detail, bringing a smile to her face. She lay on a beach, the sun shining down on her, the aroma of salt in the air. Waves crashed nearby, she saw her dress lying on a nearby rock, discarded for a swim. The warm water lapped at her toes. Her smile grew; it was such a happy memory.

Josie shot upright, her eyes wide. The memory that had been so comforting to her, she realized, was not her memory. She had never visited that beach. She had never owned a dress like that. She swallowed hard; it seemed she had just experienced another one of her visions.

A voice from a distance broke her thoughts. She focused her mind on the noise. "JOSIE!" Footsteps pounded up the stairs. "JOSIE!" the voice called again. She recognized the voice as Michael's.

"Just a second!" she called back, hurrying out of the tub and toweling off quickly before slipping into her bathrobe. She opened the door of her en suite, finding Michael standing inside the doorway of her bedroom.

"Josie! Why haven't you been answering your phone? I texted you as soon as I was out of my meeting, then I called, I texted Damien and he hadn't heard from you, then I tried calling you again and got no answer, I've been worried sick."

"Oh, sorry, I was taking a bath, I didn't have my phone."

"Seriously? It didn't occur to you to update me or Damien to tell us you were home and what the doctor said?"

"Sorry, no, I guess I just wanted to get home and decompress. I wasn't thinking."

He sighed. "Okay, well, anyway, what happened at the doctor's?"

"Oh, um, nothing really. He didn't prescribe anything, just said to relax and wait for Wednesday's session and we'll go from there."

Michael cocked his head to the side in disbelief. "He called you into his office for an emergency appointment and then didn't prescribe anything and told you to relax and wait? What was the point of you going?"

"No idea. I guess once we talked he decided to try another session before prescribing anything."

Michael was annoyed, throwing his hands in the air with frustration. "All of that and he did nothing. On Wednesday I'll go in with you and have a word with him. This is ridiculous."

"He's the professional, I'm sure he knows what he's doing."

"Well, I'm glad you consider him a professional because so far, I'm not impressed."

Josie remained quiet, hoping his frustration passed before she was forced to tell more lies about her morning excursion.

Michael eyed her for a moment. "Why are you wearing that necklace?"

"Oh," Josie said, clasping at it. She forgot she put it on while in the bath and, in her rush to get out, had never taken it off. "I just put it on while I was in the bath, no particular reason."

Michael didn't answer for a moment. "I guess," he said, loosening his tie, "I'll let you get back to your bath. I'm home for the rest of the day, I'm going to grab my laptop and do some work downstairs."

"Okay," Josie said, giving him a weak smile. As he left, she turned, grabbed her phone and headed into the bathroom, locking the door behind her. She glanced at herself in the mirror before sitting down on the edge of the tub. She had no intention on getting back into the bath, but she didn't want to be disturbed so she let Michael conclude that's what she intended to do.

Instead she toggled her phone on. She saw several missed messages and phone calls. She ignored them and opened her text message app, sending a text to the mysterious man she met with earlier: *What can you tell me about my visions?*

As she waited for the response, she cleared her notifications and sent a text to a very worried Damien, telling him she was fine and that the doctor prescribed nothing for her.

As she sent the message off, she received a reply from the man: *Have you had another vision?*

Frustrated she sent back: *Why can you never just answer me? Can you answer this... what is your name?*

Within a few moments the response came back: *I want you to remember my name. It's better if you remember on your own... explaining it will sound crazy like you keep telling me*

Josie responded: *I can't remember your name... I don't know you*

He responded: *You'll remember and then it will all make sense... let's meet again*

Although unsure, the person she most desired to talk to was this man. Why, she wondered, was she so drawn to him? She considered his proposition, again unsure when she could meet him. As she considered her options, another text came through: *We could meet in the morning, during your jog... if you don't want anyone to find out*

Josie was taken aback. How was he aware she jogged, and that she did it alone? Moreover, how had he surmised that she was keeping this from her friends? Even with the unsettled sensation the message gave her, Josie found herself typing an affirmative message back to him, telling him to meet her tomorrow morning at the end of her road around 5:30 a.m.

He texted back a confirmation, and the two ended their conversation for the moment. Josie decided she would re-dress and try to finish some work while Damien gave her a tongue-lashing about her lack of response earlier.

The afternoon and night crawled. Josie tried to focus on

her work and the mundane details of her day but found herself unable to do so. Her mind continued to return to her strange visions and the conversation that she had earlier in the day. She had another restless night, not getting much sleep with the apprehension of the meeting coming up the next morning. At least, she contemplated as she lay awake, this was one way to avoid the nightmare.

CHAPTER 12

*J*osie rose early the next morning, dressing for her run, driven by nervous energy. Despite the early hour the clock showed, she was anxious to get going, so she figured she would wait for the man to arrive before finishing her run.

Much to her surprise, as she approached the end of the road, she spotted a car. She slowed to a walk, approaching it. The man was leaning against the car, waiting for her. As she approached, he walked toward her.

"Good morning, Josie," he said, as he approached her.

"Good morning," she said, suddenly concerned this might not be a good idea.

"Did you sleep?"

"No."

"You had another vision, didn't you?"

"I did. Of a beach somewhere." She covered her face with her hands. "I don't know what to think."

"It's okay. You'll figure it out. I imagine the hypnosis can help."

"Yeah, sorry, I'm not comfortable going somewhere with

someone who won't even tell me his name and then being hypnotized by someone else whom I've never even met."

The man snorted a laugh. "Oh, I always admired that feistiness you have. You don't have to come with me, your doctor can do it. I expect it might take longer because your doctor doesn't understand what to trigger, whereas mine does. But it's up to you, whatever makes you comfortable."

"So, you're not opposed to me saying no and going back to my doctor?"

"Other than you struggling for a longer time, no, I'm not opposed."

"Why can't you just tell me what is happening? You keep hinting at it but you won't tell me. It's frustrating."

"Josie, you wouldn't believe me if I told you, that's why you've got to come around to it on your own."

"Why are you so concerned about me 'remembering' and not struggling and whatever?"

"Because I care about you." He paused. "And because, truth be told, I need your help, desperately. We all do. The sooner you remember, the sooner you can help."

"You need my help? With what?"

"Well, I need Celine's help. And again, you wouldn't understand even if I tried to tell you, you wouldn't believe me."

Josie sighed, crossing her arms and walking a few steps away, turning her back toward him. "Why does this have to be complicated? You won't tell me your name, you won't give me any information. The only thing I have to go on is someone else's memories, this Celine person's memories. I mean, how do I have them? Do I have multiple personalities or am I possessed or something?"

"No, no nothing like that," he said, smiling as he approached her again, he put his hands on her arms, giving them another squeeze. "Hey, you better be getting back.

Consider my offer, okay?" he said as he backed away from her toward his car.

Josie turned to face him. He seemed more at ease this time, much less agitated. Before she could respond, he was in his car, the engine sputtered to life. Prior to driving off, he rolled down his window and shouted, "By the way, my name is Grayson. Grayson Buckley."

Grayson, yes, that named seemed to fit, Josie supposed, as she watched the car drive off. She wasn't sure why, but it made sense to her. Perhaps she was willing it to make sense because she wanted for some piece of the puzzle to fall into place. She spent another moment watching his taillights disappear before turning toward home for her jog back.

* * *

Grayson pulled away, watching her image fade in his rearview mirror. He hoped he had done enough to convince her. He had tried to hold back how dire the situation was, tried not to pressure her. The slower the process was for her, the more danger his family was in. But, he had to consider her, too. He realized how stressed she was and he had to proceed in a way that was safe for her. Yesterday she had run from him in tears. He didn't want that to happen again, he didn't want to see her cry again, he had seen that enough times before. He glanced into his mirror again; he could no longer see her. He could only wait and hope now. Hope was all he had, again.

* * *

Josie reflected on the conversation as she jogged back home. Her mind wavered back and forth between thinking she was crazy for even considering the solution this man, Grayson, had presented and wanting to find answers so badly she was willing to do anything. She considered the last few weeks; it appeared she was getting worse. Her nightmares were coming more frequently and now she had developed visions. She remembered her upcoming appointment Wednesday with Dr. Reed. Perhaps she should wait until then and reassess following that appointment. Patience was not a virtue Josie was blessed with. The doctor's lackadaisical attitude toward her issue had frustrated her. Perhaps she was being impatient, she had only had one session with him. However, he seemed unconcerned that she could speak in a language she never learned nor that she was experiencing a severe lack of sleep. She had made it clear that she was uninterested in using pharmaceuticals but he was the doctor, the one with experience, yet he acted like her problems were unimportant, making her wait for a week before another appointment.

She wrestled back and forth deciding if she was making excuses or had a legitimate complaint. By the time she had reached the house, she hadn't made a clear decision. She was still reluctant to trust Grayson but he was the only one making any sense to her at the moment.

After changing, she made her way to the kitchen to make her usual morning cup of tea. Damien was already up, pouring a cup of coffee. "Good morning," he said, "how was your night? Got some sleep, I hope."

"Not really."

"I'm surprised the doctor isn't doing anything about that. Michael may be right, we may need to be more insistent with him."

"Yeah, I don't know. I mean, I get that I've only had one session with him, but it kind of seems like he's not doing anything. He hypnotized me and I spoke French and he was just like 'yeah, ok, so come back in a week', that's it?"

"I guess he can't do much else at the moment, probably takes time to get to the root of what's causing this dream."

"Yeah, I suppose. Do you have any ideas on what is causing it?"

"Stress? At least, that's the most reasonable explanation. Why? Do you have another theory?"

"I don't know. What if it's something else? Something... bigger."

"Something bigger? Like what?"

"A warning? Memory of a past life or something?"

"Memory of a past life?" He chuckled a bit. "Yeah, you're getting way too little sleep."

Josie pinched her lips together. Damien felt guilty for laughing and approached her, putting his arm around her. "Hey, sorry, but I'm serious. I think all the sleepless nights might be getting to you. It's just some reaction to stress. Once you work through it, you'll be back to your old self, I know it."

Josie realized he was trying to be supportive and perhaps she was crazy to assume what she was experiencing was what Grayson was telling her, but something was off with the stress explanation. Still, Josie didn't want to pursue it any further with him. She patted his hand on her shoulder and said, "Yeah, you're right. Thanks, D."

"Anytime," he said, smiling. "I am working from home today so I'll be in the office room trying to fix the code everyone keeps breaking."

"Okay. I'm going to have a cup of tea on the porch before I join you and try to get some work done."

Before heading to the porch, Josie grabbed her phone. There was no reason not to get a jump-start on reading her emails while she enjoyed the summer morning. Turning the display on as she settled onto the porch swing, she opened her email and read through a few, flagging the ones that needed responses, deleting those that didn't. As she worked, a text message appeared.

After she finished with her emails, she scrolled through her text messages, finding one from Grayson: *The visions you are having... I think they are childhood memories... I'm not sure though*

Josie read it and was ready to respond when Michael came out the door. "Heading in to the office?" she asked, setting her phone down.

"Yeah, I've got a full schedule of meetings. See you when I get home, Josie." She watched him toss his briefcase into the car, climb in and disappear down the driveway through the trees. When his car was no longer visible, she picked up her phone and sent a text back to Grayson: *They aren't from my childhood... I've never been to any of those places before*

Within a few moments she received a response: *Not yours as Josie, yours as Celine*

Josie was still struggling to understand how she could be both herself and Celine, but nothing made much sense. She understood that stress manifested itself in the form of nightmares but was it capable of producing visions? The visions seemed related to when she had been hypnotized. Perhaps the treatment had unlocked some hidden depths of her memory, but she still failed to grasp how she had the memories of two people. She needed to find out before the side effects of the nightmares and visions drove her insane. An idea formed, and she went with it. She texted back: *Would your Dr. friend come to the house to hypnotize me?*

It wasn't long before she received a response: *Yes, but do you consider that wise or have you told your roommates?*

She texted back, explaining a piece of her plan: *No I haven't told them but I can say she's a colleague of my doctor... that it's some new home therapy method*

Josie had decided perhaps it was best to use another

doctor, one who understood that she was trying to unlock these "memories" that seemed to be bottled in her head. She was concerned, of course, about working with someone she'd never met but if she was here at home with others in the house, she figured it was safe.

Another text came through: *When?*

Josie considered it for a moment. If she was going to go through with this plan, perhaps it should be before her regular doctor's appointment. That way she could decide on continuing with Dr. Reed or not based on the results of the new treatment. She texted back: *Tonight? 5pm?*

The response was almost immediate: *We'll be there*

Josie texted back: *No. Just the doctor, you can't be here.*

This time his response was delayed. Josie waited anxiously for the answer. The last thing she needed was Grayson showing up and casting suspicion on the entire set up. Finally the response came through: *Ok... I understand... Amelia will be there at 5*

Josie set her phone down. That was settled. Now all she had to do was carry off the lie to her friends, and she was free to explore this option to find out if it could help her. She finished the last few sips of her tea, now lukewarm, and headed up to her office after dropping her mug off in the kitchen.

Damien was already there, working away, headphones on, music blasting. She waved as she sat down across the room from him. With a game plan in place, she was capable of focusing on a little work. For the first time, she had a sense of hope that it could help her. She worked her morning away, making good progress on a few projects. After doing another email check and responding to a few, her stomach began to growl. It was almost 12:30 p.m., so she figured it was a great time to stop and make lunch. She pantomimed to Damien, asking if he wanted some lunch. He nodded, going back to working. He was like a dog with a bone when he got going on something so she left him to continue while she prepared some lunch.

Taking it back up to the office, she handed him the plate as he slid his headphones off. "Thanks," he said, "sorry, I just wanted to finish something while my mind was on it."

"No problem, did you get your bug fixed?"

"I did, then someone broke something else," he lamented. "How's your day going?"

"Good. I got something productive done!" she said.

"Awesome, good job you!"

"Oh, before I forget," Josie said, taking a bite of her salad. "Dr. Reed's office called to see how I was doing. He's sending someone to the house tonight, some colleague. Said he wanted to try the hypnotherapy in a 'safe space' where I would be relaxed? I don't know, anyway, she's coming around five tonight."

"Oh, really? Home therapy? That's weird."

"Yeah, well at least he's doing something. I guess depending on how this goes tonight he'll decide if I should come back to the office and see him or continue at home."

"Here, there, both, whatever, I hope something helps you soon. You've got to be close to losing it entirely from the stress that you're under from dealing with this let alone whatever stress is causing this to begin with."

"Yeah, it's getting super old, I can tell you that." Josie changed the subject, chatting about work and the weather. She was plagued by guilt lying to Damien like this but she was at her wit's end trying to cope with the situation. She also recognized that he wouldn't approve had he known the origin of the new doctor. She wasn't even sure she approved.

After lunch, Josie was almost glad to return to work to avoid any further mistruths being told during their conversation. She finished up around 4 p.m. and told Damien she was going to do some preparation for dinner before her appointment. Michael was coming through the door as she headed downstairs. She explained the situation with the new doctor to him, excusing herself from any further discussion by telling him she was headed in to prepare some things for dinner.

Josie's mind lacked any focus for the hour that remained before her appointment. She fiddled in the kitchen, cutting vegetables for a pasta dish and setting out various materials for later. After about thirty minutes, she went to the living room to wait nervously. Both Damien and Michael joined her about fifteen minutes before the appointment to wait with her.

At about five to five, the doorbell rang. Josie leapt from the couch to answer it. With a shaky hand, she opened the door to find a woman, about her height, shaking her umbrella off outside. Her dark brown hair was pulled neatly into a bun at the nape of her neck. She looked at Josie with large brown eyes. "Josie Benson, I presume?"

"Yes, I'm Josie, come in."

The woman walked through the door, leaving her umbrella on the porch. "I'm Dr. Amelia Gresham. Nice to meet you." As she stepped in the room, she spotted two other people, which halted any further conversation.

"Hi," Josie said, shaking her hand. "This is my cousin and roommate, Damien Sherwood, and this is a friend, Michael Carlyle." Each of them shook Amelia's hand, exchanging pleasantries.

"So, you're from Dr. Reed's office?" Michael asked.

"Yes," the woman answered without skipping a beat. Grayson must have prepped her well. "Home therapy is a new way to approach patient care. Since Josie is having such a tough time, we consider it best to try anything."

"I was surprised he didn't give her any medication to help with the sleeping..." Michael began before Josie cut him off.

"Michael," she said, almost under her breath, giving her head a slight shake to signal that he should stop.

"Well, let's hope that this session can eliminate the need for prescription medication," Amelia said. "Josie, is there a room where we can proceed uninterrupted?"

"Oh, don't mind us, you won't even realize we're here," Michael said, motioning for the doctor to head further into the living room.

"I appreciate the sentiment, but it is important that we work in a distraction free environment where Josie is completely comfortable. That's hard to generate with an audience. It's best that we work privately. Could you lead the way, Josie?"

"Yes," Josie responded, "we can use my bedroom."

"Want me to come with?" Damien asked.

"No, no, I'll be fine, thanks."

"Not to be a pain, doctor, but, the last time, Josie exhibited some, uh, unusual behavior. It might be helpful for someone else to be present to tell Josie what happened when she comes out of it," Damien explained.

"I record all my sessions. I can make a copy for Josie if she'd like to go over what happened in her session." Turning to Josie, she said, "If you'd lead the way."

Josie led her up to her bedroom, leaving behind two unhappy men below. Once inside, Josie locked the door behind them. Moving further inside the room, she motioned to two chairs in the room positioned by the far wall. "Thanks for the cover, I assume Grayson told you I haven't told anyone who you really are?"

"Yes, he did. I'm glad you decided to see me, I think I can help."

"How, exactly?" Josie asked. "And can you tell me anything about what is happening?"

"I'd like to hypnotize you again, allow your mind to focus on capturing those memories that are coming in pieces to you until you have them all back."

"But that's the thing. They aren't memories."

Amelia held up a hand to stop Josie. "I realize that they aren't YOUR memories, but I think Grayson may have told you he thinks they are childhood memories from Celine's childhood."

"Yes, he said that. I have no clue who Celine is though or how I would have her memories," Josie said.

"I realize this may not make sense, but you have these memories in your head because you lived through them at some point. Once you have all your memories back, not just bits and pieces, this will be far easier for you to comprehend."

"Why do you both keep holding information back from me? How could I be two people? I'm beginning to believe it's because you have no explanation."

"There is an explanation, one that you will understand once you have all your memories. If I told you now, it wouldn't help you, you wouldn't believe me."

Josie stared ahead, trying to make sense of the response. "Okay," she said after a moment, "so, you'll hypnotize me? And try to 'unlock' these memories?"

"Yes, shall we begin?"

"How can I trust you are not planting these 'memories' in my head?"

"You have been experiencing these symptoms long before I hypnotized you, so the source is not me."

"Good point," Josie admitted. "So I guess we can get started."

Amelia set a tape recorder on the small table between the two chairs and started recording the session. "Okay, Josie,"

Amelia began, removing a bright gold medallion hanging from a gold chain from her pocket. "I want you to get comfortable and concentrate on this medallion. I want you to focus on this and the sound of my voice." Josie focused on staring at the medallion, concentrating on how it caught the light as the doctor twirled the chain between her fingers.

"Josie, you are starting to relax. I'm going to count backward from ten and when I reach one, you will be completely relaxed and will be in a calm, peaceful trance." Amelia began counting backward as Josie's eyelids began to grow heavy and close. When she reached one, Josie was completely relaxed.

"Josie? Are you calm and relaxed?"

"Yes," Josie responded.

"Okay, now I want you to let your mind be open. I don't want to talk to Josie right now. I want to talk to Celine. Is Celine there?"

Josie's forehead pinched together as if in deep thought but she didn't respond.

"Celine? Are you there?" Amelia said again.

Josie's breath became faster and more ragged, her forehead pinching together tighter.

"Relax, you are safe. There's no reason to be upset. I would like to speak with Celine. Celine, are you there?" Amelia asked again.

After a moment, Josie responded. "Oui, je suis là."

Amelia directed, "Celine, speak English."

"Sorry," Josie responded, "Yes, I am here."

"Hello, Celine," Amelia said. "It's good to hear you are still here. You've been trying to appear for some time now, haven't you?"

"Yes. Yes, I have always been here. It's almost time but I cannot return."

"Celine, you must. We need you."

"No, I cannot. Josie must remain."

"We must let Josie decide that for herself. You must give her all the information she needs to do that."

"No, I must protect her, it is our only chance."

"Celine, you must allow her to make her choice with all the information. You must allow her to access everything, all of your knowledge, all of your collective memories."

There was no response.

"Celine? Please, you must. Grayson, Alexander, everyone, we need you. Josie needs you. She is being tormented by your memories, you must give her access to everything. You must integrate with her."

"I will let her see more, but I must protect her. She is fragile."

"Celine, we don't have much time." There was no response. "Celine?" Amelia paused. "Celine?"

There was no response. She was gone. "Okay, Josie, I'm going to bring you out of the trance now. I will count backwards from ten and when I reach one, you will awaken, refreshed and rested."

The doctor counted backwards and when she reached one, Josie's eyes opened. She glanced around. "What happened?" she asked.

"We made great progress!" Amelia answered.

"Progress? Did you find out why I'm having these dreams and visions?"

"I would expect you to continue to have both, but I hope they will be a little less taxing for you. I'd like to see you again, perhaps Thursday. Let's skip a day to let your mind settle."

"What? That's it? No solid answers? I don't feel much different, I mean I feel okay, but I didn't learn any more than I did before."

"Josie, we need to let your mind come to its own understanding. But I'd like to push your mind to do that faster, I recognize the toll it's taking on you. I think you may find that you do feel different overall, particularly with respect to the visions."

Josie sighed. "Okay, okay, I'll trust you for now. Thanks, Millie." Josie paused a moment before looking at Amelia, surprise on her face. "Where did that come from? I'm sorry, Dr. Gresham."

"It's ok, Josie. It's my nickname."

"Yeah, but you never told me that. How did I know it?"

"I told you things would be different. The memories you have of me are starting to integrate into your mind."

"I'll take your word for that." She shook her head in disbelief.

"I'll take that and see you again Thursday to help you remember more." Amelia clicked off the tape recorder, standing and putting it in her purse.

"You said I could get a copy of that?" Josie said, also standing.

"I'd be happy to share it with you after I've had the chance to write my notes on the session. I can share it with you on Thursday."

"Okay. Well, thanks. What time Thursday?"

"Anytime that works for you, Josie."

"Can we do it around noon?"

"Sure. I will come by Thursday at noon."

"Great. I'll walk you down."

Josie unlocked the door and took Amelia downstairs. Both men stood as they walked down the stairs. "Thanks again, Dr. Gresham." Amelia left, retrieving her umbrella from the porch. Josie closed the door, turning to find both Damien and Michael staring at her.

"Well?" Michael prompted.

"She said it was a productive session. She said I would be

more settled and see improvement. And I feel better, since I woke up I feel decent. She said I might still have the dreams and stuff but she said we made good progress. She said we'll have another session on Thursday."

"What, that's it?" Michael asked.

"Yep. I am, however, starving, so let's go make dinner."

"Did she give you a copy of the tape?" Damien asked.

"Ah, no, she said she would bring one on Thursday, she wanted to make notes."

"So, you don't know what happened in the session?"

"No, I don't. Maybe that's for the best though. Maybe knowing what happened last time was worse for me. Now can we please go eat?"

"Sure," Damien said, glancing at Michael.

After dinner, Josie suggested they settle in to watch some T.V. and try to relax for the rest of the evening. As they settled down, she checked her phone, noticing a text from Grayson: *How are you?*

Josie answered: *Fine, not much different, but no worse so far*

Gray answered her immediately: *I'd like to see you*

Josie considered it for a moment before answering. She wanted to see him, too. She couldn't explain it but the reluctance she had experienced before seemed to be diminishing. She texted back: *Ok, tomorrow morning... mid-jog?*

He answered quickly: *See you then, Josie*

Josie put her phone down and settled into the couch next to Damien. For the first time in weeks, she felt relaxed; she hoped that translated to a more pleasant night's sleep.

* * *

Amelia unlocked the motel room door. "Well?" Grayson demanded, jumping off the bed as soon as she entered the room.

"Well…" She sighed. "You were right, Celine is still there."

"I knew it!" he exclaimed. "Did you get through to her? Does she remember?"

"I talked to Celine, but she wasn't very helpful, so no, Josie doesn't remember yet."

"You talked to Celine? What did she say?"

"That she couldn't return and that Josie needed to be protected. I think in the end she may have agreed to allow Josie to share more of her memories. I told her that Josie was being tormented by the snippets she was getting. I'm hoping that works. I see her again Thursday."

"Thursday? Why not tomorrow?"

"Give her mind a chance to relax, Gray. We'll find out more Thursday."

He nodded his head. "Okay. Okay, sorry, Millie, I'm just impatient."

"I know, Gray, I know. But we're getting there, this is real progress."

Progress, finally, Gray thought, or at least he hoped so. He wanted to see her, needed to see her, needed to observe if the progress was real. He sent her a text and waited for a response. It seemed like lately all he was doing was waiting.

CHAPTER 13

The next morning Josie's alarm woke her. For the first time in weeks, she had slept, experiencing no nightmares. She basked in the sleep she had gotten for a moment before rising from her bed. Getting up, she opened the music box. As she started to dress for her jog, she remembered that she was meeting Grayson this morning. The idea brought a smile to her face.

She hit the road with a spring in her step. She had almost forgotten how revitalizing a good night's sleep could be. As she approached the end of the road she saw Gray, leaning against his car. She continued toward him when a pain shot across her head. She slowed to a stop, shutting her eyes for a moment. As she did so, a memory formed in her mind. It was Gray; he stood in a large room, a glass of brandy in his hand. He turned to face her. "There you are, darling," he said, smiling. As quickly as it came, it passed.

Opening her eyes, Gray stood in front of her, having rushed toward her when she stopped. "Josie," he called, grabbing hold of her, "Josie, what's wrong? Are you okay?"

"I'm fine," she answered, looking at him as if for the first time, "I had another vision."

"Another vision? Of what?"

"You," she answered.

"Me? Do you remember me?"

"No," she said, breaking from his grip, "no, just that one fleeting memory, but I feel different. You seem so familiar to me, but I can't place why or anything specific though."

"Josie, that's great!"

"Is it? I still don't understand anything."

"You will, this is progress."

"Perhaps I should meet with Amelia again sooner?"

"No, she said you need to let your mind relax."

Disappointment filled Josie, but she understood. "Maybe she's right. Perhaps it's best not to push it too fast. This is the best I've been in weeks. I didn't have the dream, and the vision wasn't too painful." She turned to face him again. "I had better get going."

"Okay, text or call me if you need anything," he said, putting his hands on her arms and rubbing them.

"Okay, I will," she said, grabbing his hand and holding it for a moment before turning to leave. As she jogged toward home, she turned back, giving him a quick smile before turning back around and heading away from him.

Josie felt different, she wasn't sure if it stemmed from a good night's sleep or if something had clicked into place for her after her session with Amelia. Either way, she planned to take full advantage of it, she resolved, as she powered through the rest of her run.

The house was still quiet when she arrived home. She tiptoed upstairs to change and back down to make her cup of tea. Everyone must be sleeping in, though she couldn't fathom why. No one had mentioned anything about it to her. As the sun began to rise over the horizon, a yawning Michael appeared in the doorway. He stretched as he came out to join her on the porch swing, still in pajama pants and a t-shirt.

"No work today?" Josie asked.

"I'll work here, I'm not going in to the office," he said, half-asleep.

"Rough night?"

"I'm a little tired, yeah. How about you? Did you get any sleep?"

"Yes, I did! That session with Dr. Gresham must have helped, I slept through the night, no nightmares. Must have been a rough night for Damien, I see he's still in bed."

"I don't know." Michael shrugged. "Did you put coffee on this morning?"

"Yep, it's ready."

"I'm going to grab a cup, be right back."

As he entered the house, Damien came out, coffee cup already in hand, yawning. "Ah, good morning," he said, still mid-yawn.

"Good morning, yikes, what's with you two? Late night playing video games?"

He sat down next to Josie on the swing, "Yeah, video games, yep."

Josie considered the response odd. She could tell when Damien wasn't telling the truth, and this was one of those times.

"Everything okay?" she asked, trying gently to pry.

"Yep, all good, everything is all good."

"D…" she began, but Michael's return interrupted her.

She looked between the two of them. There was a weird vibe between them, she wasn't sure what it was. "So, are neither of you going to the office today?"

"Nope, just going to work from home," Damien responded.

"Yep, same here like I said before, working from home."

"Oooookay. Well, I'll let you guys get at that then. I'm going upstairs to start some of my work."

Josie headed upstairs to her office. She surmised that she could actually be productive today. She checked her phone before diving into her emails. Grayson had sent a text: *How was the rest of your jog?*

She smiled at the message and answered: *It was good, thanks :)*

Setting her phone down, she opened her email account and began sorting, flagging, answering and deleting emails. The task took her almost two hours to complete. When she checked her phone next, it was approaching 10 a.m. Damien wasn't up here yet which surprised her if he was planning on working from home. He must have gotten embroiled in another video game battle with Michael. Boys, she thought, rolling her eyes. She saw another text message waiting for her: *I'm glad that session with Millie helped*

She was about to type a reply when she heard Michael calling her. "Josie, hey, Josie, can you come down here for a minute?"

"Sure," she shouted back, wondering what they needed. If they called her down there to get them a snack or a drink while they played video games she would give them a piece of her mind. She headed downstairs, as the living room came into view, she saw Damien sitting on one of the arm chairs, Michael at the bottom of the stairs. Someone sat on the couch. Even though her back faced Josie, she recognized her mother. What was her mother doing here, she wondered?

"Mom?" she asked, glancing to each of them for an explanation.

"Hi, Josie," her mom started. "Come sit down."

Growing suspicious, she asked, "What is going on?"

"Michael has been telling me a little about what is going

on," her mom began, "About your stalker. Josie, we need to talk, I need to tell you something."

Josie's eyebrows raised, her eyes wide. "You called my mom?" she said to Michael.

"Yes, I called your mom because I was at a loss about what else to do."

"What do you mean you were at a loss about what else to do? Are you kidding me right now?"

"You're acting crazy, Josie. You're distant and secretive. You've been lying to us. You're all over the map, so yeah," he said, his voice growing heated.

"I've been lying? Seriously? What exactly are you accusing me of?" Josie blasted back.

"Yes, you've been lying. Your little story about going to Dr. Reed's on Monday and the 'home therapy' you had yesterday. I called Dr. Reed's office. He didn't meet with you Monday and he's never heard of a Dr. Amelia Gresham."

"So you called my therapist and discussed my treatment with him and then you took it upon yourself to call my mom like I'm a kid?"

Josie's mom stepped in between them. "Stop this, you two, it's not helping anything. I am glad Michael called me. I didn't realize what was going on or the extent to which you'd been suffering with these nightmares. I certainly didn't know you were being stalked." She walked Josie to the couch as she talked, her arms around her shoulders. Sitting her down on the couch, she sat next to her, taking her hands. "I realize now what a tough time you've been having. I'm sorry to say, I have some difficult news to share with you. It may have some bearing on what you're experiencing and may help with your treatment." She turned toward Michael and Damien. "I'm sorry, but would you two mind giving us some privacy?"

"Sure, no problem," Michael said.

"Absolutely, just yell if you need us, we'll be upstairs,"

Damien said. They both left the room, leaving Josie alone with her mom.

"I'm not being stalked, this is all blown out of proportion. I'm fine, really," Josie said, once the men had left.

"Josie," her mom began, "this has been weighing on my mind for a long time. I hoped never to have this conversation with you but I feel guilty keeping it from you now in light of what's going on. I worried when you received the jewelry box but I hoped it was just some sort of a mix-up and nothing more came of it. But when Michael called me, I knew I had to come. There is something you need to know and I don't want you to hear it from someone else. I want to be the one to tell you."

"Michael had no right to call you and upset you, Mom. I'm fine."

"Josie, please. This is hard enough for me, please let me talk."

"About what? What are you trying to say?"

"Josie," she began, squeezing Josie's hands. "Your Dad and I, well, we, well, you know we love you more than anything. And, well, there is no easy way to say this, so I'm just going to say it. The fact is, you're not ours."

"What?" Josie said, struggling to understand what her mother was stumbling to say.

"Biologically, Josie. You're not our baby. I mean you'll always be my baby, but I didn't give birth to you."

"What?!" Josie said, shocked. "I'm... I'm adopted?"

"More or less, yes."

"More or less? What does that mean?"

"Your father and I were desperate to have a child. We were on the waiting list for adoptions but they told us it would be years before they even considered us for adopting a baby. We were desperate to have a baby."

"So, what? You were suddenly moved to the top of the list? What?"

"No, we, well, we received a letter in the mail from a private adoption agency offering us the opportunity to adopt you. It said we had been selected from a list of potential parents and they had a baby for us."

"What? How?"

"They offered us a baby, they told us you had no home and no parents and you could be ours if we promised to provide a loving and stable home for you. Well, of course, we accepted. We were so desperate, and you were so perfect." She tucked a lock of hair behind Josie's ear, smiling.

"Are you serious? You got a random letter saying they had a baby for you?"

"You weren't some black market deal." Her mother shook her head as she answered. "We had no reason to expect they weren't legitimate. It was a certified letter from a private adoption agency. We assumed we were doing something good and fulfilling our own dream of being parents. We thought you were just an unplanned pregnancy. We had no reason to question them nor did we want to. We were desperate to have a child, and you were beautiful."

"Some random agency sent you a random letter saying they had a baby, gave the baby to you and you didn't question it?"

"Of course we asked some questions, Josie. But the man we met with had reasonable explanations and documents and we only had a limited amount of time to decide. We were told because they were a private agency this would be a quiet adoption. We assumed perhaps to salvage the mother's repu-tation. We weren't prepared for it, it took us by surprise!"

"Yeah, I'll bet. Where is there even an agency who just mails random letters to people?" she asked rhetorically.

"Maine. The agency was in Maine. We had to travel to a

little town called Bucksville, I'll never forget it. We didn't even have time to get a car seat for you. I held you in my arms the whole way home. Oh, Josie, I'm so sorry we never told you, but it made no difference to either of us that you weren't biologically ours. We never thought it was important, you had no health issues or anything that would have prompted us to look into your background and like I said, we were just thrilled to have a child. We thanked the Lord every day for you and did our best to live up to the promise we made." Her mom's eyes filled with tears.

Josie's heart went out to her mother. She kept the secret for almost twenty-five years and now she was forced to tell it. She knew her mother, she realized how terrifying this must be for her, how afraid she was of how Josie may react, petrified of being rejected by the daughter she had raised. The truth was Josie wasn't angry, and she held no resentment toward her parents. They had lived up to their promise. She had a wonderful childhood that she wouldn't have traded for anything. It didn't make much difference to her that they weren't her biological parents. They were her parents in every way that counted. She squeezed her mom's hand. "It's okay, mom. It doesn't matter to me either that we're not biologically related. You'll always be my parents."

Josie witnessed her mother's relief. A few tears fell from her eyes; she wiped them away. "I'm glad to hear that, Josie. But I am concerned about this stalker. I wonder if he has any connection to how we got you."

Josie was wondering the same thing, and she intended to find out, but she didn't need her mother hovering over her to do it. Knowing Josie had met with the man who had been following her would make her mother sick with worry. "I don't think it does. I haven't seen that man again; I think he just followed me because I basically fainted in his arms at the mall. It was so embarrassing."

"Well, now that I've told you the truth, at least nothing can take you by surprise. Oh, Josie, I hate to rush off and leave you with everything going on, but I have a surgery scheduled on one of my patients this afternoon and I've already asked a partner to cover my morning rounds. Oh, Josie, if anything ever happened to you…" Her voice trailed off.

"Mom, I'm fine. I doubt he's still around and even if he were, I'm practically on house arrest with these two around, so no one can get to me," she said as a joke to put her mom's mind at ease. "And, you're only an hour and a half away, you're not far. You can check on me with text any time."

"And you'll tell me what's going on?"

"Yes, I'll tell you what's going on. I didn't want you to worry like you're doing now. I'm fine. SOMEONE," she said, emphasizing the last word, "made a mountain out of a mole-hill. There isn't a stalker, my nightmares aren't that bad, I had a great night's sleep last night, I'm much better, everything is fine."

"Are you sure? I can't change my afternoon surgery but you could come home with me."

"I'm sure. I'll be fine. I have tons of work here to keep me busy. I appreciate you changing your schedule to drive out here to tell me this in person, but I realize your patients need you. You don't have to stay and you don't have to worry."

"Okay, if you're sure. It does ease my nerves that Damien is here, and Michael, too, to be honest. Do you promise to tell me if this man reappears? By the way, what did he look like?"

"Tall, slim, medium brown hair, blue eyes, not bad look-ing, actually."

"Oh, that makes it a tad better."

"It makes it better that my stalker is good-looking?" Josie joked.

"No. But it's not the description of the man from the adoption agency, so hopefully it has nothing to do with that. That man was short, round and balding. He wasn't much to look at either, between us girls."

Josie filed the information away for later and smiled at her mom in response as she rose from the couch. "Well, it wasn't much of a visit but I'm sure you're busy with work. If you need anything, call or text. I love you, Josie." Her mom pulled her into a tight hug. After giving her a kiss on the cheek, Josie walked her to the door and watched as she pulled out of the driveway, waving as she honked the horn.

The smile disappeared in an instant from Josie's face as she entered the house, slamming the door shut behind her. As if on cue, Michael and Damien appeared at the foot of the stairs. "I can't even fathom where to begin with you two. Honestly, I can't," she said, shaking her head in disbelief. "So, I'm not going to until I've had a chance to think through everything my mom just told me."

"What did she tell you?" Damien asked.

"Well, I just found out I'm not really my parents' child."

"What?" Damien said, shocked.

"Yeah, they just adopted me from some private agency that gave me to them when I was a baby."

"Josie, I had no idea. I just wanted her to help us get you back on track," Michael began.

Josie held her hand up. "I don't care what you wanted. I am furious with you right now. But I need time alone to process all this."

"Yeah, I'm sure, totally, I get it," he answered.

"Jos," Damien started, "I… I…" He fumbled, at a loss for words but wanting to comfort her from the bombshell that had just dropped. While she realized this was Michael's idea, it was clear Damien had been complicit; Michael did not have her mother's number and probably had gotten it from Damien.

"D, I'm really not in the mood," she said, disappearing up the steps. Her mind was a whirlwind, but she needed some answers. She retrieved her cell phone from her office, opening her text app. She sent a message to Grayson: *Need 2 c u*

Heading to her room, she gathered her purse and went downstairs to retrieve her keys before heading out the door.

"Whoa, where are you going?" Michael asked, following her as she stormed out the door.

"Out," she called, not stopping.

"Hey, are you serious? I don't care what kind of bull you wanted to tell your mom but there is a stalker and you know it," Michael shouted, following her.

Without a word, she got into her car and pulled away before he could say anything else.

He flung his arms in the air with disgust. "Grab my keys," he shouted to Damien, "we'll follow her."

"No need," Damien answered.

"What? Are you going crazy, too? Who knows where she is going! Or who might be there! Come on, we've got to go!"

"I know where she's going."

"You do?" Michael asked, shocked.

"More or less, yeah. We can track her. Josie is terrible about losing her phone. A while back we installed a tracking app. I still have it on my laptop, I can follow her phone wherever she goes."

Michael smiled at him. "Damien, you are a rock star. Let's find out where she's headed."

CHAPTER 14

*J*osie blasted the air conditioning in her car. The sun had made the car warm just as the morning's events had made Josie overheated. She considered everything on her way to the motel. Was Grayson connected to her adoption? He wasn't old enough to be her father; that much was clear. Could he be a brother? A cousin perhaps? Was this what he meant about her being Celine? But if she was a baby when the man had given her to her parents, how would she have childhood memories from when she was Celine. Nothing fit, nothing made sense. Were the two connected? If they were connected, she needed to know how.

She turned onto the road Mountain View Inn sat on and swung her car into the parking lot. She spotted Grayson's car parked right outside of room seven, where he had said he was staying. She parked her car next to his in the half-empty lot, got out and headed to the door, banging on it.

The door opened. Grayson stood at the entrance. "Josie," he said, surprised. "I got your text, but I didn't realize you were coming here."

Josie pushed past him into the room. "I need answers and I need them right now. No more nonsense, I have to know."

He closed the door. "Okay, what do you want to know? And why the sudden need? Did something happen?"

"Yes, oh yes, something happened all right."

"What? More memories? Another vision?"

"Oh, no, not another vision, nope. I just had a visit from my mother, courtesy of an overzealous ex-boyfriend, who told me she thinks you're stalking me because I'm not biologically her daughter. Yeah, some agency just gave me to her when I was a baby."

Grayson listened as she rehashed the morning's events. Josie continued, "So I want to know what you know about that?"

"I don't know anything about how your parents got you."

"Really?" she retorted, crossing her arms. "You don't know anything about it?"

"No, I do not."

Josie stared at him a moment, considering what he had said and whether or not she believed it. "Are we related?"

He pursed his lips, taking a deep breath. "Celine and I are related, yes."

"Please stop with the nonsensical answers. I can't take any more."

"Josie, please, sit down. I'm sure what your mother told you was a shock but it will all make sense as soon as...."

Josie cut him off. "Yeah, I know, I know, as soon as I remember, if ever. I don't want to sit down and relax; this talking in circles is driving me nuts. I need some answers, now." Despite her protestations, she sunk onto the bed, burying her head in her hands. The stress of the day caught up to her, and she began to sob. She felt someone next to her, then arms wrap her in an embrace. She picked her head up.

"Hey, it'll be okay," Grayson said, stroking her shoulder.

She wiped a tear from her face and took a deep breath. "Where are you from?"

"What?" he asked, the question taking him by surprise.

"Where are you from? Where did you come from? Where do you live?"

"I doubt you've heard of it, why are you asking?" he asked, his face a mask of confusion.

"Just answer, please."

"I'm from a town called Bucksville. It's in Maine. See, I told you you wouldn't have heard of it."

Josie's heart dropped. It couldn't be a coincidence. He was from the same town that her parents had gotten her from. "How are we related?" she asked.

"Josie, I…"

"HOW?!" she demanded.

"You're my wife."

* * *

"Looks like it's right up here," Damien said, tracking Josie's phone with the map on his phone.

Michael crept along the road, searching for where Josie's car may be. "There it is!" Damien said, pointing out the window. Michael eased the car into the parking lot and pulled into a space on the opposite end of the lot, far enough away to be hidden to the casual observer but with a view of Josie's car.

"Mountain View Inn," he said, reading the sign posted at the entrance. "What is she doing here?"

"No idea, but that's her car for sure."

"Guess we'll wait and see."

"Should have brought snacks, I didn't realize we were going on a stakeout."

* * *

The revelation hit Josie like a ton of bricks, it was the second time today that an admission had shaken her to her core. She sat in silence trying to process the information. She had prepared herself for him to be some long-lost relative, someone connected to the dumped-at-birth story her mother had confessed to her but she had never expected this. A brother, a cousin, perhaps even an uncle, but not a husband.

She shook her head; it was impossible. She had been given away as a baby and she'd never been married before, certainly not to Grayson. He couldn't be telling the truth. But why would he lie? It was too much for Josie to process. "No," she stated, "that can't be. I've never been married."

"I can't explain it, but we are husband and wife. Well, Celine and I are husband and wife."

Josie stood. "No, no, no, you're lying. I'm not married to you. I was given away as a baby and I've never been married." She headed for the door, wanting to be away from here.

"I'm not lying, Josie, please wait."

"No, I'm leaving," she said, distraught. She opened the door and rushed out into the blinding sunshine toward her car.

Grayson caught up to her before she could get in, grabbing her arm. "Josie, please, wait. We have to talk about this."

"No," she asserted, pulling her arm from his grip. "No, this is nonsense. I'm not listening to any more of this."

"Where are you going?"

"None of your business." Josie climbed into her car.

"Josie, you're upset, please, wait, don't leave like this."

It was no use; Josie slammed the door, fired the engine and raced out of the parking spot and lot. "JOSIE!" Gray called behind her but she did not stop.

* * *

Michael and Damien watched the motel room door behind Josie's car open. Josie came rushing out, followed by a man. They appeared to be arguing.

"We have action," Michael said, calling Damien's attention to the drama unfolding near Josie's car. "Who is that?"

"No idea, never saw him before."

"Boyfriend, perhaps? Looks like they're arguing about something."

"Boyfriend? I doubt that."

"What else explains it?"

Damien pondered it for a moment. "Nah, it doesn't add up. Josie isn't that sneaky, why would she lie about seeing someone new? And it's not her style to meet him at some cheap motel."

"Who is he, I wonder? I have half a mind to go ask him."

"I'm not so sure that's a good idea."

"Probably right. Whoa, there she goes. We should follow her." Michael started the car, throwing it into gear and heading after Josie.

"Yeah, wow, whoever he is she sure is mad at him. Don't get too close, I can still track her phone so we'll see where she's going."

* * *

Josie drove down the road, trying to remain calm and not drive erratically but she was a ball of emotions. She couldn't even pinpoint what emotion she was experiencing. Was it anger, shock, upset, sadness, disbelief? Was it some combination of them all? It had been one shock after another today. The day had started off well and tumbled from there. She was glad she had gotten a good night's sleep or else the day may have proven too much for her sanity. As it was, she had no idea where to go or what to do right now. She considered driving herself to her parents' house but she didn't want to alarm her mother. She had no desire to go home and deal with her roommates nor did she want to deal with Gray.

Josie drove without direction for a while, eventually ending up at the local park. Josie parked the car and made her way down the closest path. She had no particular destination in mind but the walking helped her focus on something other than the insanity that she had heard earlier today. She came to a bench shaded by a large oak tree. She sat down on it and watched the others in the park, laying out on the large grassy area or playing with their dogs. This had been her a year ago, carefree, happy, living life without thinking too much. Now her life was a wreck. She was on the verge of a mental breakdown and it seemed the man she invited into her life had already had one.

She took some deep breaths, trying to calm down and focus her energy on creating a plan to get herself back together. She watched life pass by her for a good while until she gathered enough strength to return home. She still had no interest in discussing anything with anyone but she needed to be home.

As she stood to leave, pain shot across her head from temple to temple, forcing her to sit down again. She gasped, grabbing her head and squeezing her eyes shut. Visions shot across her mind, all pouring in at once. Gardens outside of a large white house, swimming in salty water near the beach she had seen before, Grayson smiling at her, holding her hands as they sat in front of a large fireplace, a dark haired man with white streaks at both temples handing her a drink, a blonde woman, her hair in an up-do laughing with her. Some visions she barely had time to process they all came so fast. Her brain pounded as though it was ready to explode out of her head. As quickly as it had began, it passed. The pain subsided; the thoughts stopped spilling into her head at lightning speed.

She didn't grasp what was going on, but the experience left her shaken and wanting to go home. She hurried back up the path to her car and turned toward home.

When she reached her road, she glanced in the rearview mirror. There was a car following her. As it came closer, she recognized it. It was Michael's car. They both pulled into the driveway.

Josie jumped out of her car. "Were you following me?" she asked, her voice loud and shrill.

"Who is he, Josie?" Michael said, slamming his door and approaching her.

"So you were?"

"Who is he, Josie?" He persisted with his question. "New boyfriend? Is he the guy that set you up with the new doctor? Is this why you've been sneaking around?"

"I'm not doing this with you. It's none of your business," Josie shouted as she began to head to the house.

Michael wasn't giving up. He followed her into the house, continuing the argument. "Is this the reason you broke it off with me? Were you already seeing him?" Michael was livid with jealousy, still raw from the one-sided end to their relationship.

"I said I'm not discussing this with you, not after what you did calling my mother, following me, and not when you're in this mood."

"Oh, I'm sorry if I'm in a mood. I'm sorry that I'm wondering if the guy you just met in a motel room was the reason our relationship ended so abruptly. And I'm sorry I was concerned about some crazy person stalking you so I followed you to make sure you were okay."

"You are a real piece of work, you know that? You insisted

on staying here because you had to be the hero and save me from this so-called stalker. Then you call my mother to come 'handle me' and then you follow me to spy on me. Are you serious? And the real reason has nothing to do with keeping me safe, it's all about whether or not this guy is competition for you."

"Yeah, I love how you keep avoiding answering that question. Is he?"

"Guys, maybe let's take it down a notch? It's been a really stressful day for everyone," Damien interjected.

Michael sighed, placing his hands on his hips and shaking his head. Lowering his voice, trying to remain calm, he said, "Look, Josie, I'm sorry. I'm trying to understand what is going on. You know I still care about you and yeah, I'm jealous if you're seeing him but mostly I just want you to be okay."

"He's not the reason we broke up. I hadn't even met him then."

It took Michael a moment to comprehend the information. "So, who is he, Josie?"

"I'd like to know that, too," Damien added.

Josie wasn't sure how to explain but she couldn't keep hiding it, they had both seen her with him, there was no sense in lying. Taking a deep breath, she began, "It's hard to explain, I don't even really understand it myself but he's the guy who brought the music box, and caught me in the mall when I fainted, and was talking to me the next day at the office supply store."

Michael's face did little to hide his shock. "Wait, what? The stalker? This guy is the stalker. And you met with him... alone... in a motel room. Josie, are you crazy?"

"No, I'm not crazy," Josie said, her voice becoming heated again. "He said he could help, and I needed help."

"What about Dr. Reed? Is this guy the one who sent that other quack?" Michael asked.

"Millie is not a quack," Josie defended her.

"Millie? Do you know her?" Michael asked.

"Yes, no, I don't know, it's all so confusing," Josie said, burying her head in her hands.

"He's really been helping you, I see," Michael said, rolling his eyes.

Josie, overwhelmed and upset by the conversation unfolding, squeezed her lips together trying to determine a way to explain it that made sense. But she wasn't sure she even could make sense of it.

"So, has he cured you, Josie? Has he told you why you're having those strange dreams? What they all mean?" Michael continued.

"No," Josie said, fighting back tears.

"Yeah, I didn't expect so. Let me guess, he told you he had all the answers. He could help you, he could make you whole again. And let me keep going with my guess here, next he failed to give you any actual information. Am I right so far?" Josie didn't respond. "Then he told you he could send a doctor to help you. A doctor who probably put stuff in your head that he was this nice guy whom you could trust. This guy is crazy, Josie, crazy. I don't know what his end game is, but this ends now." Michael started up the steps.

"Where are you going?" Josie asked, surprised that he was walking out of an argument. Michael never left an argument until it was settled, usually in his own favor.

"To get rid of the thing that started this mess."

"What?" Josie followed him, Damien trailing behind them both.

"That damn music box," he said, bursting into her room and making a beeline to it. "This thing started all this trouble, and it needs to be out of this house now."

"What? No!" Josie shouted. "Give that to me!" She reached for the music box, now in Michael's hands.

He pulled it away from her. "No, Josie. This thing started all this madness."

"Give it back, Michael. I was having nightmares long before that."

"But you weren't meeting with stalkers in motels before it came. You act weird every time you're around this thing," he said, moving it overhead out of her reach and trying to skirt around her to the door.

"GIVE IT TO ME!" Josie shouted, jumping for it. She grabbed hold of it and the two struggled for a moment before Josie lost her grip. She tumbled backwards, flailing to regain her balance but losing that battle. She smacked her head hard on the footboard of her bed before collapsing to the floor. The impact was enough to knock her unconscious for a few moments.

"JOSIE!" Damien called, rushing to her side. Michael dropped the music box, also racing to her side. It clattered to the floor, landing on its side and open. Tinkling music filled the air as the two gathered around Josie's slack form.

Michael held her hand, checking her wrist for a pulse. "Her pulse is okay," he choked out. "Josie, Josie, wake up," he said, patting her hand.

"Breathing looks okay, I don't see any blood where she hit her head," Damien said. "Jos, hey, Jos, wake up." He patted her cheek.

"Should we call an ambulance?"

Before Damien could answer, Josie began to moan a little, knitting her eyebrows and moving her head. "Wait, here we go, maybe she's coming to," Damien responded. "Josie, Josie, that's it, it's time to wake up now."

Josie's eyes fluttered open, staring straight at the ceiling. "Josie? Josie, are you okay?" Damien asked.

Josie did not respond, she continued to stare at the ceiling. She blinked a few times then clutched her head with both hands, covering her eyes. She moaned as though in pain.

Michael and Damien exchanged glances. "I think we had better get her to the ER," Michael said, swallowing hard. Damien nodded in agreement.

Josie began to sit up. "Whoa, whoa, Josie, easy, you took a nasty spill and hit your head. You should lie still," Damien said.

"I feel sick," she whimpered. "My head, it hurts so much." Waves of nausea passed over Josie and the pain in her head screamed across her temples. She was deathly pale. Her breathing became ragged and her vision was closing to a pinpoint. Blood rushed through her ears and her hands began to tremble.

"Yeah, you hit your head pretty hard, just take it easy, we're going to take you to the ER," Damien said, looking to Michael, unsure of what to do. Damien was never good in a crisis.

"Here, I'll carry her to the car," Michael said, putting his arm under her knees and around her shoulders. As he did, Josie shrieked in pain then went slack, losing consciousness again. "She passed out. I'm going to lay her back down. Perhaps we should call an ambulance."

"Maybe," Damien said, not sure what to do. He was distraught at seeing Josie this way, his hands shaking.

Michael stood, opening his phone to make the emergency call. "Wait, she's coming around again," Damien exclaimed.

Josie's eyes shot open, and she bolted upright. She glanced around the room as though she had never seen it before and was getting her bearings. Her breathing appeared normal, and she was no longer complaining of nausea or pain. The color seemed to have returned to her face. "Josie, oh, Josie, thank God," Damien said upon seeing her looking better.

Josie looked at him oddly, then at Michael. After a moment, she found her voice. "I'm fine. I'm fine. Help me up."

"I don't think that's a good idea," Michael began.

"Yeah, I agree, you just hit your head pretty hard and passed out and then woke up and passed out again after saying you were really sick and in lots of pain."

"Well, I'm fine now. My head is a little sore," she said, rubbing the spot she hit. "But I'm fine." She began pushing herself up to stand.

"Whoa, okay, wait. Here let me help you," Michael said, grabbing her hand to help steady her. "You okay? Woozy at all?" he asked once she was upright.

"No, I am fine."

"Perhaps you should sit down for a minute," Damien motioned to the bed.

"Sit down? No, no, I need to go. There's something I need to do. It can't wait."

"What?" Michael asked. "No, you need to go to the emergency room and check that you're okay. Now, come on, I'll drive."

"No, I'm fine. I need to go." Josie began to leave the room.

"Josie, are you kidding?" Michael reached for her.

She pulled away. "Don't."

"Josie," Damien began, "I don't…"

Josie cut him off. "You two have done enough damage so far," she said, picking up the music box and its contents and setting it on a nearby dresser. "I'm fine. I need to go. I'll be back later."

She disappeared from the room, leaving behind two stunned men. "Ah, I'm not sure she should be alone nor should she be driving. She may have a concussion," Michael managed to get out.

"Yeah, me either. She was acting… weird."

"Should we follow her?"

"That was what led to this disaster. We could wait and track her phone?"

"Good point. As much as I don't like this at all, perhaps we shouldn't give her any more reasons to go berserk. Start tracking that phone."

CHAPTER 15

*J*osie pulled into a spot at the Mountain View Inn next to Gray's car. Sliding out from behind the wheel, she approached the door and knocked. The door opened, Gray stood inside. Josie pushed inside past him.

"Josie! I'm glad you came back; I was worried sick about you. I'm sorry about before. That's the reason I was cautious about how much I told you. I didn't want to tell you a lot. I knew how you'd react, that you wouldn't understand…"

"You can cut the apology, Gray, it's me."

Gray's forehead wrinkled, and he knit his eyebrows together, trying to understand. "Celine?"

"More or less."

"You remember?"

"I remember everything, yes. There's no danger of breaking poor Josie anymore by telling her the awful truth about her past, or rather, mine."

"Celine, thank God." He raced over to her, intending to pull her into his arms.

She pushed him away. "No, Gray."

"Celine?" he questioned. "Listen, you're right. There's no time for that now. We have to go home."

"No. Like I said, I remember... everything. I remember the end, I remember the pain and misery, I remember the bargain I made, I remember all of it, Gray."

"Celine, I realize you were unhappy toward the end, but we need to put all of that aside now. The family needs you; you must come home with me. I thought we would be okay after you left. But this is different. It's something we've never dealt with before. We need you."

"I'm sorry. I can't. I only came to say goodbye. You need to leave, go home, I can't help you. I have my memories but that's all. I'm not like I was. I can't go back to that. I have one chance, one. I'm not giving it up. I have a normal life here, I don't have long until I'm twenty-five and then I'm home free, and I'm planning on staying normal."

"Celine, you HAVE to come home."

"No, Gray, I don't. You know I was never meant to live that life. I have my chance at a normal life. I'm taking it."

"Celine..."

"It's Josie. I'm Josie now," she said, turning to leave the room.

"Celine, wait," he called after her.

"Goodbye, Gray," she said, as she closed the door and went to her car.

* * *

The door closed behind her. That was Celine, all right, he thought. Gone was the self-doubting, wide-eyed innocence of Josie, replaced by all the confidence that he remembered of Celine. So, she remembered, but she still wasn't willing to help. He had won the battle but failed to win the war. He needed to convince her. He sat on the edge of the bed trying to think.

There was another knock at the door. He rushed to it, hoping it was Celine, hoping she had changed her mind. Opening the door, he found Millie. "Was that Josie I just saw leaving?"

"Yes and no," he answered, wandering back over to his perch on the edge of the bed.

Millie closed the door behind her. "What do you mean by that?"

"That, my dear Millie, was Celine." He watched the shocked look pass over Millie's face. "Yes, she's back, and she remembers everything. And she's not too happy about it either. She couldn't care less about helping us; she just wants her normal life as Josie. So, yes, she's Celine, but she'd rather stick with Josie."

"She remembered? How? When?"

"All questions I don't have answers to. She wasn't in a very sharing mood. Like I said, she came by to tell me to leave her alone."

"The important thing to focus on is that she remembers."

"Yeah and a fine bit of good that'll do us for her to remember and do nothing about it. For God's sake, we're nearly out of time, all of us!"

"Yes, I realize that, but let her assimilate all of this information then go back to her and convince her. You don't have to hold back anymore, she knows the truth now, and you know her better than anyone, use that, convince her."

Gray pondered for a moment. "There may be a way. But you're right; it's best to let it sit for now. When she's being stubborn, there is no convincing her of anything. Looks like we wait… again."

* * *

"Okay, her phone is being tracked."

"And?"

"Give it a minute, she's barely out of the driveway." Damien said, watching the dot moving on the map. "Turning left onto Highland Road." He waited a few more moments. "Okay, looks like she's headed back to the motel."

"The stalker motel?"

"Yeah, the stalker motel. Yep, she's stopped there."

"Unbelievable. What is going on with that?"

"No idea, but I agree, it's really strange for her."

"Should we go over there? Confront them? Find out what's going on?"

"Do you really think that's a good idea? I mean, the last time we confronted Josie we almost killed her."

"We didn't almost kill her. I'm not happy about what happened, but we didn't almost kill her."

"Well I thought we had."

"And you're not worried about her being almost killed now? Or disappearing? Running around after a head injury with some crazy stalker."

"Yes, I'm worried about her, but I think perhaps now that we have some new facts we can go about it differently, maybe get the information without causing her to, you know, be knocked unconscious in a fight," Damien said, shrugging.

"I guess."

"Oh, movement, look, she's on the move again."

"Where to now, I wonder? And is he with her?"

They watched the dot moving along the map for a few minutes. "Umm," Damien said, pausing. "Looks like she's coming home?"

"Looks like it."

"Yep, she's turning on Highland. Almost here."

The two stared at the screen for a moment longer before

Michael suggested, "Ah, yeah, maybe we should sit down, pretend we haven't been spying on her."

"Yeah, good idea." They raced to sit down, Michael plopping onto the couch and grabbing the newspaper, quickly opening it, Damien threw himself into an arm chair, grabbing his iPad.

Within minutes, Josie came through the door. She eyed the scene in front of her, stopping herself just short of rolling her eyes. "Oh, hey, Jos," Damien said, "still feeling okay?"

"Yeah, you sure you two are feeling okay?"

"Yeah, why do you ask?" Damien asked.

"Well, Michael is reading the paper upside-down and you are working with a blank screen on your iPad."

Michael scowled. "Okay, you caught us. We are upset and worried about you. We weren't concentrating on what we were doing. I still think we should have taken you to the emergency room."

Josie looked at them both. How frustrated she had been with them earlier. The moment had passed, she was ready to move on. This was the life she was choosing. She could understand how upset they were. She walked over, joining Michael on the couch. She sighed. "I'm fine, I don't need to go to the ER. And there is no reason to worry. I am fine. And to put your minds further at ease, I said goodbye to Gray. I told him to leave me alone."

"Gray? The stalker guy?" Michael asked.

"Yeah, the stalker guy. Time to get back to normal."

"That sounds great, Josie," Damien said. "We can go to Dr. Reed's with you tonight. We want to help you get back to normal."

"I'm not going, I'm canceling the appointment."

"Are you sure that's wise?" Michael asked. "Sorry, I don't mean to push you, I'm just asking."

"I think it is. I can always go back if things don't continue to improve but I think I've turned the corner."

"Okay, well, that sounds like a plan then," Michael said.

"All right, well, I'm going to cancel that appointment and then what do you say we order something to eat? Pizza?"

"Awesome, yes, please!" Damien said.

"Great." Josie rose and disappeared upstairs.

"Wow, talk about a complete turnaround, huh?" Damien exclaimed.

"Yeah, I'm almost afraid to believe it. Seems too good to be true. You mind if I hang around another week or so just to be sure she's okay?"

"Nope, I don't mind at all. When you're around, she's so busy being mad at you she never gets mad at me." He grinned.

"Glad that's working out for you," Michael joked back. "Hey, while I'm here, keep that phone tracker on. Just in case."

"Sure thing," Damien said.

CHAPTER 16

*W*hen Josie awoke early the next morning, she remembered experiencing the dream again, running through the cave, hands bloody. Now that she remembered everything about her past, the dream had made much more sense and felt much less overwhelming. Still, she had assumed once she remembered everything the dream would no longer trouble her. Why she had the dream again perplexed her. Was it a remnant of stress from remembering her past?

She laid in bed for a few moments before she got up to jog. She considered her day; there were a few work items to take care of this morning. She hoped everyone else in the household was going to the office today, leaving her time to embrace her newfound memories and begin to act like Josie again. She had acted very "un-Josie-like" yesterday; she had to be careful to continue to behave like Josie. She wanted things to return to normal. She didn't have long before this could become permanent; she had to make it through.

After changing clothes, she checked her phone. A text

message from Gray was waiting: *Celine... need to see you... urgent*

She rolled her eyes and sighed. This was not what she needed. Not only did she not want to continue involving herself with Gray, but she also did not want her roommates finding out that she was still involved with him. She texted back: *Told you yesterday I can't help you*

The response was almost immediate: *Celine, please... I heard what you said, but I need your help... just for a few minutes.*

Perhaps the best way to deal with Gray was to meet with him and reinforce to him she could not help him. If she ignored him, he'd likely show up when she least expected him, probably at the worst possible moment. She texted back: *Meet me at the end of the road... leaving for my jog now*

Before she received a response, she left. She spent the first half of her jog setting her mind to deal with Gray. She had to remain steadfast in her long-term goal, which was to remain far away from the drama of Buckley life. As she approached the end of the road, she spotted Gray's familiar form, leaning against his car. She steeled her nerves for the encounter and pushed ahead, jogging up to him.

"Good morning, Celine," he said, still leaning against the car, arms crossed.

"What do you want, Gray? I already told you I can't help you."

"I know what you said, I don't accept it."

"Well, that's too bad for you. Soon there'll be no choice. So either accept it now, then or not at all. Either way, the result is the same."

"No, Celine. It's not. You've still got time to change your mind and you've got to."

"I will not continue having this argument with you. I'm not changing my mind; nothing will make me change my mind. Go home, Gray."

"I can't. I can't go back without you, we need you too much."

"How did you find me, anyway?" Josie asked, curious how he tracked her down after the events twenty-five years ago.

"Your sister, Celeste, she's back, she helped us."

"Oh, well now I'm sure I'm not going back. Whatever problems Celeste has brought to your doorstep you can handle yourselves," Josie said, holding a hand up.

"Damn it, Celine, we don't have time for your stubbornness," he exclaimed. "You've got to come back."

"I told you no, I meant it, stop asking me, stop texting me, go home." Josie turned to leave; finished with the conversation.

"Celine," he called as she started to jog away, "it's serious. It's the Duke. He's back."

Josie came to a stop, processing the information. She shook her head after a moment; she couldn't let herself become involved. "Sorry, Gray, I can't help you," she said and resumed jogging home. She forced her mind to stop dwelling on the conversation. She could not afford to become involved. She had one chance at a normal life; she had to take it. She had to walk away.

When she returned home, the house was abuzz with activity. Michael and Damien were getting ready to go to work. She would be alone in the house today; that would make things much easier. By 7 a.m., everyone was heading out of the house, leaving her to enjoy her cup of tea alone on the porch. Josie watched them both head off down the driveway. It was the first day of her new life and she planned to enjoy it.

* * *

Michael and Damien both pulled down the drive, with Michael trailing behind Damien. Within minutes of getting on the main road, they both turned off into a small parking lot outside of a now-abandoned pizza shop. Damien pulled his car around the back of the building. Michael followed him. Damien got out of his car, locked the doors and hopped into the passenger side of Michael's.

"She still at home?"

"Yep," Damien said, checking the phone tracking app.

"All right, well, let's double back and get this stakeout started."

"Cool. I brought snacks this time," Damien said, grabbing his backpack. "We got soda, chips and candy, all kinds of stuff." Damien eyed Michael for a moment, "You seriously going to stay in dress clothes all day?"

"No, I brought a change of clothes, I'll change when we get there."

"I can't believe we're doing this. She'll be so mad if she catches us."

"Yeah, she will, but," Michael said, easing the car back onto the road, "the complete one-eighty yesterday didn't sit well with me."

"Oh, I totally agree. I've known Josie all my life, she was acting nothing like Josie. I just can't figure out why she'd lie. I mean I get not wanting her mom upset, but why lie to me?"

"Well," Michael answered, pulling back onto the road the house was on, "we'll soon find out." He pulled the car past the driveway of the house before easing it off the road into a clearing of trees. The car was hidden from the house but they could keep tabs on Josie's location, follow her if needed and watch the house. After parking, Michael hopped out to change clothes then climbed back in behind the wheel. "Okay," he said, "let's get this party started."

They didn't have long to wait. By mid-morning, Josie had

a visitor; a car pulled into the driveway and headed for the house. "Let's check it out," Michael said, opening his door.

The pair crept through the woods closer to the house. Michael took out a pair of binoculars and trained them onto the house.

"Seriously?" Damien asked.

"What? I want a clear view," Michael retorted. "Okay, who do we have?" A figure exited the car.

"Well?" Damien asked, "who is it?"

"It's the guy from the motel. Here, check it out. Good thing I brought these, huh?"

Damien looked through the binoculars. "Yeah, good thing. Yep, that's him all right. What's he doing there, I wonder?"

"Yeah, she said it was over. Doesn't look over to me."

They watched as the man rang the doorbell then knocked on the door and waited a few minutes before Josie opened it. They stood talking for a moment or two before he disappeared inside the house.

"I wish we could hear what they are saying," Michael said.

"Yeah, should have bugged the place."

"Wait, can you do that?"

"What? Are you serious?"

"Well, it'd be useful at a time like this."

"I mean, yeah, but I've never done it. I imagine she might figure it out if we're setting up bugs all over the place."

"True, but if this continues it may be something to consider. Well, get comfortable I guess, let's see how long he's here."

* * *

Josie heard the doorbell ring, then a knock. She hoped it was a delivery person, but she had a sneaking suspicion it wasn't.

She headed downstairs, leaving her office. She peered out of the window next to the door. It was Gray. She sighed, opening the door. "What do you want?"

"To talk to you. Can I come in?"

"No, Gray, you can't come in. This is crossing the line. I've already told you I can't help you."

"All right, fine. I'll come back later. Perhaps around six tonight, perhaps you'll be in a more receiving mood then."

Josie grimaced. She stood aside, allowing him entrance. "Thought you'd see it my way," he said, stalking into the house.

She closed the door. "You have five minutes, Gray. Although, there is nothing you can say that will change my mind."

"You're being stubborn, although I'm not surprised, you've always been stubborn. It's one of your most enchanting yet exasperating qualities."

"Four minutes."

"Are you really enjoying your life here? This mundane existence? The daily grind?"

"Three minutes."

"You can't tell me this is what you want. Come on, Celine. Can you look me in the eye and tell me this is what you really want?"

"Two minutes."

"You can't, can you? You can't do it, that's why you're just trying to wait me out, that's why you won't discuss anything."

"I can, Gray. I can. This is what I want. I like my life. I am happy as Josie."

"You didn't know any different, not until yesterday anyway."

"I'm not coming back. I can't."

"Celine, please. We need your help."

"I can't help you. Especially if the Duke is involved."

"Celine, you're the only one who can help if the Duke is involved. You know that."

"I think your time is up, please go." Josie walked to the door and opened it.

"Celine, please. There are children involved here. We need your help. Now, please, stop being stubborn."

"How dare you? Don't you try to guilt me into this."

"I'm simply telling you what is at stake here. If you can let two innocent children be tormented by the Duke, much the way you were, then fine, I'll go. But I don't think that's in your nature, Celine. At least it wasn't. Perhaps Josie is that selfish, you were not." He walked through the door. "Think about it. I'll be in touch."

Josie slammed the door behind him. She was furious. How dare he show up at the house unannounced and then try to guilt her into changing her mind. She tried to convince herself that she wasn't being selfish. It was worth it, she deserved a life too. Sacrifices had to be made. She had to stay the course. Days remained, only days, that was all it would take. She took a deep breath; she had to maintain her normal life. She forced herself to climb up the steps, determined to focus on work for the afternoon. She hoped to use it as both a distraction from her recent conversations with Gray and an affirmation that this was the life she was choosing.

"Here we go, he's coming out," Michael said, "that was a short conversation."

"He doesn't seem upset, he's not yelling like yesterday."

"No, he wasn't in there long enough."

"There he goes, and he's off."

"Yep, hmm, well, should we go back to the car?"

"Yeah, it's way too hot out here already. Plus, time for a mid-morning snack."

They headed back to the car, Michael turned on the engine to run the air conditioner to cool the car off for a bit. "So, who do you think he is?" he said, cracking open a soda that Damien brought.

"No idea. I never saw that guy before yesterday. Here wait, I'm going to text her and see what she says."

"Wait, you're going to text her about this guy?"

"No, I mean, sort of. I'm going to just 'check in' and ask her how it's going, is she okay and all of that."

"Oh right, yeah, okay, good idea. See what you get back from her."

"Okay, here we go. I sent it, said 'everything going okay?' Let's see what we get back."

Within a few minutes, Josie responded: *Yep, all good here :)*

"So she's still going to lie," Michael said.

"Looks like it. It's too obvious to ask if she's had any visitors. Hmm, perhaps I can say… I've got it. 'No disturbances?'" he said as he typed.

His phone chimed indicating a response: *Nope, nothing to worry about, D!*

Damien responded: *How's your head?*

After a moment, he received a new message: *Seems fine, doesn't hurt, no bump or anything*

"Anything?" Michael asked.

"Nope, she's admitting to nothing. Looks like that was a bust." He threw his phone down, grabbing a bag of chips and popping it open.

"Well, I guess the stakeout continues."

* * *

Josie answered the text messages from Damien. She was surprised it took him this long to check in. It seemed he was walking on eggshells around her, not wanting to come across as overbearing. She settled in to her chair and pulled up her email application. Nothing new there. She opened a few reports and a word document to continue working on creating a summary for a client.

She typed a few words and added a chart. She fiddled with adjusting its size and location and added a caption. She stared at the document. She typed another word and stopped. She found herself distracted. She tried to push ahead, finishing the statement. She deleted it and rewrote it twice then was stuck again.

It was no use, she couldn't focus. She still had about an hour before lunch so she decided she would relax with a bath. She headed for her room. As she prepared for the bath, she noticed the music box sitting on the dresser where she had put it the night before. She shook her head, turning to face away from it as she changed.

After the tub was full, she slipped out of her bathrobe and into the tub. She laid back, closing her eyes, trying to relax. After a few moments she opened them. Staring ahead, she found she could see the music box from where she was in the tub since she had left the door ajar. She couldn't catch a break today, she thought. She closed her eyes again, shutting it out. They popped back open after a few moments. It was no use this wasn't relaxing her either.

She gave up on the bath, climbing out, toweling off and redressing. Perhaps she needed to get out of the house, she thought. She wasn't sure where she would go, but anywhere was preferable to sitting at home unable to focus on anything. She grabbed her purse and keys and headed for her car.

* * *

"Got movement again. There goes Josie's car." Michael announced.

"Got the tracker up, let's see where she goes."

Michael looked over Damien's shoulder watching the red dot move around on the app's map. "Where are you going, Josie?" Damien asked his phone.

"Mall trip?" Michael asked, finishing his soda.

"Perhaps. Lunch break?"

"Could be. Doesn't look like she's heading to the mall."

"Nope, doesn't look like she's heading to any of her favorite lunch spots either," Damien said, studying her movement. "Actually, it kind of looks like..."

"She's going to the motel," they said in unison. Michael fired the engine and backed out onto the road. He put the car in drive and sped off down the road.

* * *

Josie pulled out of the driveway, knowing she did not want to stay at home. She didn't aim for any particular place. She wove around the back roads in what she thought was an aimless pattern. Before she realized it, she was turning onto the road that housed the Mountain View Inn. She sighed, frustrated with herself for not being able to stay away.

She pulled into the parking lot. Gray's car was there in front of room seven. She pulled in next to it. She climbed from the car and knocked on Gray's door. After a few moments, Gray opened it.

He smiled at her and stood back to allow her to enter the room. He glanced around outside before closing the door, shutting the world out.

"It's good to see you, Celine. I'm glad you came back."

"I'm not 'back,' Gray. Not the way you want me to be. But I didn't like the way our last conversation ended."

"Neither did I. I don't like fighting with you, never did. Now, can we start again? Perhaps discuss things fresh?"

"I'm not selfish, Gray, Josie isn't selfish either, but I made a bargain, I can't go back. You must understand that. You were there at the end, you know what I suffered through."

"Yes, I know. I wanted to help you. I wanted to be there for you. But you went ahead and did this without discussing it with me. Stubborn, like I said before."

"I wasn't being stubborn, come on, Gray."

"You were. It always has to be your way. I wanted to help, you wouldn't let me. You pushed me away. We were a team, Celine, at least I thought we were. By the time I knew what you had done it was too late, and it's almost too late again. I refuse to lose you a second time."

"You don't have a choice, Gray. I can't be involved. I can't do this again."

"Celine…" he began.

"No!" Her voice rose sharply. "No, Gray, we're finished. I just didn't want to leave things the way they stood. I need you to understand."

"Well, I don't understand. Not at all, I will never understand. So if you've come here looking for some absolution from me you can just turn around and go because you're not getting it. Not today, not tomorrow, not ever, Celine."

Josie shook her head, clenching her jaw. "Okay," she said after a while. "I'll go." She went to the door, opening it. Before leaving, she looked back at Gray. "But you should go, too, because I'm not changing my mind, absolution or not."

Josie left, almost running into Millie on her way out.

"Oh, Celine, nice to…" she said, her voice trailing off a bit as Josie pushed past her.

"Not in the mood, Millie," Josie said and kept going to her car.

"What was that about?" Millie asked, entering the room.

"She's mad because I won't let her off the hook, tell her it's okay to not come back, let her keep living her pretend life as Josie."

"She sounds like she has her mind made up. This is the third time she's told you that, isn't it?"

"Yeah, it is. But she will change her mind."

"How can you be so sure?" Millie inquired.

"Because she came here looking for validation. She's looking for an okay from me that what she was doing is right."

"But you told her you didn't agree, and she still didn't change her mind."

"No, she didn't, but she will."

"I don't understand your sudden confidence, Gray. How can you be so sure?"

Gray gave her a half-smile. "Did you already forget what you told me, Millie?" Millie looked puzzled. "I know her, remember? If she hadn't come back, it would have concerned me. But the fact that she did suggests that she's thinking about it, reconsidering, feeling guilty for saying no. She came back because it's bothering her and as long as I don't tell her it's okay, as long as I keep the pressure on her, she will keep being bothered. The guilt will grab hold of her conscience and squeeze until she changes her mind. I'll text her later, keep the pressure on her, she'll come around soon, I know it."

"I hope you're right," Millie said. "I just got a text from Alexander. Things are continuing in a downward spiral. So, for all our sakes, I hope you're right."

CHAPTER 17

osie drove back toward home. The conversation with Gray still bothered her. She wasn't sure what she expected from him when she went to the motel. How could he accuse her of being selfish? He, of all people, should understand what she went through twenty-five years ago. She wouldn't let him bother her. She needed to put it out of her mind.

She considered getting lunch at a favorite restaurant, anything to distract her mind, but she wasn't hungry. Perhaps some shopping would help, she surmised. She aimed her car for the mall, parking outside of her favorite department store. She wandered around like a zombie, not able to focus on anything. When her watch read almost 1:30 p.m., she supposed that she had better eat.

As she headed for the food court, the memory of her last experience here plagued her. Every place she turned, memories of Gray and his pleading for help haunted her. She left without eating, heading home to grab a light snack instead.

At home, she gathered her snack and forced herself to finish her report generation, sending them off before deciding to call it quits for the day. She was mentally and physically exhausted and spent the rest of the afternoon on the front porch swing, trying to remind herself of her end goal. She anxiously awaited the return of her roommates and the distraction that they would provide for her.

* * *

"Wonder what all that was about?" Michael asked, as they pulled back into their hiding spot near the house.

"Seems like she's trying to distract herself, that's what she usually does when she's upset by something. Retail therapy. Ever seen her closet? She does it a lot."

"She wasn't at the motel or the mall long though, and she purchased nothing."

"Yeah, that's the part that's got me concerned."

"That she didn't purchase anything?"

"Yeah," Damien responded, lost in thought.

"Of everything going on, her lack of purchasing has you concerned? Seriously?" Michael asked.

"Yes. Well, I mean, it's totally out of character. When Josie has a problem, she shops it away. Do you know how many pairs of shoes she bought when she didn't get a big contract once?"

"No?" Michael phrased his response as a question.

"Well, it was a lot. Broke up with a boyfriend, that's like a five dress minimum. Bad day at work, she buys a new sweater. Fight with her mom, going rate is about three blouses and a new skirt. The fact that she met with that guy, whoever he is, then went shopping and came out with nothing is majorly concerning."

"Hmm," Michael said, enlightened to the stress-relieving mechanism employed by Josie. "So, what's it mean when she buys nothing? Nothing is bothering her?"

"I'd say just the opposite. Something so significant is bothering her, she can't even shop. So that's like something scary serious."

"But what could it be?" Michael mused. They both sat in silence for a few minutes, lost in their own theories about what might be bothering Josie. After a few minutes, Michael said, "So, how many dresses did she buy when she broke up with me?"

Damien looked up at the roof of the car, thinking, "Um, three dresses and two pairs of shoes, I think."

Michael made a face. "Not bad, did I do good then?!? So what's this guy's story that she's bought nothing."

"That's the million dollar question."

"I'm getting stiff." Uncomfortable, Michael shifted around in his seat. "Good thing I'm not a cop. I couldn't do this often."

"Might not have to, looks like she's calling it a day. She's on her swing."

"Maybe we should 'come home from work early,'" Michael suggested.

"That'll work for me. One of us should circle around a few times so we're not back at the same time."

"Rock, paper, scissors for it?" Michael asked.

"Okay," Damien responded, as they both made fists. "Figures, that's my luck," he said after losing, his rock being covered by Michael's paper. "Okay, drop me back at my car and I'll drive around for about fifteen minutes then come back."

"Sounds good," Michael said, firing up the car and backing onto the road. They drove to where Damien had left his car.

"See you soon," Damien said as he exited the car at the abandoned pizza parlor parking lot.

* * *

Josie laid in bed, unable to sleep. Despite both Damien and Michael coming home early, they did little to distract her from her conversations earlier in the day. She had made a good show of it, but finally night had come and she was alone with only her own thoughts to plague her.

From her position in bed she could view the music box in front of her. She stared at it. She should have put it away earlier today, but she didn't. Now it served as a constant reminder of her past. She considered putting the thing away now. She rose from bed, intending to do just that. After grabbing hold of it she took a moment, sitting back on the bed, holding the box. She clutched it to her chest, an over-whelming sense of sorrow filling her. She opened the box, letting the music fill the air. She decided against putting the music box away for the moment, setting it back on the night table and climbing back into bed.

As she set the box down, she noticed the notification light blinking on her phone. Picking the device up she checked her notifications and found a text message waiting for her. She opened the message; it was from Gray: *Here is a picture of Max and Maddy, Avery's two children... I thought you might want to see what's at stake*

Attached to the message was a picture of a smiling boy and girl, standing on either side of Avery. The last time she had seen Avery, she had been a child smaller than the ones in the picture. Now Avery had children that were about ten and eight.

How much things had changed yet also how little. Gray realized guilt was weighing on her, and he was exploiting it; how well he knew her. Using her guilt to his advantage was smart, but also maddening. She stared at the picture; at those two little faces.

Shutting her phone off, she set it back on the night table. She rolled over, facing away from it, trying to shut the image out of her mind as easily as she had shut off the phone's display. Unfortunately, it wasn't that easy. Even though she recognized what he was doing, she couldn't ignore the text. Rolling back over, she retrieved her phone and responded: *Meet tomorrow morning to talk?*

She didn't know what she would say, but it bought her some time to reflect. She got up, pacing around the floor while she waited for the response. Her phone chimed: *Can we meet tonight?*

She sighed; Gray would not let this go. He had a hook in her and would use it to his advantage. She responded: *Usual spot?*

It wasn't long before Gray texted back: *See you there soon*

Josie changed out of pajamas and into casual clothes, sneaking out of the house and down the driveway. It would take her a little longer than usual since she would not jog the route. She had made it almost to the end of the road when a car approached. It was Gray; he rolled down the passenger window. "Hop in," he said.

"Can I trust you not to drive me straight to Bucksville?" she joked.

"No, but it's a chance you'll have to take," he joked back as she slid into the passenger's seat. He swerved around, turning back toward the main road. "So, you haven't changed your mind then, I take it?"

She sighed, "I can't do it." He frowned at her response but said nothing. "But," she continued after a moment, "I can't do nothing either."

"So, you'll come?"

"I haven't decided. There's no good ending for me. I'm at a loss."

"The worst ending for everyone is the one where you do

164

nothing. Now I've shown you what is at stake, it's a tragedy waiting to happen." He pulled off the road into an empty parking lot.

Josie stared straight ahead into the darkness in front of her. "I can't be what I was."

"But if you aren't we have no hope."

"I'm not so sure about that."

"Well, I am. We need you, Celine."

"Perhaps I could help in another way."

"Another way?"

"Yes, I mean, I know a lot, I remember everything. I remember…" She paused, struggling to get the words out. "I remember the Duke. Perhaps I can help even if I'm just as I am now, just Josie."

Gray considered it for a moment. "Okay, there's a train leaving early tomorrow morning. I'll meet you at the end of your driveway at four thirty tomorrow morning."

"Okay, I'll be ready."

Gray turned the car around and pulled back onto the road. "So you're okay with this?" Josie asked him after they were back on the road.

"You're coming home, I will take whatever you're giving me right now, so yeah, I'm okay with it," Gray responded.

Within minutes they were pulling back onto Josie's road. "Just leave me off at the end of the driveway," she said.

"Okay," he said, pulling to a stop across the driveway. "See you tomorrow morning, four thirty, don't be late."

"I won't be. See you then."

Gray pulled away, swinging around to head back toward the main road. Josie made her way to the house. She needed to pack. Worry plagued her. She hoped this wasn't a mistake, but she had a nagging suspicion it might be.

* * *

Gray entered the motel room, throwing his keys onto the nearby table. Millie was waiting in a chair, having known he was meeting Celine. "Well?" she asked as soon as he entered.

"Well, we leave tomorrow morning, pack your bags, Millie, we're going home."

"She agreed?"

"More or less."

"That doesn't sound good."

"She agreed to go and no more."

"Is that any use to us?"

"It's a win, she's going, I'll worry about the rest when we get home."

"That's a brave attitude."

"It's the only attitude that I can have, Millie. Now, let's get packed up, we pick Celine up at four thirty in the morning."

CHAPTER 18

*J*osie stood at the end of the driveway. There was a chill in the summer morning air. Josie couldn't help but wonder if it foreshadowed what was to come. She pulled her sweater around her tighter as she watched the car lights approaching. The car pulled up alongside her. She took a deep breath knowing this was her last chance to back out before the ball started rolling. Josie would have been indecisive at this moment; Celine was not. She recognized what she had to do.

"Good morning, Celine," Gray said, jumping out of the driver's side to put her luggage in the trunk.

Josie slid into the backseat on the passenger side. "Good morning, Celine," Millie said from the passenger seat. "I'm glad you're joining us." Josie didn't answer.

Grayson slid in behind the wheel and swung the car around toward the main road. "Time to go home, Celine," he said as they pulled away from her driveway.

Josie stared back for a moment watching her driveway and mailbox disappear behind her. She couldn't help but feel this was the end of an era for her, that she might never lay eyes on this house again. Returning her gaze to the front, she made a silent vow that this would not be the case. She would help but she would remain strong, she would return as Josie.

* * *

A loud rapping at the door startled Michael awake. He rushed to the door, opening it to find a flushed and flustered Damien. "What's wrong?" he asked.

"We got trouble," Damien answered, a bit out of breath.

"Trouble? Is it Josie? Is she sick? What?" he asked, pushing through the door past Damien and racing toward Josie's room.

"She's gone."

"What? Gone? Where?"

"Looks like the city, perhaps the train station? I only looked quick. I came to get you right away."

"Train station? What?"

"Well, I've been tracking her phone. I wrote my own little application to track it that will also alert me to out-of-the-ordinary occurrences, like odd times or locations or..." Damien began.

"Yeah, okay, get to the point."

"Oh, right, well, it alerted me this morning. According to my little tracker, Josie left the house around four thirty this morning and traveled into the city, see?" he brandished his laptop with the blinking red dot.

Michael looked at the screen. "Four thirty? Seriously? Where is she going?"

"No idea, but it might be worth following her."

"Yeah, I'd say so, let me change and we'll head down there."

"Okay, me too."

The two parted ways to dress for the trip, meeting back

in the living room a few minutes later. "Okay, I got phone chargers, laptop, some clothes, basic toiletries, snacks, and I grabbed a few waters. Perhaps you should throw some clothes in just in case? It looks like she's at the train station, she could be going anywhere."

"How did you do that so fast?" Michael said, running back upstairs to grab a few things.

Damien followed him up the steps. "Oh, it's my go-bag."

"You have a go-bag?"

"Yeah, doesn't everyone?"

"No?" Michael said grabbing a few things and tossing them into his duffel bag before running to the bathroom to throw a few toiletries in.

"Oh. Hmm. Well, anyway, you ready?"

"As I'll ever be," Michael said. The two headed downstairs and continued out the front door. Damien locked it behind them and double-checked that the lights were all out before heading to the car. "Come on, what are you doing?"

"Sorry," Damien said, throwing his bag in the backseat and climbing into the passenger's side of Michael's SUV, "Josie'll kill me if I left a light on or something."

"Let's hope it doesn't come to that. Perhaps she's seeing the weirdo from the motel off or something."

"Doubt it, her car is here, so wherever she is, she went in someone else's car so I have this bad feeling that it's not that."

Michael turned the car around in the driveway and made his way down the drive, turning toward the main road. Both of them were silent, lost in thought, wondering what they might find when they caught up with Josie at the train station.

About thirty minutes into their one hour drive to the train station, Damien's app beeped an alert. "She's on the move again. Heading north it looks like."

"So, she's not coming home, that's for sure," Michael responded, knowing they lived west of the city.

"Nope, wonder where she is going. Do you think she's on a train?"

"It's a little after six o'clock, can you check the train schedules to determine what trains are pulling out now and where they are heading?"

"Good idea," Damien answered, pulling up his web browser on his phone and heading to the station's website. "Let's see," he said as he scrolled through to find a list of departures. "There's a train that departed at 6:05 a.m., heading up the coast, final destination is somewhere in Maine."

"The time frame fits, what are the other stops, I wonder."

"There's a list of them here, but there'd be no way of knowing unless we knew what ticket she bought or we wait for her phone to show us."

"Once we get to the train station perhaps we will get some information. We'll use the phone as either a confirmation or back-up."

"Sounds good, I'll keep an eye on my app to see if she stops moving before we get there but I doubt that."

They finished the rest of their ride in silence with Damien staring at the phone tracker, watching Josie move further and further north. They pulled into the lot and parked. Grabbing their things from the backseat, they made their way into the train station. This early in the morning, it wasn't very busy. There was only one person working the ticket booth. "I'll see if I can find anything out from her," Michael said, pointing to a girl at the ticket window.

They both walked over to the ticket agent. "Good morning," Michael said, flashing a smile. He planned to use his good looks to charm the girl out of some information.

"Can I help you?" she said, in a monotone voice.

"Ah, I hope so. We're supposed to travel north to meet a friend. In fact, she just left on the earlier train. We slept in, oops," he joked, flashing another smile, "anyway, we're heading to the same place she was so we need the same ticket."

"Final destination?"

"Ah, same as hers was."

The girl looked at him, expressionless. "Final destination?" she repeated.

"Well, okay, this is embarrassing, but... " Michael said, leaning in toward the window and lowering his voice, "neither of us remember what stop she told us to get off at. I was hoping you could help me out and give us the right tickets, you know, based on what she bought."

"Why don't you just ask her?" the girl said, annoyed.

"Like I said, we slept in and she's already going to be mad about that. On top of that, if I tell her that we forgot where we're going she will be super mad. I would rather avoid that if you know what I mean." Michael winked at her.

The girl sighed. "I don't remember every ticket I sell so looks like you're out of luck."

"Ah, well if it helps, she was on the six-oh-five, with a tall, dark-haired guy. Here's Josie, our friend," Michael said, pulling out his phone and flashing a picture of him with his arm around Josie. "Do you remember where they were going? I'd really, REALLY appreciate it if you could help us out." Michael also flashed a one hundred-dollar bill.

The girl rolled her eyes, but slid her hand over the cash, pulling it discreetly toward her. "Two tickets to Bucksville then?" she asked, tapping around on her computer.

"Yep, that's right, how did we forget that?" he said, turning to Damien and playing along. "Bucksville! Awesome, well thank you so much, Cara," Michael said, eyeing her name tag. "Two tickets on the next train to Bucksville, please."

Cara sold him the tickets. "Train leaves off platform B at 8:35 a.m. Got a long wait," she said, handing the tickets to him and turning away to avoid any further discussion.

"Thanks," Michael said, taking the tickets. They turned around, scoping out the area.

"How about the seats in the corner? Quiet spot and there's a plug," Damien said, waving his phone to indicate the need for the plug.

"Good idea." They both headed toward the corner, setting their gear down and taking seats on opposite walls. Damien took out his charger and plugged his phone in. Michael said, "Well, that worked out. We'll only be about two and a half hours behind her. Let's see when we get there. A little after six thirty tonight. Why is she going to Timbuktu, Maine?"

Damien continued to watch the little red dot moving further north on the map. "No idea, I will be happy when we are moving in the same direction. Oh, I should call off work."

"Me too, I'll leave a voicemail for my secretary, tell her I won't be in today."

Both men left voicemails taking the day off with their respective employers then put their phones on chargers. "Okay, now with that done," Damien said, taking his laptop out of his bag, "let's discover what we can learn about Bucksville." He tapped the keyboard, entering the town's name into the Internet search bar. "Top result is a Wikipedia article, let's find out what it says." He began to read from the article, "Bucksville, Maine is a small seaside town on the Maine coast. Population blah blah blah, it was founded by the Buckley family in 1754. The Buckley family is still the largest landowner in the town and its surrounding areas, owning both personal property and commercial ventures including the town's shipping fleet and cannery. Um…" He scanned through the rest of the brief article. "There's not much else here, nothing really of note."

"Is there a section called 'Why would anyone go to Bucksville?'" Michael joked.

"No, also no information on why Josie might go there."

"Burning desire to visit a cannery?"

"She's always thought Maine was pretty, but she's never been there herself that I am aware of. Do you think this is related to what her mom told her? About being given away as a baby?"

"Could be, but why not tell us?"

"Yeah, that's the weird part," Damien said. "She's always been open with me." He watched the little red dot moving further and further away. "I'll be happy when we're moving, too. Where are you going, Josie?"

"It's okay, man," Michael said, detecting his upset, "we'll find her, it'll be okay."

Damien nodded to him. The two sat in silence for a while until Damien's phone chimed an alert. Checking it, he shifted forward onto the edge of his seat. "It's a text from Josie!"

"What's it say?" Michael asked, leaning toward him.

"Let me get it open, come on, phone! There we go. Okay, she says 'By now you probably noticed that I am gone. I'm fine, I hope to be back soon, I'll explain later… too much to type.'"

"That's it?"

"That's it. I'll answer her and see if I can get more information."

"Okay, but don't let her know we're following her."

"Okay, I won't." He read aloud as he typed his response. "Yeah, we noticed and have been worried. Where are you and what do you mean by soon? And… how do I know you're really okay?"

They waited with bated breath for her response. First,

they received a selfie with the message: *I'm fine, see?* A smiling Josie looked out of the phone at them. She did, indeed, look fine. Next came a lengthier message: *It's just something that I have to do... I'm not sure how soon... now you can stop worrying*

Damien sighed in frustration reading it. "She's being intentionally vague. I'll ask her straight out." He typed back: *I am still worried... can you at least tell me where you are?*

She responded: *No... I don't want you following me.*

"Too late," he said to Michael before typing back: *Keep in touch at least? Although I wish you'd tell me what's going on... you've never been this secretive with me*

Josie responded: *I'll keep in touch... sorry D but it'll all be over soon and I'll be home and life will be normal*

"Well, I guess that's that," Damien said. He sighed. "Only an hour left to wait for this stupid train. And then another eleven hours to Bucksville."

"Yeah, that gives us twelve solid hours to prepare."

"Prepare for what?" Damien questioned.

"The inevitable tongue-lashing she'll give us when we show up wherever she is," Michael said, only half-joking. "Hey, I'm starving, I'm going to see if I can get a breakfast sandwich at the little shop that just opened. Want me to grab you something?"

"Yeah, breakfast sandwich and a coffee would be awesome, thanks."

After having some breakfast and fueling up with coffee, the two had only about fifteen more minutes to wait, so they packed up all of their stuff and headed to the platform. Not long after, they were seated on the train, ready for the long journey to Maine.

Damien watched the countryside roll by as they journeyed up through Boston and on toward Maine. Michael used his phone to answer various emails and review some work documents. The journey seemed to take forever, and the two made little conversation along the way, both of them more focused on finding Josie once they arrived at their destination.

When the train stopped in Bucksville, it was close to 7 p.m. They disembarked, finding little to nothing near the train station.

"Looks like the town is that way," Michael said, pointing to his right. Following his finger, Damien spotted a cluster of lights.

"Yeah, and it looks like we're walking," Damien said. "At least we're traveling light." Damien shrugged his backpack onto both shoulders.

They made their way toward the lights. They found the main street and began walking down it on the sidewalk. A short way down the road they came across the Bucksville Inn. "Should we stop in here, rent a room, and ask around about Josie?" Michael posed.

"Good idea. With any luck, we'll get some information there. Perhaps she's even staying here and we'll find her."

"Looks like it's the only place in town to stay so there's a good chance."

They pushed through the door and entered the small lobby. There was a small desk to their left, a call bell sat on top. No one was standing behind the desk so Michael wandered over and rang the bell. To the right was a little café. Damien approached Michael at the desk. "Looks like there's a café, might want to grab something to eat once we get our bearings."

"Yeah, I could use something to eat, I'm starving," Michael said as an older gentleman approached the desk.

"Help you?" the man said, pushing his glasses higher on his nose.

"Yeah, we were hoping to get a room for the night."

"All right. Have you filled out this paper with your information. Will you be paying cash or credit?"

"Credit card," Michael said, pulling his wallet out of his pocket and handing over his credit card then filling out the form.

"Need two keys, I guess? Got a nice room with two double beds, room five. Diner's open 'til eight so if you want to eat better get in there. Anything else I can do for you?"

"Thanks, yeah, we're going to head there right after we dump our stuff. There was one other thing," Michael said, pulling out his phone. "We're looking for our friend." He showed the picture of Josie on his phone. "You wouldn't happen to have seen her, would you? She got into town a few hours ago."

The man adjusted his glasses and peered at the picture. "Oh, ah, yeah, Mrs. Buckley. I didn't realize she was back in town, haven't seen her in a while. If she's anywhere, I'd guess she's up at the big house."

"Big house?"

"Yeah, the Buckley place up on the hill. Locals call it Buckleyham Palace." He chuckled. "All in good fun, of course. Head straight out of town on main street and turn right at the first road, follow it all the way up to the gates, can't miss it."

"Thanks a lot, we'll try there after we grab a bite. Oh, any place we can rent a car for the weekend?"

"You're welcome. Car? Nope, no place to rent a car in Bucksville. If you need anything else, just give me a holler. Name's Cunningham, Bill Cunningham."

"Thanks, Bill," Michael said, stuffing his phone back in his pocket with his wallet. Turning to Damien he said, "Let's dump the bags and get something to eat, then we can see about getting up to that house."

They made their way upstairs and left their bags in their

room. It was small, decorated with a quaint nautical theme. They headed back down to the lobby and into the café, finding themselves the only ones there.

"Take any table you want," the waitress called from the counter. They chose a table in the corner, as far from the counter as they could so they could talk without being overhead. The waitress delivered the menus and left them to look over their choices. Within a few moments she was back to take their order then gone again to deliver the order to the kitchen.

After the waitress left, Damien said, "I got a text from Josie. She said she's made it to her destination safe and is fine. I texted her back and asked again if she could tell me where she was, she hasn't answered though."

"The old guy thinks she's up at the house on the hill."

"Yeah, but why did he call her Mrs. Buckley? She's never been married."

"Maybe he needs new glasses. Maybe she looks like Mrs. Buckley. Oh, maybe," Michael said, growing excited, "Mrs. Buckley is her real mom and she looks like her?"

"Hmm, could be. That's the only thing that makes sense so far."

The waitress returned with their order, each having a simple burger and fries. "You boys from out of town? Don't think I ever saw either of you before," she said as she set the plates down in front of them.

"Yeah, looking for a friend."

"Well, good luck. Bucksville isn't that big so he shouldn't be too hard to find." With that the waitress disappeared, returning to wiping up the counter and cleaning up as she readied to close the café for the night.

"What is Josie doing here? It must have something to do with her birth parents. Could stalker guy be a relative? But why the arguing?" Damien asked, stuffing a fry into his mouth. "Mmm, this is surprisingly good," he added.

"Maybe he wanted her to come here and she refused? Perhaps they were arguing about that and then she ended up deciding to come."

"Again, why not tell us?"

"I don't know."

"I mean, okay, say it has to do with her birth family. So why not say, 'Hey guys, that guy is my long, lost brother' or something, just explain it. Why all the secrecy and sneaking around? It would make much more sense for her to just tell us and not keep it secret. Then we wouldn't be worrying, following her around or chasing her across the country."

"Well, she doesn't know we're chasing her yet."

"No, but still, she must realize this is coming across super odd to anyone on this end."

"Perhaps she's afraid I'll call her mom again."

"Okay, so then just say 'Don't call my mom again' right? I don't get it."

"Me either, fingers crossed we'll find out soon though."

They finished their meal, paid the bill and headed out into the night. It was cooler here than it was at home, the night breeze had a crispness to it similar to a fall evening.

"Well, looks like we're walking," Michael said. They saw no signs of a cab anywhere on the streets.

"Straight out of town to the first road on the right," Damien imitated the innkeeper.

"Okay, let's go!" Michael said as the two set off on foot toward the house on the hill.

CHAPTER 19

*J*osie took a deep breath as they rode up the long, winding driveway toward the house. It had been many years since she had been on the estate. A nervous energy filled her and her stomach clenched into a knot.

Henry, one of the estate caretakers, had picked them up at the train station and drove them to the house. He maneuvered the car alongside the front entrance. The house loomed large over them in the waning sunlight. Josie took another deep breath as she exited the car and stared up at the house's dark frame. It had been decades since she had last been inside, yet it seemed as though it were only yesterday.

Grayson climbed out of the front passenger seat. He slipped his hand around hers. "Welcome home, Celine," he said. He gave her another moment before saying, "Shall we go in?"

"Why put it off?" Josie said.

She took another deep, steadying breath before she pushed through the double doors into the entryway and the main foyer. The house had changed little; it was still as grand as she remembered with its wide stairway leading to the second-floor gallery-style hall. There was a large sitting room to the left. On the wall that separated it from the foyer had hung a large painting that now appeared to be missing. Grayson noticed her gaze fall upon the missing element. "The painting of Mina disappeared a few months ago, that's when we realized there was trouble on the horizon."

"Disappeared? You're right, that's not good news." Josie answered him.

Josie saw movement coming from the sitting room and within a few seconds Charlotte Buckley-Stanton appeared in the doorway. "Celine! How lovely to see you again, I'm so glad you've come back. Won't you please come in and sit down? Millie, good to have you back." Charlotte approached Josie to give her a brief but sincere hug, slipped her arm around her waist and led her into the sitting room. Charlotte, Avery's mother, was always the picture of grace. Widowed at a young age, she had raised Avery on her own from the age of eight and had remained a fixture in the Buckley house.

Charlotte led Josie to the sofa, and the two sat down, with Gray taking an arm chair across from them. "How was your trip? I trust you're not too tired to have dinner with us?"

"It was fine, thank you," Josie answered.

"We've had a long day, Char, but we can make it through dinner," Gray said. "Would either of you like a brandy before dinner? I'm having one." He stood to pour himself a glass from the drink cart.

"Oh, yes, I'll take one, thank you, Gray," Charlotte answered.

"No, thanks," Josie said, wanting to keep her wits about her.

"Celine, I put you in your old suite, I hope that's suitable?"

Charlotte asked tactfully, trying to determine whether or not she would be sharing a room with her husband.

"It's fine, Char, we'll work it out," Gray answered first.

"Yes, it's fine, Charlotte," Josie agreed.

Charlotte's behavior would never betray the underlying trouble Gray had described to Josie. She was the quintessential hostess, working hard to make her household at ease regardless of the circumstances. The Buckley house could be crumbling around them and Charlotte would still be poised on her couch with a demure smile calmly telling her housemates that they should find the nearest exit.

"If you don't mind, I'll head upstairs to freshen up before dinner," Josie said, excusing herself.

"Of course. We dine at seven," Charlotte answered.

Josie excused herself from the room and made her way up the massive staircase. She had no trouble navigating to her old room, finding it had also changed little. Henry had already brought her luggage up from the car; she found it sitting on the bench at the end of the bed. Opening it, she found a few personal items and carried them to the bathroom.

She stood for a few moments gazing into the mirror. It was hard for her to believe she was back, yet here she was. It was so familiar to her, so easy to slip right back into the fold. She had to make sure she didn't stay in this house.

* * *

"Hey, what are you two doing over there?" a man's voice yelled.

"Ah, hello, hi," Michael said, waving his hand. "We're looking for someone."

"Looking for someone? Do you realize you're on private

property? The 'No Trespassing' sign on the gate should have made that clear," the man said.

"Yeah," Michael said, looking back at the open gate marked with the sign he and Damien had ignored. "Yeah, I realize this is private property, but the gate was open. I didn't see any signs. We don't mean to intrude but we're looking for a friend. The man at the hotel suggested we try here," he fibbed. "Perhaps you can help us?"

"Old Bill Cunningham told you to come to the Buckley estate?"

"Yeah, that's what Bill said. Here, I have a picture of her," Michael said, pulling out his phone and bringing up the picture of him and Josie on the screen to show the man.

"That's your friend?" the man asked, almost as though he didn't believe them.

"Yep, that's her," Michael said. "Have you seen her?"

"Well, yeah, of course. I dropped her off at the house a few hours ago. She didn't mention guests coming, though."

"Oh, well, we were a few hours behind her on the train, she might not have known when to expect us," Damien joined in.

"Did you walk here? If I'd have known, I could have picked you up at the train station. Or you could have had old Bill call me to pick you up at the hotel. Like I said, I didn't realize you were coming, Mrs. Buckley didn't mention anything."

"Oh, no problem, the walk was nice. Like I said, I'm not sure Josie, ah, Mrs. Buckley knew what train we were on," Damien lied, rephrasing Josie's name to the name the man had used to add credence to their story.

"Well, no matter, hop on in the car here and I'll take you up before I head into town."

"Oh, no don't worry about it, we can walk it," Michael said.

"Walk it? It's about a mile up to the top there. Nah, I'll drive you."

"No, really, it's fine, we're fine," Michael declined again as politely as he could.

The man made a face at them. "Why are you two acting so sketchy?"

"Sketchy?" Damien said, with a nervous laugh. "Hahaha, nah, we don't want to trouble you, that's all."

"It's no trouble, will only take a few minutes."

"Well, umm, it's actually, umm... it's getting late. It's nearly nine," Michael said, trying to act nonchalant, "perhaps it's best if we try back tomorrow. We don't want to disturb them, they're probably getting ready for bed."

"You two walked from town all the way here, ignored a 'No Trespassing' sign, came onto private property and first you say you'll walk up but now you say it's too late for me to drive you? Listen, you two are either going to get into that car or I'm going to call the sheriff because something isn't right here."

Michael and Damien gulped, glancing at each other. "Well," Michael said, "I guess we'll take the ride then."

"You sure this is a good idea?" Damien whispered as they approached the car to get in.

"Well, better this than getting arrested. Let's hope Josie is up there and isn't too mad to vouch for us."

Without a word, the man slid behind the wheel. He fired the engine and swung the car around toward the house. Within a few minutes they were approaching a large, gothic-style house. Michael and Damien peered from the windows of the car at it.

"That's one spooky house," Damien mumbled.

They pulled up to the front door, and they all exited the car. "This way," the man said. He motioned them through the front door. They entered the foyer, both of them gaped around at the entryway. They noticed a woman coming across the foyer. "Oh, Mrs. Stanton," the man said.

"Yes?" the woman answered.

"I found these two characters hanging around near the end of the driveway. Claim they know Mrs. Buckley."

"Oh?" The woman eyed Michael and Damien. "Well, let me get her, she's in the sitting room. Celine? Celine!" The woman called through the doorway.

"Umm," Michael began, "I think there's been a mistake, we were looking for..." He stopped mid-sentence as Josie appeared at the doorway, accompanied by the man from the motel.

"Celine, Henry discovered these two men on the property. They say they're friends of yours?"

Josie was staring at them both. Damien surmised if looks could kill they'd both be dead many times over. She sighed. "Oh yes, I know them."

"Oh, I'm sorry Mrs. Buckley, had I known, I would have picked them up from the train station, they didn't have to walk from town." The man turned apologetic.

"No problem, Henry. I didn't realize they were coming. They weren't expected," Josie answered, glaring at the two of them.

"Well, I'm glad you made it, would you all like to join us in the sitting room for a nightcap?" Charlotte asked, the picture of politeness.

"I'd like a moment to speak to them alone and then I'm sure they'll need to be on their way. I assume they've got an early morning train to catch back home."

Michael opened his mouth to answer but Henry beat him to it. "No, won't be another train passing through all weekend, Mrs. Buckley. They don't run trains no more on weekends here. They won't be able to get out of town until at least Monday."

Josie closed her eyes a moment, gathering her thoughts. Before she could respond, Charlotte was taking over, always the gracious hostess. "Oh, heavens, well, I'm sorry to hear that you're stranded here! Of course, you'll be staying with us?"

Josie watched the situation spiraling out of her control, unable to stop it without looking suspicious to someone in the room. Gray stepped in, sensing her tension. "I'm sure they have a room at the inn, Char, perhaps it's best they stay there."

"Oh, nonsense, they are friends of Celine, they'll stay the weekend with us. Henry was just heading into town, he can pick up your luggage and bring it up on his way back." She smiled graciously at the two of them then at Josie.

"Well, thank you, Mrs., uh, Stanton, was it?" Michael said, matching her gracious smile. "We would be more than happy to stay and are so grateful for your hospitality."

"Oh, wonderful. I'll have Mrs. Paxton prepare two rooms and Henry, if you would be so kind as to gather their bags on your way into town?"

Michael handed him the key to their room. "Room five, thanks a lot!"

Charlotte left to attend to having their rooms made up and Henry headed out the door to the car, leaving Michael and Damien alone with Josie and Grayson. "Well, you worked that out pretty well, didn't you?" Josie said, crossing her arms.

"I think it's best if…" Gray began.

"Gray, can you give us a minute alone, please?" Josie requested.

"You sure?" he asked.

"I'm sure, thanks."

"I'll be upstairs," he said, squeezing her arm and making his way across the foyer and up the grand staircase.

"You want to explain to me what you two are doing here?" Josie said with her arms still crossed.

"Do you want to explain to us why they're calling you by another name here and think you're married?" Michael countered.

"No, I do not. Nor do I want you here at all, let alone for the entire weekend. So, here's what will happen. Tomorrow morning you two will make an excuse, I don't care what, and go back down to the inn and stay there and leave on the first train out Monday morning."

"Josie," Damien said, "we're really sorry, we were just worried about you. I mean, you disappeared this morning then sent some cryptic text, you've been having a lot of trouble with those nightmares and stuff and then meeting that weird guy and then finding out you were adopted. We're worried, so we came after you. We just want to be sure you're okay and help."

"I don't need your help, I'm fine. And how did you follow me, anyway?"

The two exchanged a glance. "Well," Damien began swallowing hard.

"Just dumb luck," Michael said.

"Dumb luck? That makes zero sense, how did you find me?"

Damien hesitated. "Damien," she intoned with emphasis.

"I tracked your cell phone," he croaked out just above a whisper.

"What?" she asked.

"I... I... I tracked your cell phone. I had that app still and then I wrote another app to track it with more precision. It works pretty well, I'm thinking about putting it on the app store. I built notifications in it and everything to inform you if there's unusual movement and..." he babbled.

"DAMIEN!" she shouted.

"Sorry, yeah, so anyway, it told me you left this morning, chimed when you got to the train station and we followed you there and we asked a girl and she said you bought a ticket to Bucksville and so we got on the next train and now we're here. Like I said, we just want to help. I realize the news you got from your mom was a shock and I want to be there for you, Jos. We've never had secrets before, I just want to help." The distress was obvious on Damien's face, not only from the overall situation but also from upsetting Josie.

Josie felt sorry for him. He was a genuine and nice person; he was honest in his effort to help her. She might not have been able to pinpoint Michael's motives, but she recognized that there was nothing sinister about Damien's. Softening, she said, "I realize you're trying to help and I'm sorry there are secrets between us, but I can't explain it, not right now. I wish I could. I know it's hard for you, but I can't. You have to trust me, trust that I know what I'm doing and that soon everything will be back to normal."

Damien nodded at her, still upset but willing to not push things further right now. "I'm sorry I upset you, Jos."

"You didn't upset me, D." She moved to him and gave him a hug. "But you need to leave while I sort this out."

"Why? What is the big secret?" Michael chimed in.

"You know, I'm not mad at him, but I am mad at you. You don't get to ask questions," Josie said, pointing at him.

Josie was about to continue but Charlotte returned to the foyer. "Mrs. Paxton has your rooms ready. I'm sure you two are tired after your long day. Have you eaten? I can have something sent up for you if you'd like?"

"Oh, no, thank you, we had dinner at the café," Michael answered.

"Oh, I hope you enjoyed it. Our little town does have good food. Wells, let me show you up to your rooms. Oh, unless I interrupted your conversation?" She turned to Josie for an answer.

"We're finished, thanks, Char. I'm going to bed, too, see you in the morning."

"Good night, Celine," she said as Josie headed up the steps. "Follow me," she said, turning to the two men. As they walked up the steps and down the hall she continued, "I had Mrs. Paxton put you in the same wing as Celine and Gray, not too near so you'll all still have your privacy. I put the two of your rooms together. Henry should be back within the hour with your luggage; I hope he won't be disturbing you by bringing it up. If you plan to retire for the evening, I can leave a note for him to put it in the foyer for you."

"No, he won't be disturbing us, thanks!" Michael said.

"Oh, wonderful. Mrs. Paxton sets breakfast out on the sideboard by seven; please help yourselves. Well, here we are, I hope you are both comfortable. If you need anything, please let Celine or me or Mrs. Paxton know. Celine and Gray are just down the hall through those double doors."

"Thanks," they both said in unison.

"You are very welcome and sleep well." They entered their respective rooms. Damien looked around the room. It was large with refined furnishings including a large four-poster bed, a few dressers, and a sitting area near a large window that overlooked the cliffs and ocean. A door on the nearside of the bed led to a bathroom which he assumed he shared with Michael given its placement and the door on the opposite end leading to another space.

Damien wandered to the window and peered out, opening it. He could hear the waves crashing on the shores below. Exhaustion was setting in. The day's events combined with the concern over his cousin, Josie, and the lack of information in general were snowballing. The worry was wearing on him.

A knock on the door distracted his thoughts. He made his way across the room and opened it. Michael walked in as soon as he opened the door. "Okay, I thought we bought a ticket for Bucksville not Weirdsville," he joked as he made his way into the room.

"Yeah, really," Damien retorted.

"Oh, sorry," he said, after sinking into a chair by the window, "were you going to bed? I assumed you'd be staying up."

"I'm tired but I wouldn't be able to sleep. Too many things going through my mind."

"Yeah, exactly, like why is Josie here? Who are these people? Why are they calling her by another name? And why is she acting like it's totally normal?"

"Yep, all that and why is she not telling me? And why are they acting like she's married to motel guy and why is she going along with it? Are they drugging her? Mind control perhaps? Did that doctor lady plant something in her head?"

"No idea, this whole thing gets weirder by the second. I mean, you two have always been together from the time you were kids, right?"

"Yep, we grew up like siblings. Went to school together, college together. Even got our master's degrees at the same place."

"And she's never been on her own even for a short duration where she could have gotten married and you didn't know?"

"No. I lived with her from the time I was five. I went on every family vacation, every trip she's ever been on. She's never been away from me long enough to meet someone and marry. It gets weirder by the second and her behavior is weird, too. I mean I get maybe not telling you but she's never acted like this with me before."

"Okay, we need a plan. Because my thinking is we ALL

leave on Monday together or none of us leave. In short, my plan is we don't leave until Josie does."

"I agree. I'm not comfortable leaving her here no matter how much she insists she's fine. This is too weird. And this house is creepy."

The two spent another forty-five minutes discussing various aspects of what was happening then turned in after Henry brought their luggage to their rooms. Their plan was to be up early and meet most of the household at breakfast.

CHAPTER 20

*J*osie sat at the table sipping tea, a plate of eggs and toast in front of her. Next to her, Gray was sipping coffee, reading the morning paper. Charlotte was already up as well and had joined them for her morning coffee and toast. Not long after they had all settled in, Michael and Damien appeared.

"Oh, good morning!" Charlotte said in a cheerful voice. "Did you sleep well? Breakfast is on the sideboard."

"I slept great!" Michael said. "And breakfast smells delicious, thanks!" The two made their way to the buffet and helped themselves to eggs, toast, bacon and a cup of coffee.

As they were making their way to the table, another woman entered. Petite and blonde with a shoulder-length bob, Josie recognized Avery. "Well, good morning everyone," she said. "I see the children aren't up terrorizing you all yet," she laughed. She poured herself a cup of coffee and sat down at the table.

"Good morning, darling. No, the children aren't down yet. Michael, Damien, this is my daughter, Avery. Avery, this is Michael and Damien, friends of Celine's."

"Hi, I'm Avery," she said, extending her hand to Michael, then Damien.

"Nice to meet you," they both said. There was a lull in the conversation.

Avery sipped her coffee then said, "So, how was your first night back in the house, Aunt Celine?"

Michael and Damien exchanged a glance at the mention of the word "aunt" as Josie answered. "Ah, it was fine. You know, I think I'll take a walk," she said, springing up and leaving some of her food on her plate.

"I'll come with you," Damien said, jumping from his seat.

"No, you finish your breakfast, I'll be back later," Josie said, already heading toward the door.

Damien, not sure of what to do, returned to his seat to finish his breakfast, not wanting to appear rude to the rest of the family in case they needed to extend their stay beyond the weekend.

"That was abrupt. Was it something I said?" Avery said, laughing. She looked at Michael and Damien, "Don't worry, if you were hoping Aunt Celine would give you a tour after breakfast, I'm sure that my kids, Max and Maddy, would be more than happy to show you around the house, the property, and most likely the town."

"Thanks. We may take them up on that," Michael said. "I bet they're great tour guides."

"Oh, the best. They'll show you every dark corner and cobweb this place has," Avery said as two children came through the door. "Speak of the devils. Here they are now. Max, Maddy, come over here, meet some of Aunt Celine's friends. This is Michael, and this is Damien." Both children shook their hands, and they all exchanged pleasantries. "I was just telling them you'd be willing to give them a tour. Aunt Celine had a few things she needed to take care of this morning and she can't show them around."

"Oh, yeah, we'll show you all around," Max said.

"Yeah, ALL around," Maddy added. "I hope you aren't afraid of ghosts."

"We are," Michael said, "but we'll have you to protect us, right?"

"Yeah!" both children said in unison, giggling.

"Okay, well first, let's get you both something to eat and then you can commence on your grand tour of the estate," Avery said.

The four of them finished their breakfast and Max said, "Okay, are you ready? I need to grab some flashlights and we'll meet in the foyer. Maddy, why don't you take them there?"

"Be sure you give them the full tour now, don't skip anything," Gray said.

"I expect they'll have you traipsing all over the house and into every forgotten corner. I apologize ahead of time if they wear you both out!" Charlotte said, smiling.

"I think we can keep up. It's an interesting house, I can't wait to explore every corner!" Michael said.

The two followed Maddy into the foyer. They waited a few moments before Max appeared with an armful of flashlights, passing one out to each of them. "Ready?"

"We're ready, Max," Maddy said.

"Okay, you probably already saw this part when you came. The best part of this room was the portrait of Mina Buckley. It used to be there on that wall." He motioned to a blank wall. "But it went missing a while ago, no one knows where it is and everyone is really upset about it."

"Upset about a missing painting?" Damien asked.

"Yeah, no one can find it and everyone is in danger until we can."

"What? Because there is an art thief on the loose, you mean?" Michael asked.

"No, because the legend says that painting was hung there over two hundred years ago to protect this house and everyone in it and as long as it hung there, everyone in this house was safe. Mina Buckley was always watching over everyone in the house for as long as the painting hung in this foyer. But now it's gone, so Mina isn't here to watch us anymore. Now we're all in danger."

"I see. Sooooo, Mina Buckley was a friendly spirit who took care of the people living in this house?" Michael asked.

"Yeah, that's right. And someone took her away and now we're all doomed," Max said, matter-of-factly.

"Doomed? That's a little dramatic, isn't it?" Damien asked.

Max shrugged his shoulders. "That's what all the grown-ups said when the painting disappeared. They said 'We're doomed' and then Uncle Gray said he had to find Aunt Celine, she was the only one who could help."

"Your Aunt Celine was the only one who could help with what?" Michael asked.

"She's not really my aunt. She's not even really my mom's aunt. Uncle Gray is my grandma Charlotte's cousin not her brother, but my mom still calls them Uncle Gray and Aunt Celine."

"I see, what is it that only Aunt Celine can help with?" Michael pressed.

Max shrugged again, "No idea. Hey, you wanna see something cool though?"

"Sure," Michael said.

"Come here." He waved them into the sitting room. "Wait, first," he said as he closed the door behind them, "you have to BOTH swear to secrecy on your lives to never tell anyone about this."

Michael and Damien exchanged a glance then shrugged. "Okay, sure, we swear," Michael said.

"Do you swear?" Maddy asked Damien.

"Yes, scouts honor!" he said, holding up three fingers.

"Okay. Behind this chair here," Max said, pulling aside a chair placed against the wall, "it is a secret panel that leads to a secret passage that goes to another part of the house!" He pressed on the wooden wall panel and it popped open. "See!!!"

"That's so cool!" Damien said and actually meant it.

"Come on, let's go through it!" Max said, thumbing on his flashlight.

They all crowded into the small passage. Max closed the panel behind them so "no one could follow them." They followed Max as he snaked around the passage hidden behind the walls, pointing out where they were in the house a few times.

"So, Max," Michael said, as they wound around the passage, "do you remember Aunt Celine much?"

"No, I've never even met her. She lived here a long time ago before I was born when my mom was little."

"She lived here when your mom was little?"

"Yeah, my mom said she remembers her, but she was only about Maddy's age or younger when Aunt Celine lived here before." Michael and Damien glanced at each other. The facts weren't adding up, unless the child was wrong about what he was saying. "I can't wait to meet her, though."

"Oh, why's that?" Damien asked.

"Because Uncle Gray said she was the most beautiful woman he'd ever seen. I bet she's really pretty."

"Yes, she's really, really pretty, I bet," Maddy parroted.

They reached the end of the passage, Max fiddled with something and opened a doorway into another room of the house. This one was not being used, it was dark with furniture covered in dust sheets and random items placed around in storage.

"I bet," he said, "if there is a painting thief, they'd hide somewhere here. Hey, maybe the painting's even hidden here! Come on, let's spread out and search for it!"

"Okay, buddy, we'll check over in this corner!" Michael answered, drawing Damien to the opposite side of the room. Once they were away from the children, he said in a hushed voice, "Okay, so new theory, crazy motel guy thinks Josie is the reincarnation of Celine."

"Seriously?" Damien asked.

"Yeah, seriously. Did you hear what the kid said? Aunt Celine lived here when my mom was little. Now, he's like what, nine or ten? His mom looks like she's somewhere in her thirties, around my age, give or take a year. Say she was ten when Aunt Celine was here, that's twenty-five years ago. Josie would have been a baby, it doesn't fit."

"Do you really believe a kid who thinks a kindly spirit lives inside a painting here? Perhaps he just got his timelines confused."

"He can't be that confused. He's never met her and like I said, he's around ten? Even if Celine was here until he was three or four, before he can remember, Josie would have been too young to be Gray's wife and living here."

Damien considered it. "Yeah, no matter which way you work this, Celine and Josie can't be the same people. So, what's she doing here?"

"Hey, are you guys looking over there?" Max yelled over.

"Yep," Michael called back, waving his flashlight around, "nothing but cobwebs here!"

"I mean, is she just playing along? Is this guy crazy, and she feels bad for him? Is he threatening her? Are they controlling her mind somehow?" Damien continued to muse aloud.

"I don't know, but we've got to talk to her, convince her to at least give us some clue as to what is going on."

"Yeah, perhaps we can convince the kids to take us outside and see if we can find her."

"Good plan. Let's head back over," Michael said, starting toward the two children. "We didn't find anything, how about you guys?"

"Nope." Max scuffed his foot against the floor. "I really wanted to find it. I'd be a big hero, I bet! They'd probably even let me eat ice cream for dinner!"

"Maybe it's not in the house, I bet your family already looked everywhere in here for it. Can we try somewhere else on the estate?"

"Hey, maybe you're right!" Max looked off into space, thinking. "Let's see, there's Uncle Alexander's house, the caretaker's cottage, the garage, the stables, and a few sheds. Where should we start first?"

"I bet you Aunt Celine is already out looking. She left early this morning from breakfast, probably to start searching, maybe we should head out and track her down and find out where she's checked and then we can narrow it down," Michael said.

"Hmm, okay! We can finish looking around the house tomorrow, it's going to rain, anyway. Do you know where she started her search?"

"No, we'll need to rely on you two to find her," Damien said.

"Oh, I bet she went to visit Uncle Alexander first thing this morning," Maddy said. "Uncle Alexander told me they were really good friends. Let's go there."

The children led them out of the room and down a series of dark hallways until they reached a part of the house that was lit and lived in. Michael and Damien still had no clue where they were until they got to the main gallery hall that circled the foyer below. The kids bounded down the steps toward the front door. "We better keep the flashlights with us!" Max said as he pulled the door open.

The bright sun was peeking in and out of fluffy white clouds, forcing them to shield their eyes when it was uncovered. "Uncle Alexander lives this way, down this path. He built himself a house that looked like the one the Buckleys had over in England. Come on!" Max yelled.

Max and Maddy raced down the path with Michael and Damien rushing to keep up with them. The path contained a few twists and turns. The children seemed to have no trouble navigating, turning off when necessary to another path. After weaving through several paths, a large white house appeared in the distance. It didn't appear to be as large as the main house or as grand but was still impressive.

They pushed on toward the house, the children reaching it first. They used the large brass doorknocker to knock at the door. The door opened as Michael and Damien caught up to them. It was Henry, the caretaker they had met last night. "Help you? Oh, Mr. Max and Ms. Maddy, how are you?"

"Hi, Henry," Max said. "We're here to find out if Uncle Alexander has seen Aunt Celine."

"Oh, yeah, he's seen her, she's here, but, uh, they can't talk. They're real busy."

"Are they looking for the painting?"

"Painting? Oh, you mean Mina's painting? No, they're just talking. But they can't be disturbed."

"Oh, we'll just wait for her here," Max said, pushing his way into the house with Maddy. Michael and Damien pushed through with them.

"Oh, well, I'll tell them you were here but they might be a long time, so it's best that you be on your way."

"We're not in any hurry, we'll wait," Max said.

Henry became impatient. "Now, I just told you that you can't wait here. Now you get going," he snapped.

"Listen, Henry, this is our fault," Michael interjected, "We were looking for Jos, eh, Celine, and we asked the kids to help us. It's important that we find her."

"Yeah, really important," Maddy said.

"Like I said, I'll tell her you were here, but it's best you're all on your way."

"We'd prefer to wait for her. Perhaps you could let her know we're here?" Michael said.

"Now I told you they're busy and can't be disturbed! What part of that don't you understand?!"

Michael was ready to respond when a new voice entered the conversation. "That's rather rude, isn't it, Henry? These people are guests on the estate." Both Michael and Damien spotted a man coming down the stairs from the second story. Josie was with him.

"Well, Mr. Buckley, you were talking to Mrs. Buckley, and you said it was important, I didn't want to disturb you."

"It's fine, Henry, I'll handle it from here," he said, reaching the bottom of the stairs. "I'm Alexander Buckley, it's a pleasure to meet you, and you're both friends of Celine?" Alexander shook both of their hands.

"Hi, Uncle Alexander," Max said. "Wow! You must be Aunt Celine, you're as pretty as Uncle Gray said!"

"Yeah, you're so pretty," Maddy interjected.

Josie smiled at the two children. "Yes, I am Aunt Celine and thank you!"

"Were you looking for the painting, too, Aunt Celine?"

"Um, in a way, yes. In fact, I'm leaving right now to keep working on it."

"We'll check at the stables and the sheds if you take the other spots, Aunt Celine!" Max said before she could leave.

"Okay, sounds good, thanks," Josie said, trying to make a quick exit.

"Jos, Celine," Damien said, shaking his head, "we need to talk."

"We'll talk later," Josie said, heading out the door.

"Umm, a pleasure to meet you Alexander, but we need to talk to Josie, eh, Celine. Sorry to rush off," Michael said, already heading out the door. Damien followed behind him. They rushed to catch up to Josie on the path.

"Josie!" Damien called behind her. "JOSIE!" They caught up to her and Damien grabbed her elbow. "Josie, please, wait."

"D, sorry, this isn't the best time. I'm busy trying to get things figured out so we can get back to normal. Now, please, let me go. Go back to the house. Read a book or something and go home on Monday."

"No, Josie!" Damien said, "I will not accept that. No way!" Damien's insistence surprised Michael.

"D, please, I can't explain it now, I can't but I definitely want you and Michael to go. I'm pleading with you to leave."

"Why, Josie? This is beyond bizarre and I'm not leaving without you. I want you to come home with us."

"I can't come home yet, D, I can't."

"Why? Please, Josie."

"There is nothing to worry about. But I can't come home." She turned to leave.

"Josie, come on," he said, grabbing her arm again. "You can't expect us to go home and leave you here. Do you realize how bizarre this looks to ANYONE on the outside of it?"

She pondered for a moment. "I realize how bizarre it is, yes. It's as bizarre as it was to me when Gray first approached me but it makes sense, it does, but I can't explain it. Now, please..."

"No, Josie," Damien continued, "no. I'm beyond worried

about you. I'm exceptionally concerned. This bizarre story about you being someone named Celine who that kid told us lived here when his mother was a kid, these people bringing you here, you going along with it, have they brainwashed you? Are they threatening you or someone in our family?"

"No and no. I'm not brainwashed. They are not threatening me. I am here of my own free will, believe it or not. And I have other things to do. Now, please," Josie said, pulling away from Damien's grip and heading off down the path.

Damien opened his mouth to call after her but gave up, surmising it would be useless. Michael clapped a hand on his shoulder. "Well, we're right back where we started, still no information, but a terrible feeling that something is wrong."

"Something is wrong," Damien said, turning toward him. "And if Josie won't tell us, then I'll confront the guy who brought her here. One way or another we're getting some answers. Come on!"

The new fire in Damien's belly impressed Michael, and he followed him down the path back toward Alexander's house. Alexander exited the house with the two children. "I was just about to return them to the house. Were you able to catch up to Celine?"

"Yes. She was in a hurry, like she said, so we didn't talk much. We were just coming back to get the kids and have them continue our tour," Damien said.

"Oh, wonderful, then I leave you in good hands, Max and Maddy. A pleasure to meet you both, I hope we can see each other again before you depart."

"Nice meeting you," Damien said, then turned to the children, "ready?" Alexander disappeared back into the house.

"Yeah!" Max said. "Did Aunt Celine tell you where to check next?"

"Well, in a way," Damien answered. "She told us to find Uncle Gray and talk to him about it."

"Oh," Max said, looking dejected.

"What?" Damien asked.

"She just doesn't want us to find it, that's all. Or she would have told us where to check, not sent us to Uncle Gray."

"Well," Damien said, "I think she's kind of sending us on a scavenger hunt. She doesn't want it to be too easy!"

"Scavenger hunts are fun!" Maddy said.

"Hmm, maybe. Okay, let's go back to the house, I bet Uncle Gray is there."

"Okay, you lead the way," Damien said.

"Smooth," Michael said as they followed the kids down the path back toward the house.

The children had them back at the main house in about ten minutes. They rushed through the front door yelling for Grayson. "Hey, what are you children yelling about?" a woman wearing an apron said to them as she passed through the hall.

"We're looking for Uncle Gray," Max said.

"Yeah, Aunt Celine said we need to find him right away!" Maddy added.

"Oh, she did, did she? Well, I think he's in the study. Hey, no running!" she shouted after them as they ran down the hall with Michael and Damien following them.

They raced half way down the hall and burst through the door. Max shouted, "Uncle Gray! There you are!"

Seated at a desk across the room, Gray's attention was drawn from his book. "Max, Maddy, what's going on?"

"Aunt Celine said we needed to find you," Max said, as Michael and Damien came into the room.

"She did? Is she okay?"

"She's fine," Michael said, "Max, Maddy, Aunt Celine said

once we found Uncle Gray to tell you to check in the scariest part of the house for the painting. She said you'd know what that meant."

"I know exactly where she means, yeah!" Max exclaimed. "Come on, Maddy!"

"Okay!" Maddy answered, and the two disappeared from the room.

"Mind explaining to me what that was about?" Gray asked.

"Sorry, necessary distraction," Michael said.

"We need to talk to you," Damien added. "We need answers and I'm rather sure you have them. So you're going to answer some questions. First why did you bring Josie here? And why are you calling her Celine? How did you get her to come with you and buy into whatever crap you're feeding her?"

"Why not ask her yourself?" Gray retorted.

"I'm asking you," Damien persisted.

"You know what I think? I think you've asked your Josie, and she's not talking." Gray said, standing from the desk, crossing his arms with a smug smile.

Damien faltered, not sure what to respond with. "That's probably because you brainwashed her somehow."

Gray chuckled. "I didn't brainwash her. No, I didn't do anything to her. The fact is she made a choice, and it didn't involve you."

Gray was slowly but surely backing down the more timid Damien, but Michael wasn't about to let it happen without a fight. He approached Gray, getting into his personal space, meeting his eyes. "She might have made a choice, a stupid one, but the next one she makes won't involve you, you can take that to the bank."

Gray smiled again, turning away from Michael. "We'll see."

"You smug, arrogant son-of-a-..." Michael started.

"What's going on here?" Millie asked, walking through the door.

Michael backed off a bit. "I need to speak with Gray, would you two please excuse us?" she asked, noticing the tension in the room.

"This isn't over," Michael warned before leaving the room with Damien.

Michael sighed once outside the room after Millie had closed the door on them. "Well, that didn't go as well as I hoped," Damien admitted.

"I didn't expect he'd give up much information, but I hoped his arrogance might have tipped his hand."

"I'm betting the shady doctor won't give us anything either, no sense in waiting for her."

"Nope, they're thick as thieves, those two," Michael answered, shaking his head. "Our best bet is to keep appealing to Josie. We have to find a way to get through to her."

"Yeah, I hope we can do it. Perhaps we should take our own tour of the house and see if we can find anything interesting or helpful."

"Okay, sounds like a plan," Michael said, setting off further down the hall. "We should also try to keep an eye on Gray, following him we're almost bound to find something."

"Good idea, we'll stick close so we don't miss him leaving."

Josie sat on the swing under the gazebo, facing the ocean as the sun lowered behind her in the sky. The swing glided as if in a slow waltz under her as she gazed at the sky, painted like a rainbow by the setting sun. Gray approached from behind her. "I thought I'd find you here."

"I'd forgotten how beautiful it is here," she answered, without taking her eyes off the horizon.

Gray sat down on the swing next to her. She gazed at him. How many times had they sat in this exact spot together? How many problems had they solved here? She felt like this problem was insurmountable; it had no good solution. No matter what option she chose, she would disappoint someone. She looked into his crystal-clear blue eyes. She couldn't be what he wanted; she couldn't do what he wanted. "Gray," she began.

"Don't, Celine. Don't say anything."

"But, Gray, I…" she started again.

He put his arm around her, pulling her closer to him. "No. We don't need to discuss this now."

Josie squeezed her lips together. Her first day back had been easier than she had expected. It wasn't a trend she expected to continue. If the Duke was here and the portrait of Mina had gone missing the situation was likely about to explode. She realized the normalcy that she experienced through this day was because of Gray. He had been careful not to overwhelm her with the troubles he had relayed to her before she came back. She glanced up to him; leaving him would not be easy when eventually she needed to return to her life.

She pushed the thoughts from her mind; she couldn't dwell on that now. "We must make sure Michael and Damien are on the first train home on Monday."

"I agree. I had quite the unpleasant visit from them earlier."

"What?"

"Yes, they somehow convinced the children to lead them to me and then proceeded to grill me on how I tricked you into coming here. They are more than a little curious why everyone here calls you Celine."

"They can't learn the truth, they need to leave. I wish they could have left earlier."

"You're worried about them getting hurt here?"

Josie nodded her head in affirmation. "And stumbling on information that they shouldn't have."

"Monday will be here before you know it."

"But will they leave?"

"Celine, if they don't, it's on them, you need to accept that."

"No, Gray, they MUST go."

"Is there some other reason you want them to leave? I understand the danger and the complication of finding out the truth about you, but this seems like something more."

"Every day that they stay here leads me one day closer to not being able to be me."

"By me you mean Josie?"

"Yes, you knew when I came that I intended to stay Josie and return to my old life once this was settled." Gray pulled his arm away, leaning forward on the swing. "I need you to make sure they leave on Monday." He didn't answer. "Gray?"

"Yeah, I'll make sure they're gone."

"Thank you," she said, putting her hand on his shoulder.

He smiled, settling back into the swing and wrapping his arm around her, giving the ground a kick sending the swing sailing faster. "You're welcome. You know I always have your back, Celine."

Josie returned her gaze to the water. She knew what he said was true. He did always have her back, and she trusted him. Leaving Gray would prove difficult, but she had more pressing concerns now. She focused her gaze on the beauty in front of her, the calm before the storm. She would need every bit of strength she possessed to get through this, she couldn't waste it on needless worrying.

CHAPTER 21

*D*amien laid in bed, listening to the silence in the house. He couldn't sleep; too many things raced through his mind. There were so many unanswered questions, things he couldn't figure out, things he couldn't process. He had never seen Josie like this; she was different somehow. It wasn't only how she was treating him; it was also her general behavior. There was a shift in her personality. It had to be something they were doing to her. Were they drugging her? Was it some form of mind control? He struggled to find answers, solutions that made sense. One aspect that bothered him was how familiar she was with these people. She exhibited a level of comfort with them he'd only seen her display with her own family.

As he grappled with the situation, a bloodcurdling scream ripped through the silence. He shot upwards to sitting, listening in the darkness. At first he heard nothing more, but then he overheard voices, one sounded like a child crying. Within a few moments footsteps pounded toward his room. They stopped nearby, and he overheard Charlotte's voice.

"Gray, it's Maddy, something's wrong. Get Celine, perhaps she can help."

Damien crept out of bed and opened his door a crack, peering out. Moments later, both Gray and Josie came racing past. "What happened to her?" Josie asked Gray.

Gray responded, "I'm not sure. She's been having nightmares, talking strange…" their voices faded as they disappeared down the hall.

Damien exited the room, creeping down the hall after them. As he rounded the corner into another wing, light streamed from a door that was ajar. Voices came from inside. Sneaking closer, keeping to the shadows in the hallway, he listened to the commotion coming from inside the room.

Maddy was still sobbing. Damien crept closer, risking a glance around the corner into the room. Josie was sitting on the bed, holding the child in her arms. Gray sat on the bed's edge on the other side of Maddy. Avery was looking on from the foot of the bed. Her mother, Charlotte, had her arms around Avery. Damien crept back so he would remain hidden but within earshot.

"No, no," Maddy shouted through tears, "I don't want to close my eyes, I don't want to see him again."

"It's okay, Maddy," Gray said. "Aunt Celine is here now. What did I tell you before I left? I said I was bringing Aunt Celine back to help you. She won't let anything happen to you."

"But I still saw him tonight."

"I know, but Aunt Celine wasn't here with you, but she is now. She won't leave you for the rest of the night, she'll make sure you're okay."

"That's right, Maddy. I'm here now, just close your eyes, I'll make sure everything is okay," Josie said to her.

Was this the reason that Josie agreed to come, Damien wondered? Was it to help this child?

"Tell you what," Josie continued. "We'll both get under the covers and get comfy. You don't have to close your eyes until you want to. Okay?"

"Okay," the child said, sniffling but seeming to calm down.

"Okay," Josie said. Damien overheard the covers rustling. "There, comfy?"

"Yes," Maddy said, still sniffling.

"Put your head down, that's it. You relax, I'll be here with you, I'm not leaving."

"See? I told you she'd take care of you," Gray said. "Do you want me to stay, Cel?"

"No, no, we'll be fine, thanks," Josie answered him.

Everyone said their good nights to them both as Damien slipped back down the hall to his bedroom. He doubted he'd sleep now after the excitement; his mind abuzz with fresh information. He considered knocking at Michael's door but decided it could wait until morning. He headed back to bed to wander through the maze of his thoughts alone.

* * *

A knock woke Damien from a deep sleep. "Yeah?" he called, groggily pulling himself out of bed, lumbering to the door and opening it.

"Sleeping in?" Michael asked.

"Ugh, I barely got any sleep last night."

"Too much on your mind?"

"Yeah and the midnight excitement didn't help any."

"Excitement?"

"Yeah, didn't you hear it? The kid, Maddy, was screaming like crazy last night."

"I didn't hear anything, must have slept right through it. What was she screaming about? Do you know?"

"Something about not wanting to go back to sleep and see some guy. She must have had a nightmare. But the weird thing is, it wasn't her mother comforting her."

"Who was?"

"Josie!? Gray told Maddy that that's why he went to find her, so she could help her. It was weird. It made no sense again, but perhaps this is how he convinced Josie to come? Told her it was a kid who needed her help?"

"Maybe. I mean, why Josie? You'd think it would be Avery who wanted to be with her and that Maddy would want Avery not Josie, she doesn't even know Josie."

Damien pulled a shirt on over his undershirt and changed into jeans from pajama pants. "Yeah, the whole thing was weird. They seemed really, really concerned about this nightmare. I mean, kids have nightmares, right? Why act like it's that big of a deal?"

"No idea. Let's go down to breakfast."

"Hungry?"

"Yes, but I also have an idea to obtain more information. Come on."

When they arrived in the sunroom for breakfast, everyone else was already there except for Maddy and Avery. Josie looked exhausted, like she hadn't slept at all. "Good morning, everyone," Michael said, acting as though nothing had happened.

"Good morning," Charlotte answered. "Oh, I hope you slept well, and we didn't disturb you last night. Maddy had a bit of an episode."

"Oh?" Michael said, "I hope she is okay?"

"Oh, she'll be all right, children are resilient. Well, I'm glad it didn't disturb you."

Michael smiled as he poured coffee and carried his plate and cup to the table. Damien followed suit. As they sat down, Josie stood. "I'm going to lay down for a bit."

"Of course, I hope you get some rest," Charlotte said.

Gray grabbed her hand, "I'll check on you in a bit." He held her hand a moment longer before Josie left the room.

"Oh, Mr. Buckley, excuse me," Mrs. Paxton said, entering the room, "Mrs. VanWoodsen is here to see you. I told her the family was still having breakfast, but she insisted. She's in the office waiting."

"That's fine, Mrs. Paxton, I'll go to her now," Gray said, standing. "If you all will excuse me." He folded his paper, laying it on the table and left the room.

"So, Charlotte," Michael said, "Max and Maddy did a wonderful job of showing us around yesterday."

"Oh, I'm so glad they didn't tire you too much, they can be rambunctious at times."

"Not at all. They were telling us the story of a painting that used to hang in the main foyer. Uh, someone named Mia or Mina?"

"Oh, yes, the portrait of Mina Buckley. Yes, it recently went missing."

"That's what Max told us. The way he described it, it sounded very grand. I was wondering, do you have a picture of it? I'd love to take a look at it."

"Oh, yes, we have one. It's in a volume in the library. I can show it to you as soon as you're finished with breakfast."

"Oh, great! Well, just give me a minute to finish my coffee then!" Michael said.

"Oh, Mrs. Stanton? Avery is asking for you."

"Oh? Oh, tell her I'll be right up. I need to show Michael something in the library first."

"Oh, please, go to Avery. Just point us in the direction of the library, I'm sure we can find it ourselves."

"Are you sure it wouldn't be too much trouble?"

"Not at all, we'll have fun finding it!"

"You're so gracious. Mrs. Paxton, please show them to the

library when they have finished with their breakfast. You'll find the photo albums in the cabinet on the back wall. I'll go up to Avery now." Charlotte set her napkin on the table and disappeared from the room.

"Okay," Michael said, swallowing one last sip of coffee, "lead the way, Mrs. Paxton."

* * *

"Ah, so you ARE back," Celeste said as Gray entered the office. She sat across the room in the desk chair. Her long, blonde hair pulled up into a high ponytail. Her blue eyes sparkled even from a distance, her full lips curled into a slight smile at the edges. "I take it you found Celine?"

"Yes, I found her," Gray said.

"And she's here? She's back?" Celeste asked.

"She's here."

"But?"

"But nothing, she's here."

"Something is amiss. She's here but not really. She didn't agree, did she? She's not like she was, is she?"

"What do you want, Celeste?"

"I want to see my sister."

"She's resting. Maddy had another episode last night; Celine was up most of the night with her."

"So, she's getting worse? Gray, if you can't get her to…"

"Yes, I know." Gray cut her off. "I know. Now, look, you can't see her today. Like I said she was awake most of the night. And besides, she doesn't want to meet with you. She said as much before she came. So, it's best if you go." Gray opened the door, motioning her out.

"Okay, I'll go, but I'll be back. I WANT to see my sister, Gray." She stepped into the hall, Gray followed her. Michael and Damien were coming down the hall led by Mrs. Paxton.

Celeste eyed them both as they passed. After they had passed them, she whirled to face Gray, asking, "Who are those two men?"

"Friends of Celine's."

"Friends? She brought them with her?"

"No, they followed her here. She was not too happy about it. They'll be leaving tomorrow, she insisted."

"No, they mustn't leave."

"What?" Gray asked, confused, his brow wrinkling.

"If you want your Celine back, as she was, the real Celine, you must do everything in your power to keep them here."

"What? Why? You've got to tell me what you mean."

"I can't tell you more than that, but I'm certain. Do as I say and whatever you do, don't tell Celine I told you."

* * *

Michael and Damien followed Mrs. Paxton down the hall and into the library.

"Here you are," she said. "Anything I can help you find?"

"No, no we're just going to poke around at a few things Charlotte mentioned this morning. Thanks though!"

"Suit yourself," she said and turned to leave.

Once Mrs. Paxton left, Damien said, "Did you notice that woman in the hall?"

"The blonde with Gray?"

"Yeah. Was it me or did she totally look like Josie?"

"Yeah, yeah I guess she did."

"The hair, the eyes, the lips. All the same. How weird is that?"

"Possibly a family connection? Are all these people involved with her biological family?"

"Maybe. So, what's with your sudden interest in discussing art with Charlotte?"

"Not art, really. I was hoping though that we'd be able to find some photo albums or something here. That's why I asked Charlotte about the portrait."

"You want to see pictures of paintings?"

"No, pictures of the family. If Celine was here when Avery was a kid maybe they have some family photos of her. Maybe we can determine if she looks like Josie or when she was here, anything that may give us more information."

"Ohhhh, good idea, nice ruse!"

Michael nodded at him, proud of his plan. As the two began to look around thunder clapped overhead. "Sounds like a storm is blowing in," Michael said.

"Yeah, I'm not going to lie, this house is spooky so I am totally creeped out already by a potential thunderstorm."

"Well distract yourself by looking through the photo albums, come on, let's get to it."

* * *

Josie folded her shirt in haste, tossing it back into the suitcase she had dragged onto the bed. She took some of her frustration out slamming the clothes down. The bedroom door opened, Gray entered the room. Straight off, he noticed her packing. "Celine, what are you doing?" he demanded.

"Packing."

"Why?"

"I'm leaving tomorrow with Michael and Damien."

"What? You can't be serious. Why?"

"I'm going home, Gray. I'm useless here."

"No, no, you're not. You're the only one who can help us, Celine."

"No, I can't help you. The old Celine could help you, Josie can't."

"That's not true, you helped Maddy last night."

"I didn't help her, Gray. I sang her a lullaby, lied to her and hoped for the best. I can't help her, not really. I can't stop what's happening." Josie continued to throw items into the suitcase.

"Celine, please. You're the only one who can help."

"I can't help."

"Stop, stop," Gray said, taking the shirt from her hands and setting it down before taking her hands in his. "Celine, stop. You can help, you're just tired. You haven't slept, you need some rest."

Tears escaped from Josie's eyes. "I can't help her, Gray. I can't help anyone here. I shouldn't have come."

"Shh, stop," he said, wiping her tears. "You need some sleep. You're tired. After all, you're only human. Please, lie down for a little while then we'll talk."

Exhaustion overwhelmed Josie. She looked at her half-packed suitcase, sniffling. She nodded. "Okay, I'll try to get some sleep."

"Good. Let me move this," he said, removing the suitcase from the bed. Josie climbed into bed, snuggling into the covers. Gray opened the music box. "You always liked to listen to this." He sat on the edge of the bed next to her.

Josie's eyes were already getting heavy. She reached out to take Gray's hand. He smiled at her. She looked at his hand, noticing that he still wore his wedding ring. "You still wear your ring," she said.

"Of course I do," he answered, caressing her cheek. "You'll always be the only woman for me, Celine Devereaux."

She smiled at him again, suddenly recognizing her own bare ring finger. "Get some rest," he said, leaning over and kissing her forehead. He stood and made his way across the room, stopping at a jewelry box on top of a dresser. He opened it and reached in, pulling out something small. He walked back over, putting the item inside her music box.

"Your wedding ring," he said, glancing at her. "Whenever you're ready to wear it again. Sleep well."

With that he left. Josie reached over, removing the ring from the music box. She rolled it between her thumb and fingers, gazing at it. She slipped it onto her ring finger. It still fit. Before taking it off, she spun it around her finger as she let her mind wander. Within minutes, she was asleep.

CHAPTER 22

"Okay, got something!" Michael shouted across the library. Damien made his way over. "It's a book with pictures of the house. Here," he said, turning the pages to find one with pictures of the foyer, "you can sort of make out the painting here, at least I think this is what they are talking about."

"Oh yeah, looks like a portrait of a woman is hanging there," Damien agreed. "Is there a better shot of it? Turn the page."

"Yeah, here. Whoa, seriously?" Michael said, turning the page to reveal a close-up picture of the painting. The caption below the photo read: *Painting of Wilhelmina Laurent Buckley.* The men exchanged glances. "Are you seeing what I'm seeing?"

"Yeah. A painting that looks like Josie wearing clothes from two hundred years ago."

"It's a perfect likeness of her."

"It does look like her, yeah. Come on, let's see what else we can find." They perused the rest of the book, but found nothing. They continued to scan through photo albums near where they had found the book. After another few minutes, Damien found something.

"Check this out. It's a picture of Gray."

"Oh, yeah. There's no date or anything but that's definitely him."

Damien turned the page. "Look!" he exclaimed, pointing to another picture. "Josie!" On the page was a picture of Gray and Josie. His arm was around her, both smiling.

"There's another one on this page, too," Michael said, pointing to the next page. Damien looked, seeing another picture of Josie standing with the man they had met yesterday, Alexander.

"So, Josie has been here, some time. Or at least someone who looks a hell of a lot like her," Damien said.

"Let's work off of the premise that someone who looks like her was here, perhaps her mom? I mean, this picture…" He referenced the painting of Wilhelmina. "Is a dead ringer for Josie but we are certain this can't be Josie, right? This woman lived two hundred years ago. It's got to be some kind of family resemblance."

"So, you think her biological mother was from this family. That makes sense, but why call her Celine and why say she's married to Gray?"

"I'm at a loss, the more evidence that we find, the less this all makes sense. Just when we close one loop, two more spring open, I can't…" Michael was interrupted by a shout in the hall. "What was that?" he asked.

Both of them hurried to the hall. They found Max standing in the middle. "Hello, my good sirs, I hope you can help me," he said.

"Oh, hey, Max," Michael said, "did you just shout?"

"Shout? I don't recall shouting. Now, I say, are you able to help me or not?"

"Help you with what, buddy?" Damien asked.

"Could you point me in the direction of the brandy? My nerves are on edge, I feel as though I need one."

"Brandy? I don't think so, buddy, you're kind of young." Michael laughed.

"How dare you laugh at me! Never mind, I'll find it myself."

"Hey, you okay, buddy?" Michael said, grabbing Max by the shoulder. "Whoa, you're burning up. We should get someone, he's really warm."

"I'll try to find someone," Damien said, turning and heading down the hall. As he left, Max almost collapsed, mumbling and moaning as Michael caught him. He carried the boy to the sitting room, laying him on the couch. Millie raced in with Damien moments later.

"How is he? Is he conscious?" she asked.

Michael moved out of the way, "I think so, but it seems like he's delirious. He was talking weird before, asking for brandy, then he collapsed."

Millie checked his pulse, placed her palm on his forehead, looked at his pupils. Gray entered the room as she looked at him. "What's going on?"

"I'm not sure, he seems very ill. Get Celine, she may have a better idea. Would one of you carry him to his room, please?" she asked Michael and Damien.

"Sure, I can," Michael said, lifting the boy into his arms. Michael carried him upstairs and to his room, laying him on his bed. Damien followed them. A few minutes later, Josie and Gray entered the room.

"What happened to him?" Josie asked, feeling his forehead and looking to Millie for answers.

"Michael says he was acting strange then collapsed. Now he seems feverish and delirious," Millie answered.

"Acting strange? How?" Josie asked Michael.

"Ah, he was talking weird. Asking for brandy," Michael

said.

"Yeah, he was talking funny," Damien added, "calling us good sirs and stuff."

Josie turned back to Max, taking his hand in hers. Damien noticed the ring on Josie's finger. "Max? Max, honey, can you hear me?"

Max moaned, as though in pain. "What is it, Celine? Do you know?" Gray asked. Avery burst through the door before Josie answered.

"MAX!" she screamed, racing to his side. Josie stepped aside to give her room. She put her hand on Avery's shoulder.

"Millie, can you give him something to keep him quiet for now." Josie turned to Gray. "Let's talk outside."

The two exited the room, Michael and Damien followed. Josie was sure she couldn't get away to speak to Gray alone, so she chose her words with care. "It's not good. It's what happened to Avery as a child."

"You're sure?" Gray asked.

"Yeah, I'm sure."

"Can you help him?"

Josie shook her head, "I doubt it. There are a few things I can try but I'm doubtful they'll help."

"What about Celeste? Can she help?" Gray pressed.

"No."

Gray closed his eyes. "I'm not giving up, Gray," Josie said, taking his hand. "I'm going to check on Maddy."

Josie proceeded down the hall and disappeared into another room. Michael and Damien weren't sure what to do but decided they would return to their rooms. Before they disbanded, Gray said, "Could I have a word with the two of you? In private?"

"Sure," a confused Michael said.

Gray glanced down the hall where Josie had disappeared

to. "Let's head downstairs to the office." Michael and Damien followed him downstairs and to the office. He closed the door behind them, locking it.

"I have a favor to ask of you."

"A favor?" a still confused Michael said, glancing to Damien.

"Yes. Celine, uh, Josie asked you to leave tomorrow morning. I don't know what your intentions are regarding her request but I'm asking you not to go."

"Wait, let me get this straight. Josie wants us to leave and you're asking us not to leave?"

"That's right. Can I count on you?"

Both Michael and Damien furrowed their brows, glancing at each other. Was this some kind of reverse psychology? Did Gray ask them to stay with the hopes they hated him enough to do the opposite of whatever he asked and leave? Michael answered for them both, "We have no intention of leaving Josie here, so unless she's going, we're not going anywhere."

"Good, I'm glad that's settled," Gray said, turning to leave.

"Wait a minute," Damien said. "You can't just ask us for a favor and continue to keep us in the dark, we need some answers here."

"I can't give you any, I'm sorry. I can only ask you to stay. Ah, we'll say there are no trains on account of a washout on the tracks, let me handle it, just go along with me. Oh, and I'd expect Celine, Josie, sorry, to be angry, you're just going to have to deal with that." With that he departed, leaving the two speechless.

Recovering his voice, a bewildered Damien said, "And this just continues to get weirder and weirder."

"Tell me about it. Josie definitely doesn't want us here and until like five minutes ago, that guy didn't want us here either, now he's asking us to stay?"

"Yeah and did you notice the wedding ring on Josie's finger?"

"What? No! Seriously?"

"Yeah, when she was holding Max's hand, there was a wedding ring on her finger."

"Well, I'd say we need to ask her about that but I'm sure she won't have anything to say on the matter."

"I'm sure. But being asked to stay is a win in my book so maybe we'll get something figured out soon."

"Okay, well, after that morning, I need a drink."

"A drink? Seriously?"

"Yeah, seriously, hey, it's five o'clock somewhere, come on." They headed down to the sitting room. Opening the double doors, they walked in to find a woman seated on the couch.

"Oh, hello," she said, standing. "I don't think we've met. I'm Celeste VanWoodsen, Celine's sister." She extended her hand. An astonished Michael was the first to shake it, followed by an equally flabbergasted Damien. Both of them were already dumbfounded by the conversation. This was the woman they had seen earlier talking to Gray. The resemblance between her and Josie was striking; indeed, they looked like they could be sisters. Celeste noticed the lack of response from both men and added, "Let me guess, my sister has never mentioned me. How typical."

"I'm sorry to say, she hasn't mentioned you, no," Michael said, recovering a little faster than Damien.

"Well, as I said, that's typical."

"I'm Michael Carlyle and this is Damien Sherwood."

"It's a pleasure to meet both of you," she said, clasping her hands in front of her. "How are you enjoying your stay here so far?"

"It's going just great," Damien answered her, a hint of sarcasm in his voice. "The house is really, uh, interesting."

"Oh, yes, it's a lovely old house. Built hundreds of years ago. They don't make them like they used to, as they say," Celeste answered.

Before the conversation went any further, Josie entered the room. She took a moment to stare at the scene before her, taking note that both Michael and Damien were conversing with Celeste before speaking. "Hello, Celeste. I'm sorry, would you both excuse us? I'd like to have a private conversation," she said, turning to Michael and Damien.

"Sure," Michael said, "we'll be in the library. Speaking of private conversations, could you stop by after? We needed to talk to you about something."

"I'll do my best, but I'm rather busy," Josie answered, pouring herself a drink. She waited until both men left the room, closing the doors behind them for privacy.

"So, you are back," Celeste said. "It's good to see you, Celine."

"Yes, I'm back, and still dealing with the mess that you and Teddy created so long ago."

"Straight to business, is it? No sisterly greetings?"

"Sisterly greeting?" Josie huffed at her. "I didn't even want to see you, Celeste."

"So I was told. Gray mentioned it earlier, but I had to come. It's been years since I've seen you, and you are my baby sister."

"Hmm, where was this sense of familial obligation all those years ago?" Josie murmured.

"Always back to that. Well, let me tell you, Celine, I've thought long and hard about it all those years you were gone. I am sorry for what happened and the position it put you in, truly I am. I have missed you, I'm glad you are back."

"Is that all?"

"I hope you're here to stay, Celine, I really do. Gray has

missed you, too. You're wearing your ring, I hope that's a good sign."

"Unless you have something meaningful to say, Celeste, I am very busy managing the mess here."

"All right. I can accept that you're still upset and I'll leave it be. But I meant what I said, I hope you are here to stay. And on that note, I think it would be wise for you to stop pretending to be this other person and become who you truly are. For all our sakes', Celine," she said, putting her hand on Josie's arm and squeezing it. "I do love you, sister dear."

Celeste left the room; Josie heard the main door close a few moments later. She closed her eyes, reflecting on the conversation. It had been so long since she had seen Celeste, her older sister. There was a strong connection between the two of them. The inner child in her had wanted to throw her arms around Celeste in a sisterly hug. But even with the time and distance, she wasn't sure she would ever forgive her sister.

Exhaustion still consumed Josie, having only caught a short nap before Max had taken a turn for the worse. Maddy still seemed to be okay, only tired from her long night, but so far she was doing much better compared to her brother. Josie thought of the poor child, lying in bed upstairs, feverish, disturbed. She shook her head, she had to help him. She just didn't perceive how, at least as long as she still clung to who she was now.

She took a deep breath, remembering that Michael had asked to meet her in the library. She didn't want to deal with him or Damien but if she didn't she worried they wouldn't leave the following morning. She forced herself to walk to the library. "You wanted to talk to me?" she asked, pushing through the doors.

"Hey, Jos, yeah, we did," Damien said. "How are you? You look tired."

"I am tired, and I don't want to deal with the twenty questions game at this moment, if you don't mind."

"We just want to help. Is there anything we can do for Max?" Damien said.

Josie let her eyes sink to the floor. "Unfortunately, there isn't. Pray and hope for the best."

"Does he need anything? Medicine, something for the fever or anything?" Michael asked. "We could run into town and get anything he needs. Might help more than a sedative."

"No, no, Millie has everything we need to take care of him."

"Josie, he's feverish, burning up and delirious from it, and the best you and the good doctor can come up with is a sedative?" an incredulous Michael asked.

"It's not what you think, okay?"

"Then tell us what it is, because I sure don't understand why anyone would not give a fever reducer to a feverish kid," Michael continued to argue.

"His fever isn't from a virus or illness, it wouldn't help."

"Then what is causing it, Jos?" Damien asked.

Josie shook her head, "You wouldn't understand."

"Try us," Damien said. "Please, Josie, we want to understand. We want to help, you, him, anyone at this point."

"He's possessed," Josie responded, staring straight at them.

"What?" Michael said, shocked.

"You can believe me or not, but I'm telling you that's what's wrong with him."

"It's okay, Josie. We believe you," Damien said, trying to be reassuring. "We believe you. If there's anything we can do to help, please just ask. In the meantime, you should try to get some more rest."

Josie nodded. "Thanks." It sounded like the storm had

passed, she thought some fresh air may help her. She moved toward the door. Turning back before exiting, she said, "You guys might want to use the afternoon to pack up. I think the first train leaves early in the morning."

After leaving the room, she continued to the front door. Ominous clouds still filled the sky, but it was not raining at the moment. She pulled her cardigan closed against the damp air as she exited the house. She wandered the grounds for hours, spending some time gathering various natural ingredients to help Max with the fever.

After preparing them and leaving them with Max, she returned outside, making her way to the gazebo. She sat on the swing, gradually gliding back and forth. Her mind was a jumble. She thought once she had all her memories back her life would be easier; instead it felt like she had two separate entities warring inside of her. She had been Josie for just shy of twenty-five years, but Josie still clung fiercely to her life, to its simplicity. She longed to be only Josie again, to only deal with what Josie had dealt with and considered problems.

But she realized this would never be, even if she made it past her twenty-fifth birthday, she now had all her memories. Could Josie's life fulfill her? Would she ever truly be happy? Would she be able to return to that life without guilt or concern for her family? Would she always be drawn back into this dysfunctional fold? Could she live here as she was? Her mind was being torn in two different directions.

"There you are," Gray said. Her thoughts had preoccupied her so much she had not even noticed him approaching. "Mind if I join you?"

She shook her head. "You're wearing your ring. I hope that means you're considering staying?" Josie didn't answer him, searching for the right words. She pondered how to tell him she didn't have an answer to his question. "It's okay, you don't have to answer."

"I'm sorry, Gray, I don't have an answer. How's Max?"

"Holding his own. Not great, but no worse."

"It will not stop. It's just going to get worse."

"Then we'll fight, like we always do," he said, putting his hand on her knee.

"But, I can't really fight, not like I used to," she said, tears forming.

"Celine, it's okay. We'll fight the best we can. I support you no matter what you decide."

Josie rubbed the ring on her left hand with her thumb. It seemed Gray had learned some patience over the last twenty-five years. She eyed him, considering his words then nodded, grabbing hold of his hand. She would take the time-buy for now.

CHAPTER 23

*J*osie sat at Max's bedside. Avery had fallen asleep long ago, but Josie wouldn't let herself sleep, she had to be on constant watch. Despite her eyes being heavy with sleep, she forced herself to stay awake. As morning approached, Charlotte came in, waking Avery and telling Josie to go get some rest. Josie stood in the hallway for a few moments, unsure of what to do before deciding that she wouldn't be able to rest even if she tried. Instead of heading for her room, she went the opposite way, spending the final hours of darkness roaming the property.

She returned to the house at daybreak, moving like a zombie. Gray was already up, heading down to breakfast. "Are you okay? Where were you?" he asked as he watched her walk through the door.

"Out for a walk," she said.

"Are you hungry?" he asked. Michael and Damien appeared on the stairs.

"Good morning," they both said.

"Good morning," Josie answered. "Heading into town today?"

"Ah," Michael began before Gray interjected.

"No, the train is not running today. Won't be for the better part of the week. Something about the tracks being washed out. Looks like they're stuck here."

"What? Are you serious?" Josie asked. "Perhaps we can have Henry drive them to Portland and you guys can get a car there," she continued, spit balling ideas to get them home.

"We're happy to stay!" Michael said.

"Yeah, no problem here," Damien said.

"Well, I have a problem! I don't…" Josie started, becoming perturbed.

"Celine, Celine, it's okay. We'll get them on their way as soon as we can. It's fine, nothing to worry about," Gray said, putting his hands on her shoulders and giving them a rub.

"Gray, I think…" she said again.

"Celine, I'll handle it. Now, come on, you need to eat."

After breakfast, Josie checked on the children again. She made her way into the foyer. She took a few steps in before she stopped dead in her tracks. The front door opened. A man strolled in. Air gusted past her, ice cold. Her ears were greeted by the clicking of a man's dress shoes on the stone floor, the tapping of a cane alongside his feet. Josie's eyes rose slowly, afraid to identify the man entering the house.

Her pulse quickened, her heart raced, she swallowed hard. She was rendered mute as her eyes met his. His mouth curled into a half smile as he spotted her. "Celine, mon chérie, I see you are, in fact, back. Oh, how I've missed you." His British accent a familiar sound to her despite the time that had passed.

Josie stood speechless, staring at him. He hadn't changed, his regal look, standing tall with his overcoat cut in the form of a cape, his brown eyes still as piercing as ever. "Oh, come,

Celine, have I really left you speechless?" Josie still did not answer.

Michael, Damien and Gray approached the foyer. "Who is that? Josie looks terrified," Damien said, trying to push ahead of them into the foyer.

"No, don't. That's the Duke. Do not let him see you," Gray said, holding him back.

The conversation continued uninterrupted in the foyer.

"Where have you been, my dear? And why didn't I realize you were back? Wait," he said, closing the distance between them, "there's something different about you, isn't there?"

Josie mustered the courage to speak. "I don't know what you're talking about."

"Yes, yes, there is. You're not all there, are you? That's why I couldn't sense you, couldn't feel your heart beating as one with mine."

"You don't have a heart."

"Oh, you wound me, Celine." He held his hands over his heart, giving a pained look. "We are destined to be together. Come back, Celine, come home."

"Never."

He paced the room, circling around her. "After all I've done for you, Celine, I ask of you this one thing. Come back to the fold. Take your rightful place by my side. Together, we can bring this world to its knees. Then I will stand before it as a king with you by my side as my queen."

"I will never stand beside you."

He circled behind her, approaching her, his breath hot on her neck as he spoke. "I urge you to reconsider."

"No," she stated turning her head to face him.

"Then you shall pay."

"Let me guess, with my life?"

"No, my dear, not with YOUR life. THEIR lives," he said, waving his finger in a circle. Josie looked at him, terror filling her eyes. "Yes, I've already started with the children, pathetic really, that's all it took to lure you back here. I'll continue on. I will DESTROY them, Celine. And you will watch." He approached her, looking into her eyes. "I will give you until the end of the day to come to your senses, my dear." He gave her a half smile, rubbing a finger on her cheek. He leaned forward to brush her lips with his. "Au revoir, Celine." He chuckled as he made his way out of the foyer.

Josie watched him leave the house. Gray raced to her side, Michael and Damien following him. As the man made his way through the door, Josie grasped her abdomen, collapsing forward with a moan.

"Celine!" Gray said, steadying her. Josie's face was a mask of pain; she wiped her lips where his had touched her. "Come sit down, let me help you."

"I'm okay," she said, visibly shaken. "I'm okay." A tear rolled down her cheek. "I just need to lie down."

"Right. Damien, Michael, can you go with her? She shouldn't be alone and I want to check on the children."

"Sure," Damien said, taking Josie's hand from Gray. Michael took her other arm and together they led her up the steps and down the hall to the wing containing their bedrooms.

"Need anything?" Damien asked her once she was lying in bed.

"No, just rest. You can go, I'm fine."

"Jos, are you kidding me? I'm not leaving you," Damien said.

"Me either," Michael said. "Who was that guy?"

"He's a very dangerous man. Stay away from him, don't speak to him, don't look at him, if you see him coming, go the other way. Promise me, both of you, please, promise me."

"Josie, we'll be fine," Michael said.

"PROMISE ME," Josie insisted.

"Okay, okay, I promise," Michael said.

"Me, too, scouts' honor!" Damien said.

Josie grabbed Damien's hand, squeezing it. "Thank you," she said. Exhaustion overcame Josie, the encounter with the Duke had robbed her of all her energy. She closed her eyes for just a moment and sleep overtook her.

Visions and nightmares involving the Duke tainted Josie's sleep. He haunted every second of her rest. She awoke more exhausted than she was before she had laid down. Gray was at her side. "Hey, how are you feeling?"

"Exhausted, how long did I sleep? How are the children?"

"Only about an hour. Try to get more rest. The children are fine. No worse, although they both had difficulty resting while the Duke was in the house."

"He will not stop, Gray," she said, getting out of bed.

"Hey, hey, hey, I think you should rest a little more."

"I don't have time to rest. I need to see Alexander and I should talk to Celeste, too. Did you say Teddy was here with her?"

"Celine, wait, I'll get them, you wait here."

"No, Gray, I can't wait. I'm fine," she said, pulling her hair into a ponytail and grabbing her sweater. She rushed out the door, past Michael and Damien who were waiting in the hall.

"Josie? Hey, Josie?" Damien called as she rushed past.

"No time, D, be back later," she said still adjusting her sweater as she raced past them.

Gray appeared in the hall. "Celine!" he yelled down the hall.

"Should we be going after her?" Michael asked.

"There's no sense," Gray said. "She shouldn't be running around on her own but she's stubborn, she won't listen."

"Oh, believe me, buddy, we're well aware of that," Damien said.

* * *

Josie banged on the door of Alexander's house. "Alexander!" she yelled.

"Celine," he said, opening the door, "what's wrong? Is it the children?"

"No, no change with them. Can I come in?"

"Of course." He stood aside. "You still haven't told me what's wrong? You're obviously upset."

"He came to the house today, Alexander. He came to the house and I could barely keep it together. I can't help anyone here, I just can't."

"Celine, calm down, here, sit down." He led her to a sitting room off of the foyer. "You know the effect he has on you, that doesn't mean you are powerless."

"Even if I'm not just Josie, I can't help them," she said, tears streaming down her face. "I'm not strong enough no matter who I am. Alexander, please tell me you've found something that will help."

"I'm sorry, but I've found nothing. You have my help, whatever you need, but I cannot do anything alone."

Josie's shoulders sunk, her head sunk into her hands and she sobbed. Alexander held her close; she relaxed into him, letting her tears fall. "Celine, are you struggling with this because you're resolute in your decision to remain Josie?"

She wiped at her tears. "I'm not resolute, I'm starting to realize remaining Josie may be impossible. But becoming Celine solves nothing, I was unable to defeat him for centuries."

"I think you're overwhelmed, Celine. I think you might need some rest. Perhaps you should lie down here."

She pushed against him, sitting all the way up. Sniffling, she wiped the tears from her face. "No, no, I need to see Celeste. Thanks, Alex."

"Celine, are you sure?"

"I've already seen her, it's fine. I need to ascertain if she can help. Is Teddy here?"

"Yes, I believe he is. Let me get them for you, Celine, please rest here."

"I'm fine, I'll go." She stood and began walking out of the room, letting herself out the door.

Josie made her way across the property. Alexander was one person who she had confirmed could do nothing to help the situation. If she remembered correctly, Celeste and her husband, Theodore, would be at a house at the edge of the property. The house stood on a cliff near the seaside. Josie spotted it on the horizon as she made her way toward it. Her mind whirled as she pressed on, nearing the house. She forced herself to walk down the path to the house and up the steps onto the porch. Her heart raced as she pounded on the door.

Theodore opened the door, visibly shocked when he was greeted by Josie. "Celine," he said, shock in his voice, "hello, ah, it's good to see you. Come in!"

"Thanks," Josie said, walking through the door.

"I assume you're here to see Celeste?"

"Both of you."

"Of course. Make yourself comfortable." He motioned toward the living room off the front hallway. "I'll get Celeste. Celeste! CELESTE!"

Josie heard her voice from upstairs, "Yes? What is it?"

"Celine is here."

Within seconds, Josie heard footsteps coming down the stairs. "What?" Celeste's face was a mask of shock as she entered the living room. "Celine! Oh, it's good to see you. I didn't expect you to come."

"I saw him, Celeste," she said, wringing her hands.

"Oh, darling." Celeste sat next to her on the sofa, putting her arms around her. "I'm sorry. I'm so sorry."

Josie took a deep breath and continued, "I need you to do something about him. Stop him somehow."

"Celine, we can't," Celeste said. "I mean not really. We can help but we can't stop him." Celine didn't answer. "Celine, oh, my dear baby sister, I'm so sorry, but we can't do anything to stop him and he seems to be determined this time."

"Look, Celine, I realize this isn't what you want to hear, but your sister is just being honest with you, don't blame her for this," Theodore said.

"I don't blame her for this, Teddy. He seems insatiable this time, you're right. Can you help the children at least? Anything?"

"I'm sorry, Celine, we've tried. That's when Gray begged me to find you. We were out of options."

"I'm not an option at this point either, though."

"I realize that I cost you so much, Celine. I didn't understand what I was doing then, but I do now. But did you ever consider that Josie's life isn't the life for you? That you're meant to be here?" Celeste asked.

Josie didn't answer again. "I need to go," she said, frustrated.

"No, Celine, don't. Please stay, you're exhausted. Let me take care of you." Celeste said.

Josie shook her head, "I need to get back, check on the children." She stood and walked to the entrance hall. Turning back before disappearing through the door she said, "It's okay, Celeste. I'm not angry. I love you, you'll always be my sister. I understand what you did was not out of malice."

Celeste rose and rushed to her, tears filling her eyes. "Oh, Celine. How happy that makes me. I love you so much. I've missed you. You will always be my sister. You need to take care. We will help any way we can. Just tell us what you need."

* * *

Josie walked back to the main house. She was unsure she could avoid the inevitable, but she was determined to continue to try. Physical and emotional exhaustion prevented her from making any decisions. On her way to the bedroom, she checked in with both Max and Maddy. Both were resting. She dragged herself up the steps and to her bedroom. She collapsed into the bed, falling asleep as soon as her head hit the pillow.

Moments after she laid down, Josie bolted up from her sleep. Something was wrong; she could feel it. It was already dark outside; she wondered how long she had slept. The house was quiet, almost too quiet. She looked around, trying to orient herself in her groggy state. She turned the light on, but it wasn't working. She wondered if the power was out. She got out of bed to check. When she went into the hallway, a voice called her name. She followed the sound of the voice. Turning the corner leading to another hallway, she found the voice's source. It was Max, she rushed to him, fearing that he was worse and wondering what he was doing out of bed.

As she approached, she called to him but he didn't answer. When she was within steps of him, the child morphed. She skidded to a stop. Before her stood Marcus Northcott, otherwise known as the Duke. He raised his arms toward her, smiling, "Come to me, Celine."

"No," she said, shaking her head. She turned to run the other way. She made it a few steps down the hall before Marcus appeared in front of her again. "Don't run from me, Celine," he admonished.

She stopped dead, pushing through a door into an unused

bedroom. She bolted the door behind her. His voice echoed through the house. "Celine," he said in a singsong manner, "Celine, don't hide from me." She covered her ears, tears streaming down her face as his voice echoed in her head.

His voice continued to call to her, the doors and windows began to shudder and bang. Howling wind swept through the house, carrying Marcus' voice so it seemed to come from every direction. Josie slid down the wall to a seated position, pulling her knees to her chest and burying her head in them. The calls continued to get louder until they were almost unbearable to listen to.

* * *

Josie bolted upright, looking around the room. She was in her bed; the lights were still on. She must have been having a nightmare. She was almost afraid to move, afraid that the dream had been real. The bedroom door opened; her pulse quickened as she wondered who was on the other side.

Gray entered, "You're up. How are you feeling?"

"How are the children?" she said jumping out of bed.

"They're fine, are you okay?"

"Are you sure? Did you check on them?"

"Celine, they're fine. What's wrong?"

"I… I had a dream; it was awful. He gave me until tonight, Gray. He will do something. What time is it? I need to sit with the kids."

"Okay, sure, go sit with them. Let's see what happens tonight. Don't panic yet."

"Okay, it's six, six hours to go until midnight. If we can get through midnight, we may have a chance."

Josie made her way to the children's rooms, first checking on Maddy then Max. There was no change in either child. Avery left Max to sit with Maddy and Josie took over sitting with Max, holding his hand while she watched him sleep. Minutes seemed like hours as Josie waited for the night to end.

After a while, Gray joined her, rubbing her shoulders. "How are you doing? Need a break?"

"No, it's eleven, one hour to go." She sighed. Time seemed to stand still. After what seemed an eternity, the clock in the foyer struck midnight. Josie listened, every nerve in her body on edge as the clock chimed. She waited for the twelfth bell sound. As it did, she let out a sigh of relief.

"There," Gray said, "we made it. See, everything was fine." Gray hugged her close to him.

"We should check on Maddy," Josie said.

"Yes," Gray agreed. They left Max's room and looked in on Maddy, she was sleeping peacefully. They left the room. "What do you say to you getting some rest? I think you need it."

Josie was just about to agree when they heard shouts coming from the foyer. Josie glanced at Gray, a look of concern on both their faces. They ran toward the foyer, meeting Michael and Damien who were also on their way. They reached the gallery that overlooked the foyer. Josie's eyes grew wide, her heart seizing at what she witnessed.

Theodore made his way into the foyer, in his arms a lifeless Celeste. "Oh no, no, no, no, no, no," Josie said, rushing down the staircase to them. "What happened?"

"Celine!" Gray called, hurrying down after her.

Theodore laid Celeste's body on the large table that sat in the middle of the foyer. Millie was already there, having come from the sitting room. She checked her pulse, her pupils and breath.

"Is she…" Josie began, not able to finish her question.

"Yes," Millie answered, "She is dead."

Josie threw herself across Celeste, inconsolable. Sobs

wracked through her body. She clung to her sister's body as she turned her head toward Theodore. "How?" she cried out.

"The Duke. He... he..." Theodore struggled. "He took away any protection she had. Then that thug he has with him killed her. Strangled her right in front of me," he said, his voice breaking.

Josie buried her head, crying. "No, Celeste, no," she said, weeping. Throwing her head back, she screamed, "NO!"

"Celine, why don't we go sit down?" Gray asked, gently.

Josie sniffled, standing, wiping her tears. "No," she said in a low voice. She looked up toward the ceiling, spreading her arms wide and crying out in a loud voice, "I have made my choice, I call upon every power that I have ever had to return to me, make me what I was before. Return to me now, give the strength and power that I once had, give me the protection from death that I had before. Return to me... RETURN TO ME!"

Celine took a deep breath in before returning to a normal stance. "Give me a knife," she requested, staring at Celeste's limp form.

"Celine," Gray hesitated, "did you just... are you back? Completely?"

Celine threw her hand toward the gaping fireplace in the foyer; it burst into flames instantaneously. She set her gaze on Gray. "Yeah, I'm back. Now give me a knife."

* * *

Michael and Damien watched the scene unfold from the gallery. "Um," Damien said, "what the hell? Did she just snap or something? And did that fireplace just spontaneously burst into flames?"

"Yeah, yep," Michael said, in shock, "something is super

weird and I'm not sure I even want to find out what she needs a knife for."

"I'm suddenly not so sure following her was a good idea!"

Michael didn't answer as they watched in astonishment at what was unfolding in front of them.

* * *

Theodore handed her a pocketknife. Celine sliced her index finger, not even wincing in pain as blood poured from the wound. She looked down at her sister. "Celeste, my sister, blood of my blood, flesh of my flesh, I call upon you now to awaken from your slumber." She put her bleeding finger to Celeste's lips, parting them and letting the blood drip into her mouth. "Let my blood give you life, as blood will continue to give you life. Shake off the sleep of death, sister, and rise. Rise. RISE!"

Celine removed her finger from Celeste's lips, her wound already beginning to heal until it was completely healed. Within moments, Celeste's eyes opened. Confused, she rose slowly looking around at everyone. "What happened? Why am I here?" she asked.

Celine turned to Theodore, "I need to go, keep her hidden, keep her safe."

"Celine, wait," Gray called after her.

Celine was in no mood to wait; she walked toward the main entrance. The doors blew open in front of her and she left the house.

"I'm going after her," Gray said, pulling on a light jacket.

* * *

"Um, did the dead lady just sit up and talk? Was she not dead?" Damien asked.

"Yep." Michael turned his back on the scene as Josie left the house. "Are we hallucinating? Have we been drugged?"

"No idea, but I think we should... I... I... hell, I don't know what we should do. Follow Gray?"

"Getting out of this house, best idea ever, let's go." They snuck down the stairs, skirting past the people in the foyer, to leave the house.

"Gray!" Michael called, "Wait up." They ran to catch up to him. "What the hell just happened? Have we been drugged? Where is Josie, is she okay?"

"She's about to do something stupid, we need to find her, I'll explain everything later. Come on, we need to find her." They climbed into the car.

* * *

Celine walked into the bar, her eyes narrowed as she looked around until she found her target. He was sitting alone at the bar, nursing a vodka. Celine approached him, taking the seat next to him. "Stefano, fancy seeing you here," she said.

"Celine! What a lovely surprise, although it's not that much of a surprise. I thought you may visit me soon. I assume you know?"

Celine smiled coolly at him. "Yes, I know, that's why I'm here. I'd really like to step outside and discuss it with you."

The man threw his head back, laughing loudly. "Oh, I bet you would," he said, "but I'm not that stupid."

"Aww, Stefano, I don't remember you being such a coward."

He sipped his drink, wincing as it went down. "Now, Celine, let's not resort to name calling."

Celine put her hand on the glass he was drinking from. It shattered under her touch. She looked into his dark, nearly black eyes. "The next thing I break is something in your body, now let's step outside, shall we?"

He leapt out of his chair, arm cocked back to strike her but his arm was frozen, unable to move forward. "I wouldn't do that if I were you, Stefano." He set his jaw, anger coursing through him but unable to do anything about it. He reluctantly followed her from the bar into a back alley. It was deserted. Fear shown plainly on his face.

"Did you think I would let you get away with it?" Celine questioned.

"I was just following orders. Besides, I thought you were powerless, human, please."

"Please? Please what? Please make it quick? Did you make it quick when you strangled my sister?" she asked, drawing his throat into her grasp like a magnet draws metal. She lifted him off the ground, choking him. He gasped for breath, struggling, trying to pull her grip from his throat. She tossed him like a rag doll against the brick wall of the building. He collapsed into it, sliding to the ground. She lifted him again, tossing him across the alley.

She lifted him again in her grasp, tightening her grip on his throat. "Stop," he choked out, "please."

"Don't stop, Celine," a new voice joined in. "Kill him." Marcus stood behind her shoulder.

Celine's grip tightened, continuing to choke the life slowly from the man. "Kill him, Celine. Kill him."

Celine wavered a moment, brow furrowing. "KILL HIM!" Marcus urged. A memory raced across Celine's mind. A similar event, the Duke standing behind her, this time a knife in her hand. He urged her to kill the man in front of her, "Kill him," he had said, "He killed your father in cold-blood, Celine, make him pay." Her hand faltered on the man's neck.

Marcus steadied her arm. "No, Celine, kill him. Your sister is DEAD because of him."

Celine's hand began to shake. Anger and rage had filled her when she had seen her sister's dead body but if the Duke wanted her to do it, she couldn't listen to him. A tear rolled down her cheek as she looked at the man in her grasp. He deserved to pay but perhaps not at her hand.

"Celine!" Gray shouted, entering the alley with Damien and Michael racing behind him. Gray stopped short of entering the alley, ensuring Michael and Damien were kept shielded from the Duke's view. "Don't." Celine peered into Gray's eyes, then back to the man in her grip. She dropped him; he fell to the ground in a heap, gasping for air.

Marcus growled with rage. "We're not finished, Celine," he said, as she walked away from him. "You're back now, truly back, I can feel it, I can sense you again. You will be mine. You can't defeat me."

Celine walked to Gray, allowing him to take her into his arms. She embraced him for a moment before pushing back from him. "We need to talk about what will happen next. He will not stop this time."

"Okay, but I think you need to take a breath…" Gray began.

She shook her head. "No, Gray, I don't. For the first time since this started, I don't. I'm not Josie anymore. I don't need to rest or relax."

"Okay, if you're sure. What next?"

"I need to see Alexander and we should check on the children."

"I'm sorry," Damien said, breaking out of his stunned silence, "but would someone mind telling me what the hell just happened here?" He was wide-eyed, shock still plain on his face. He couldn't fathom what was happening or any reasonable explanation for what he was witnessing.

"We need to get going," Celine said, "I'll fill you in later."

"No. No way. I'm not going anywhere until I understand

what is going on. Josie, you just lifted a guy up in a choke-hold. How did you even do that, I mean, what… how…" he stammered, shock setting in as the words came out of his mouth.

Celine made a face at Gray. "We're losing him," she said, "he needs to lie down." Gray took Damien by the shoulders leading him to the car, reassuring him everything would be all right. "How are you doing?" she said, directing the question to Michael.

"Oh, just fine," Michael said, a hint of sarcasm showing through his shaky voice. "I mean I just saw a dead girl walking and talking and a fire start from spontaneous combustion and you with some kind of Hulk-like strength but, yeah, totally good."

Celine smiled at him. "I'm sorry that you had to witness that but there wasn't much I could do, everything happened so fast."

"Josie, I…"

"Ah," Celine said, wincing, "sorry, but can you just call me Celine. I realize it's weird, but I am not Josie."

Michael looked at her, surprise on his face with no understanding. "I'm sorry," she continued, "everything will be clear soon, I think."

She took his arm, leading him to the car. Damien was already sitting in the back seat murmuring to himself about what he had just seen. Michael slid in next to him, shaking his head as if to say nothing would be clear anytime soon.

"Are they going to be okay?" Gray asked as they got into the front seat.

Celine looked back at them. They had seen too much too fast; their minds could not process the events right now. She reached back and touched Damien's cheek, then Michael's, putting them both into a peaceful sleep while they drove back to the house. "They'll be fine, they need to rest."

Gray headed toward the house, taking the driveway to Alexander's rather than the main house. As they drove, he put his hand on Celine's knee. She smiled at him. "Despite everything, I'm glad you're back," he said.

"Despite everything, so am I," she said, putting her hand on his.

They arrived at Alexander's house; he ran out to meet them. "Theodore told me it was you. Welcome back, Celine," he said, opening her car door.

"Help me get these two into the house," Gray said. Celine made sure they were conscious enough to walk to a bedroom and lie down.

"Now," Gray said, once they were all in the living room, "Can you stop him?"

"Not outright, no," Celine answered.

Gray sighed. "So, you've sacrificed your normal life for nothing?"

"No, not for nothing. I can stop him for good, but I need a particular item to do it."

"What do you need, Celine?" Alexander asked.

"*The Book of the Dead.*"

Gray's mouth dropped open. "So we're doomed," he said, throwing his arms in the air.

"No one has known the whereabouts of that for centuries, Celine. If anyone has it, the Duke does and he'll never let anyone get near it. I doubt you could get near it even if he thought you were on his side," Alexander answered.

"I know where we can get the book," Celine said.

Gray looked stunned. "You do? All this time you've known where it is and you've done nothing to destroy him?"

"No, not exactly. I don't know exactly where it is but I know how we can get it. I realized it when my memories returned. Once they did, I was able to piece things together. I know how we can get the book."

"I still don't understand," Alexander said, "the last time anyone saw that book was…"

"Was the night I became what I am, yes," Celine finished his sentence.

"Did you remember something new?" Gray asked.

"No, but I met someone new. Or rather, Josie did."

Gray looked confused, as did Alexander. "That night," Celine began, "there were two men there, my English tutor and his brother, remember? I gave them the book. When I ran through the caves, I ran to them and I gave the book to them and I helped them escape."

"By opening a portal through time, yes, I remember you told me," Gray said. "But we concluded that they were inevitably working for the Duke, right?"

"Well, we were wrong," Celine answered. "They were working for me."

"You?" Alexander asked.

"Me. Like the me from right now. I sent them back to bring the book here. When I opened the time portal that night, I sent them back to me in this time."

"How do you know this?" Gray asked.

"Because I finally met the two people that helped me that night. My English tutor and his brother. I know them. Or rather, Josie did." Alexander and Gray exchanged a glance, realization dawning on both their faces. "Yes," Celine said, nodding, "They're upstairs asleep right now."

The realization stunned Gray. "You knew then, that's…"

"Why I wanted them to leave, yes. The moment they arrived here, I realized that it was too late, I realized where this was heading. I thought I could escape my fate but I couldn't."

"I'm sorry, Celine. I know you wanted a normal life," Gray said.

Celine shook her head and smiled at him. "I'm not meant

for a normal life. From the time I got my memory back I began to doubt that I could live a normal life. I prepared for this. I'll always treasure my time as Josie but this is where I belong."

Gray smiled back at her. "I couldn't agree more."

"Now," she said, turning serious again, "I will need your help. I need a letter of introduction for them to my father, and I need to write a letter to myself. We'll also need some clothes for them, Teddy should be able to help with that. Alexander, I will need your help, too. I can open the time portal again but it will take everything I have, it's not an easy task. You need to mask me while I do that, Marcus cannot have even an inkling of what we're doing."

"I can do that," Alexander said.

"I'll write a letter of introduction to your father for Michael," Gray said. "What shall I tell him?"

"Make him the heir to some American fortune, throw in the name of a middle-ranking nobility from England, something credible but not that my father would be too familiar with. Their backstory doesn't have to be that elaborate. I was almost sixteen, my father was chomping at the bit to marry me off to some wealthy American so that's all he needs to see and he'll be in."

"Consider it done," he said.

CHAPTER 24

*C*eline sat on the edge of the bed; she wanted to give Damien a few more moments of sleep. What she needed to ask him to do he would consider impossible. His mind was already struggling to wrap around what he had just seen. What he would witness her do next would break most people's grip on reality. He would need all the strength he could muster.

She hated to send him and Michael back, to ask them to do this for her, but there was no other choice. Only they were capable of retrieving the book. Still, she worried. This was her cousin, or rather, Josie's cousin. She was protective of him. He wasn't like her, like Gray, like Alexander, he was different; he was normal. She felt for Michael, too, but Damien had been Josie's family since childhood and even as Celine she had a strong connection to him.

She reached over and took his hand in hers, giving it a squeeze. He began to stir, opening his eyes and looking around without recognizing his surroundings. "You're at Alexander's," Celine said. "it's okay."

"Hey, Jos," he said, blinking against the light in the room

and squinting, "I had the weirdest dream. How did I get here?"

Celine smiled at him, at his innocence. "Unfortunately, D, that wasn't a dream. I'm sorry I can't break it to you more gently, but we're running out of time and I need a favor from you."

"A favor?"

"Yes, I need your help. Both you and Michael. I need you to get something for me, a book."

"Like from the library?" he said, comprehension escaping him.

"I wish it were that easy, but no. I need you to get a book from a very special place. There isn't much time to explain. I'll fill in as many details as I can, but you've got to get up. I've got to tell Michael, too."

Celine stood from the bed, still holding Damien's hand and gave his arm a tug. Damien stood up, saying, "Um, okay, yeah I've got no idea what's going on but I'll help however I can, Jos."

As they made their way to the door, it opened. Michael came in with Gray. "Hey, what's going on, is everything okay?"

"It will be, but I need your help. Both of you. Come on, we've got to get you dressed."

"Dressed?" Michael asked, screwing up his face and looking down at his body. "I am dressed."

"Well, not appropriately for where you're going," Celine said. "You will travel to a very particular place and retrieve a book for me."

"And I can't get this book in a hoodie?" Michael asked.

"No, you can't do it in a hoodie."

"Okay. Where is this 'particular place' where hoodies aren't allowed?"

"Martinque."

"Like the island?" Damien asked.

"Yes, the island," Celine answered. "In 1786."

"So, we need to go to Martinque? Like tonight? We'll never get a flight out that fast," Michael said, missing the last statement that Celine made.

"Wait, wait, wait," Damien interrupted, "did you say 1786?"

"I did, yes," Celine said. "I need you to travel back to the year 1786 and get the book. I'm sorry, there isn't time to explain it all but I can get you there and I think it'll be obvious after that."

Michael's eyes darted side-to-side before he uttered, "This is a joke, right? You're joking."

"I'm not. Let's continue talking about this while you're changing, we've got clothes for you. You will pose as a rich American, an heir to…"

Gray added in, "A shipping magnate," as he shoved clothes at Michael and Damien and prompting them toward the bathroom to change.

"Right," Celine continued, yelling through the door to the bathroom, "a shipping magnate, we have a letter of introduction for you. Give it to the Marquis Gaspard Devereaux. You'll find him on the outskirts of the town, he has the biggest house there, large, and white, overlooking the sea, you can't miss it. Tell him you want to tutor his daughter in English and that you hope to have the honor of courting her. And here is a second letter, give it to the Marquis' daughter in the library two days before her sixteenth birthday, just trust me on this. You'll understand once you are there. And you, D," she said, "are his brother. You've got a good sense of history, D, so make sure Michael doesn't do anything… well… stupid. You'll need to get a very special book, you'll get it from the Marquis' daughter, it's called *The Book of the Dead*.

She'll give it to you at a suitable time and help you return to us with the book, just play along until then."

Michael and Damien emerged, dressed in their eighteenth century finery, both of them pulling at their collars. "I look ridiculous," Damien said.

"Yeah, I look like a clown." Michael looked to Damien. "Is this really happening?"

"Yes, it is happening. And, no, you can't travel to 1786 in a hoodie."

"Well… I'm not on board with the whole time travel thing yet so…" Michael contended. "Oh, by the way, how do you know all this?"

"Well, you'll have to get on board with it. And I just do, you'll understand later. Now, here are the letters," Celine said, handing him letters, "follow me, we've got no time to waste."

"So, exactly how do you propose we travel back in time?" Damien asked, as they followed Celine down the hall.

"Through a time portal," Celine said, trying to sound as matter-of-fact to them as possible.

"Oh, yeah, right, a time portal. What was I thinking? That was on an episode of Star Trek," Damien said.

Celine glanced back, rolling her eyes at him. Michael added, "Of course! So do you have a key? Is there a special door?"

"She's not a normal person like you," Gray said, following behind them. "None of us are. This isn't a joke. Celine has the ability to open a time portal."

"How does anyone have that ability?" Damien said, stopping dead in the hall they were walking down.

"I told you," Gray said, stopping and facing him, "she's not a normal person like you."

"So, what is she?" he asked Gray.

"She's a woman with unique and exceptional skills," Gray answered.

"Unique and exceptional skills?" Damien asked, "what does that even mean?"

Celine returned to him, Michael following her. "I think the layperson's term would be a 'witch,'" Celine said to Damien. "Now, come on."

"Witch? WITCH? Are you kidding me, Jos?" he said, following her as she continued down the hall and stairway. "Do you fly on broomsticks and have a black cat? I've never seen you boiling any potions in cauldrons."

"It's not like that. I can't explain it and we don't have time," she said, as they reached the living room where Alexander was waiting. "Please, just trust me. You'll understand soon enough. Then we'll talk."

"If this isn't legit, it's one hell of a prank, I guess," Michael said, clapping Damien on the shoulder.

"Oh, it's no prank," Gray said.

"Ok, I'll open the time portal, when I do, go through it. Immediately! Gray, make sure they do. I won't be able to hold this open for more than a few moments. Any longer and Marcus will discover what we are doing."

"Don't worry, Celine," Alexander said, "I'll cover you as best I can so any disturbance he senses won't give us away."

"Thanks," she said, nodding to him, "ready?"

"Ready," he responded.

"Okay, here we go," Celine said, placing both of her hands straight out in front of her. She spread her fingers out, closing her eyes. Her brows knit and she squeezed her lips together, holding her breath. At first, it appeared as though nothing was happening. Then Damien felt a slight breeze circle around him, as though a window was open.

He glanced around the room, noting all the windows were closed. He also regarded Alexander in a similar stance, facing one of the windows. Within seconds, the slight breeze became a windstorm. There was a shimmer in front of him that drew his eye. Thunder crashed overhead, and the windows blew open. Wind whipped through the room from the outside, joining the gale forces that were blowing inside the room. Books and papers blew around in circles. The shimmer in front of them grew stronger until it was a large oval obscuring the wall behind it.

"That's it, the portal is open, go!" Gray yelled over the wind, shoving them both forward.

Damien and Michael glanced at each other, afraid to move. "GO!" Gray yelled, shoving them again.

They moved forward and stepped into the shimmer. Within an instant they disappeared. Gray placed his hand on Celine's shoulder. She collapsed to the floor, out of breath with the effort. "Did they go?" she asked between gulps of air.

"Yes, they went." Gray answered, as Alexander joined them, helping Gray get Celine to her feet.

Looking between Gray and Alexander, Celine said, "Now we wait."

CHAPTER 25

1786, MARTINIQUE

*M*ichael and Damien stepped through the shimmer into blackness. Within an instant, the scene transformed from pitch black to a blinding bright light. Shielding his face, he squinted his eyes open, blinking several times. "Michael," he exclaimed, "Michael, look!"

"Yeah, yeah, I see. I don't believe it, but I see it."

The pair looked around. It was broad daylight, the bright sun shone overhead. They were standing on a dirt alleyway near a building. In front of them, another dirt road crossed. Horses and carriages traversed the street. People dressed in clothing from another century bustled about. "I can't believe I'm about to say this," Damien began, swallowing hard before continuing, "but I think we just traveled back in time."

Michael didn't answer, trying to take everything in and make sense of it. After a moment, he became cognizant of the letters he held in his hand. "Maybe we should look for the big white house on the edge of town," he said, trying to focus on the mission at hand rather than the incredulousness of what had just happened to them.

"Yeah, I mean, yes, we should say yes not yeah. Okay, lead the way," Damien said.

The pair walked out of the alley toward the main road. Various small buildings lined the street. They looked right and left. "There!" Damien said, pointing to the left. "That huge white house there has to be it."

"Well, I guess we'll head there," Michael answered, moving toward it. Damien followed him. It took them only a few minutes to walk to the property. They approached the front door. Michael swallowed hard. "Here goes nothing," he said, using the doorknocker.

A maid opened the door. "Michael and Damien Carlyle to see Marquis Devereaux," Michael said, as formally as he could muster.

"Oui, monsieur, s'il vous plaît," she said, standing aside and motioning into the house. The two stepped inside, marveling at the grandeur of the house. The maid disappeared down the hall. Within a few minutes, she returned and motioned for them to follow her. She led them to an office down the hall. A rotund man sat behind a desk reviewing paperwork. As they entered, she introduced them and he stood to greet them. "I am Marquis Devereaux. You asked to see me?"

"Yes," Michael said. "I'm Michael Carlyle, and this is my brother, Damien. We've traveled from America, er, the States. I have a letter of introduction here, sir." He handed the paper to the man who opened it and read it.

"Ah, you are acquainted with Lord Blackburn. Well, any friend of his is a friend of mine. Welcome, what brings you to our humble island?"

"Well, sir, I was hoping to court your daughter, should

you and she allow it. In the meantime, I thought I may provide her with instruction in the English language."

"Ah." He chuckled. "You've heard of my daughter's beauty. Well, my dear fellow, you are not the first suitor to call at my door. You've heard tales of my daughter's disinterest in all of them? That girl will send me to an early grave."

"Yes, sir, I have. And I intend to change her mind," Michael said, trying to match the man's posture and gait as best as possible to appear legitimate.

"Well, I wish you luck there, it appears you'd be a fine match for her. And I'm pleased with the notion of her learning to speak English. I think I will take you up on your proposition, sir. You may start this afternoon."

"Excellent," Michael said in what he hoped was a stately manner.

"Just a moment, I'll have the maid fetch my daughter and you can make her acquaintance." He rang a bell, and the maid returned. He instructed her to bring Celine to his office straight away to meet Mr. Carlyle. Michael and Damien exchanged a glance at the mention of the girl's name.

"So, you're in the shipping business, are you, Carlyle?" Marquis Devereaux said as they waited.

"That's correct, yes. We have quite a fleet." Relief washed over Michael as the door opened, quashing the need for further conversation. The maid appeared, followed by a young woman. The appearance of Celine stunned Michael and Damien into silence.

"Papa, vous m'avez appelé?" the girl said.

"Oui, Céline, est-ce que je peux présenter Michael Carlyle et son frère Damien," he said to her.

She looked toward the two men, holding her hand out, palm down for them to greet her. Michael took her hand first, kissing it lightly, Damien followed. Damien was in disbelief as he took her hand. He stared down at a young version of Josie. She was identical to what she had looked like in high school minus the eighteenth century dress and hair piled on her head. Michael had a similar reaction despite not having known her at this age. The resemblance was amazing.

"Bonjour," she said, smiling sweetly.

"Celine," Marquis Devereaux said to her, continuing in French, "Mr. Carlyle has traveled from the States. I've hired him on to be your English tutor."

"Oh, Papa!" she answered in French, clasping her hands together in excitement, "I am to learn English?"

"So, this pleases you, my dear?"

"Oh, yes, Papa!"

"Excellent. You will start this afternoon; please meet Mr. Carlyle in the foyer upon finishing lunch. Now be a good student and pay careful attention."

"Oh, I promise I will, Papa!

"You may go, I will see you at dinner."

Michael and Damien watched the exchange, Michael understanding some of what was being said, Damien understanding none of it. After Celine had exited the room, the Marquis addressed them. "I am encouraged, she was quite cordial. I trust my daughter will be a good student for you. Now, if you'll excuse me, I'll have Amelie settle you into your rooms." He rang the bell again, and the maid returned. He spoke to her in French to which she nodded and motioned for the men to follow her. "Good morning, sirs, I'll see you both at dinner. And I expect my daughter to greet me in English," he said, in an amusing fashion.

"I'll do my best, sir," Michael said with a smile.

The two followed the maid upstairs to their bedrooms. Damien quickly found his way from his room to Michael's room. "Okay, this is officially bizarre," he said, entering the room.

"Yeah, that's for sure. She's like Josie but it can't be. It's the 1700s. So is Celine actually Josie later? How is that possible? That would mean she's over two hundred years old."

"I'm trying not to think my cousin is that old. Let's not talk about that, it's just too weird. So, what's the plan?"

"Well, I guess we teach Celine English and try to find out when her birthday is so we can give her this letter," Michael said, pulling the letter from his pocket, "and then try to find this book. Do you think there's a library in the house? We should have asked the maid."

"Yeah, oh, perhaps we can ask Celine. Josie said she should give it to us."

"If it's all the same to you, I'd rather find the book and get the hell home. We can try to see if she has any information. How much do you think she knows?"

"About how she's going to live to be a few hundred years old and can open time portals and kill people with her mind and stuff?"

"Yeah, about that."

"No idea, but maybe we shouldn't give away too much until we figure out how much she knows."

"Yeah, I agree. Okay, the maid said she'd see about getting us a tray for lunch. Then we're supposed to meet Celine after so I guess we've got lunch to figure out how to approach this."

As they were talking, the maid knocked, bringing a tray of lunch and asking if she should leave both men's meals here. Michael motioned for her to do so, and they resumed talking once she left. Both of them stopped their conversation though as they looked at their water glasses. The less-than-clear, murky water filled the glass. Michael made a disgusted face then said, "Yeah, I'm not drinking this."

"Hello, dehydration," Damien followed up with, pouring his water in a nearby plant.

They finished the rest of their meals then made their way back downstairs to the foyer. Within a few minutes, Celine appeared in the hallway, twirling a parasol.

"Ah, bonjour, Celine," Michael said, bowing and smiling.

"Bonjour!" Celine said, smiling at them.

They stood in silence for a few moments before Celine said, "Marcher?"

"Ah, walk?" Michael asked.

"Marcher, oui?" Celine made a walking motion then pointed to herself and the two men.

"Oh, oh, you want to walk. Yes, sure, we can walk, marcher, yes." He nodded his head. "Ah, oui, on peut marcher."

Celine nodded her head and smiled, approaching the door and waiting for him to open it for her. Michael opened it, allowing her to exit first, Damien followed behind them. Celine walked them toward the gardens. She pointed to a few flowers, requesting Michael give her the name of them. He obliged, telling her their English names with her practicing each afterwards. Michael corrected her pronunciations when necessary. Halfway through their walk through the garden, Damien noticed the Marquis looking on from a second-story balcony, watching his daughter's progress. Celine noticed him and waved to him. He waved back before turning to enter the house again.

Afterwards, Celine led them down a path that led to the beach. She smiled at them and looked out over the ocean. "Oh, uh, ocean," Michael said, pointing to the water. She giggled. "Ocean," he repeated, looking at her to mimic him.

She glanced at him then looked back at the ocean, "Yes," she said in a thick French accent, "that is the ocean."

Michael's face was struck with astonishment, as was Damien's. Damien said, "Wait, you speak English?"

"Yes, I speak English."

"So, why did your father ask me to teach you English?"

"He isn't aware and I would be grateful if you played along."

"He isn't aware? How did you learn?"

"I taught myself. I'm quite clever, you know."

"Seems so," Damien said.

"Do I have your cooperation?" she asked, facing them.

"Yeah, I mean, yes, we won't give you away," Michael agreed.

"Good."

"As long as you help us," Damien said.

"Help you?" Celine looked puzzled.

"Yes, we're new here and we know very little about, well, anything, do you mind telling us a little about yourself, your father, your family?"

Celine continued to look puzzled. "My name is Celine Devereaux, I am the second daughter of Marquis Gaspard Devereaux. My mother died giving birth to me. When I was a small child, we moved here from Lyon. I don't understand how this is helping you?"

"Second daughter? So, you have a brother or sister?" Damien asked.

"I have an older sister, Celeste."

"Is she here?" Michael asked.

"No, she lives in another town across the island. I don't understand."

"One more question," Michael said. "Is there a library in your home?"

"Yes, it is the door across from Papa's study, where we met. Why all these questions?"

"Why not tell your father you speak English?" Damien said.

"Touché," Celine said, holding her hands up in defeat. "We should go back."

The three turned back toward the house. "So, Celine, you're how old now?"

"I am fifteen, I will be sixteen in four days. Yes, I realize I'm almost a spinster, but I just have no interest in suitors. They all are such a bore. I assume my Papa is hoping you will be the next in line to court me?"

"He mentioned your rather particular taste, yes. And I admit to asking him if I may court you."

"You can try," Celine said, stalking off ahead of them and into the house.

The two exchanged a glance. "Let's try that library," Michael said. The two made their way to the library, following Celine's directions. Many books lined the shelves. "Let's split up and look around."

"Okay. Oh, how are we supposed to recognize it if we find it? I mean what are the chances it says *Book of the Dead* on the spine? We should have asked Josie what this book looked like."

"I don't know, but it can't hurt." They spent hours pouring over every book in the library without finding the specific book. Most of the books were in French. Damien asked Michael the French version of the title before looking over the books. They were just giving up when a gong rang. "What the hell was that?" Michael asked.

"Dinner gong. It announces that it's time to dress for dinner. We will have to excuse ourselves and say our luggage was lost or something since this is all we have."

"Okay, with any luck, we won't need these for much longer," Michael said, pulling at his collar. "And if we're really lucky, we won't have to drink any of that nasty water at dinner."

. . .

At 7 p.m., dinner was served in the house. Michael and Damien enjoyed a cocktail with the Marquis after apologizing for their lack of formal dinner wear and before Celine joined them for the meal.

"Hello, Papa," Celine said, feigning struggling to get the words out, "how you are?"

"How are you," Michael corrected and Celine parroted him.

"Ah, very good, my dear, very good," the Marquis answered in French, beaming with pride over his daughter's progress.

As they were seated for dinner, a man entered the room in a servant's uniform, excusing himself and handing a note to the Marquis. The Marquis opened it and read it, surprise apparent on his face. After reading it, he stood abruptly. He muttered a few words to Celine in French then turned to Michael and Damien and said, "My apologies, I have rather urgent business. It appears that I have been called back home by the Crown sooner than I expected. I must prepare to leave at once. I will make arrangements for my daughter to travel early to stay with her sister and her husband. Of course, I would be most grateful if you would accompany her with her nanny on the journey. I will send a rider with a letter to Celeste's husband, Mr. VanWoodsen, to explain and make sure you are appropriately received."

Michael and Damien both stood. "Of course, sir. We would be happy to accompany her."

"Thank you. And please, enjoy your meal."

After he left the room, they returned to their seats. They had finished the first course when the Marquis returned, holding something behind his back. "Please, be seated." He waved at them. "I just have a small piece of business with my daughter." Turning to Celine, he said in French, "Celine, I had this made for your birthday. I am so very sorry that I will not be here to give it to you on your birthday. I wanted you to have it and I wanted to make sure you liked it." He brought the object from behind his back. Damien kicked Michael under the table as he handed Celine the gold music box that they were now well acquainted with.

Celine exclaimed with glee upon seeing it. "Oh, Papa! It is lovely," she said in French, jumping from her chair and throwing her arms around him. He hugged her back, giving her a kiss on the forehead.

"Open it," he said.

Celine opened it and music filled the room. "Oh, Papa! It is the music from my first ball! How lovely. Thank you, Papa!"

After another hug, he then bid her adieu and left the room. Celine set the music box down on the table next to her, admiring it several times through dinner.

Celine explained to them as they ate that the journey to Celeste's house would take them about half a day by carriage. She informed them if they left by midmorning, they would be there in time to rest and change before dinner. They would eat a light picnic along the way. Celine was sure that her father would be pleased to have the Carlyle's traveling with her given that her nanny was quite aged and was not the most capable traveling companion for the journey.

They made light conversation for the rest of dinner before Celine excused herself to make her own preparations for the trip. Before she went upstairs, Michael took a chance in asking her if she had ever seen or heard of *The Book of the Dead*, but Celine shook her head, telling them she had never heard of such a book. Defeated, the two also retired to their rooms, hoping that their travels would bring them closer to the book.

The quartet set off the following morning around 10 a.m. in a horse drawn carriage. Michael and Damien were not prepared for the ride offered by the antiquated mode of transportation. The carriage was bumpy, and they were knocked about on the less-than-smooth roads continuously, both of them wishing they were still in the time of modern suspension.

They were grateful for the stop at midday to eat their picnic lunch and allow the horses to rest. As they approached 3 p.m., signs of life in the form of a small town appeared through the carriage window. They had reached civilization again so Celeste's house could not be far.

The carriage slowed to a stop outside a grand looking house on the edge of town. Celeste, it seemed, had done rather well for herself when she married. Michael and Damien saw several people waiting outside the home.

As they exited the carriage, they were met by a couple who looked identical to the Theodore and Celeste they had met in their time. This couldn't be a coincidence. They must be the same people. They must also have the strange gift of immortality that Celine seemed to possess. Yet, Damien still didn't quite understand how she possessed it since he had grown up with her. He had known her as a child, yet in this time, she was a teenager already. Was she reborn every so often?

When Celine emerged from the carriage, her sister ran to her, throwing her arms around her and greeting her warmly in French with a hug and several kisses. The two talked excitedly for a few moments before they all entered the house. Theodore welcomed them all, seeming pleased to have more guests to entertain. As luck would have it, the couple was entertaining Duke Marcus Northcott for a fortnight and they hoped the additional guests would make for more lively dinner conversations. Theodore was sure that the Duke would appreciate having additional people to regale with his tales of world travels. He left the staff to show

Michael and Damien to their rooms while he returned to finish some business before preparing for the evening meal. Celine, along with Celeste, withdrew to her room to get settled in, the two sisters disappearing down the hall in a cloud of giggles.

That evening for dinner, Theodore had lent some clothes to Michael and Damien since they told him their trunks had been lost in an unexplained accident and they'd had no time to track them down with the unexpected travel. The two found the new clothes equally uncomfortable, but arrived for cocktails before dinner. The day held one final surprise for them. They were astounded to meet Duke Northcott, who they had known as the Duke in their time, the source of all the problems for the Buckley family and townspeople of Bucksville.

The two sisters, Celeste and Celine, joined them in short order. Celine wore a beautiful sapphire blue dinner dress that brought out the blue in her eyes. Celeste introduced her to Duke Northcott. "Duke Northcott, please allow me to introduce my sister, Celine Devereaux."

He took her hand, his eyes never leaving hers. "Why, Mrs. VanWoodsen, I thought you to be a rare beauty, but I think your sister may have you beaten."

"Oh, please, you'll make us blush," Celeste said, batting her eyelashes. She always excelled at flirting with men.

The ladies moved away to sit on the couch with Damien and Michael joining them in two nearby armchairs. Duke Northcott and Theodore remained removed from the group, having a more private conversation. Marcus never removed his eyes from Celine.

"She is exquisite, Theodore," he said, sipping his brandy.

"Yes, well the Devereaux women are both quite beautiful, it runs in the family."

"And you said she has talent?"

"Yes, oh yes, she does. Perhaps even more than Celeste. Of course, it's raw, and she is not aware of what she is capable of but I think under my tutelage she will be quite a force."

"Absolutely not!" Marcus asserted.

Theodore looked at him, confused. "You don't want her trained?"

"I will train her. She will be under no one's guidance but mine."

"As you wish," Theodore answered.

"We will perform the ceremony on her sixteenth birthday."

"Of course, as we planned."

"What do you know of the other two, the Carlyles?"

"Nothing. I was not aware they were accompanying her until late last evening. They arrived on Marquis Devereaux's doorstep, unexpected, but with a glowing reference from Lord Blackburn. I believe the Marquis hired the eldest to tutor Celine in English with the possibility that she might accept him as a suitor."

Marcus snorted in response. "She deserves far better than an ill-mannered and ill-bred American. And doesn't she speak English? She seemed to do a fine job of it a few minutes ago."

"Ah, yes, Celine is fluent in English, however, she doesn't let on to her father. She fears he would find it a bit too modern for his daughter to have taught herself English."

Marcus smirked, turning his gaze back to Celine. "Clever girl. Learn what you can about the other two. They may be of use to us. Our group for the upcoming ceremony is rather small, the addition of two others would be preferable."

"Yes, of course. They seem like good chaps, I'm sure they could be brought around to it."

"See that they are."

They ended the conversation and moved to dinner where

the group was, as Theodore had promised, entertained by tales of Duke Northcott's world travels. He paid specific attention to Celine, whom Celeste had seated to his right. Mrs. VanWoodsen apologized for the lack of female companionship but without notice, she was unable to orchestrate a fuller party.

Everyone assured her the party was acceptable, and they found no fault with her proficiencies as a hostess. Michael and Damien paid careful attention to the relationship between Celine and the others. In private, they discussed that it seemed that the sisters were quite close; that she had not yet developed the animosity she seemed to exhibit later. It also explained the deep bond that existed between them despite whatever had caused the rift. Celine's demeanor with the Duke was congenial and polite, but nothing more. She did not exhibit the hostility and loathing that they had seen in their time.

They discussed their plan for the following day. Celine's birthday was in three days; they were to deliver the letter to her the next day. Michael would have felt more comfortable had they known the contents of the letter, but it had a seal. They could not break the seal without making it obvious that the letter had been opened. They determined to find the library the following day to try to locate the book.

CHAPTER 26

*T*he following morning, they asked Celine about her plans for the day. She remarked she planned on taking a walk after breakfast. Michael said he would like to join her, and she graciously accepted the invitation. They used the time to ask her about a library in the house. While she told them where to find it, she was inquisitive about their interest in the library and the book they sought.

They had little explanation for her other than to say it was a passing interest. They had learned of the book before embarking on their journey here and they were curious to find out if the book existed. Celine did not appear as though she believed them, but she didn't question them any further.

As they entered the house after the walk, they found Duke Northcott descending the staircase. "Ah, Celine," he said, making his way down the staircase, "what good fortune that I have come across you this morning."

"Good morning, Duke," she answered, giving a small curtsy.

"I see you have been out for a walk," he responded. "I was hoping to have had the pleasure to take in the views with you, but alas, it seems I have lost my opportunity. Perhaps though, we could engage in a mid-morning chat."

"Oh." Celine stammered a bit. "We were just heading to the library together. I'm sorry."

Displeasure was apparent on Duke Northcott's face, this was not the answer he had wanted. "Surely these fine gentleman can enjoy the library without your help," he said, glaring between the two of them.

Michael opened his mouth to answer but Celine spoke before he uttered a word. "Oh, but they can't. They aren't very good at French and several of Teddy's volumes are in French. I have promised to help them translate the passages of interest, so you see, they can't possibly go without me."

His patience was wearing thin; however, there was not much he could do without seeming impolite and risking Celine's approval. "I see," he grumbled, "well, perhaps I can fit into your rather busy social schedule for an afternoon cup of tea."

Celine was growing tired of his requests but wasn't sure she could refuse him any further. "Yes, that would be lovely."

"Wonderful. Until then, my beautiful Celine," he said, kissing her hand. "Enjoy the library," he said to Michael and Damien before turning to leave.

The trio made their way to the library, Celine shut the door behind them. She sighed, closing her eyes for a moment as she leaned against the door. Opening her eyes, she looked toward Michael and Damien and said, "Thank you and please do not leave me alone with him."

Michael raised his eyebrows. "Yeah, sure, is everything okay?"

"All right," Damien said, correcting Michael's modern English. "He means is everything all right?"

"It's nothing. I just…" She paused as she searched for the words. "How can I say it, ah…"

"He gives you a bad feeling," Damien finished for her.

"Yes, a bad feeling. Like ice going through my veins."

"How much do you know about him, Celine?" Michael asked.

"Nothing, I've only just met him, but I get feelings. My Aunt Genevieve used to have them, too, and my sister. Something is amiss with him. There is something wicked, as you say, bad."

"We'll make sure you're safe," Michael said.

"Now, what is this book you're searching for? It doesn't sound like a normal book."

"Just a silly prank, most likely," Michael said.

"A what?" Celine asked, confused by the word she was unfamiliar with.

"Prank, like a joke," he answered.

"It isn't a joke. You two are far too interested for it to be ah, what was it you said? Prank?"

"Yes, prank, and believe me, it is no doubt just that," Michael said, dismissing it with a wave in the air.

"You aren't telling me the truth," Celine began.

Damien hit Michael in the arm. "I think this is when we're supposed to give her the letter."

"Letter?" she asked.

Michael held a finger up as he gave Damien a hard stare. "Can you give us a second in private?" Taking Damien aside, he said, "Are you sure?"

"Yes, I'm sure. Didn't you listen to what Josie said before we left? She said give her the letter in the library two days before her birthday, that has to be now. Maybe that's what will get her to give us the book. Maybe she's telling us she doesn't know about it because she doesn't trust us."

"Okay, okay, right, yeah I remember her saying that. Okay, well, here goes nothing," Michael said, removing the letter from his jacket. "Celine, this letter is for you."

"For me? From whom?"

"The same friend who informed us about the book. She insisted you would be the one to give it to us, so we thought you would know about it." He handed her the letter.

Celine opened it, breaking the wax seal and unfolding it, reading with interest. It was penned in handwriting that looked similar to hers and in her native French. Her eyes grew wide as she read.

Dear Celine,

You should be receiving this letter two days before your sixteenth birthday. Events have already been set into motion that cannot be undone; they must run their course. Unfortunately, this means that your life will be drastically and fundamentally changed. I realize that this may sound insane but I cannot explain it any further, you must accept this as the truth and trust me.

You will witness things that you shouldn't at your tender age and be asked to do things no one should be asked to do. It is vital, Celine, that you do NOT give in to Duke Northcott. You must resist him with every fiber in your being. Do not trust him, or Teddy or even your sister, Celeste. You can trust Michael and Damien. It is also crucial that you retrieve the Book of the Dead from Duke Northcott and give it to Michael and Damien. After this, you must help them return to their own time. They are not from your time, Celine, which I'm sure you already suspect. Once they have the book, you must open a time portal for them to return. While this may sound impossible, you will have the strength to do it, you have learned much from Aunt Genevieve, use what she has taught you and what is told to you below.

Be safe, Celine, take care, and know that you will survive.

What followed was a set of instructions to open the time portal. The letter was unsigned. She set her jaw and looked at the both of them. "Is this some kind of joke? Prank?"

"No," Michael said, peering over the top of the letter. "What does it say?"

Celine pulled the letter close to her, folding it and slipping it into a pocket in the folds of her dress. "Things that shouldn't be said, that shouldn't be known, that couldn't be known. How do you come to be here?"

"We came in the carriage with you," Michael answered.

"Enough pranks," she said, using her newfound word, "you must answer some questions and you must be honest with your answers. How did you come to be at my father's house?"

Michael and Damien exchanged a glance. Michael gave Damien a questioning glance. "Time to lay it on the table," Damien said, then turned to Celine and began, "as unbelievable as this may seem, we're from another time, the future. We know someone there who told us she knew a lot about you. She said that you'd be able to give us a book she needs, *The Book of the Dead,* she said she needs it to get rid of that Duke guy. He's in our time, too, and he's being a really, really bad guy there and hurting many people. We need your help. I realize it sounds crazy, but it's the truth."

Celine stood pondering for a moment, then said, "I believe you. But I know nothing of this book. From the letter, it looks as though it may belong to Duke Northcott. Perhaps his room would be the best place to search?"

"Oh, okay, that makes perfect sense, but there is no way we can search for it in there, if he catches us I don't want to find out what he'll do to us. From what I gather, this book is extremely important, and undoubtedly important to him," Michael said.

"Yeah, I agree, sorry, I'm just excited that everything is out in the open and we can at least be normal with you," Damien said, breathing a sigh of relief.

"You're right, if my feelings are correct, he is not a good man. But perhaps I can help you search there. I can distract him. He seems intent on speaking with me alone. I can arrange it so you can have some time to search. Perhaps tomorrow morning? I can suggest that we take a walk together."

"No," Michael said shaking his head. "No way, he's dangerous, at least where we're from and you got a bad feeling from him, there's no way we will let you do that."

"I'm not sure I can avoid it, and besides, I will control the situation as much as I can, make sure we are outside where other people can see so I cannot be in any danger."

"We're not sacrificing you," Michael insisted.

"You are not, I am sacrificing myself. As I said, I am not sure I can avoid his advances entirely. Perhaps when I've made myself clear that I am uninterested he will leave me alone and hopefully by then you will have retrieved the book. You can not change my mind. When we leave the house after breakfast, you will search for the book."

"You are as stubborn as our friend told us," Damien said.

Celine smiled, standing straighter and pushing her shoulders back, wearing the statement as a badge of honor. "Then it is decided. Now, I am going to my room before afternoon tea. Please make sure you are there, I don't want to be alone with him this afternoon."

"We'll be there," Michael said, nodding his affirmation.

They all waited through the rest of the day on pins and needles, waiting to enact their plan the following morning. They made polite mealtime conversation, doing their best to be gracious houseguests.

After dinner, Duke Northcott cornered Celine over nightcaps, having a private conversation with her while

Theodore and Celeste insisted the Carlyles join them in a card game. The Duke's constant hovering over Celine distracted Michael but he did his best to remain engaged so as not to cause any suspicion.

"Good evening, Celine," Duke Northcott said, blocking her from continuing toward the couch.

"Duke Northcott, good evening," Celine said, giving him a fake smile.

"How fortunate we were that your father was called away early."

"Fortunate?" Celine questioned.

"Yes, it has allowed me the good fortune to enjoy your company for two more nights than I should have."

"How kind," Celine said, trying to take a step toward the center of the room.

Duke Northcott blocked her again, stepping to the side to prevent her from moving.

"I must confess that kindness is not the primary motive."

"Oh?" Celine asked, playing innocent, knowing full well where this was likely headed.

He rubbed a finger against her cheek. "Oh, Celine, you must realize how beautiful you are." Celine smiled at him but did not respond. "And you must be able to see how enamored I am with you."

"I imagine with all your travels you have had the good fortune to meet many beautiful women," Celine said, dodging the statement.

"None that have set my heart on fire as you have," he said, his eyes piercing hers with intensity as he closed the distance between them.

Celine wasn't sure she could take much more without becoming nauseated. This man repulsed her, yet he gave her no reason to react this way. Still, she could not shake the perception, it was rooted deeply inside of her. "Oh, Duke Northcott, you mustn't speak this way."

"I am sorry, Celine, I know you may find it improper but I cannot help myself."

"We've only just met," Celine said, putting him off again.

"It does not matter, I am a decisive man, I know what I want. Perhaps we can steal away for a more private conversation?"

Celine had no desire to be alone with this man beyond what was needed for her plan. She had to think fast. She swayed on her feet, feigning unsteadiness. "Celine? Are you ill?" Duke Northcott asked, catching her as she swooned. The other men jumped to their feet.

"Oh, I am so terribly light-headed," Celine lied, throwing her hand across her forehead in a dramatic motion.

Celeste rushed across the room with Theodore. "Perhaps you should sit down for a moment," she said.

Theodore poured a small glass of brandy and brought it to her. "Here, Celine, drink some of this, to steady yourself."

Celine accepted the glass, taking a small sip. Celeste stroked her hair. "Are you feeling any better, my darling?"

"A little."

"Perhaps she should go to bed?" Michael suggested.

"Is that necessary? She said she is better," Duke Northcott commented.

Celine stood. "Yes, I am feeling…" her voice trailed off as she collapsed to the couch, continuing to feign her illness.

"I think you may be correct, Mr. Carlyle. Perhaps the best thing would be rest. Celine? Celine," Celeste said, rubbing her hand, "are you able to walk to your bedroom?"

"I'll help her," Michael said.

"Surely you do not expect her to walk," Duke Northcott said. "She almost collapsed. Stand aside," he said, pushing between Damien and Michael. "I shall carry her." He lifted

Celine from the couch, carrying her from the room as Celeste scurried in front of him, opening doors.

"My poor Celine," he said as he carried her through the foyer and up the steps.

"I fear your forthrightness has overwhelmed me, Duke."

"Please, call me Marcus. My sincerest apologies, but I am a man who speaks his mind."

She smiled at him as they reached her bedroom, more so because the experience would soon be over than from his comments. Celeste pushed the door open and Duke Northcott gently laid her on the bed.

"Thank you so much. What a bother I've been," she said to both of them.

"Not at all. Please get some rest, Celine. I hope you are soon recovered." He kissed her hand.

"Yes, thank you, Duke, I'll take it from here," Celeste said, prompting him to leave. He closed the door behind him. "I think he fancies you," Celeste said, helping settle Celine, removing her dress and getting her nightgown.

"He scarcely knows me," Celine said, wobbling on her feet, trying to keep up her ruse.

"Oh, that doesn't matter. He's a man who knows what he wants." Celine rolled her eyes. "I know how to read a man. He fancies you, Celine. It would not surprise me if he offers marriage soon."

"We shall see, Celeste. Now, I am exhausted, I'd like to get some rest."

"Of course, sister dear. I hope you are feeling better soon," Celeste kissed her forehead and left her to sleep.

Celine lay in bed, unable to sleep at first. The events of the night rattled through her mind along with the letter's warning. She hoped the plan worked and the Carlyles soon found that book. She wanted to rid herself of this man as soon as possible and she was not looking forward to their conversation the next morning. Celeste may be correct and if so, she wanted to avoid that situation at all costs. Still, she had agreed to help, and was determined to carry out her end of the plan.

Settling her nerves, she dozed off. When she did, Duke Northcott filled her dreams. He pursued her relentlessly, calling to her as she ran through the house trying to hide. He told her there was nowhere she could run, nowhere she could hide that he wouldn't find her; that he would pursue her to the ends of the earth and beyond.

CHAPTER 27

*T*he following morning arrived, although not soon enough for Celine. Michael and Damien met Celine in the hallway. "Are you feeling better?" Damien asked.

"What happened last night?" Michael added.

"I am fine. I must confess," she whispered, "I was not sick. I just wanted to rid myself of that dreadful Duke and his advances."

"Oh," Michael said, glancing at Damien. "Maybe we should forget about today's plan."

"No, absolutely not!" Celine said, raising her voice above a whisper. "You must find that book. We continue as we planned."

They all agreed to the plan one final time before heading to breakfast. As Celine entered the dining room, she found Duke Northcott already at the breakfast table with Theodore. He stood as she entered the room. "How much brighter my morning has become," he said, holding a chair out for her to sit. "It's as though a ray of sunshine has entered the room."

She smiled at him as she sat. "You are too kind, Duke."

"I trust you are better?" he asked her.

"Yes, I am much better. Thank you."

"I arrived early at breakfast today in the hopes of being the first to ask for the pleasure of your company on a morning excursion. It appears though that I may already be too late," he said, glancing at Michael and Damien who had entered the room with Celine.

"Oh," Celine said, trying her best to flirt. "No, you are not too late. I have no plans as yet."

"Then you'll accept my invitation?"

"With pleasure. I enjoy morning walks."

"Wonderful, I look forward to the conclusion of breakfast with enthusiasm."

Celine smiled, risking a glance to the two men with whom she shared the secret plan. She then returned to eating her breakfast, trying to maintain a neutral expression.

At the end of her breakfast, Duke Northcott offered her his arm. "Shall we, my dear?"

Celine accepted, standing from the table. As she stood, Michael and Damien also stood, excusing themselves. They followed Celine and Duke Northcott to the foyer, watching them as they passed out the door. Celine gave one final glance back to them. Michael winked as she disappeared out of the door.

Celine walked into the bright island sunshine. "What a beautiful morning," she said, trying to make pleasant conversation.

"The beauty of the morning pales compared to yours, Celine."

"Oh, Duke Northcott, you flatter me too much."

"Please, call me Marcus. I speak only the truth. Certainly you are accustomed to the attentions of men." Celine gave a nervous smile. "I know you find me too forward, yet your beauty compels me to be so."

They walked through the garden, Celine took the time to admire the flowers. "I fear I may be giving you…" she began, trying to curb the discussion before it went any further.

"Celine, please," he said, stopping to face her. "I must speak to you frankly even if it overwhelms you. I believe that we are an excellent match. I can provide you with a life of great means and position. As my wife, you would want for nothing."

"Oh, Duke Northcott…" she began.

"Marcus, please, Celine. I am a far better match than the ill-bred American who has his sights set on you." When Celine didn't answer, he continued, "I can offer you something more, something that he cannot. Furthermore, I can provide you with something else that he cannot." Celine met his eyes. He turned her toward a gazing ball which stood in the middle garden. She saw their reflection. Standing behind her, he put his hands on her arms, his head next to hers. "You are a stunning woman. What if your beauty could last forever?"

"But it cannot," she stated.

"That is not true. Celine, I can offer you a life of status and position and so much more. I am a powerful man, Celine, in many ways. I can offer you more than just a lifetime, I can offer you an eternity." Celine knit her brow, not understanding the whole of his comment. "Eternal life, Celine. Eternal youth and beauty." He traced his finger down her jawline. "I know you know of what I speak, your Aunt Genevieve made you aware of the dark arts. But with my instruction you can become a powerful entity. And together no one could stop us, together the world will beg at our feet."

Celine watched his face as he spoke through the mirrored gazing ball. The circular ball twisted and distorted it, making it almost gruesome at times. His breath on her neck made her ill and his grasp sent icy shots through her. Her mind raced to the letter, the warning that she had received. "All you must do is say the word, Celine," he said, fingering a lock of her hair. "Say the word and the world is yours."

"But at what cost?" she whispered.

"No cost that should concern you, my dear," he said, kissing her neck. "Now, Celine, will you say yes?"

"No," she exclaimed, setting her jaw and trying to stand firm.

He smirked, giving a small laugh. "I am not a man accustomed to hearing the word 'no,' Celine."

"I'm sorry, Duke, but that is the only answer I have."

"Oh, Celine, think carefully. I know you find my affections too forward but I am offering you the opportunity of a lifetime. Marry me, Celine, become my wife."

She spun around to face him. "I said no!" she said defiantly. He grasped her arms tightly. "You're hurting me!"

"You are being a fool. I suggest you take some time to give my offer more consideration. Perhaps to consult your sister, Celeste, who certainly has more experience in these matters."

"I have my own mind, my answer is no."

"I advise you to reconsider. I am not a man you want as an enemy," he said through clenched teeth.

She struggled, twisting away from his grasp. She backed away from him before turning to run to the house. "I can offer you the world, Celine," he called after her. "Don't be a fool."

Celine ran to the house, shutting the sunlight out with the large wooden front doors. She was breathless and tears spilled from her eyes. Celeste was making her way down the stairs. She rushed to Celine, taking her in her arms. "Mon chérie, Celine, whatever is the matter? Are you ill again?" Celine clung to her, sobbing. "Oh, my darling, let me take you to your room to rest." Celeste helped her up the stairs. She was too bleary-eyed to notice Michael and Damien slipping from the Duke's room and into their own. Celeste was too concerned tending to her distraught sister to have noticed them either.

Celine collapsed onto her bed, catching her breath as Celeste stroked her hair. "Now, my darling, please tell me what has happened to trouble you so."

"Duke Northcott has proposed marriage."

"Oh, Celine, that's wonderful news! These are not tears of joy?"

"They are not."

"Why ever not? He's quite the catch, many women have tried and failed to catch his eye."

"Celeste, there is something amiss about him, something wrong."

"Wrong? I don't understand."

"Yes, wrong. Celeste, he told me he could offer me eternal life, he said he could make me powerful enough to rule the world at his side. These aren't normal things, Celeste."

"I'm sure he meant that he is an incredibly powerful man. He is well-bred. He possesses a fortune and good position. He is fifth in line to the British throne! It would be a very good match if you became his wife, Celine. You would want for nothing. You would be the toast of society."

"No, he told me that but then he told me that through the dark arts he could offer me more."

"Celine, you're being childish. It is a good offer, take it."

Celine was skeptical, eyeing Celeste incredulously. The words from the letter she had received echoed through her mind. *Do not trust your sister, Celeste.* Celeste continued her lecture, "You grew up with no mother, and I tried to be the best substitute, yet I know I was not a suitable replacement, but even so your behavior is untenable. You must settle at some point, you cannot continue this childish behavior of refusing to even consider suitors. Furthermore, the Duke's offer is something to be grasped at, not avoided. Few women can claim such prizes."

"What of love?" Celine asked, trying to steer the conversation away from the Duke's promises.

"Love is for children's books and fairy tales. Appropriate marriages are never begun based on love. Love will come later, when you are settled and provided for."

"He was rather violent with me, Celeste. When I refused him, he grabbed at me, I think he bruised my arm."

"Is it any wonder? I'm certain he's not used to being told no, assuredly not when he is making such a generous overture. I'd say he showed incredible restraint." Celine didn't answer, she was frustrated and feeling betrayed. Celeste stood up, handing her a handkerchief. "Dry your eyes and make yourself presentable. Spend the afternoon in serious consideration of your life. This evening after dinner, I expect you to accept the Duke's offer." With her final comments made, she left the room, slamming the door behind her.

Celine wiped her eyes and used the washbasin to splash cold water onto her face. She fixed her hair and tried her best to cover her red eyes and nose. When she was presentable again, she peeked into the hallway, hearing and seeing no one, she tiptoed down the hall and tapped on Michael's door. Within a few moments, the door opened, and she darted inside.

"What happened?" Damien asked, rushing to her.

"Did you find the book?"

"No luck," Michael said, "we searched high and low, not a trace of it. What happened? You were crying when you came back."

"I'm fine, I was just, ah, shocked."

"What happened?" Michael pressed.

"He proposed marriage. He wasn't happy when I turned him down."

"Did he hurt you?" Damien asked.

"Not much. Although I did not give him an opportunity to do worse."

"Is your sister asking him to leave? I saw her with you, did you tell her?" Michael questioned.

"Yes."

"And is she asking him to go?" he pressed.

"No. She has advised me to accept his offer and would like me to do so this evening after dinner."

"What? That's crazy!" Damien said. "He's deranged, why would your sister want you to marry someone who hurt you?"

"She thinks he showed considerable restraint in not doing more. I do not plan to change my mind, no matter what she says. I will skip dinner this evening so as not to cause any scenes."

"We'll be here for you, Celine. We'll make sure you're okay," Michael said.

"Thank you," she said, smiling up at them. "Please excuse me, I would like to lie down. Since I plan to avoid dinner, I will see you tomorrow morning."

"We will check on you later. Get some rest," Michael said.

CHAPTER 28

*M*ichael and Damien made their way down to the sitting room for cocktails before dinner. They found themselves met with only the men, both ladies conspicuously absent. Theodore apologized for the lack of beauty in the room with Duke Northcott commenting that the ladies were likely fussing over their clothes or hair. The gentlemen shared a laugh over their brandy. After several more moments, Theodore excused himself to check on them.

Heading upstairs, Theodore overheard arguing coming from Celine's room. He announced himself at the door before entering. Inside, he found Celine in a dressing gown and an exasperated Celeste in her eveningwear. Upon seeing the scene, he bellowed, "What is the meaning of this?"

Celeste breathed a frustrated sigh. "She is not coming to dinner, she claims she's ill."

"Ill?" He turned to Celine. "Is this true?"

"Yes, I'm not well, rather woozy, in fact, I thought it best to stay in bed and not disrupt the meal in case I should be overcome by another episode like last night."

"You'll disrupt the entire household even further if you continue with this childish behavior," Celeste scolded her.

"Childish behavior?" Theodore asked.

"Yes. The Duke has proposed marriage to her and she, in her infinite wisdom, has refused him and now continues to act as a child, feigning illness and refusing to come to dinner. It's an embarrassment, Teddy, we will be considered socially inept."

"Has he? And you have said no? May I know your reasoning?" he asked Celine.

"No," she said, crossing her arms.

"I must insist," Theodore said.

Celine remained silent. "Celine, while your father is away, you are under our care. Now, I must insist that you give me your reasoning for what I consider to be a very foolish decision."

Celeste answered for her. "She was blubbering earlier about him being rough with her and about love. Have you ever heard a more ridiculous reason for marriage?"

"Celine, I will speak plainly to you. As your brother-in-law, I care for you. I want to see you succeed and settle into a good marriage. This is a good match offering you a good position and incredible wealth, love will come later. I would be remiss in my duties as your guardian if I did not stop you from making a grave error."

"I will not marry him."

"You are being impossible," Celeste said, her face growing red with frustration.

"Can you give me a reason you cannot marry him?" Theodore asked her. She did not answer. "Perhaps another man? Perhaps Mr. Carlyle? Is there an understanding between you?"

Celine considered the question. Lying would provide the easiest solution. However, she did not want to thrust that position on Michael. It would be unfair to him, particularly if the Duke challenged him for her hand. "No, there is no understanding."

"Well, then there is no obstacle preventing you from accepting the Duke. I must insist that you dress at once and find your way to dinner. I also urge you in the strongest possible terms to reconsider and accept the offer, assuming it still stands with the utmost haste," Theodore said.

"Perhaps it does not. And would you wish me limp in my chair, having fainted away from illness at the dinner table?"

"It wouldn't hurt, perhaps Duke Northcott will take pity on you and forgive your error in judgment," Celeste said.

"Either way, Celine, I must insist that you dress and attend dinner and I encourage you to make an opportunity to speak with the Duke in private following dinner. Even if you are still wavering on an answer, tell him you were too hasty and are considering his offer," Theodore said.

"Yes, ill or not, it's time you grow up, Celine, you can't claim illness and hide yourself away at every turn. You are soon to be a married woman if all goes well and you will need to learn to manage your moods and be a gracious hostess and dependable wife," Celeste advised. "Now, come," she said, calming her voice, "I shall help you ready yourself. Perhaps the rose dress, it brings out the pink in your skin, it will make you look quite becoming for Duke Northcott."

"Why must I? Have I no rights to my own opinion? No ability to make my own life?"

"Celine! My patience is wearing thin," Theodore said with a clenched jaw. "Must I resort to threats to encourage appropriate behavior? Perhaps the Carlyles create too much of a distraction. You spend a great deal of time with them. Perhaps I need to ask them to leave at once, maybe this will allow your mind to focus."

"No. You mustn't," Celine begged.

"I must if I consider it in the best interest to those in this household," Theodore threatened. "There's a good girl," Theodore said to Celine as she plopped herself in front of her dressing table.

Theodore exited the room, rejoining the men downstairs.

"I hope there isn't a problem?" Duke Northcott inquired as he entered the room.

"No," he assured him with a smile, "just a little indecision over which dress is most becoming for the evening."

"Ah, I can't imagine either woman in an unbecoming ensemble," Duke Northcott said.

"Well, you know women, everything has to be just right, particularly when the evening is important," he hinted. "The poor girl has herself in quite the tizzy over it. Luckily my beautiful Celeste is an expert in such matters and should have everything smoothed over soon."

The two women entered the room within a few moments. True to his word, Celeste had Celine pulled together smartly in a rose gown and bejeweled hair barrettes. "My deepest apologies," she said to everyone.

"There is no need to apologize, Mrs. VanWoodsen," Duke Northcott said, approaching Celine, "you were both worth the wait." He kissed Celine's hand.

"How kind of you, Duke Northcott. What an under-standing man you are," she answered, shooting Celine a glance.

"Careful, my dear, I may become jealous," Theodore said, laughing. "Shall we? I believe Cook may become impatient with us."

They entered the dining room. Polite dinner conversation was made, as usual, before the ladies went through to the sitting room to play cards while the men enjoyed a final drink and a cigar. Before joining the ladies, Duke Northcott asked if he could speak with Theodore, sending Michael and Damien to the sitting room ahead of them.

"I assume you've heard by now that I offered marriage to Celine?" Duke Northcott asked once alone.

"Yes, I did. I advised her, as did Celeste, that it is in her best interest to accept the offer. It is my understanding that she is considering it."

"She has declined my offer."

"A childish and impulsive reaction, I'm sure. The poor girl doubtless didn't know what to say, you are quite an imposing man."

"Don't patronize me, Theodore, I am not in the mood. Either way, we must proceed. I will not take any chances. Since she has not expressed interest on her own, we proceed as discussed previously. Is everything prepared?"

"Yes. Although I think you may find that she may have come 'round to the idea now."

"We shall see. What of the two Carlyle gentlemen? Have they been approached?"

"No, but I plan to this evening."

"Good," he said, turning to leave the dining room.

Theodore and Duke Northcott joined the others in the sitting room. They found the four engaged in a game of cards.

"Oh, Celine," Theodore said, already sipping a brandy, "I'm sorry to delay you, I know you wanted to take a walk this evening."

Celine's heart sank. She was hoping to avoid this, but Theodore would not allow her to get away without facing it. "Yes," she said, reluctance filling her voice.

"I could accompany you, I'd like to get some fresh air, too," Michael said, standing.

"Oh, Mr. Carlyle," Theodore said, holding a hand up, "I

was hoping to discuss a rather important matter with you and your brother."

Celine forced a weak smile. "Thank you, Mr. Carlyle, for your kind offer, but perhaps Duke Northcott would be kind enough to accompany me since you are unavailable."

"I would be only too happy to," Duke Northcott said, nodding toward Celine.

"You may want a shawl, sister dear, you wouldn't want to catch a chill. If you come with me, I will fetch mine for you to borrow. Duke Northcott, if you would be so kind as to meet us in the foyer, I promise we will not be more than a moment."

"Of course, Mrs. VanWoodsen."

Celeste guided Celine from the room and up the stairs to her bedroom, retrieving a shawl and wrapping it around her sister's shoulders. "Be charming, Celine. Apologize for being too hasty, beg his forgiveness, and accept him. If he should question you, tell him you were feeling ill and exercised poor judgment, but make him aware that it is only on the rarest of occasions you do this. Don't be foolish, Celine. I shall look forward to a blushing announcement of engagement from you when you return." Celeste fussed with her hair, pinched her cheeks to give them color, and pushed the bust line of her dress down just a tad. "There, I think that should do." She turned her around, pushed her out the door and down the stairs toward the waiting man.

Celine felt as though she were being ushered to the gallows, every step another one closer to her doom. The words in the letter reverberated in her mind constantly, warning her not to trust Duke Northcott, Theodore or Celeste, urging her not to give in to him. If she didn't, Theodore had threatened to remove her only two allies. Sometimes winning the war was more important than winning the battle. She plastered a smile across her face and approached him across the foyer.

Smiling, he offered her his arm and she, feigning graciousness, accepted it. Celine glanced back at her sister who nodded to her as they made their way out the door.

"Everything is so beautiful in the moonlight, wouldn't you agree, Celine?" he said as they entered the garden.

"Yes, it casts a romantic glow," she said before taking a deep breath and beginning her performance. She stopped walking, turning to face the Duke. Her heart beat hard in her chest. She hoped he didn't notice the sweat forming on her brow as her nervous instincts went to fever pitch. She glanced down at the ground then up to him. "Duke Northcott," she began, then fluttered her eyelashes as she had seen her sister do so many times when charming a man, "Marcus." She offered a small smile. "I must apologize for my behavior earlier and beg your forgiveness." She paused, unsure if she could continue without choking on the words. "I haven't been feeling well and I believe it has had an unintended effect on my judgment."

Duke Northcott tilted his head, considering her words. "Have you a different answer than you had earlier?"

"Have you the same offer?" she asked demurely.

"Yes, my offer remains unchanged."

"Then I should choose to accept it. Oh, please know that I am not always so imprudent in my decisions."

"I should hope not. I will need my wife to be a sensible woman. Let us consider the matter forgotten and begin our engagement with a fresh start, shall we?"

"I would appreciate that very much. You are an understanding man, Marcus," Celine said, choking back the bile creeping up into her throat.

Duke Northcott leaned forward, sweeping her into his arms. He kissed her lips hard. "Together, my dearest Celine, we will conquer the world." She smiled at him. "But I shall need you to trust me and obey me, do you understand?"

She nodded. He smiled at her. "Tomorrow we shall wed and I shall secure your place next to me for eternity."

"Tomorrow?" she asked, shocked.

"Yes, Celine. There is no reason to wait. Tomorrow on your sixteenth birthday you shall become my wife for all of eternity."

Celine was in absolute shock. She had planned a long engagement in light of her father's absence, then she could fulfill the obligations tasked in the letter, return home and break off the engagement. "My father is away, we mustn't marry without him."

"Oh, my darling, he'll understand."

"No!" Celine said, pulling away from him.

"Celine," he said, growing serious. "Do not test my patience, again."

She set her jaw, turning to face him, no more demure looks, no more batting eyelashes. "No."

He grabbed her wrist, pulling her close to him. "Do not dare to defy me again, Celine. You try my patience. I will not tolerate this kind of behavior."

She pulled at her arm, trying to break free of his grip. "You're hurting me," she squealed.

"I shall do more than that if you don't learn to obey me, my dear. I will soon be your husband and you my wife, you will obey me!"

She struggled and broke free, taking a few steps back. "I will not obey you! And I will not marry you!" she shouted before fleeing back to the house.

* * *

Celeste, Celine and Duke Northcott left the room, leaving Theodore alone with Michael and Damien.

"I'm glad we have this opportunity to speak," he said to them. "I have what I think is an intriguing offer for you gentlemen."

Michael turned his head, showing interest.

He smiled. "I have a small club of men, like-minded, successful, interested in furthering their fortunes in the world. Tell me, do either of you gentlemen have any experience with the occult?"

"The occult?" Michael looked to Damien who shook his head. "No."

"Then I have an interesting opportunity for you. I'm having a small meeting tomorrow night and two spots are open. It is a very exclusive offer since Duke Northcott will be in attendance and he is well-versed in the occult. In fact, one may never come across an opportunity like this again. What do you say, gentlemen? Interested?"

"Very interested," Michael said. "It sounds like an intriguing offer."

"Excellent," Theodore said, smiling at them, "excellent, then I shall expect you to be ready at ten o'clock. I shall meet you in the gardens outside."

"We will see you then," Michael said as Celeste entered the room.

"Well, will your sister be warm enough on her walk?" Theodore asked her, ending the conversation.

"Oh, I hope so, I worry about her," Celeste answered, pacing the room.

"Come and sit down, my dear, I'm sure she will be just fine. Duke Northcott will let nothing happen to her, I'm sure."

The four made light conversation before Michael and Damien excused themselves announcing that they were retiring for the evening. A few moments after Michael and Damien departed, Celeste and Theodore heard the front door open and slam shut. Footsteps raced across the foyer moments before the door opened again and closed. This time footsteps approached the sitting room. The door opened and Duke Northcott entered.

Both Celeste and Theodore stood as he entered. Celeste looked around him, anxiously hoping to find her sister, but fearing the worst. "If you are looking for your sister, you won't find her. She has refused me again, Mrs. VanWoodsen."

"What?" Celeste was incredulous. "How dare she? I shall speak to her again. Please, Duke, give her another chance."

"She is out of chances. I much preferred her to come to me of her own accord but now she must be made to do what we want," he answered her.

"Of course." Celeste dropped her eyes to the floor.

"By any means necessary, wouldn't you agree?"

"Yes, of course we agree, Marcus. Please, tell us what we can do to help," Theodore said.

"You must follow every direction I give you and never question me. I may need to employ some rather extreme tactics to achieve our goal. You must give me your absolute and unfettered loyalty."

"Yes, you know we do, Duke," Theodore answered.

"Celeste?" Duke Northcott said, turning to her.

"You know you have my unwavering support. I am sorry for Celine's heedless behavior."

"Your apology is unnecessary, Celeste, your steadfast support will be enough. What of the Carlyles, Theodore? Has that end of our plan cooperated?"

"Yes, Duke, they are very interested."

"Excellent. Then we proceed as planned. By tomorrow night, Celine will be ours for eternity."

CHAPTER 29

*C*eline heard a quiet knock at her door then a whispered voice said, "Celine? Celine, it's Michael and Damien, are you in there?"

She raced to the door, throwing it open and ushering them inside while checking that no one saw them. "Quickly, come in."

"Are you okay? You weren't at breakfast, we were worried," Michael said.

"I am fine, although… " Celine paused, lowering her eyes to the floor. "I am afraid that I may have ruined your chances to retrieve the book."

"What do you mean?" Damien asked.

"Assuming that Duke Northcott has the book, he'll never give it to me now. Never!" she cried, covering her hands with her face. "I'm sorry."

"What happened last night?" Michael asked. "Did he hurt you again?"

"I tried my best, really I did. I played along, apologized and accepted his proposal as my sister instructed me to do. He said we were to marry today. I panicked, I didn't know what to do, and I refused. He became angry and I could not pretend anymore. I told him I would never obey him nor marry him. He must be furious, as must my sister be, surely she knows by now. We should prepare to leave the house," she said, unable to hold it all in.

Damien put his arm around her, pulling her close and rubbing her arm to reassure her.

"No, you did the right thing. You can't marry him, you had to keep yourself safe. Don't worry about it; we'll figure out a way. We may already have one, in fact," Michael said.

"You have a way?" Celine asked.

"Your brother-in-law asked us to join him in some secret ceremony tonight. If that book is going to make its appearance I'd put money on it being at the secret occult ceremony he's taking us to tonight," Michael explained.

Celine considered it. "Yes, you may be right. But it may be very dangerous. Surely you cannot risk it."

"It's more dangerous for the people from our time if we don't risk it," Damien said.

Celine nodded. "Then I will go, too," she said.

"No!" they both replied in unison.

"I can help!"

"You can help us by staying here, safe," Michael said.

"That is ridiculous," Celine said, crossing her arms.

"Hey, we need you to help us get back to our time, so we need you safe. We'll meet you back here as soon as we get that book and you can send us back," Damien said.

Celine frowned but acquiesced. "Agreed, but only because I am a necessary part of the plan."

"We're meeting Theodore at ten, so expect us maybe two or three hours after that," Michael said.

"I'll be ready. Do you suppose the book will be there and you'll be able to take it?"

"I'm not sure but it's our best shot so we will have to make it work," Michael replied.

"Good luck. You should be going, I expect my sister to visit me soon. If she found you here, it would be the end of our brilliant plan."

Damien gave her a quick hug. "By the way, happy birthday, Celine."

She smiled at him. "Merci! Now go!" The two opened the door a slit, checking the hallway. It was clear, so they made their way out and to their own rooms.

Celine paced the floor for a few minutes then sat down at the desk in the room, preparing to write a letter to her father. She had only recorded the date and heading before she heard a knock. "Celine? Celine! It's me," Celeste's voice called out, "Please open the door. Sister, please. I am not cross, I just want to talk."

Celine put down her quill and, unlocking her door, let Celeste into the room. She was carrying a tray. "Happy birthday, sister dear!" Celeste said brightly. "I brought you some breakfast and some tea. Teddy told me you were not in attendance for breakfast this morning."

"Thank you but please, Celeste, I am not hungry."

"Oh, Celine, please try to eat something. I worry about you."

Celine was silent, afraid if she spoke she may say something to her sister that she would regret.

"Please, Celine, can we talk?"

"I do not feel well enough to talk," Celine said.

"That's fine, Celine, then just listen," Celeste said, setting the tray on the bed and drawing Celine to sit down with her on the edge. She took her sister's hands in hers. "I heard that you did not accept Duke Northcott's proposal." Celine began to pull her hands away but Celeste kept a firm grip on them. "I am not cross, perhaps I pushed you too hard. Perhaps you are not ready, particularly for such an imposing man. Please, sister dear, can you forgive me for the short-tempered words that we exchanged yesterday?"

Celine looked into her sister's eyes, a match to hers in every way. She searched them for any signs she was lying. Was her sister letting her off the hook? "Oh, Celeste, of course I forgive you! You are my sister, you will always be my sister and I hate it when we fight." Moving closer, she threw her arms around Celeste in an embrace.

Celeste let out a sigh of relief and a laugh. "Oh, I love you, Celine, really I do, that is why I sometimes get so cross. I want only the best for you."

"I know," Celine said, leaning back to face her sister again.

"Now," Celeste said, "don't think I have gone too soft and agree with you. I still believe that Duke Northcott is a good match for you and I know that he is still interested. You have made an impression on him, sister dear. I hope that I can convince you of that, but I do not want to quarrel with you over it. Not before your breakfast anyway." She laughed, motioning to the tray.

"Celeste, please, I don't want to quarrel with you either, but I do not agree he is a good match. He is a violent man. And I did initially accept his proposal last night," Celine said, eating a bit of the porridge and taking a sip of tea.

"You did? Whatever happened for you to change your mind so quickly?"

Celine nodded as she ate another few spoonfuls of porridge. "I did as you and Teddy advised. Oh, Celeste, I really did try. He insisted that we marry today. I disagreed. I wanted Papa to be here. I did not understand why we should be so quick to marry. I would be married before Papa even learned I was engaged."

"And?" Celeste prompted, waiting as Celine ate more and sipped more of her tea.

"And he did not react well. He grabbed my wrist, twisting it until I was in pain and told me I must learn to obey him. His sudden turn frightened me and I called it off."

Celeste considered the story for a moment while Celine finished her porridge. "You know, Celine, I don't always agree with Teddy, but I do as he sets forth, that is part of being a good wife. You are so young to understand and it must seem terribly unfair, particularly since Papa has let you do as your heart pleased for so long. He has spoiled you." She smiled, tucking a lock of hair behind Celine's ear. "But it is my job as your older sister to make sure you will be looked after."

"You think I should have agreed then?"

Celeste stood, walking a few steps away from the bed, contemplating the question. After a moment, she responded, "You reacted hastily. You should have sought me out for counsel. Together we would have sorted things out. Teddy and I are your guardians at the moment, we could have intervened."

"I did not expect you would have listened, Celeste."

"And for that I am sorry," she said, turning to face her.

Celine sighed. "It is over now," she said, stifling a yawn. "I am feeling very tired. I must confess, I did not sleep well."

"Oh, yes, no doubt from the upset. Again, I apologize for my part in that but I hope it is resolved and we can put it behind us."

Celine smiled sleepily. "Yes."

"Here, let me help you into bed," Celeste said, pulling the covers up around her, "rest now, sister dear, rest." Celeste kissed her forehead as Celine's eyes closed and she drifted off to sleep.

Celeste moved the tray from the bed, setting it on the dressing table before opening the door. "Is it done?" Duke Northcott asked, entering the room.

"It is. She is sleeping, the sedative acted as we expected."

Duke Northcott approached the bed, staring down at Celine. He traced a finger down her cheek before leaning in to kiss her slightly parted lips. "Soon, my dear Celine, you will be mine," he whispered.

"Duke?" Celeste said gingerly, "If I may be so bold as to say I believe my sister was earnest in her acceptance of you last night. I believe she may have been overwhelmed and frightened when she behaved so poorly."

"I admire your sister's strength and steadfastness to her convictions," he said, fondling her hair as he admired her. "She will make a loyal follower once she has joined us."

"She is still very young. Perhaps if you were to approach her just one more time, showing her tenderness, she would respond to your liking."

Standing, he turned to face her. "I will not be told how to conduct my affairs, Celeste."

"My apologies, Duke," Celeste said, her head sinking to her chest, "I was only attempting to help your cause."

"Then do as you are told."

"Yes, Duke. I will do everything you ask."

"Good. See that she stays sedated until we are ready," he said, leaving Celeste alone to look after Celine.

CHAPTER 30

$\mathcal{M}$ ichael and Damien made their way to the garden around quarter to ten in the evening. They hadn't seen Celine since earlier this morning after breakfast. She had not appeared for lunch, tea or dinner. Celeste apologized on her behalf, stating that she was ill and resting in bed. The explanation did not sit well with Damien and Michael. Aware of the circumstances of what had transpired between Duke Northcott and Celine, they hoped it meant she was avoiding further contact with the Duke and an impossible social situation and was not indicative of a deeper problem.

They waited in the moonlight, looking at the cloudless sky. "It's amazing how many stars are up there," Michael said.

"Yes, you never notice what light pollution drowns out until you witness a world without it," Damien responded.

Soon there was movement along the path and they could make out a figure coming toward them, from the opposite direction of the house. As he approached, they recognized the form of Theodore. "Gentlemen," he said as he approached. "I hope you are ready for the evening. It promises to be most interesting."

"We are ready, sir!" Michael said, trying to sound enthusiastic.

"Looking forward to an interesting evening," Damien added.

"Good, good. You've come on a good night," Theodore said, leading them down a path toward the shore. "We are inducting a new member this evening, so you can witness a little of the process that is required of you to become a full member."

"Member, sir?" Michael questioned.

"Yes, oh, it's a very exclusive club. You were fortunate to have found your way to us."

"I see," Michael answered. "What all does the club do?"

"Oh, mostly dalliances here and there, but let me tell you there are great benefits to joining."

"Benefits?"

"Why yes, many men have seen a positive change in their fortunes after joining. The already fortunate have grown more so. As a young lad starting out in your own ventures, this could be useful to you to build your fortune, attract a good wife, and build a lifestyle other men can only envy."

"I see, well it sounds like we were very fortunate to have happened upon you when we did," Michael surmised as they neared the beach.

Theodore stopped just short of the sand, moving toward what looked like a stone wall. Michael and Damien were surprised to see it was a cave opening as they neared the rocky outcropping. They followed Theodore into the cave after exchanging a wary glance. This was not the best place to be, given only one entrance and exit existed, however, this was most likely what the group intended.

They followed Theodore through a series of tunnels that

wound further and further into the cave. The air grew cold and damp, the walls wet to the touch. Deep inside, one of the tunnels opened into a large cavernous space. Candles were placed around, casting shadows throughout the space with their dim light. Theodore picked up a few black robes that had been placed on a stalagmite near the cavern's entrance and passed one to each of them, donning one himself. "Please wear these robes and take your place over there." He motioned toward the back of the cavern. "I caution you, do not interfere with the ceremony in any way. You are here only to observe, your time for entry into the group will come after a series of tests, tonight being one of them. Do you understand?"

They both nodded their agreement and took their place near the back of the cavern.

"I am completely creeped out right now," Damien whispered.

"Me, too. What is under that black sheet?" Michael whispered back.

"I don't know. Looks like some kind of altar. Oh man, I really hope it's not like a sacrifice or something."

"Why did you have to say that? Now that's all I'm thinking about."

"Celeste is here, too, see her blond hair poking out of her hood up there? Near the altar."

"Yeah, looks like she's a member, along with her husband. I don't see the Duke."

"Me either, or Celine, but look, next to Celeste, a book. Could that be the *Book of the Dead?*"

"I don't know but I'd bet it is. How are we going to get it?"

"No idea, but I think I spotted an opening behind us. It's hard to tell, it's so dark back here, but we might be able to run out through there if we have to."

"Good to know," Michael said, as a gong sounded. "Here we go."

At the sound of the gong, a low chant began to fill the chamber. From another tunnel, Duke Northcott appeared, wearing a similar long black robe, the hood thrown back. He approached the altar, stopping in front of it. The chanting continued growing louder and louder.

"Tonight," he said in a loud voice as the chanting lowered to a murmur, "we welcome a new member to our group. A very important member, a member who will stand by my side as we continue to make our mark on the world. Let us begin."

Turning toward the altar, he pulled the black cloth off of the altar revealing what was underneath.

"Oh my God," Damien said, putting his hand over his mouth that was agape. "It's Celine."

Celine lay on her back, unmoving; her eyes were closed as if she was asleep. Duke Northcott fingered a lock of her hair, staring down at her for a moment before continuing. He removed something from his pocket and leaned toward her. "It's time to wake up, Celine, dear," he said, holding something under her nose.

Her face twisted as though the smell was putrid and her eyes shot open. She blinked a few times, her brow furrowing with confusion. Duke Northcott leaned over her, stroking her cheek. "Celine, darling, how are you? Here, take a drink of this, it will steady you." He offered her a chalice. She sipped it. "Can you sit up?" he asked, helping her to sit up. She was dazed, as though she was drugged, unable to comprehend what was happening.

"Should we be doing something? What is he giving her?" Damien asked.

"I don't know, I don't think there's anything we can do," Michael whispered back.

"Where… where am I?" she mumbled, her words slurred. She placed her hand on the Duke's arm as she swayed, coming close to falling off the altar.

"You are at your initiation ceremony, my darling," he answered her.

"What?" she said, shaking her head.

"Your initiation ceremony. Tonight you will join our ranks, my ranks. You become one of us, sign your name in the *Book of the Dead* and you will stand beside me as we conquer the world. All these people are here for you, Celine," he said, waving his hand to encompass those in the cavern. "Your sister, your brother-in-law, even your new friends, the Carlyles."

"Okay, that was low," Michael said, "he's trying to make her think we're here for whatever sick game he's playing with her."

Celine's breath quickened, she put a hand to her chest. "My heart is racing," she said.

"Yes, that's just the drink taking effect. It will make you more alert. Can you stand now?"

She slid down off of the altar to her feet. She swayed a bit as though drunk, grasping at Duke Northcott to stay upright. Within a few moments, she gained her footing, seeming to become hyper alert. Her eyes darted around the cavern frantically. "Celeste?" she asked, seeing her sister.

"She's in a trance, she cannot communicate with you. Now, Celine, it is time, time for you to become one of us. Your powers are impressive, but you need guidance. I can provide that for you, but you must join us."

Celine looked at him, questioning. "Join us, Celine. You know I offer you eternal life, eternal youth. Your power joined with mine will bring the world to its knees. But first you must be initiated." He nodded toward a black-robed figure standing near a tunnel. The man disappeared and reappeared, pulling another hooded figure into the cavern. He removed the man's hood and shoved him forward. Duke Northcott removed a dagger from within his robe, placing it in Celine's hand. He grasped her hand in his and raised the dagger to point toward the man. "You must kill him, Celine."

Celine swiveled to face him. "I will not!" she said, incredulous.

"Celine, you must draw blood to become one of us. I order you to kill him, now kill him."

"I do not wish to become one of you. You and your... your cult, it's evil."

"No, Celine. This man is evil, we are ridding the world of evil, kill him." The man looked pleadingly at Celine, his eyes silently begging her not to kill him. "This man has committed many crimes, he must be punished. Kill him."

Celine pulled her hand from his. "Only God shall judge," she said, stepping away from him.

Duke Northcott sighed. "Your stubbornness will be your undoing, Celine. I did not want to show you this but you leave me no choice." He nodded again toward the man who had retrieved the accused criminal. The man disappeared again into one of the tunnels, returning slowly this time, dragging something. "Look, Celine, behold one of this man's many crimes."

Celine turned to identify what the robed man was bringing. Her eyes grew wide as it became clear he was dragging a body. He flung it into the middle of the cavern. The body rolled, landing face up. Michael and Damien gasped as they recognized the face. "NO! PAPA!" Celine shouted, racing to the body. She lifted his head in her arms as she wept over him. She cried out toward the heavens in an agonizing pitch.

Damien made a move to go to her but Michael held him back. "Don't, we can't risk it yet, we all need to make it out of here alive." Damien reluctantly agreed, remaining visibly bothered by the scene unfolding in front of him.

Duke Northcott approached her, caressing her hair. "There, there, my darling, Celine. We are your new family. We will take care of you now." He pulled her to her feet. She clung to him, still wailing with heartbreak. He walked her away from the body, back to the prisoner. "Now, my darling," he said, brushing her hair from her face and holding her face in his hands, "kill this man."

Tears continued to stream down her face. She looked like a frightened child as she stared up at him, in complete and utter shock. He placed the knife in her hands again. "This is the man responsible for your father's death. When your father departed, he robbed him on his way to the ship and then killed him. He killed your father for a few pieces of gold, Celine. Now, I want you to make him pay for his crimes. Kill him, Celine." He pointed the knife toward him, holding her hand in his again.

"No," she sobbed, "no, I cannot."

"Celine, listen to me, kill him. You can and you must. I will guide your hand, I will provide you with the strength you do not have, but you must kill him." Pulling her closer, he pressed the knife forward until it was touching the man's chest.

Celine sobbed, tears rolling down her cheeks. "Please," the man said to her, his lip quivering.

Celine squeezed her eyes shut for a moment. Duke Northcott moved around so he was behind Celine. "Celine, he killed your father in cold blood, make him pay," he growled into her ear. "Do it now, Celine."

Celine was wide-eyed as she peered at the man then scanned the room. She sniffled and choked additional tears out as her eyes darted between her intended victim and the others. "Celeste?" she asked again.

"She cannot help you, Celine, she is in a trance. Now, concentrate, Celine. Finish your task and you shall see her again."

Celine looked toward Damien and Michael. Michael shook his head slightly showing that he did not agree with what was happening. She glanced back at the man in front of her then back to her friends. Damien mouthed the word "book" to her and darted his eyes toward it. She followed his glance, noting the book. She looked back at him, giving him a slight nod.

"NO!" she shouted, pulling her hand from the Duke's hand and letting the knife clatter to the floor. She took a few steps back away from him, moving toward the book. "No," she shouted again, "I will not do it, I will not join you."

"Celine," Duke Northcott warned in a loud voice.

"No, Marcus, no. You are evil and I will not join you," she said, backing up further.

"Celine," he warned again, "do not do something you will regret."

She shook her head, "The only thing that I would regret is joining you." Then she looked toward Michael and Damien and shouted one word to them. "RUN!"

Immediately after issuing her warning, she spun around, grabbing the book from its place on the altar near Celeste and fleeing through one of the nearby tunnels. She hoped her co-conspirators followed her lead and disappeared down the tunnel behind them. While these tunnels were a maze, she was sure she could navigate to them and give them the book.

"CELINE! NO!" Duke Northcott howled behind her. "FIND HER!" he demanded of his loyal subjects. Celine heard footfalls running, they seemed to be coming from every direction. She weaved through the maze of tunnels, having explored enough of the cave while visiting her sister on previous occasions to move through them with ease. She tried to put as much distance between her and the cavern as possible while also making several turns so there was not a straight path to her.

After several minutes of running through the tunnels, she stopped, clutching the book to her chest and breathing in a belabored manner. She closed her eyes, listening, trying to determine the best path to take going forward. After a few moments, she opened her eyes, peering into the blackness. She thought she detected a noise to her right, so she moved left. She went around a corner into a small circular opening. Standing in front of her was the man Duke Northcott had asked her to kill. In his hand, the knife she had dropped earlier.

He smiled at her. "I'll be taking that, miss," he said, motioning to the book with the knife, a grin crossing his grizzled face.

"No, I cannot give it to you, I'm sorry," she said, clutching it to her chest tighter and turning to leave.

"I wasn't asking, miss," he said, grabbing her arm and turning her around.

He grasped the book, trying to pull it from her. "I said no!" she shouted. He let go of the book, nearly causing her to fall backwards.

"And I said I wasn't asking," he said, plunging the knife into her abdomen. Intense pain surged through her body as the knife pierced into her belly. She dropped the book, grasping at the knife now stuck in her stomach. The man chuckled as he picked up the book. "You screamed less than your daddy. I'll be seeing ya, miss. And I thank ya, this will get me back into the Duke's good graces." He disappeared down a tunnel.

Celine sunk to her knees, pain narrowing her vision to pinpoints. She grasped the knife and pulled it from her body, shrieking as it slid out of her wound. Clutching her belly, she struggled to stand. She looked at her hands, covered in blood. She leaned against the cave wall, feeling its dampness as she labored in pain to move. She heard a noise behind her. "Oh mon Dieu, I must go, he is coming," she said aloud, motivating herself to move.

She struggled to move forward, staggering a few steps forward before almost collapsing. "Celine, stop," a voice said behind her. She recognized the Duke's voice and sobbed as she tried to push forward, realizing that she could not escape him.

"Marcus," she said, turning toward him, tears again streaming down her face. She began to collapse forward.

He noticed her clutching her stomach, the blood that covered her hands and dress. "Celine, no!" he shouted, rushing toward her and catching her as she collapsed. "No, Celine, my darling," he said holding her in his arms and surveying the wound, "who did this to you?"

"I did, gov'ner," the criminal said, entering the cavern again. "But I got the book back for ya, see?" he said, brandishing the book.

Duke Northcott set his jaw, letting Celine slip to the cave floor and rising. He grasped the knife that Celine had discarded, covered in her blood. "You fool, do you know what you have done?"

"Got ya the book, gov'ner. Now I reckon that's worth a good bit to you, in'it?"

"Yes, it is, give it to me."

"Then we're even right?"

"No," the Duke said, clenching his teeth, "I'd still owe you something."

"Well, that sounds a bit of all right to me," he said, handing the book over.

The Duke accepted the book, then plunged the knife into the man's heart. "There, now we're even," he said, pulling it back and allowing the man's shuddering body to collapse to the floor where he took his last few agonizing breaths before his spirit left his body.

Duke Northcott returned to Celine's side, setting the knife and book down, he leaned over her. "Celine, I will not lose you," he said. He sliced his hand open with the knife then placed his hands over her wound, squeezing his blood into it. He murmured words in Latin, then facing her said, "My blood will give you life. My blood will become your blood, my heart will beat with yours, Celine."

Celine groaned as the pain worsened for a moment. Within seconds, she felt the pain subsiding. She wondered if she were taking her last few breaths, slipping away from the pain of the world. But as the pain subsided, she began to feel stronger not weaker. She looked down, and it appeared as though her wound was closing. She looked up at Duke Northcott, bewildered. "You will be all right now, Celine," he said, stroking her hair and breathing what appeared to be a sigh of relief.

She sat up, there was no more pain in her abdomen, no more blood oozing from her body. She looked to him. From the corner of her eye, she saw the book. He had just saved her life, but she knew she had to deliver the book to Michael and Damien. If she was correct, the Duke could be injured but not killed. His hand had bled but was already healed. A deep wound could buy her the time she needed. "Thank you," she whispered, then added, "I'm sorry."

His brow furrowed with confusion, then his face twisted with understanding as he felt the knife pierce his gut. She grabbed the book and fled from the room. The knife clattered to the floor behind her but she dared not look back.

"Celine!" she heard a voice call out. She did her best to head toward it, recognizing it as Michael's. Threading through the tunnels, she made her way to the mouth of the cave. She could see two figures standing at the entrance and she raced toward them, practically running straight into their arms.

"I have the book," she said, out of breath. "Come quickly, we must get to the beach and send you on your way."

"Okay. Oh my God, Celine!" Damien said as she emerged into the moonlight.

"I'm fine, not even a scratch on me, come, he isn't far behind."

They followed her to the beach, she selected a spot that shielded them from view. Handing the book to Michael, she said, "Are you ready?"

"Yes, we're ready," he answered.

"Wait," Damien interrupted. "Come with us, you aren't safe here."

"I cannot," Celine said, "I am safe now, no physical harm can come to me."

"But…" he protested.

"There is no time to discuss it. You must go. Now be ready when the portal opens."

They nodded in agreement. Celine nodded back. "Good luck," she said, stretching her hands in front of her and squeezing her eyes closed. The wind picked up around them and a twinkling started on the rock face in front of Celine. They waited until the wind was blowing in a near gale force and the portal began to open. Once it was fully opened, they raced toward it.

Damien looked back once, seeing Celine's hair twisting in the wind, her dress blowing wildly. "Come on!" Michael shouted ahead of him. Damien turned and followed him into the portal, leaving Celine and the eighteenth century world behind in a brilliant flash.

CHAPTER 31

PRESENT DAY, BUCKSVILLE, MAINE

Celine sat at Maddy's bedside, placing a cool rag across the child's forehead. The children were getting worse, feverish, and spouting random and strange utterances whenever they were awake. Millie used a mild sedative on the children in an attempt to ease their discomfort. There had been disturbances in the village, too: unexplained animal deaths, diseased crops, and fits of madness.

They had moved the children to Alexander's house, yet the trouble seemed to follow them there. They were careful to keep Celeste hidden away, too, lest Marcus Northcott discover she had returned from the dead. Things were at their breaking point; if the book did not arrive soon, there may be no recovering.

Celine shifted in her seat, trying to get comfortable. She pulled her legs up to her chest and onto the chair, propping her head up with her hand. Gray entered the room, putting his hand on her shoulder. She looked up at him, giving his hand a squeeze.

Out of nowhere, a rogue breeze rustled her hair. No windows were open in the room. Her brows furrowed for a moment then she leapt from her chair.

"What is it?" Gray asked.

"They're coming back," she said, making a beeline out of the room and to the living room where they had last seen Michael and Damien. In the living room, she found Alexander. The air stirred even more when she reached the room. "They're coming," she said. Alexander stood and together the three of them waited for Michael and Damien to appear.

Within moments the gale force winds blew through the room and a glimmer appeared, growing larger by the second on the far wall. Within seconds, it covered most of the wall and within a few more, Michael and Damien were standing in front of them, Michael clutching a book to his chest.

Celine breathed a sigh of relief at the sight of both of them, appearing no worse for wear. She ran to them, pulling them both into a hug at the same time.

"We got it," Michael said.

She stepped back, "Are you okay?" She looked between the two of them, knowing the terror that they had just lived through. Centuries of living had not dulled the memory for her and they had just lived through it.

"Yes, yes. We're all right, more or less," Michael said.

"I feel awful that we had to leave you that night, Celine. What we witnessed you go through was horrible. I can't imagine what you went through after we left," Damien said, worry crossing his face.

"I survived. And now, thanks to you both, the Duke will not," Celine answered.

Michael gave a small smile. "I hope not, that guy's a real bastard."

He handed the book to Gray. Celine smiled at his comment, her arms still around them. "I hope it's the right book. I've never seen a book look anything like this," Michael said.

"Oh, that's the book, all right," Celine answered. "And I doubt you have. I don't think there's ever been another one like it. Bound by leather made from human flesh and filled with pages written in blood, it is as horrific as its name."

"And just as unhelpful it seems," Gray said, looking through the book with Alexander. "Other than a list of names, it appears to be gibberish." He slammed it shut, throwing it down on the couch in frustration.

Celine smiled. "It's written in a language only a few gifted people can understand. People like the Duke."

"What good does that do us? Is he going to help us read the book so we can destroy him?" Gray yelled.

"No, but you forget, I am as powerful as he and his blood runs through my veins, which means I can read it."

A smile spread across Gray's face. He handed the book to Celine who opened it, scanning it. "So, does it tell us how to destroy him?"

"Not destroy him, but banish him from this world. See these markings? They tell us how the coven was created, who it serves and how to handle a problem, should one arise."

"And the names?" Alexander asked, as he, Michael and Damien grouped around Celine.

"The names are those in his coven."

"Your name's not in there," Damien said, seeing the end of the list without having seen her name.

"No, I never pledged my loyalty to him, never signed the book in the blood of another. I never belonged to him, despite what I became that night," Celine explained.

Damien nodded in understanding. "So what do we need to do?" Gray asked.

"We need to hold a special ceremony, call forth the Hellbeast he serves and ask him to take him back to whence he came. It will not be easy. As much as I'd like to do this alone, I will need all of you, including Teddy and Celeste. Alexander and Gray, you're going to have to help me control the Duke once we get him on site, along with Teddy. Celeste will have to lure him there. I'll perform the ceremony."

"What about us?" Michael asked.

"Stay with the children, watch over them. You've done your part."

"We want to help!" Damien exclaimed.

"I know, but you have," she said, grabbing his hand. "Please, this is very dangerous for someone who isn't immune to it like we are."

Damien nodded. "Okay," he reluctantly agreed.

"When and where, Celine?" Gray asked.

"No time like the present. The beach just up from the cave. Celeste can lure him down the path through the cave and out of the cave's mouth onto the beach, he'll walk right into our trap without ever seeing us."

"How can we be sure this Hellbeast will banish him?" Gray questioned.

"This Hellbeast will not be pleased that he's not gathering up a following, increasing his coven. Simply put, he will be fired for not doing his job. That's one of the 'problems' the book states. If someone isn't carrying their weight, they can be banished from the earth."

"Well, let's get started with the banishment then," he answered.

"Good luck," Michael said.

"Be careful," Damien added.

"We'll see you when this is over," Celine said, reassuring them.

CHAPTER 32

*C*eleste made her way to the home that sat on the edge of the cliffs. She could see lights inside burning away the darkness around the home. She was careful to keep to the shadows, using her black cape to stay hidden until she wanted to be noticed. Reaching the house, she ascended the steps to the porch in silence and approached the front door. She removed the note from her pocket and slid it under the door. Celeste retreated down the steps as stealthily as she climbed them and stopped a few feet from the house. She stood visibly in the path, pushing back the hood of her cape, allowing the moonlight to bathe her hair and face. There she would wait for the note's recipient to find her.

She did not have to wait long, within minutes, she spied through the windows the note being handed off to the Duke. He looked at the envelope, on which she had scrawled *Marcus.* Opening it he read the note, then vaulted from his chair and made his way to the front door. Celeste knew the words by heart and she read them aloud as he read the note. "Marcus, I have information you must know regarding Celine. Meet me later, C."

The mysterious note undoubtedly piqued his interested, as they had presumed it would. He opened the door, still pulling on his cape-like coat. Glancing up, he caught sight of Celeste standing in the moonlight. Celeste paused a moment, allowing him enough of a look to be sure he recognized her. Then she moved down the path, pulling her hood over her.

She risked a glance back. Satisfied that he was following her, she continued into the woods and toward the cave path's entrance. She made her way through the narrow passages, winding her way down to the beach. He was fast on her tracks. She paused again at the mouth of the cave, then darted onto the beach.

* * *

Celine made her way to the beach, accompanied by Gray, Alexander, and Teddy. They picked a spot close to the cave opening, but hidden from its view by a rocky outcropping. Celine carried with her the book. They positioned themselves in a semi-circle, facing the cave entrance. Celine began reading from the book, invoking the Hellbeast that Marcus Northcott had sold his soul to long ago.

In a loud voice, she called out, welcoming him to join their group. "I call upon the Hellbeast, Bazios, he who forged a pact so long ago with the one who calls himself Marcus Northcott. He who has allowed him to live many lifetimes to serve his master. Come to us and behold what a poor servant you have chosen. Come to us! Come forth from the eternal hellfire where you are banished to live for all eternity and join our circle so that you may punish your unworthy servant. Come, Bazios, come."

As she called to him, a pattern snaked through the sand. Then the sand began to swirl in front of them. It twisted and danced upward until it formed a writhing serpentine figure with the head of a man and the horns of a goat. "You called to me?" it hissed.

"Yes, Bazios, we did."

"Who calls to me?" he demanded.

"Celine Buckley calls to you."

"I know of no Celine Buckley."

"No, you wouldn't," Celine countered, "but I was intended to be one of yours, brought to you by your servant Marcus Northcott. Marcus failed to deliver not only my soul but the souls of many others. See, here, how the book you and he signed in spilled blood has no new entries. For centuries you have allowed him to walk this earth and for centuries he has played you for a fool."

"Why do you call upon me to tell me these things?"

"Because I want you to reclaim him and take him to the depths of hell with you."

"Why should I do your bidding?"

"Because your book demands it. Or are you too weak to make him pay for his lack of obedience?"

The sand snake quivered in anger. "Must I do your job for you, Bazios? What will your Dark Lord say?" Celine continued to needle at him.

He growled with rage. "Bring him to me and I shall deal with him."

"You're in luck, Bazios. For he approaches us now, he is close. Watch and observe how your so-called servant displays his arrogance, throwing your pact to the wind as he pursues the only thing he has for epochs, his own gratification by making me his."

Without a word, the sand serpent slithered his way to a nearby rock. Hidden in the shadows he waited. Celine saw Celeste approaching the circle. Celeste nodded her head discreetly. "He's coming," Celine said in a low voice.

As Duke Northcott approached the group, confusion

plain on his face at seeing Celeste alive along with the other members of the group, Teddy shoved his hand forward, jolting him with a shock. He stumbled to the side, not expecting an attack. Following Teddy's lead, Gray launched his attack, jolting him from the other side. He reeled as Alexander launched a frontal attack.

With the element of surprise gone, Marcus was quick to recover from the latest attack. He threw his arms out, blowing the three men down with one strike. "What is the meaning of this, Celine?" he demanded.

"It is your end, Marcus."

He threw his head back laughing. "Your minions can't harm me," he said, deflecting an attack from Alexander and firing one back at the same time. "See? Not even Celeste, whom I notice you have managed to bring back from the dead. Impressive, my dear, but then you always were an impressive specimen."

"Hence your interest."

"Indeed," he said, "but not even you, impressive as you are, can defeat me, Celine. Which is why you should join me." He pointed his palm toward Gray, a lightning bolt shooting from it, pinning Gray down. He kept his hand there, continuing his assault on Gray. Celine blasted him with a fireball, stopping the assault. Gray still lay in pain on the beach. "How pathetic. You had to save him again, Celine. Because he is weak, he pales in comparison to your power, he might as well be human. And, of course, you even tried to escape him yourself by becoming human again. Celine, you deserve better."

"By better, you indubitably mean yourself."

"Without a doubt, Celine. My power combined with yours would make us an unstoppable force. Join me."

"I didn't fall for this centuries ago, Marcus. I will not fall for it now. You have wasted centuries chasing no one but me."

"Not wasted, my love, toiled and labored after you. You are the only thing that matters."

"Aww, that's sweet, Marcus, but you know, it's not the reason that you have been permitted to live for centuries."

Duke Northcott looked at her, puzzled by her words. Celine continued, "And now it's time that you paid for that by being dragged back to the depths of Hell by the Hellbeast you made that unhallowed pact with."

Marcus' face turned stone serious, realization dawning on him. "No, Celine, don't do this."

"Too late," she said.

"But you couldn't have the..."

"The book?" she finished.

"Yes," he said.

"This book?" she asked, holding it up. His face was a mask of shock. Celine jolted him with another fireball, dropping him to his knees. "Bazios, you heard him yourself. Now come and do your job and drag him back to the underworld where he belongs."

"No, no, Celine, no!" he shouted. The sand snake slithered toward him. "Bazios, I can explain," he began.

"SILENCE!" the snake shouted. "Your soul belongs to me and I have come to collect it." The snake reared back and lunged forward, mouth opening, devouring him in a cyclone of sand. The shrieks were deafening. As the mouth of the serpent reached the beach, the shrieking ended, and the sand settled back to the ground. The wind stopped howling, and the beach became quiet. Silence surrounded them, only broken by the pounding of the waves against the rocks.

CHAPTER 33

*C*eline rushed through the doors of Alexander's house. "Well?" Michael asked as he and Damien rushed to the door.

"It's done, how are the children?" she asked.

Avery was making her way down the stairs. "His fever has broken!" she shouted.

Charlotte followed Avery down the stairs. "Did you say Max's fever broke? Maddy's did, too!"

Celine closed her eyes, breathing a sigh of relief. Gray and Alexander clapped each other's backs. Celeste and Teddy threw their arms around each other. "It's done," Celine said, a tear rolling down her cheek. "It's finally over."

* * *

Celine sat on the swing under the gazebo, rocking gently as she watched the scenery. Damien approached her. "Figured I might find you here," he said. "Can I join you?"

"Sure," she said, sliding over as he settled onto the swing with her.

They sat for a moment in silence. Celine reached out and took his hand. "You okay?"

"Yeah, yeah. There's just so much that I don't understand."

"Ask away, D, I'm an open book."

"Ha! Thanks, Jos, oh, well, uh, I guess that should be Celine."

"You called me Celine right after you got back from Martinque."

"Yeah, but it still takes a little getting used to. You'll always be Josie to me."

"I am Celine but a part of me will always be Josie."

Damien nodded, lost in his thoughts. "So, how did you end up like you are, Celine? You didn't kill anyone that night, right?"

"I didn't follow through with killing that man, no, which is what would have bonded me to Marcus' coven. But killing someone and then signing the book with their blood was always Marcus' own requirement. He deemed it exhibited the deepest pledge of loyalty. The only 'requirement' is to draw blood from someone else."

"And you did that?"

"Yes. That man, the one Marcus ordered me to kill, I came across him in the tunnels. He wanted the book, Marcus had sentenced him to death, most likely for disobeying him. The man presumed retrieving the book for him might redeem him somehow. He was willing to kill for it, in fact. He stabbed me, took the book and left me to die."

The admission stunned Damien. "So, what happened? Why didn't you die? Not that I'm complaining!" he said, holding his hands up and waving them in front of him.

"Marcus. He found me bleeding to death. He killed the man and then healed me, he cut himself and poured his blood into me."

"So that's what you meant when you said his blood ran through your veins. Wow, for once he did something noble."

"Well, I'm not sure how noble it was. I was a great power for him to possess."

"True. So, what happened next? How did you manage to get the book from Marcus?"

"After he healed me, I saw the book and the knife. So, I took the knife, plunged it into his gut, grabbed the book and ran."

"You drew his blood which…" Damien began.

"Made me what I am, what he was."

Damien pondered for a moment, analyzing it all. "So, how did you become Josie? I mean, you're immortal, right? But we've been together since we were kids. How?"

"Yeah, Celine is an immortal. Josie was a human. Years ago, I was so exasperated and exhausted by centuries of being chased by Marcus that I made a deal. I went to an adjudicator, a neutral party. I wanted to be human. I wanted out. So, I bargained for a new life. I was literally reborn, given to a human set of parents and given twenty-five years. If in twenty-five years I did not change my mind, never took my powers back, I was free to live my human life in peace. I didn't quite make that cutoff."

"No, by the way, happy belated birthday."

She laughed. "Thanks, D."

"So, do you have a handler or whatever like the Duke?"

"No, I don't, I don't owe my soul to anyone. I always try to do good with the powers I was given."

"Hmm," he said, pondering the conversation.

"Hey, guys," Michael said, coming up from behind them. "Admiring the scenery?"

"Yes," Damien said. "It is beautiful here."

"Yes, we finally can enjoy the beauty and peace here," Celine said.

"I'm glad for that," Damien answered, sighing. "I don't know how I can go back home without you." He stared down at the ground.

Celine looked over at him. She would also be heartbroken if he left her. She had already given the situation hours of consideration. She could understand what Damien was suffering through. She had left her family before, she would not do it again. "About that," she began, "I was thinking, you've been talking about going one hundred percent remote with your company, perhaps now is the time to do that."

"How would that help? Then I'll be alone even more in that house," Damien answered, kicking the ground with his foot.

"Not if you stayed here with us."

Understanding filled his face, along with a smile. "You mean... move here?"

Celine nodded. "Yes, move here. Then I wouldn't miss you and you wouldn't miss me and besides we could always use a good person like you to help us fight the darkness. The Duke is gone, but evil will always exist."

His smile broadened. "I would like that. I will talk to my supervisor first thing tomorrow morning."

With Damien settled, Celine turned to Michael. "How about you? Are you okay to go home?"

"Well, it looks like I'm losing two of my friends, but at least there's the internet. And I'm not sure there is a normal life for me after what I just experienced. I just feel this connection I don't want to lose. Unless..."

"Unless?" Celine asked.

"Unless we open a branch here. I could oversee it, live in town."

Celine smiled. "Well, we make a good team."

"Will there be more trouble?" Michael asked.

"Like I said, there's always evil in the world," Celine answered.

"So maybe I should stick around like Damien," Michael said.

"Maybe you should," she agreed.

"You should. We are a team...a team of shadow slayers! Besides, we already have our next task," Damien joined in.

"We do?" Michael asked.

"Yeah. As far as I know, that painting is still missing. Which, according to the legend, means no one is safe. We need to find that painting!"

EPILOGUE

*C*eline fell back onto her backside, blown backward by the force of the portal closing. She blinked, clearing her eyes from the intense wind as the sand settled back to the beach. They had vanished, both of them with the book. They had made it to wherever they were going, she hoped. "Good luck," she whispered.

"Celine!" she heard a voice shouting. "CELINE!" She saw Celeste running toward her. "Are you all right, Celine?"

Celine stood without answering, brushing herself off. "Yes, I am just fine, sister dear," she said, disdain filling her voice. "No thanks to you."

Celeste looked surprised at her comment. Celine continued her rant. "Our father is dead, Celeste, murdered by the Duke's orders. My life hung by a thread tonight and now I'm…"

Duke Northcott joined them before she could finish. "I assume they have gone?" he inquired.

"Yes, safely away from you."

"With my book. Damn it, Celine. Do you know what you have done?"

"Yes, I stopped you. That is what I have done."

He shook his head. "It doesn't matter, you are mine now," Marcus said, lording the fact over her.

"No, Marcus, you are mistaken. Yes, it's true, I am like you, but I am not yours and I never will be." She turned to Celeste. "As far as you are concerned, Celeste, I will never forgive you for your part in this tonight. You've stolen my life and our father's life." She turned back to Duke Northcott. "And as for you, I shall fill my days searching for that book and use it to destroy you."

Marcus laughed. "You can try, Celine, you can try, but you will never be rid of me. I will always be with you."

The End

Stay up to date with all my news! Be the first to find out about new releases first, sales and get free offers! Join the Nellie H. Steele's Mystery Readers' Group on Facebook! Or sign up for my newsletter at www.anovelideapublishing.com!

* * *

Now that Josie has found her true self, continue the adventure and find Celine's painting! Check out Book 2, *Stolen Portrait Stolen Soul*, now!

* * *

Like cozy mysteries? Check out the Cate Kensie Mystery series. Misty Scottish moors and a quirky castle. Read Cate's first adventure, *The Secret of Dunhaven Castle*! You can also read Jack's version of the story!

* * *

If you love cozies, you can also check out my newest series, Lily & Cassie by the Sea. Grab book one, *Ghosts, Lore & a House by the Shore* now!

* * *

Love immersing yourself in the past? Lenora Fletcher can communicate with the dead! Can she use her unique skill to solve a mystery? Find out in *Death of a Duchess*, Book 1 in the Duchess of Blackmoore Mysteries.

* * *

Ready for adventure? Travel the globe with Maggie Edwards in search of her kidnapped uncle and Cleopatra's Tomb. Book one, *Cleopatra's Tomb*, in the Maggie Edwards Adventure series is available now!

* * *

If you prefer adventures set in the past, try my newest pirate adventure series. Book 1, *Rise of a Pirate*, is available for purchase now!

Made in United States
Orlando, FL
26 March 2022

16170134R00187